And It Was Full of Light!

Finding the courage to overcome
homophobic bullying and hate

Robert W. Littlefield

authorHOUSE®

AuthorHouse™
1663 Liberty Drive
Bloomington, IN 47403
www.authorhouse.com
Phone: 1-800-839-8640

First published by AuthorHouse 11/1/2010

ISBN: 978-1-4520-5492-6 (sc)
ISBN: 978-1-4520-5493-3 (hc)
ISBN: 978-1-4520-5494-0 (e)

Library of Congress Control Number: 2010914211

Printed in the United States of America

This book is printed on acid-free paper.

The central Texas town of Dunston is purely fictitious. All other
cities, towns, and geographic features mentioned in this story,
including those in Texas and Massachusetts, are real places.

Acknowledgements

Writing a first novel is a long journey—taxing, exhilirating, cathartic, emotional, and intellectually stimulating. In hindsight, the easy part was the first huge gusher of writing. Then came the editing and re-writing! Of course many people provided encouragement along the way. One of the best decisions I ever made was to choose Author House in Bloomington, Indiana, as my publisher. My team leader, Teri Watkins, patiently guided me through every step of the process. Thank you, Teri, and thanks to Bethany Grubb, Alan Bower, Becca Bass, the editorial staff, and the rest of the team for your wonderful and highly professional support.

This story wouldn't be in its current form if not for noted novelist and biographer William J. Mann. During a writing class and a subsequent one-on-one mentorship, Bill inspired me and helped me shape and improve my writing into the style that resulted in the story you are now reading. Thank you, Bill.

My editor and good friend from Worcester, Bill Gagnon, was exceedingly generous with his time, unstinting in his critiques, and liberal with encouragement. His critiques—blunt, honest, somewhat difficult to accept at first—by and large turned out to to be right on the money. He, more than anyone, helped sharpen the story line.

And then there are the good people of Texas who provided so much information and background during my research trip to Llano, Brady, Mason, and Ivie Reservoir. My wonderful bed and breakfast hosts in Brady, Jack and Cindy Whitworth, provided countless insights into central Texas culture, geography, ranching, and government. Their introductions to local officials led to valuable insights about Texas schools, the football culture, and law enforcement. Special thanks to Sabrina Hill of Midland, Texas, for her insights into Texas culture, and her son A.W. Hill, for helping with the vernacular and idioms of Texas teens.

I've been blessed with friends and family, many more than can be mentioned here, who served as a sounding board, provided insights, and boundless encouragement. Thanks, everyone.

A special acknowledgement must be reserved for one of my most special friends, Roger Reynolds. It was his deep interest and encouragement that led me to continue this project early on. He was the first person to read the entire original manuscript and tell me it was not only a worthwhile project, but an entertaining and compelling story. Thank you, Roger.

Prologue

Friday afternoon, May 1, 1998

Look at him, a teenage Greek god on the dance floor, muscles bulging, abs chiseled, skin so smooth and perfect it almost glows, devastating bedroom eyes that can make every girl in school (and one gay boy) weak in the knees at fifty yards; delicious, kissable lips set perfectly on a face that would make both Abercrombie and Fitch drool; his tanned body streaked with trails of sweat glistening under the club lights, his hands pumping to the pounding beat of a hot trance mix—surprisingly delicate, beautiful hands that can throw a football so high above the stadium lights it disappears for what seems like a full minute; and he's motioning—to me!—come here, come dance with me, so he can nuzzle his cheek tightly against mine and wrap his arms around me and squeeze his body into mine and rub his hands over every inch of my skin. Beautiful, stunning, sex god Kyle Faulkner at long last wants to dance with me ... and he's naked! Oh, this feels so good, so—

"Hey, Bobby, what's up with you?"

"Danny! Jeez, you startled the crap out of me."

A bit dazed, I'm looking around to get my bearings. Yep, still here in this stupid little food court in this pathetic excuse for a mall in cow town Dunston, Texas, a hot boy in my arms still nothing but a dream. Danny, my best friend since I moved here freshman year, edges closer.

"You looked like you were just staring off into space. You all right?"

"Yeah, I'm fine," I reply. "Really, I'm fine."

Okay, maybe a little flustered is more like it. At least Danny's looking at me and not my shorts. He'd be on my case big time if he knew I was having a fantasy about Kyle, not only the most perfectly gorgeous boy who ever lived, but lately, the biggest jerk too.

Danny gestures with his thumb back toward the sandwich wrap shop where he works.

"I haven't had a single customer in half an hour."

"Everyone's at the new Wal-Mart. This place was a joke to begin with, and now it's like a morgue."

"Got that right," he says. Trying for that cool look, Danny plants a shoe against the wall close to the corner where the food court and the mall meet, folds his arms over his slender chest, and slouches down so close we're almost touching.

A quick peek to compare our heights confirms what I've been suspecting: I'm maybe an inch taller than his five feet seven, the happy result—well, for me anyway—of this spring's growth spurt. Not that I'd tease my best friend. Not once did Danny ever tease me about being small and scrawny all through high school. A true friend, he's stuck with me through everything, like those wild hair- and clothing-challenged times I'd rather forget, those awful days and weeks after I was told Dad was never coming home, and … don't think about it, don't think about it!

"You're still upset about Kyle, aren't you?" he asks, absently brushing a lock of thick black hair out of his eyes.

I react with a snort of disgust.

"Two weeks since the prom and he's still being a jerk. I heard Kathy broke up with him Wednesday night. After the shit Kyle's been pulling, I can't say I blame her."

"Did you try talking with him again?" Danny asks through a yawn.

"Talk to him? Danny, he won't even look at me. I'd leave him another note, but the two I left last week ended up as confetti."

"What a jerk. One of his friends was talking about your dance music, and Kyle goes, 'I'm not into of any that gay shit.' And he called you the gay kid."

I only react by leaning my head back against the wall and noisily blowing out a deep breath. I've been lying to Danny and everyone else about why Kyle has been such a jerk these last two weeks. No one would understand if I told them what really happened.

"I was hoping you'd be really happy when we graduate, especially seeing the prom went so well," Danny says.

"A few more weeks, then it's sayonara, Dunston High School, and good-bye, Texas," I tell my friend. "Hey, what are you doing out here anyway? Aren't you supposed to be behind the counter working your butt off?"

Danny peers over my shoulder toward the little sandwich wrap shop, not so much to check for customers as to watch out for his boss. His mouth curls into a smirk.

"Just taking a break from serving all the customers. And what are you doing at Dunston's finest shopping experience?"

"Sneakerama, then eat."

"And I know exactly where."

"Peruvian Chicken!" we shout together, bursting into idiotic laughter and jumping to exchange a high five. It was Danny who introduced me to their charcoal-roasted chicken and sweet potato fries when we were freshmen, and since then, I've eaten there, what, 4 million times?

"Too bad you can't get a job there," I tell Danny with a gentle prod of my elbow. "It's the only place in this dump that does any business. But at least you get to wear the cool uniform."

Danny rolls his deep-brown Cambodian eyes and ignores my snickering, made worse with both hands clamped over my mouth. For once, he doesn't bust me in return. I've ranked on him so many times about his maroon-and-orange Daffy's Rollwich uniform—especially the cute little paper hat with the cartoon duck—that it's become a running joke.

"So how's the new car?" he asks to conveniently change the subject.

"Oh, totally awesome. Chloe said she really likes the electric blue—"

"Hey! What are you doing out there?"

It's Danny's boss, glaring at us red-faced, his fat belly straining his apron, his eyes bulging like a cartoon character's. Every time I come here, this fat idiot is yapping about something or other, but Danny just rolls his eyes.

"I'd better get back," he mutters. "He's been all over my case today, so I don't want to piss him off even more, you know what I'm saying? Hey, if you're going to be around tonight, how about we catch the new Godzilla flick? Chloe wants to see it too."

I answer with a thumbs-up and make a mental note to call my friend Chloe.

As his boss steams, Danny ambles back to the sandwich shop, now mobbed with exactly one customer. He might not last the summer working for this guy, plus he's bored out of his mind with so few people shopping here. Maybe he can get a summer job at Wal-Mart.

Still leaning against the wall near the food court, I happen to glance at my reflection in the store window across the mall. I study myself, still not quite believing it's really me. After looking this way and that to make sure no one's watching, I stand tall, pump my chest out, and flex my right bicep, just like a jock showing off for his girlfriend.

Six months ago, I would never have flexed my arm in public, let alone worn a sleeveless shirt, but now that my workouts have added more than twenty pounds of muscle just since last summer, I'm starting to like how I look. Maybe still too skinny, especially compared with Kyle and some of the other football jocks, but this is by far the best that little ol' me has ever looked.

Ah, but what does it matter? I still need to get the hell out of this place. Too much pain, too much misery, never once a hot boy in my arms, and now all this shit with Kyle. Maybe I'll leave for Stanford right after graduation and get an apartment in Palo Alto. I could deejay or join a band or something, anything, to get away from Dunston High School and straight boy Kyle Faulkner and this stupid, football-worshipping cow town stuck out in the middle of nowhere.

"Hey mister, move along or I'm calling mall security," my friend Danny calls out in a bad cop voice made worse by his stupid grin. He gets the finger in return.

I'm just slipping out to the mall, grinning back at Danny—

"Hey!"

I screech when someone blindsides me so hard I'm smacked right onto the tile floor. Oh no, it's Kyle! In a flash, his hands are gripping my shirt, lifting me almost off my feet to pin me against the wall. Danny shouts at me, but with Kyle so angry he's baring his teeth six inches from my face, I'm too scared to answer.

"You stupid queer, a lot of this is your fault," he says through clenched teeth.

An instantaneous flash of blinding, white-hot anger is followed by the unique sound of Kyle's air being expelled when my knee slams into his crotch. Doubled over, collapsing to the floor, Dunston High School's football god groans in agony.

"Oh, no," I moan, frozen in astonishment at what I just did. It only takes a few seconds to realize he's going to kill me.

Danny shouts again as I tear through the food court, crashing through the door into the brightness of the parking lot.

Shit! Why did I do that? I'm dashing to my car when, to my horror, I realize I parked all the way at the other end of the mall.

Gasping for air, I stop to bend over with my hands on my knees. Just as I'm thinking Kyle will be too hurt to chase me, the food court door blasts open with an awful bang. Against every instinct to run, I look back. Red in the face, chest heaving, eyes two pinpoints of rage, Kyle springs at me like a lion charging prey. I take off, running faster than I ever thought possible.

But not fast enough. I should have known better than to think I could outrun Kyle. I'm not halfway through the lot when he's grabbing at my arm. Kyle swings me around, grips my shirt with both hands, and slams me against the side of a white van so violently my head bounces off with a hollow bang. Not a word is said.

The force of the blow, more noise than anything, instinctively causes me to curl up and clench my eyes shut. Kyle's powerful grip, however, is holding me against the van, my shirt trapping me like a harness.

His hands let go. Here it comes …

Just Surviving

Chapter 1

Three years earlier

The mall food court is jam-packed and loudly buzzing with the usual Saturday afternoon swarm of shoppers. I can't even begin to steady my nerves as I hastily scan the tables for Danny and Chloe. I'm so nervous my tummy's doing flip-flops. That's when I get a whiff of the familiar, irresistible aromas coming from Peruvian Chicken, all the excuse I need for a food detour.

Just at that moment, a somewhat plump, dark-skinned girl with a bright red headband accenting a gigantic mop of frizzy black hair bounces up in the far corner, waving wildly and shouting my name. Of course it's Chloe, who else? Oh, and there's Danny slouched in his seat, hand over his eyes, trying to be inconspicuous as Chloe carries on with one of her milder public spectacles.

I laugh, but it's a half-hearted attempt to appear calm as I squeeze past crowded tables to reach them.

Wrappers and half-empty cups of soda litter the table.

"Gee, thanks so much for waiting," I tell my friends.

"Sorry, we were starving," Danny mumbles. "Go get something to eat, go!"

"Hey, are you okay?" Chloe asks. "You look kind of nervous."

"I'm fine." She's giving me a squinty look. "Really, I'm fine. I'll be right back."

Standing in line at Peruvian Chicken, waving with a forced smile at my friends, I admit to myself I'm not fine, I'm just plain scared. Will they make a big scene? Will they still be my friends? Please God, I pray, please let this goes okay.

Pacing near the counter and anxious for my number to be called, I don't even remember ordering. I hope it's roast chicken and fried sweet potato.

"*Ciento diez, ciento diez, number one hundred ten.*"

This is it!

"You guys want some fried sweet potato?"

"Not me," Chloe says, finishing the last of her drink with a raspy burble through her straw. "So are you going to tell us the big mystery?"

I'm hesitating and she continues.

"When you called, you said meet us at the mall and it's important, then you wouldn't tell us why. Come on, let's hear it." That's Chloe: insistent, impatient, right to the point. She's always full of laughs and so outrageous sometimes I think that girl is demented. On the other hand, she doesn't let me get away with anything.

"Hey, I'm glad you guys made it. Did you do some shopping?" As Danny and Chloe impassively wait me out, I catch myself drumming my fingers on the tray with rapid, loud thumps. I self-consciously put my hands in my lap.

Chloe's patience runs out. "Will you please tell us what's going on? We're your friends, right?"

"Absolutely. You guys are my best friends."

Chloe studies me with a squishy-nose look. "Are you in some kind of trouble?"

"No, I'm not in trouble," I tell her, "I'm just a little scared right now."

"Scared? What do you mean, scared?"

"I'm scared of you. And you too, Danny."

My best friends exchange a puzzled glance.

"I don't get it. Why are we scaring you?" Danny asks.

"You're not. I'm just scared of how you'll react when I tell you something." I haven't taken one bite of my food. My mouth is dry and when I pick up my Coke, my hand is actually shaking enough to make the ice tinkle. Chloe gives me a strange look.

"Jeez, would you just relax?"

"Yeah, man, whatever it is you're trying to tell us, just spit it out,"

Danny says, raising his voice and throwing his hands in the air. *That's typical Danny.*

"Sorry, this is really hard, but I've got to tell someone. It's why I asked you guys to meet me here." My heart is thumping so hard it's scary. I swallow hard. Here goes—

"Is it a huge problem for you guys if you're eating with a gay boy?"

Nothing. No shocked looks, no big scene, no storming out of the food court, just complete silence—and Chloe's raised eyebrows. Fearing the worst, I wait them out.

"You're really gay?" she finally asks at her usual bullhorn volume.

I'm sinking lower in my seat. "Yeah, I'm really gay."

While she thinks this over, Danny, on the other hand, isn't reacting except for that easy-to-miss smirk he gets when someone says something totally stupid or really obvious.

"Excuse me, what did you just say?" It's one of three older girls at the next table. I don't know them all that well, only that they're going to be seniors.

"I said I'm gay."

"You mean, like, for real?" the one nearest me says.

"Say, aren't you Bobby Fowler?" another asks.

"Yeah, I'm gay, for real."

"This is a joke, right?"

"He said he's gay, got it?" Chloe snaps. "Now do you mind if we talk?"

"It's okay, Chloe. Look, it's not a joke. I'm gay."

Open-mouthed amazement is followed by whispering and giggling, which quickly becomes higher-pitched and more excited. My attention returns to my two friends. I still can't quite read Danny.

"Is this a total shock?" I ask him.

"Nah, I pretty much had it figured out," he replies with a smirk, "especially with some of the guys like Jason calling you a homo and stuff like that last year. I'm cool and it's no big deal, at least for me."

"It's no big deal?"

"Come on, man, just chill out," he says.

"I'm wicked surprised, but thanks." I turn my attention to Chloe. "Is this freaking you out?"

"No, not really, maybe a little surprised. Maybe I shouldn't be surprised, you know? There were times last year when I wondered about you. Like you'd see a humpy-looking boy walk by and you'd say, 'Oh, that guy is *so* athletic.'" She completes the imagery with a little wave of her hand, nothing more than a flick of her wrist. Chloe follows with a fit of giggling.

I giggle too, and at last take a deep breath. This time it really does ease some of the tension. I feel good. *Everything* is starting to feel good, like a colossal weight has been lifted off me.

"Like Danny said, it's no big deal," Chloe continues. "It will just take a little getting used to, that's all."

"Thanks, Chloe. Thanks, Danny. You guys are my very best friends, and I wanted you to be the first to know."

"You're my best friend too, and I'm glad you told us, but look," he says, nodding toward the front of the food court. "Those girls are leaving, and it's going to be all over town in the next six seconds. You're going be the first gay kid in the history of Dunston High School."

I'm twisting my paper napkin into a tight little spiral as Danny's comment sinks in. An instant stab of fear knots my stomach before I decide being gay can't be *that* big of a deal. Danny and Chloe were cool. And besides, it's who I am and I can't keep it inside any longer.

"I hope people leave me alone," I tell my friends. Relieved beyond words, I'm still so keyed up I can hardly eat. Ever since I was little, I've known I like boys, but spitting out "I'm gay" the first time sure was scary. "Hey, maybe I'll meet someone when I go back to school," I go on. "At least one hot boy will be gay and will ask me out. And I would just die if it's someone half as hot as Kyle Faulkner."

Chloe's head sinks into her hands. "Oh, this will take some getting used to," she moans.

"Sorry, I didn't mean to weird you out, but I don't want to go through high school and not meet someone. I want what you guys want, but for me, it has to be a guy."

"It's okay," she says, rubbing my hand. "I want you to be happy."

"Yeah, that's what I want," I say. "I want to be happy again."

Chapter 2

I'm feeling pretty satisfied. After a good ten minutes of failed attempts, a dropped stick, and some swearing here and there, I finally nailed a complex new drum riff. Oh, and there was that little matter of telling Danny and Chloe the most important thing in my entire life. And there I was so scared I almost peed my pants.

My break is interrupted by the rapid flicking on and off of the light at the foot of the stairs.

"Hi, Chloe."

The words are hardly out of my mouth when familiar, heavy footsteps clomp down the stairs, followed by the loud creak of that loose step halfway down. I tense, thinking all sorts of bad things about why she's here.

Giving me one of her biggest smiles, one that can brighten up my darkest moods, Chloe parks herself right in front of my drums. "I could hear you from outside," she says. "Have you been here long?"

"I came straight from the mall to practice and work on a new remix. Did you hear my new riff?"

"Yeah, it sounded great. Look, I stopped by to tell you something."

"Oh crap, you're not cool with my being gay?"

She hesitates and squints a bit, the way she always squints when she's serious. "Of course I'm cool with you being gay. Bobby, I was thinking about how nervous you were and what you told us, you know, that you wanted me and Danny to be the first to know. It made me feel special. I could see it was really hard to say you're gay, and it must have taken a lot of courage. I stopped over to thank you for sharing something so special in your life."

It takes a moment for all of this to sink in, as well as to start breathing again. "You know, you're the most special friend I ever had," I tell her. I hop around my drums to wrap my friend in a tight embrace. Chloe is more than a friend, she's my soul mate. "I love you, Chloe," I whisper.

"Are you okay now?" she asks. "You were so nervous you were shaking."

"I'm fine. I was shaking a little, wasn't I?" I snicker thinking about it, prompting a fit of high-pitched giggling from Chloe. "Now it feels like this huge relief, like … oh, I don't know how to even explain it," I tell her. "Everything feels really good. The whole universe just feels right."

"Well, I'm happy that you're happy, and I'm glad this feels right." Chloe absently taps one of my cymbals with her fingernail, just enough to make it ring lightly. "What's this about a new remix? Do I get to hear it?"

"Yeah, it's just not finished."

Flipping power switches on my recording equipment and amps, I'm grinning to myself anticipating Chloe's reaction to my newest track. It's what I call Hi-NRG techno trance, because it sounds like this gay dance CD I sent away for and that's what it said in the notes.

The finished room I call my recording studio takes up almost half the cellar. Chloe and Danny, like me, think it's totally cool, the perfect place to hang out.

Amps, two synthesizers, speakers, a medium-sized subwoofer, a forty-channel mixing board, and lots of other electronic equipment are stacked on tables and shelves opposite my drum set. The first time he came down here, Danny flipped out. He said most sci-fi flicks don't have this much electronic equipment. Except for my desk chair and two purple bean bags, a ratty old couch the previous owner left behind is the only other furniture down here. We still laugh about the time Chloe was so grossed out she brought an old sheet to cover it.

"Here we go," I warn Chloe.

The room begins shaking to my latest gay dance music. I was right! Look at that girl, a silly smile mixed with this goofy wow expression as she starts to boogie. I'm cracking up, she's ignoring me, and in moments we're both dancing and gyrating in the middle of the cellar, thinking we're totally cool while the subwoofer vibrates the air so strongly it might microwave us.

"Bobby, this is awesome," she shouts as she carries on with her unique brand of high-energy dancing. I always crank up my dance music really loud because I heard that when you go to gay clubs, it's ultra loud. The first time I ever played music for Chloe at this volume, she shrieked and blocked her ears. Then I told her it's supposed to be this loud. Oh, yeah, I told her that parents hate it. That did it.

The music ends with only the bass beat thumping out of the subwoofer.

"It'll take a few more days to overlay eight tracks of percussion and melody to get this finished," I explain as I eject the CD.

"Wow, that's all I can say. I have no idea how you do it, but that was your best ever," she says. Chloe decides to play around on my drums, but after a few cymbal crashes and half-hearted taps on the snare drum, she sits there, staring once more with that tight-lipped, narrow-eyed look.

"Well what?" I finally ask.

"Why don't you make a CD of your dance music?"

"Make a CD? Girl, you can't be serious."

"You finished a whole bunch of tracks, right?"

"Yeah, at least a dozen."

"Listen, that music made me want to dance. My feet just didn't want to stay still. Bobby, my whole *body* wouldn't stay still. You don't know how good you are, and Danny agrees with me."

"Hmm, my own CD ... oh, I don't know about this. Who'd want to buy it?"

Chloe has to think about this for a few seconds. "I know. Maybe at first you could hand out copies at school."

"Yeah, then everyone will think I'm cool. We'll have to think up a name for my record label."

"That will be fun." Chloe bangs on the drums again and stops. Actually, it's her routine: play, talk, play, talk, the talking by far outweighing the playing.

"Thank heavens for your music," she says. "At least you've been able to use your dad's house and work on your music to help you get by."

"Yeah, but you and Danny helped more than anything."

Chloe smiles sweetly, and when she returns her attention to my drums, I think about what she just said. *Dad's house.* I call it my house, like anyone would, but to Danny and Chloe, it's always "your dad's house."

It's been almost six months since I was told Dad had died overseas, although they've never found his ... I still can't even think it. He moved me here from Massachusetts three months after Mom died. I live in a foster home, only a few hundred yards down Farm Road 1951, a lightly-used country road that passes through fields and grazing land five miles from the center of town.

After Dad died, I was sure this house would be sold and I'd lose my recording studio and a place to play my drums, but it's maintained because of a trust Dad set up. I'm here every day, sometimes for hours. I even have my own key.

My friends and I use the lap swimming pool and the hot tub that Dad put in last summer. Dad taught me to do laps and flip turns. Imagine that, unathletic me doing flip turns. I even bought goggles.

Chloe's right. My music—which I couldn't have done without being able to use this house— helped me get through some really dark times.

A local county judge, Judge Garrity, is the trustee of the trust Dad had set up to take care of me in case anything happened. The judge is also my legal guardian, to say nothing of my friend and mentor, which is what he calls himself. He stops by frequently to visit and take a dip in the pool, but I know he's checking up on the place as well. So does my foster mother, Mrs. Robles. I've kept my promise that my friends and I wouldn't mess up because otherwise, this place is history.

"Hey, I better get home for supper. I don't want to get yelled at," I tell Chloe.

"Does Mrs. Robles still yell at you?" she asks.

"Nah, not as much. I'm still trying to make this work so we get along okay."

She seems to be thinking this over. "Are you finally getting comfortable with your foster home?"

Hot anger rushes to my face. "I only said I'm trying to make this work. I'll never be comfortable in a foster home. It's just not fair. She says she's trying but she's not my mother. *She's never going to be my mother!*" Chloe's face tightens in a frown. "I'm sorry, Chloe. I need to take your advice and not get so steamed up about being in a foster home."

Chloe, always calm and comforting when I'm out of control, gently rubs my shoulder. "It's okay," she says. "I know it's hard. Maybe as time goes by things will get better."

"Hey, gotta go," I tell her.

At the foot of the stairs, it hits like a flash of lightning. "Oh, no! It's all over town," I tell Chloe with a slap to my forehead. "I don't want the judge to find out from someone else I'm gay. Shit!"

"So maybe you'd better tell him. Like tonight?"

"Oh, crap," I moan.

"Jeez, Bobby, weren't you going to tell him?"

"I guess so, but later, maybe a lot later. I didn't mean for everyone in town to find out so soon."

"Bobby, you told those girls."

"I wasn't thinking. What am I going to do?"

She tries to calm me down, rubbing my shoulder again and talking softly. "It's going to be okay. You'll see. Just don't let him find out from someone else, okay? You've been so close and he's helped you so much."

"But what if he freaks out? What if he throws me out of here? Oh shit, I'm screwed."

Saying nothing, my best friend gives me another wonderful hug. It's her way of saying everything will turn out okay, and if not, she'll still be here as my best friend.

Chapter 3

Up and down, up and down, in perfect, metronomic cadence. I'm lying on my bed, reliving today's little drama at the mall, tossing a tennis ball up and down. I do it a lot, just lie here, sometimes daydreaming, sometimes not thinking about anything at all. Tonight, I'm still wired from everything that happened today.

My eyes slowly unglaze, only to focus on that stupid light over my bed. I hate it. It looks so completely fake, like fake lanterns on a fake ship's wheel. My bedroom, at one end of the house off Mrs. Robles's kitchen, is small and simply furnished. The only picture I brought from my house, the one of Mom and Dad and me at Nauset Beach on Cape Cod when I was eleven, sits atop the bureau. The only other furniture, a small wooden table that serves as my desk, is tucked under the window. It's so close to the bed that I hit it if I push the chair back too far. Sometimes I sit at my desk, staring out at the trees backlit by dusk, feeling sad, wondering what will happen to me, asking God why Mom and Dad had to die.

Other than my Marky Mark poster on the closet door and a picture of Jesus over the bed (I guess Mrs. Robles's daughter put it there before she died), that's about it. I was going to take the picture down but was afraid I'd get in trouble with either Mrs. Robles or Jesus.

Another weird thing: Mrs. Robles's house, a small ranch house with a long dirt driveway, is only a few hundred yards down the road from my house. I can see it from my bedroom window.

Toward town, only one other house is visible; the others are hidden by gently rolling hills. Actually, they're more like bumps than hills. Up past my house are huge ranches, each with its own gate. Here, no-

nonsense guys with huge pickup trucks raise cattle and goats; otherwise, it's nothing but miles of open country.

I'm a visitor here, that's all. The house up the road is my real home, my empty, real home, the place Dad never came back to.

Mrs. Robles—I still can't bring myself to call her *Mom* or anything like that—didn't say anything when I came in for supper. Of course not. Softly snoring in her recliner, a stupid game show blaring from the TV, a glass of that fizzy gin drink she likes sitting half-empty and flat on the end table under the ugly lamp with the little glass dangly things, my foster mother was asleep. I finished getting supper ready, part of my chores anyway, and made a fresh pot of coffee. "You'll earn your keep," she had told me early on.

After supper, I escaped to my bedroom to read and avoid the never-ending updates about her relatives, their latest illnesses, her friends, their problems, the latest gossip, and all that other stuff I don't give a crap about. Sometimes I nod, pretending to listen. She doesn't really know me or how I feel. She's not my mother.

Once in a while I get yelled at, especially when she says I ignore her when she's talking, or I'm not respectful if I don't say *yes, ma'am* and *no, ma'am*, or that I'm cross, or she thinks I'm not taking my anti-depressants. Yeah, well screw that. She isn't the one who got put in a foster home. She's keeping me here because the judge pays her a lot of money each month for taking me in.

I promised I'd try to make this work and I have, but it still doesn't seem fair. *Me* in a foster home? It doesn't seem possible. This can't be happening to me! But it is. I'm in a little bedroom in a foster home in a little town in the middle of Texas. I'm surviving, that's all this is, I'm just surviving. The tennis ball is bouncing off the ceiling now, harder and harder.

Last week, the judge told me to look ahead and try not to dwell on the bad things after I got upset and yelled at him at his house. Maybe I should think about how I lucked out when I called him tonight after supper. I was so scared he could hear it in my voice. It must have taken me fifteen minutes to spit it out. And when he said he knew I was gay since the first day he met me, I was stunned. He thanked me for sharing something so special in my life, just as Chloe had, and promised we'd talk more tomorrow at our usual Sunday breakfast at the Ramada Inn.

Maybe I'd better tell Mrs. Robles, especially since she goes to breakfast with us. What if it doesn't go well? What if she kicks me out and I have to go to another foster home? What if it's a long way from here and I can't use my recording studio or play my drums? They better not do that to me. I'll run away to Boston or Australia and do my music stuff there.

Eleven o'clock; still way too revved to sleep. Once again, just like last night and every night before that, all these memories flash back. I can't control them. Tonight, my brain is in warp drive.

* * * * *

Dad is shaking me awake. He looks funny, like his eyes are red. "Bobby, I have to tell you some very bad news." I'm struggling to wake up. "Mom was hit by a drunk driver leaving work," he says, his voice strangely shaky. "They had to call an ambulance. Bobby, Mom won't be coming home. On the way to the hospital, she … she died." Those words burned into me forever.

I wish I could stop remembering that night, just two days after my big thirteenth birthday party, when all my friends and neighbors showed up. When Dad came up to my room to tell me, I didn't believe it. The next morning, when the horror finally sank in, nothing seemed real. At the funeral and for weeks after, I was numb. It was like a dream except I was awake and I couldn't escape. I couldn't believe Mom was gone, I just couldn't believe it.

I still miss you, Mom. I wish you were here, sitting on my bed, making me feel better like you always did, even when I was bad. I'm sorry about all those times you had to yell at me.

Dad, I miss you too. I miss you so much.

Shit, I'm out of tissues.

Chapter 4

Dad tried to go on like everything was normal, at least in front of me, but nothing was the same. During supper not quite three months later, Dad told me something that I could hardly believe.

"We're moving *where?*"

"Mason Air Force Base in central Texas," he explains. "We'll be living in Dunston, the nearest town. Why don't you look it up in the atlas?"

"But why? I don't want to go to Texas. Come on, Dad, why can't we stay here?"

"I've taken a job with General Cantwell. You remember General Cantwell, don't you?"

"But can't I do eighth grade here with all my friends and then move?"

"Bobby, I'm sorry, but we're leaving in two weeks."

Two weeks goes by in a blur and just like that, in the cool mist of a July dawn, we're on the road to Texas. Before leaving town, we stop at the cemetery. I try to hold back tears but can't. It makes Dad uncomfortable when I cry, and I try hard not to. Everything is weird. I'm leaving the only home I've ever known, my school, my neighborhood, all my friends … everything, all because of a drunk driver. It doesn't seem possible that strangers will be moving into the only house I've ever lived in.

We arrive in central Texas after three boring days on the road. I should be happy the trip is over, but Texas is nothing like home and worse, we're out in the middle of nowhere. I take it we're on the outskirts of Dunston when we come to a huge billboard: "Dunston, Deep in the Heart of Texas. Home of the Warriors, state champions 1945, 1959,

1962, 1963, 1980." It doesn't say which sport, but I have a feeling it wasn't hockey.

Everything around here is wide open with huge farms and cattle and goat ranches—goats!—everywhere. And every single ranch has a gate, some modest, some spectacular, with flags and plantings and fancy iron gates. We stop to check out the cactus growing like weeds along the roads. The Texas sky is impossibly huge, and it isn't just hot, it's nuclear. We pass by the first farm supply store I've ever seen, and everyone sells hunting supplies, even gas stations, just like back home everyone sells donuts. These supplies include weird-looking huts that Dad found out are deer blinds. Later, when we shop and talk to people, I'm amazed at their accents. They even talk slower.

After spending my entire life in the well-to-do, old coastal town of Hingham, Massachusetts, I've arrived on an alien planet.

* * * * *

Great, just great. School starts early in Texas—real early, like the second week of August. I get cheated out of three weeks of summer vacation. It doesn't matter that I'm bored out of my mind. I throw a total fit. Dad ignores me and takes me to enroll in eighth grade. The principal at the middle school reads my transcript and has me take a whole bunch of tests. Several days later, they call back and surprise Dad and me by asking us to meet with the high school principal.

"Mr. Fowler, I can assure you we'll provide excellent educational opportunities for your son," says Mr. Lessard, the high school principal. He's really tall and big, and while friendly, there's something about him that makes me think it would be a mistake to get sent to his office. "Well, Bobby, you must be excited about going directly into ninth grade. Just think, you're going to be in high school, young man. Every eighth grader will be very envious of you."

"Yes, sir," I answer, more polite than excited.

"I'm a little concerned," Dad tells him. "Bobby's always been small for his age. I don't want him to be intimidated by boys a year older."

"I understand," Mr. Lessard replies. "My sense is Bobby will do just fine. He's very bright and he's certainly very personable. I don't think he'll have any trouble fitting in."

I can hardly believe I'm going to be skipped a grade. Someone behind the counter says I'll be the youngest in a class of 289 students. I have a very bad feeling about this.

"Bobby, classes begin tomorrow," Mr. Lessard informs me. "Report here at half past seven, and we'll give you your homeroom assignment and your class schedule. I'm expecting your very best," he concludes with a stare that reminds me he's my new principal.

He and Dad have a few more words, and when they shake hands, I realize, quite unexpectedly, my high school years are about to begin.

* * * * *

It's after 7:30. I've been standing at the counter in the administration office for twenty minutes and no one's helping. The older woman behind the counter appears overwhelmed with telephone calls and people shouting questions at her every two seconds. Crap, my first day here and I'll be late for my first class.

"Excuse me, I'm Bobby Fowler. I'm new here and I'm supposed to report here first."

The woman, identified by a little plaque on the counter—Madeleine Henson, Administrative Assistant—looks up.

"Well, hello there. Shouldn't you be at the middle school?"

"Excuse me?"

"Aren't you starting seventh grade?"

"No, ma'am, ninth grade. Mr. Lessard told me I have to skip a grade."

"For mercy sakes," she says. She sticks her head into Mr. Lessard's office. I can't hear what they're saying, but when she comes out she's shaking her head and running her hand over the bun in her gray hair. She seems nice, though, like someone's grandmother.

"Let me get your file and then you'll be on your way to your first high school class," she says with a reassuring smile. "You must be so excited."

Excited? Try nervous. Not only am I in a new school, but everyone in my class will be a year older. As I watch her rummage through unruly piles of colored folders, I wonder if I can get my usual straight A's after skipping a grade.

"Here we are. Let's see, your first class is English in room 344," she says. "Your homeroom is with Mr. Evans in room 229. He's very nice," she says, looking over her glasses. "Here, Bobby, this is a map of our school. We're here …"

I half-listen, trying to be polite. This is definitely not Hingham Middle School. Everything feels different and strange and this campus, which includes the middle school and sports fields sprawling all over the place, is big and confusing. There's even a huge football stadium with lights and a two-story press box. Everyone looks different. The boys are big and they sure don't look like the boys in Hingham. One kid outside was wearing a cowboy hat!

Here it is, room 344. Just what I was afraid of—class is underway. Great, now I have to walk in and everyone will look at me. Maybe I can hide in the boys' room until it's time for my next class.

I gingerly open the door, trying to be as quiet as possible. Of course, everyone looks. The teacher—a large, older man with thin gray hair, a big red nose and a big gut—stops what he's doing at the blackboard and stares, annoyed that I interrupted.

"Son, seventh grade is not in this building. Are you lost?"

"No, sir. Mrs. Henson told me to report to this class. I'm Bobby Fowler. I'm supposed to give you this." I hand him my class assignments. With everyone still staring at me, I try not to look too nervous. *And I'm not in seventh grade!*

The teacher glances at the paper and then stares again, looking down his big red nose.

"And you are how old?" he asks, his voice cold and unfriendly.

"Thirteen … and a half, sir."

He pauses with a slight, not-very-nice smile. "Shouldn't you be in eighth grade?"

"Mr. Lessard told me I have to start ninth grade." The mention of the principal's name seems to be magic.

"Oh, I see. Well then, I'm Mr. Sawicki and this is freshman English. We sit alphabetically here. Let's see…" he says, putting on reading glasses to scan a chart on his desk.

"Davis … Falls … Faulkner. Kyle Faulkner, raise your hand. Tomorrow you'll sit behind that boy, understand? The rest of you students adjust your seating. For today, just sit over there by the windows."

Wow, that guy Kyle Faulkner is super good looking and I get to sit behind him.

"Okay, class, let's get back to breaking down this sentence," says Mr. Sawicki, cracking a piece of chalk on the board. "Can someone tell me the verb?"

JAMES ILLEGALLY PARKED HIS CAR NEXT TO THE FIRE HYDRANT.

Everyone's just sitting there. What's the matter with these kids? Are they stupid?

"Anyone? Come on, class, this is just a review. Anyone at all? Yes, Mr. Fowler."

"Pahked."

"Excuse me?"

"Pahked," I repeat, louder. Several students giggle.

"I see. Maybe you can you tell us the object?"

When I answer "cah," everyone snickers. Even Mr. Sawicki grins.

"You must be new here. From that accent, I'm guessing you're from England, is that correct?"

"Oh, no, sir, I'm from Hingham, Massachusetts, right near Boston." Mr. Sawicki grins again.

"Young man, you might want to learn to talk like a Texan real soon or no one around these parts will understand a word you're saying."

The classroom erupts in laughter. Heat rising in my face, I glare back, but Mr. Sawicki ignores me and returns to the board. Two boys next to me whisper loudly enough for me to hear.

"Hey, Josh, get a load of the dweeb."

"He sure talks funny—"

"—and he thinks he's smarter than us."

"He looks like he needs diapers." Josh and his friend try to suppress a laugh.

Mr. Sawicki's voice cracks across the classroom.

"Jason! Josh! That's enough!"

After that little humiliation, I keep my head down, but every now and then, I sneak peeks around the room, checking out every single boy. Quite a few are big and athletic and some, like that boy I'll sit behind tomorrow, and even these two jerks, are wicked cute.

At the bell, I check the schedule for my next class. Oh, dear God, please help me. I'm about to have my first-ever gym class.

Chapter 5

The awful smells hit me the second I open the door—deodorants, sweaty clothes, damp, musky odors. Excited chatter and laughter echo through the locker room. I have no idea what to expect. If anything, this is worse than walking into Mr. Sawicki's class.

My brand-new purple-and-white gym bag plops onto the floor next to a mostly empty bench. Now comes the part I've been dreading. Somehow I manage to get my long-sleeve shirt off and my white gym T-shirt on without anyone making fun of me, or worse, that look of disbelief that anyone could be so unathletic.

The two who made fun of me in English class just came in, and right behind them is that dreamboat I'll sit behind tomorrow. Kyle. I can't remember his last name but it doesn't matter because he's hot!

Just my luck, they sit right across from me.

"Think they'll bring you up to the varsity?" Josh, the tall, lanky one with a big mop of curly blond hair, asks Kyle.

"I know I'm good enough," Kyle replies, "but Aaron's being recruited by Texas Tech and both backups are really good, so why would they need a freshman quarterback? Maybe if I play safety …"

My gosh, is Kyle good-looking. The three of them are. A lot of the boys in here have smooth bodies, but Jason has more muscles than I've ever seen. The muscles on his arms stick out like balls and his chest is—his chest is gorgeous. Every bulging muscle in his legs looks sharp. He's taking his boxers off. Look at all that pubic hair, look at—

"Hey, punk, what the fuck you looking at?"

"Nothing," I answer in a little squeak.

"Hey, Jase, what happened?" Josh asks.

Jason slams his wire basket into the rack with a loud clank. "Nothin'."

Kyle's staring at me. Great, I just messed up in front of the cutest-looking boy I've ever seen.

Out in the main gym, divided by huge doors, everyone is standing around waiting for our P.E. instructor. Most of the guys are in little groups, talking and laughing and horsing around; most are bigger and more athletic than me. I feel different. I'd like to be somewhere else, anywhere else, especially when I notice Kyle, Josh, and Jason glancing at me and then laughing.

"Did you hear the news?" Jason asks Kyle with a goofy grin. "He already beat you out for third-string quarterback."

"Up yours," Kyle answers. He lands a hard punch on his friend's muscular shoulder. Jason doesn't even flinch. He's just standing there with a satisfied grin.

"Listen up, everyone." I assume the fit-looking guy striding into the gym, wearing long pants and a tight T-shirt with a whistle dangling around his neck must be our P.E. instructor. "I'm Mr. Boucher and this is phys ed for freshmen." He proceeds to review the rules. Everything he says, he shouts.

"Okay, two lines, one against the wall here, one over there. Let's move it, *now!*"

To let everyone know who's in charge, he blows his whistle really loud. Kyle is on my right, and standing next to him, I feel especially self-conscious. He's taller by four or five inches. Not only is he incredibly good-looking, he's built like a younger version of the Greek god Mercury I saw in a book. I sneak a quick peek at his arm. His completely hairless skin is a perfect bronze. How I'd like to run my hands all over that gorgeous skin. How I'd like to kiss—

"Listen up. Today we're going to introduce you to freshman P.E. with a little dodgeball," Mr. Boucher shouts as he marches up and down between the two widely-separated lines. "Here, Jason," he says, handing muscle boy the ball.

Jason is opposite me. He whispers to the kid next to him with an evil grin, winds up, and wings a fastball right at my head.

I yell and duck as the ball rockets toward me at impossible speed. The ball hits the divider doors with a smack so loud it echoes around the gym.

"What's the matter? Scared of the ball?" Jason shouts. Everyone laughs, even the guys on our side as I scamper to pick up the ball. It's slightly deflated, and I'm having a hard time gripping it.

"Well, throw it back, moron," someone on my side says.

I toss it back, but it falls out of my grip, bounces halfway, and dribbles toward Jason. More laughs. Of course he winds up and wings another, even harder, right at me. At least this time, I don't yell. I can't believe how hard he throws. Another throw back, this time to someone else, anyone but Jason, but when I lob the ball, all I get are more laughs.

The kid who picks it up whips it right back at me. It hits my arms crossed in front of my midsection so hard it stings.

"*That's enough!*" Mr. Boucher screams.

Everyone's laughing, even Kyle, who's doubled over and hanging on to Josh, who's equally hysterical. *Please, God, get me out of here.* At least for the rest of the period, I'm spared further humiliation.

But in not aiming at me anymore, there's another message: *I'm not included.*

"Everyone hit the showers. And girls, no pissing in the shower. Now get going!" Mr. Boucher screeches as we file into the locker room. Most boys head into the steamy shower wrapped in towels, but Kyle is naked. I manage one quick peek at the most awesomely perfect body I've ever seen as he strolls into the shower. A shiver shakes my shoulders.

The open showers offer no privacy. The room is oddly L-shaped, with the smaller section off to the right where maybe I can take my shower and no one will see me.

"That kid can't weigh ninety pounds soaking wet," I hear Josh say in a whisper that's a little too loud.

"He screams like a fucking girl," Jason answers, way too loud.

Someone snaps a towel at me so hard I yelp. I desperately want to be somewhere else, anywhere else. Like back home.

* * * * *

As a reward for finishing the first week of gym, Mr. Boucher gave us the option of shooting baskets or trampoline. Long lines of guys wait their turn at the two new trampolines, and just me and one other boy are shooting baskets. Actually, the other kid is shooting baskets and I'm just standing off to the side, staying far away from more humiliation. I watch Kyle acrobatically bounce way up and down. He even performs a few flips.

I wish I could do stuff like that. Yesterday, everyone laughed when I kicked the basketball away trying to dribble and again when I couldn't shoot the ball anywhere near the basket. Jason was pissed. I overheard him in the shower, which was easy because he was loud, saying, "Every guy should be able to put the fucking ball in the fucking hole."

Kyle finishes his turn. After a few high-fives, he glances my way and walks halfway across the gym, right up to me.

"Hey, you're not going to try out the new trampolines?" he asks.

"Maybe when the lines go down," I mumble back.

He smiles ever so slightly. "How about if I show you how to dribble?"

"*You* want to help *me?*"

"Yeah, why not? You looked lost out there yesterday." Kyle picks up a ball and holds it in front of me. "Keep the ball on your fingertips, like this …"

He starts by teaching me to dribble in place. At first, it's hard to control the ball, but little by little, I get the feel of it. I begin to like the way I can control the bounce, much like I precisely control the bounce of my drumsticks. Then he has me walk and dribble. It's awkward, but I'm getting a little better. We practice faster and faster until I can run, well maybe jog, and dribble. I'm totally in heaven. The best-looking boy in gym class is helping me one-on-one. I'm eager to do everything he says.

"Stand over here," he tells me, pointing to a spot on the floor. "I'm going to show you how to put the ball in the basket. Try to aim for the backboard, keep a bend in your knees, and throw off your fingertips, like this …"

I try. And try. Shots are flying everywhere, high off the backboard, short of the basket, clanking off the side of the rim.

"I'll never do this," I mutter after another try misses everything.

"Come on, keep trying. It'll come," Kyle says. "Keep your eyes glued on the bucket and remember your follow-through … *that's the way!* See? Your first basket."

I actually made a shot! I'm standing under the hoop with the ball cradled against my hip. I can't quite believe I shot a basket. Kyle's smile is so bright and so perfect, with such white teeth, I can't help but stare.

"Is this the first time you ever played basketball?" he asks, sauntering over to join me under the hoop.

"Yeah, sorry. I'm not very good at sports."

"Did you ever do any sports back in … where was it?"

"Hingham, Massachusetts, just south of Boston. I never really got into sports. But I can skate pretty good with hockey skates," I add, hoping he'll be impressed.

Kyle crinkles his nose as if I told him I do ballet. "Hockey? There's no ice hockey around these parts," he says in a perfectly sexy Texas drawl. "Hey, did you ever see the Red Sox?"

"Yeah. My dad took me to Fenway Park every year."

"Dude, there's an 'r' in Park. You sure talk funny."

"Well, you sure sound funny to me!"

He hesitates, I think surprised that I came right back at him.

"Sorry, but you know you're going to get teased. Okay, time for the big test. Let's see you do a layup."

I hesitate, not wanting to look like a jerk with Kyle standing under the basket watching me. "Come on, you can do it," he says, encouraging me with a two-fisted salute.

I cautiously dribble down the court and heave an awkward shot off the backboard. It's rolling around the rim … it's rolling … it goes in! *How did that happen?* I can't believe I did a layup just like the basketball players do. Kyle, however, is not impressed.

"Four more," he says without any sign of a smile. Four more tries, three go in, one rolls off the rim when the screech of Mr. Boucher's whistle ends our little training session.

"Not bad for a beginner," he says with another irresistible smile. To top it off, I get a high-five. Kyle Faulkner just gave me a high-five! I feel faint.

Everyone has showered and is getting dressed. I'm in a bathroom stall when I hear Jason's voice over the loud chatter in the locker room. "What do you think you were *doing?*"

"Give me a break. I was just helping the kid." It's Kyle's voice. "Why are you all stressed out about him anyway?"

"Dude, he's a fucking little sissy, that's why. He's been sneaking peeks at me, and he sure seemed happy you were helping him."

"He was okay."

"Fine, you help him all you want. He'd better stay the fuck away from me, that's all I can say."

"Come on, Jase, I felt bad for him," Kyle explains. Jason snorts something in disgust while I cower in the stall. Oh, God, help me get through this.

Chapter 6

"Everyone gather 'round," Mr. Boucher says in his usual booming voice. I'm about to find out what all these blue mats are for. "We're going to learn the basics of wrestling. I'm going to demonstrate the beginner's starting position and the first take-down. Over the following four weeks, you'll learn much more and we'll have plenty of practice matches."

Oh, God no. I'm going to die.

"Jason, front and center," our PE instructor says. "Okay, Jase, assume the starting position."

I call him Dodgeball Boy. He's not just hunky and muscular, his short, blond hair is thick and perfect, and he's unspeakably good-looking. It's totally unfair. That boy is so hot he makes me nervous just to be near him. I see him hanging around with Kyle and Josh and this other kid, Dustin, all the time. They're known as the Four Amigos. Girls, even upperclass girls, ogle and flirt and talk about them in giggly, excited whispers, especially Kyle. Boys try to stay in their good graces and hang around with them. From what I can see, the Four Amigos are the most popular boys in the entire class.

"Okay, boys, now pair off and practice," Mr. Boucher announces after he and Dodgeball Boy finish their demonstration.

Thank goodness I'm paired with Tyrone, a shy, skinny kid from the school's nerd culture. He's a head taller than me and doesn't seem to be very athletic. That's why, I think, he made his way over to me. When it's my turn, I'm very gentle when I get him in the starting position. Another loud whistle rattles around the gym.

"Okay, boys, now all of you practice the first take down move a few times," our instructor shouts. "Listen up. If you wrestled in eighth grade, pair off with a boy who has never wrestled and show him how to do the move."

Please, God, please let me get paired with Kyle!

He's already grappling with Josh, and now they're both on the mat, screeching and laughing as they roll all over the place.

"Come on, guys, let's get serious," Mr. Boucher says, more laughing than upset. "Jason, you help that boy over there."

To my horror, Mr. Boucher is pointing at me. When Dodgeball Boy sees who Mr. Boucher is pointing at, he doesn't look too happy. Now I'm scared, and not just because he'll throw me right through the floor. I'll have to be close to that gorgeous body—really close.

"Coach, I'm not wrestling with him," Jason announces in a huff.

"Maybe I can practice with Tyrone?" I meekly ask.

"You two just get going. Jason, you take it easy and show him how to do the starting position and the first take-down."

Kyle, with Josh right behind him, saunters over. "Come on, man, you're the best," he says to Jason. "Just show him, that's all."

Jason waves him off. "Come on, Coach, I might kill the little sissy."

"That's enough of that. Just go nice and easy and get going … *now, please.*"

Mr. Boucher hurries off to break up a shoving match. Down on my hands and knees, I'm wishing I was paired with Kyle, or anyone else. Jason gets down into the starting position. His hot breath close to my neck excites and scares me. Not two seconds later, I'm lifted in the air. Then so fast I can't even begin to squirm out of his hold, I'm slammed onto the mat hard enough to make my head bounce. Little flashes of bright spots sparkle in front of my eyes. It's the oddest thing, but my field of vision narrows.

"Don't ever wrestle with me again, you little homo!" he screams as he gets up, face red and fists clenched.

As Jason stalks off, the dead silence in the gym is finally broken by Kyle's voice. "Come on, Jase, whatcha do that for?"

Everyone is looking at me sprawled flat on the mat, unable to move. I can make out Mr. Boucher peering down. I think he's asking if I'm okay.

"Yeah, I'm fine," I croak in a pathetic attempt to show how tough I am.

He reaches down, grabs my hand, and lifts me to my feet. My vision goes gray. I'm swaying and my knees are unsteady. A hand pushes my head down to my knees.

"Go to the locker room, drink some water, and keep your head down between your knees for a few minutes," Mr. Boucher says. "You, go with him to make sure he's okay," he tells someone.

At least I don't cry. Every part of my body hurts. I feel dizzy and sick and totally humiliated as I wobble to the locker room. Worse, Jason screamed that nasty word in front of everyone. I hear Mr. Boucher shouting at him, but right now all I want to do is sit down before I pass out.

* * * * *

"Just what do you think you're doing up there?" Of course, Mr. Boucher notices me sitting up in the bleachers. A day after getting slammed to the mat, there's no way I'm wrestling.

"I hurt my elbow."

"Well, come here, let's see." He looks skeptical as I hop down the steps of the retractable bleachers. When he grabs my skinny little left arm and feels a tiny abrasion on my elbow, I grimace, pretending it hurts.

"Okay, sit up in the bleachers for a few days," he says.

If I'm relieved, so is he. He relates so well to Kyle and the other athletic boys. I overheard in the locker room that Kyle and Dodgeball Boy were brought up to the varsity football team when two players were injured. Of course they were; they're so athletic it's scary. There's nothing they can't do, and they make everything look easy. I don't know what I am to Mr. Boucher, but he treats me differently than the way he treats them.

* * * * *

After three days of sitting in the bleachers, I'm totally bored. I'm invisible, not even an afterthought. At least I get to watch Kyle wrestle. I daydream of him wrestling me to the ground and lying on top of me, his lips close to mine, his breath hot on my face. Dodgeball Boy is another matter. Tyrone told me that Mr. Boucher yelled at him pretty good that day and made him do a hundred pushups in front of everyone. Now he'll be out to get me. He's so hot I want to watch his every move, his every drop of sweat, but if he catches me staring one more time, he'll beat the crap out of me for real.

Sitting up here can't go on forever, and I'm sure Mr. Boucher will make me rejoin the class soon. I can't go back to gym class, I just can't. I need a plan.

* * * * *

I'm so scared of getting caught skipping gym, I can't concentrate. Every little noise in the band room or just outside makes me jump, and then I look around to see if someone's watching. The little scrap of music I've written for my fake special assignment is junk.

I picture Mr. Boucher storming into the room to drag me back to gym class after giving me a hundred detentions, and then Dodgeball Boy beats the living crap out of me to the cheers of the entire class.

But nothing happens and the bells ring. No more gym class, no more getting body slammed, and no more yelling nasty names at me. There is a God!

Chapter 7

Chloe breaks into hysterics the moment she comes out of the crowded lunch line and spots me at the back of the cafeteria. I'm standing and waving my arms wildly at our usual table. I think some of my friend's energy and wild sense of fun has radiated off on me.

We met in algebra and hit it off instantly. It wasn't long before we were hanging around after school at each other's houses. I share thoughts with Chloe I've never shared with anyone. When I told Chloe and her mom how hurt I was from losing my mom and leaving my home and all my friends, both surprised me with warm, tender hugs.

An attractive, slightly built Asian boy is following her past crowded tables.

"Bobby, this is Danny Tranh. He's one of my best friends and I wanted you guys to meet."

"How do you do?" he says as we shake hands. "Chloe told me all about you, and I've been looking forward to meeting you." His politeness is a surprise. A friendly, engaging smile reveals perfect white teeth, a wonderfully bright contrast against golden-brown skin. He shakes a lock of shiny black hair out of his eyes, beautiful hair so coarse and thick, each strand could be a little radio antenna. I can't help staring, but when he notices me looking him over, I quickly look down.

"In case you were wondering," he says with a cheery smile, "I'm Cambodian with a little French mixed in. When we moved to Texas, everyone thought I was Chinese."

"Hey, man, how's it going?" I ask in my best straight-boy voice.

"So, are you still hiding out in the music room?" Chloe asks with a wicked grin. "Oh, don't worry. I told Danny about your adventures in gym class, and he's cool." Danny's grin is just as wicked.

"I got caught yesterday by Mr. Reynolds, so I'm back in gym class," I explain. "He was going to give me detention, but then I told him I'm flunking gym. You know, I'm not all that athletic, and I'm intimidated by Mr. Boucher and some of the aggressive guys. I'm sure he talked to Mr. Boucher."

"Is it okay now? And what about Dodgeball Boy? Is he still bothering you?" she asks.

"It's better. I stay away from him, and he stays away from me."

"Dodgeball Boy?" Danny wants to know.

"This kid Jason. See him way over there? He's the muscle guy with the short blond hair. He's really been on my case."

Danny turns completely around to follow my point. "Oh, Jason. I've known him ever since I got here in third grade. You know, I think he's a nice guy, but sometimes his hormones are out of control."

"Nice guy? Well, anyway, Mr. Boucher apologized and made Jason apologize. He sure didn't look too happy, and I felt awkward."

"At least the jerk apologized," Chloe mutters.

"Mr. Boucher asked Kyle and a couple others to help me out. Maybe he isn't as bad as I thought."

"Kyle? Kyle Faulkner's in your gym class? Oh, what a total doll!" Chloe says while fanning herself with her fingers.

I totally agree—but can't tell them. Danny's rolling his eyes. I can see he isn't too impressed with Kyle Faulkner's incredible body or stunning good looks.

"Chloe's been raving about how you play drums. That is so totally cool," he says.

"Yeah, I'm in the concert band and I have a set at home. Maybe next year, I'll try out for marching band. Playing drums is the about only thing I've got going for me."

Chloe scowls and wags a finger at me.

"That is so not true."

"Come on, Chloe. I'm younger than everyone else and I'm not an athlete. Sometimes I feel like such an idiot."

Chloe reacts with a low, frustrated growl. "Listen, you've got so much going for you," she says, this time jabbing her finger at me. "Your music talent is off the charts, you ace every test, and you talk so well in class. Don't you understand? You're a really nice guy and you're funny and you've got a lot going for you. And I'm glad you're not some stupid, stuck-up jock."

I'm too stunned to react. No one has ever said anything like this to me, ever. Well, Mom, but that doesn't count.

Danny quickly starts making jokes about how fat and stupid Mr. Sawicki is. We tease and laugh, and when we leave the cafeteria for afternoon classes, I'm happy I've made a new friend.

I'm retrieving books from my locker, thinking about the nice things Chloe said, when Kyle, Jason, Dustin, and Josh appear. Students part to let these studs strut down the middle of the corridor. Even though we're going to the same class, they pass without a greeting, a nod, or anything indicating I exist. Chloe's nice words recede as I stare at their athletic arms and tight bodies and everything else that makes them the most desirable boys in school.

How I wish I could be like them.

Chapter 8

"All right, everybody, take your seats and settle down." Our music teacher, Mr. Reynolds, is setting a snare drum down in front of the 110 members of the concert band. Rehearsal is about to begin. I'm so nervous I have to pee.

"Band, I found out a very talented musician has joined our group," Mr. Reynolds announces. "I've asked our newest and youngest member, Bobby Fowler, to give us a demonstration on snare drum. Bobby, can you come down here and play something?"

Every head turns to watch me squeeze my way down through the flutes and clarinets. A murmur spreads through the tightly packed ranks of musicians.

"So what did you decide to play?" he asks.

"'The Connecticut Halftime.'" All eyes are focused on me adjusting the height of the drum. A dead silence drapes the room when I look up, ready to play a fun but demanding piece of drum music.

"All set?" Mr. Reynolds asks. Okay, one, two, three, play ... are you ready?"

"Sorry, sir, but that's really slow."

"Okay, again. One, two, three ... Bobby, what's the matter?"

"It's still too slow," I tell him. "Can I just start?"

Without waiting for Mr. Reynolds to say yes, I take a deep breath and tap my foot four times. I begin fast, faster than I've ever played this. I'm whaling through the music, hitting every accent hard. The band room is filled with a wall of percussive sound. In spite of the volume, I hear a girl in the front row exclaim, "Oh my God!" Inspired, I pick up the tempo slightly.

By the last part, I'm playing so heavy and so fast I'm grimacing a little. At the end, I hammer the final accent so hard my head snaps back.

Instantly, every member of the band jumps to their feet, clapping, cheering, whooping, hollering. At first startled, I reply with a little wave. What's really amazing are the guys in the percussion section going crazy, even the seniors. How cool. I've been walking a tightrope ever since I joined the band. I try to defer to the older drummers and not threaten them, while at the same time trying not to hold back on what I can really do.

Mr. Reynolds isn't clapping or doing anything other than standing there with a little grin of disbelief. When at last he offers a handshake, he's hesitant, like he can't believe what he just heard.

Practice is over, I've come back down to earth, and now, still low in the band pecking order, I'm collecting all the music in the percussion section when the most popular girl in the entire class approaches. I know who she is even though we haven't met. Every boy drools when she walks by, leering at her tight, athletic body, and talking big about what they'd do with her on a date. Her wavy blond hair is shampoo-ad perfect.

"Hi, I'm Helen. I play flute," she says, her blue eyes sparkling with warmth and friendliness. "I've never heard anyone play like you did. Golly, that was amazing."

"Thanks. It's really nice to meet you."

"How did you do that?"

"Oh, I don't know. I've been playing drums since I was five," I tell her.

"Aren't you the one who moved here from Boston?"

I shake my head that I am.

"Look, don't let it get to you if people tease you about how you talk," Helen says with a sweet smile. "We probably sound weird to you."

"Ah, it's okay. I'm getting used to being teased."

"Well, I'm sorry I didn't do this when school first started, but welcome to Texas and welcome to Dunston High School."

She offers her hand with a bright, sparkly smile. *One of the most popular girls in the entire class is welcoming me!*

We talk a bit more about my drumming and, for some reason, Texas barbeque. With her looks and social status, Helen could be a stuck-up snot, but she's really nice and she seems genuine. I like her a lot already.

She leaves for home, and as I finish storing all the music, I'm trying to picture Danny's reaction when I tell him Helen Albrecht stayed behind to talk to me. He'll be jealous. Maybe I'll tell him we "got along well." Yeah, that's what I'll do so he won't be suspicious.

Mr. Boucher being nice after all, my new friend Danny, my drum solo, meeting Helen—wow, what a day!

Chapter 9

I remember that day, the best day of my freshman year, as if it happened yesterday. Still, freshman is so—young. In August, I start tenth grade, and next spring, can you believe it, I'll be fifteen.

"Sophomore," I say aloud in my room, hardly believing I'll be in tenth grade.

Sophomore.

It sounds so mature.

I'm too excited to sleep. I'm still lying here staring at the ceiling and the stupid light, tossing my tennis ball up and down when one more memory intrudes. It forces its way in front of my eyes even though I desperately want to stop reliving it. Sometimes I wonder if God is unhappy with me.

"Bobby, we're going over to Mrs. Robles's at eight tomorrow morning," Dad tells me for the second time. "Just make sure you're all packed tonight." Dad and I are cleaning up in the kitchen after once again having take-out for supper. "I'm expecting you to behave for Mrs. Robles and do your homework, understood?" I don't answer. "I said, is that understood?"

"Yeah."

"Yeah? What kind of talk is that?"

"Yes, Dad, I promise," I reply, forcing every word out.

"Remember, I'm gone for two weeks and I'll be home on the twenty-second. We'll have time for some shopping, and don't forget, the Cantwells have invited us for Christmas dinner."

"Sure thing, Dad."

Christmas? I don't feel any joy or excitement or anything about Christmas. I don't care about putting up a tree, decorating the house, buying gifts, singing Christmas carols, or Christmas dinner with anyone. I don't want any gifts. With Mom dead, there's no joy and no celebrating in me. There's just no Christmas in me, and now Dad's leaving.

"Why do you have to go off on one of your trips?" I ask him.

Dad gives me one of those looks as if he can't believe I actually asked.

"How come, Dad? Why can't you just work here?" I ask, getting louder.

"Because I can't, Bobby, you know that."

My anger feels like heat deep down inside rushing to my head. "You won't even say where you're going!" I yell at him.

"For the hundredth time, I can't. I start by flying to Ramstein Air Force Base, okay? Why are you acting like a little kid?"

"You moved us here and now you're leaving," I scream. "Why can't we just go home?"

"That's enough!"

"Go to hell!"

I've been curled up on my bed for a while when I hear the doorknob turn with a little click. Light from the hallway spills into my room. I stay completely still, not even breathing. I know he's waiting and watching in the doorway.

"Good night, Bobby," he says in a soft voice, almost a whisper. The door latch gently clicks and my room returns to complete darkness.

Mom would have come and sat on the bed. She would have run her hand through my hair and made me feel better. Dad can't do that. I know he loves me, but that's just not my dad. When I was little, Mom used to call Grandma back in Texas and sputter about how reserved Dad could be and "those New England Yankees." All I know is he's my dad and that's the way he is.

I hold back angry tears. I want Dad to be proud of me, but he's leaving in the morning. He's leaving me all alone.

* * * * *

Standing here waiting to say good-bye on the dirt driveway of our next-door neighbor, Mrs. Robles, a chilly, swirling wind cuts through my jacket. A shiver jolts my shoulders. I know it's not just because it's cold and gray.

Nothing was said at breakfast, as if last night never happened. Dad even made my favorite, french toast with real maple syrup, so maybe he feels bad too. I didn't say much and it didn't help that I had an awful nightmare last night. On the way over, I again had to promise to study hard and behave for Mrs. Robles. She's older and she's nice enough. Dad said her only daughter died suddenly from a brain something-or-other some years ago, and she had a foster child awhile back, and she's had a tough life. Maybe Dad wanted me to feel bad for her, but right now I really don't care about her problems.

She's trying to be extra cheerful. When I banged my heavy suitcase through the front door, she offered to help. I'm trying to be polite, but I'm in no mood for her goody-goody smiles. I hope she just leaves me alone.

Dad's ready to go. He can't look right at me and he's stiff and awkward. Nothing new there. Dad's always like this when he has to say good-bye.

"Bobby, make me proud."

We shake hands. He pats me on the shoulder.

"Bye, Dad."

He gets in the car and just like that, he's leaving. Dad's watching me more than where he's going as he slowly backs the car down the long driveway. I give another little wave and he waves back, hardly moving his hand back and forth and not smiling. He can't take his eyes off me. And just like that, he's driving away.

I'm shivering and alone in the driveway of some woman I've only met a few times. I feel a little like I did after Mom died. It's odd because I'm not sad or scared or anything. I feel nothing. I feel nothing at all.

Chapter 10

Dad will be here tomorrow night. Mrs. Robles is nice; she even gave me the key to the house so I can play my drums and work on music. Still, I'm really looking forward to Dad coming home. And, if I know him, I'll get an unusual gift from some exotic market, maybe Istanbul or Cairo, or, like last time, Karachi. Oddly, though, it's been six days since I last heard from Dad, unusual because he's been calling every other day.

Mrs. Robles is rapping on my bedroom door.

"Bobby, can you come out to the parlor, please? Someone's here to talk to you, dear."

Great, another of her nosy friends wants to check me out. I'm an exhibit at the zoo.

A handsome, crew-cut man in a gray suit is standing in front of one of the overstuffed chairs in the living room. Tanned and lean, I think he's about Dad's age.

"Hello, Bobby," he says. He offers a stiff handshake but doesn't introduce himself. His faint, nervous smile quickly disappears.

Standing next to him is a thin, older black woman with large eyeglasses dangling on a silver chain and a worn leather briefcase at her feet. She extends her hand without any smile whatsoever. I'm getting the feeling they're not here to visit with Mrs. Robles.

"Well, why don't we all sit," Mrs. Robles says with an odd shake in her voice. I think she's expecting the guy to say something, but he's just sitting there staring back. Except for a nervous glance, Mrs. Robles can't seem to look directly at me. After several more moments of awkward silence, she loudly clears her throat.

"Bobby, this man flew all the way from Washington to see you, and this woman is from Child Protective Services. I'm afraid there might be a development you need to hear about. Here, come sit, dear."

Every nerve in my body goes on alert as I very carefully ease myself onto the sofa where Mrs. Robles is patting the cushion.

"Do you remember me?" the guy asks. "I'm Dick Huntington. I work for the same company as your dad. Actually, Dave's one of my best friends. We were roommates at Harvard."

Now I remember. I nod in reply. He came to our house a few times, and he's the only guy who ever gave Dad a hug. Beads of sweat dot his forehead; he's fidgeting with his hands.

"I'm afraid there's been a bit of trouble," he says. "We've lost contact with your dad. At the moment, he's missing, which I'm sure is just temporary. Bobby, please don't be overly alarmed, but the plane he was in … his plane went down. We're quite sure your dad got out. The State Department and other government agencies are doing everything possible to locate him and bring him home. It's just that—" As he hesitates and swallows hard, every part of my body tenses a little tighter. "I don't think he'll be home for Christmas."

I can't move. I can't speak. I can't think. All I hear is a rushing sound in my head. When I don't reply, Mr. Huntington continues.

"Bobby, listen to me. We're going to get your dad back home. The government has committed a lot of assets, and we're doing everything possible to find him and get him back. I'm not authorized to tell you what country he's in, but their government is actively cooperating. I promise you, we're doing everything possible to get your dad home, and we will."

This isn't happening. This can't be happening.

"Bobby, I'm so sorry, hon," the woman says. "I know this is a shock, but everything will be okay. They just have to locate him. I'm Mrs. Clark from Child Protective Services, and we're here to look after you. Is everything going okay staying here with Mrs. Robles?"

"Yes, ma'am," I tell her, although it feels like someone else spoke.

"Mrs. Robles has agreed to have you stay awhile longer," she goes on, "just until they contact your father and bring him home. Hon, I just know these good folks will get your father back home right after Christmas. The Good Lord is looking out for him."

They stay longer, but I hear nothing. Dad's plane went down. Dad's missing. The rushing sound in my head is worse, and there's an awful feeling in my stomach. Everything is black. Everything is very, very black.

Chapter 11

Some Christmas. I've pulled the bedcovers up tightly, thinking maybe I can sleep through the day or at least stay in my room. Dad's still missing. With no more news, I'm hoping Christmas will go away. Upset to the point of getting sick, I missed the final two days of school, mostly staying in bed and using the bedcovers and science fiction novels to keep the terror at bay.

Mrs. Robles tries to be kind, but everything about Christmas in her house is weird. I don't like her decorations or the fake tree or the blinking lights and there's no wreath on the door. I don't like the sixty-degree weather or the bare ground. I just don't like anything about Christmas in Texas. A knock on my door makes me shudder.

"Bobby, it's noontime. Time for gifts. Okay, dear?"

Well, that plan just went out the window. I numbly sit on the side of the bed, rub my head and face roughly, and somehow find the energy to put on my jeans and shirt. I'm half-awake when I drag myself to the living room where she put this awful silver tree. Dad and I always went to a tree farm to cut our own. This year, he said, we'd have to go into town to buy a cut tree, but this!

"Here you go, dear. I know your father will bring presents when he gets back, but my goodness, we can't have Christmas Day without presents."

"Yes, ma'am," I mumble.

Mrs. Robles reaches under the tree for two wrapped packages and hands them to me. I open the larger one. It's a pair of gold corduroy shorts.

When I open the second gift, I find a flashlight with an emergency flasher. I wanted gifts even less than before Dad went missing, but these are beyond stupid. She's waiting expectantly.

"I made a trip into town just to get your gifts."

"Thank you, Mrs. Robles," I mumble.

She reaches under the tree for another gift and reads the tag. She says it's from her sister Ruth in Arizona. When she opens it, she screeches and carries on when it turns out to be an oversized pink sweatshirt with "Texas" in sequins. I'm going to barf. There are more gifts under the tree, and I've got to sit through it all. My head is way down, almost to my knees.

"Are you okay, dear?"

"I don't feel very well."

"Why don't you lie down and maybe you'll feel better when dinner is ready, okay, dear?"

I get to my room, throw her dumb gifts on the desk, and curl up in a ball on top of the bed. Not only do I have to get up later and pretend I'm enjoying dinner, I have to go through this all over again tomorrow with the Cantwells.

I'm just too upset to eat much dinner. When I think about Mom not being here and Dad hurt and stranded in some far-off place, I start to tear up. Afraid of losing it, I ask if I can be excused. I flee to my room.

It's early evening. Hunger forced a reconnaissance from the safety of my bedroom. After guzzling a huge glass of milk and demolishing almost half of a chocolate pecan pie, which thrilled Mrs. Robles, I realize it's been five days since I talked to either Danny or Chloe. They know nothing of what's happened.

"Mrs. Robles, may I use the phone to call Chloe?"

"Certainly. Just don't talk too long, dear."

"Alone?"

She shrugs, puts my dishes in the sink, and retreats into the living room without a word. To be sure she can't hear, I stretch the telephone cord all the way into my room and shut the door almost tight.

"Chloe?"

"Bobby! Merry Christmas. Were you sick?"

I'm on the verge of tears. She's waiting, but if I try to talk, I'll cry instead.

"Bobby, what's wrong? Are you okay?"

"I need to talk to you. Please, Chloe, I really need you," I gasp after a long silence.

"Oh my gosh, what happened?" she asks when I start crying. "Bobby, what's going on?" I'm losing it and can't answer. "Hey, hold on a sec …" she says.

There's a long silence. I hear muffled voices in the background before she picks up.

"Mom's driving me over."

I hear the car pull in, followed almost instantly by the slam of the car door. Two seconds later, the doorbell rings. She and Mrs. Robles talk in the living room, but I can't make out what's being said. I'm on the edge of the bed with my head in my hands when I hear a light tap on the door.

"Come in, Chloe," I reply so softly there's another little tap as the door squeaks open.

When I look up, Mrs. Robles's large frame is silhouetted against the bright light of the kitchen. She comes into my darkened room quietly. Easing herself onto the bed right next to me, she gently rubs my back.

"I know you need your friend, but I'm here for you too, okay, dear? I know I'm not your mother and I'm not supposed to be, but I want to help, okay, dear?" Everything with her is "okay, dear," but what she said really gets to me.

"I'm sorry I spoiled your Christmas, Mrs. Robles." As I look up, tears fill my eyes.

With another couple rubs of my back and a peck on the side of my head, she leaves as quietly as she had come in. In the kitchen, she motions to Chloe.

She sees my teary eyes and gasps. In her concern and excitement, she almost shouts. "Bobby, what the heck happened? Mrs. Robles said you're very upset, something about your father's missing."

I'm trying hard to control myself and tell her what happened, but now that she's here, a floodgate opens. I begin sobbing so hard I'm shaking. Chloe grabs me and holds tightly while I completely fall apart and bawl on her shoulder. All the hurt, all the fear is gushing out.

Not understanding what's going on, Chloe hugs me and rubs my shoulders without saying a word until I calm down to teary eyes and sniffling. I manage to spit out everything that happened, including my hunch that Dad's on an intelligence mission in the Middle East.

"There's more …" I'm hesitating, afraid to say it. Chloe patiently waits and rubs my shoulder. "I'm really scared Dad's never coming back," I choke out, sobs again filling my bedroom. It's at this instant I understand the terrifying implications of something else: not only did I yell at Dad the night before he left, I didn't even tell him I love him when he drove off, just like I had never told Mom the evening she left for work.

Chloe again wraps me in a hug and rubs my back. "Come on, you said lots of people are looking for him. You watch, they'll bring him home real soon. I just know they will. Everything's going to be okay."

I desperately hope so, but deep down is a knot of fear that just won't go away.

Chapter 12

Completely engrossed in a new composition, I'm almost jolted right out of my chair by the loud rapping on the door at the top of the cellar stairs.

"Bobby Fowler? May I come down?" comes a loud voice. It's a guy and he sounds older. I answer that it's okay, although I can't imagine who's coming to see me.

Unlike Danny's daredevil, three-step jump down the stairs, the cadence of creaks down the wooden steps is slow and deliberate. My curiosity peaks when a dark suit is revealed from the bottom up.

He's tall and he's definitely older and he's distinguished looking, with perfectly groomed white hair and a handsome, reddish face highlighted by bushy white eyebrows. The instant he sees me, his entire face lights up in a friendly, bright smile, but it's his eyes that catch my attention, eyes that are full of warmth. With the suit and shiny blue tie, he looks a little like the lawyer who helped Dad after Mom died.

"Hello, Bobby, I'm Judge Francis Garrity, but please just call me Judge. Mrs. Robles told me you'd be here." When he offers his hand, I'm surprised to see a heavy gold chain on his wrist.

The judge begins looking around the room. He takes in my drums to his right and synthesizer and speakers to his left. The judge smiles again, walks over to the sofa, and slowly eases himself down the way old people always sit.

"I'm terribly sorry I interrupted your music, but now that I've sat down, can I stay a few minutes?" he says with a wink.

"Yes, sir," I reply with a shrug of my shoulders.

"So, I understand you spend a lot of time here. I heard some of your music when I came in. It was … ah, it was interesting. What was that?"

"It's just some experimental music I've been working on, sir. It's all synthesized."

"Synthesized?"

"Yes, sir. It's artificially manipulated sound. Here …" I press a few keys that make percussive pops. After flipping a couple rocker switches and adjusting a slide, the same keys make chime sounds with reverb. "I can make lots of sounds, but this synthesizer doesn't have many features. Mom and Dad gave it to me last Christmas. I could do lots more with better equipment."

"And the drums?" he asks, nodding toward my white pearl set.

"Yes, sir, I *love* playing drums."

"Well, me boy, let's hear something."

It takes a couple deep breaths to relax and focus. I begin my basic solo, starting with just my hi-hat and snare, and gradually adding in everything else. Then I'm off to the races. I'm running complex, high-speed jazz riffs over my snare drum and toms and cymbals. It's not the rock-and-roll shit most kids play to impress their friends with a lot of noise and not much else. After several minutes in a total groove, I end with a few extra loud pops on cymbals and bass drum.

"That was my Buddy Rich ending," I tell him. "He was a drummer." There's no response from the judge except a grin and a surprised, almost disbelieving look.

"Was that okay?" I ask him.

"Jesus, Mary, and Joseph, you'll go far with that talent," he says.

"Thanks. I've been practicing."

"Listen, me boy, it's a beautiful day outside," he says with a heavy Irish accent and a grin. "I need to chat with you and I thought we might take a walk. Is that okay with you?"

I nod that it is. How odd. It's in the high thirties today, a lot colder than the sixties we've had all week, and he wants to talk outside? He follows me up the cellar stairs to the hallway where I left my jacket.

Stepping out into the calm, crisp air, the mid-January sun is so bright I squint. I try not to grin when I see his mint-condition older black Cadillac further down the driveway. It's the perfect car for an old guy. My smile disappears, however, when we start down the driveway at a surprisingly fast pace.

"So tell me, are you doing well with your studies?" he asks as we march up the road.

"I guess so."

"And Mrs. Robles? Is everything going well staying with her?"

"I guess so."

"She cooks your meals and takes good care of you?"

"Yes, sir." He looks at me, expecting more. "She doesn't cook as good as Mom used to. Nothing's the same."

"I'm sure everything seems very different, and I'm sure it's upsetting. Bobby, you must have some friends at school, someone you can talk to."

"Yes, sir. Danny and Chloe, they're my best friends. Sometimes they come over to hang out, and once in a while, they listen to my new compositions. I told Mrs. Robles how good they've been since Dad went missing. She said they're true friends, you know, friends who stay with you when things really suck."

"Mmm ..." is his only response as we walk along a field now brown and barren from winter winds.

"You're certainly a good-looking boy. Interested in any girls at school? Or are any interested in you?" he says with a wink.

I hesitate, although I didn't mean to. "No, sir, I don't have a girlfriend."

Out of the corner of my eye, I catch a trace of a smile. We continue walking—actually, we're marching—up the road.

"I stopped by to talk to you about a few things," he says after a few minutes of silence. "First of all, a few months ago, your father had the foresight to set up a trust. Your father and I met several times. I must say, he's a fine man, a Harvard man, just like me. This trust is money he set aside in case anything happens, like right now. I'm the trustee. Do you know what that means?"

"No, sir."

"It means I control the trust and make disbursements under the terms and conditions of the trust agreement. I know this is all legalese to you, so let me tell you in practical terms. The trust keeps your house going while your father's away and pays for your support and expenses. You really enjoy your music, don't you?"

"Yeah! I mean yes, sir. I play my drums and work on music every day."

"Well, as the trustee, I can release funds for special needs. Young man, I might not be an expert, but I know enough to recognize talent. How would you like to get some more of this synthesizer equipment?"

"Yeah! That would be awesome."

"Why don't you let me know what you want and we'll see what we can do."

"Yes, sir." *Wow, a new synthesizer; maybe an amp and a subwoofer too.*

"In return, I get a promise from you. Actually, you've got to promise two things. Your first promise is to study hard at school."

The judge stops and holds me by my shoulders. "I know you're discouraged, and I'll bet you're scared out of your mind. I talked to your principal and I know you're having trouble with your grades. Bobby, don't mess up your life because you're scared and hurt now. I promise you, someday, young man, there will be rays of sunshine. I know you think that's just a crock, but I really mean it. When things aren't so dark and scary, you're going to need a good education."

"I can't concentrate. Besides, nothing seems to matter anymore."

"I know this is very difficult. I just want your promise you'll try hard," he says with a pat on my back.

"Yes, sir. What's the second promise?"

"Well, first of all, when I report back next week, the court will appoint me as your legal guardian. I'll be responsible for your care and development, and I'll report to the court. But you're more than just a legal responsibility to me. Your second promise is that you let me stop in a couple times a week, or even more if you wish. You are a very special young man, and I feel very bad about you losing your mother and now your father's missing. I want to help in any way I can, and I want to be here for you. I hope that's all right with you."

"Yeah," I reply so softly I'm not sure he heard me.

"There's one more thing," he says as we resume our walk.

Is this the bad news?

"My father grew up not far from Hingham. He was from Southie—South Boston. He went through some very bad times when he was young, just a year or two older than you. Like you, he lost both parents and had five younger brothers and sisters to care for. My father quit high school when he was sixteen to go to work and support the family, and this was when it was still hard for Irish to get good jobs. He used to tell me it took courage and faith to make it. I know this is a lot to ask of a thirteen-year-old boy, but sometimes life throws some very bad breaks at us, like it did to my father. It takes courage and faith, Bobby, courage and faith."

I don't reply. I've only been half-listening anyway.

"You probably think these are just words from some old guy, but please don't forget that I'm here for you. And you can even call whenever you need me or even just to talk. Bobby, I will be very, very pleased to have you pick up the phone and call. Here's my card with my private number on the back. I don't want you to feel all alone in a strange place. Just remember, I'll always be here for you."

He hands me a business card with a hand-printed number on the back. He's nice but he's old. *Why would I want to talk with him?* We start back, again at a fast pace.

"So you like being able to use your father's house to play drums and compose music?"

"Yes, sir. And like I said, Danny and Chloe come up and they listen to new stuff I've composed or we just mess around."

"I'm going to let you continue to use your father's house and I'm giving you your own key," he says. "You just can't mess around too much."

"Sir, what do you mean?"

"Come on, Bobby, you're just kids. I mean, unsupervised teenagers in a house? You have to take good care of the house, make sure it's secure and alarmed, no drugs and no drinking, only two friends at a time, things like that. I'll check up on you from time to time, and I'll ask Mrs. Robles to do the same."

"We never really … mess around, you know?"

"Yes, I'm sure," he says. My heart almost stops when I remember the huge dent in the paneling right near the sofa where he was sitting. That was from a couple days ago when I got so angry at a drum riff I couldn't get right. I screamed "fuck" a few times (well, maybe quite a few times) and threw my drummer's seat clear across the room. Maybe he didn't notice. "Please just keep it that way. Promise?" he asks.

"Yes, sir, I promise."

"And no more throwing stuff at the walls," he says with a sly grin. I don't reply while heat rushes to my face.

We continue for several minutes in silence. He's become tense and he's even walking slower. Our driveway is not too far up ahead.

"Bobby, about your father …"

Every part of my body instantly tightens. An icy cold grips me.

"He's been listed as missing by the State Department. Is that your understanding?"

"Yes, sir," I tell him in an already-shaky voice. "A friend of my dad's, Mr. Huntington, he calls every few days. He said lots of people are still looking for Dad and not to give up hope." My heart is hammering so hard I can hardly spit the words out. We stop on the side of the road. He's looking out across a gently hilly field dotted with trees and cactus.

The judge exhales hard. I'm trying to steel myself for what's coming next.

"I've talked with Mr. Huntington as well," he goes on. "I've also done some checking around on my own. I have contacts in the government and I've talked to people at your father's company, including one woman who was with your father overseas."

"Someone saw my dad?"

"Only before they lost contact. Bobby, the State Department and your father's employer agreed that I should talk to you. This is extremely difficult, but I have to tell you, your father won't be coming home. They're certain that your father … they're certain he died. There's just no physical evidence except for his ID tags and some other evidence they wouldn't discuss. I'm so very sorry, but it's not fair to keep you hoping for your father to come back home. The State Department will continue to list him as missing in action, but he just won't be coming home. Bobby, I'm so very sorry."

I think it odd that I'm not crying, I'm not screaming, I'm not asking questions. I'm standing here doing nothing. I try to think of something to ask, but my brain isn't working.

"As I said," he continues, "sometimes the only thing we have left is courage and faith. And sometimes we have nothing left, and it's okay to lean on someone else."

We continue to walk back slowly, his arm around my shoulder. I feel almost disconnected from everything around me. I'm not crying, but hot tears stream down my cheeks, quickly becoming cold in the winter air.

It's weird, but just as we get to the driveway, I notice for the first time the beauty of this clear winter day and the warmth of the bright sun. I feel grateful for it, as if it's a message that there is still a universe filled with goodness and light and a God filled with love. It's all there is to keep the overwhelming sadness from crushing me.

"Mrs. Robles is very upset," he tells me. "She will apply to become your foster mother. Bobby, I'm very concerned about you. I'm going to stop back here tonight, if that's all right with you."

I want to make my mouth work and say something, but when I look up, nothing comes out. The judge wraps his arms around me. When I look up and see his moist eyes, I bite my lip and try hard not to cry.

"You're in a strange place," he says. "I'm sure you feel all alone, but you're young and resourceful. Things will get better someday, but right now, you need time to grieve and time to heal. And remember, I'm here for you. I'm here to help you get through this. And, Bobby?"

I look up again, still unable to say anything, tears still on my cheeks.

"You knew, didn't you? I'm sure you didn't want to hear the words from me, but I'm guessing you pretty much expected this."

The shock and sadness are overwhelming; it's hard to admit what he just said.

"Mom never came home," I finally manage as my voice begins to crack. "I was scared Dad wasn't coming back either."

The judge, this kind stranger who I've known for an hour, puts his arms around me as I lose control and sob. Oblivious to the chilly winter air and the brilliant, crystal-clear blue sky, the two of us—this tall, older man with the friendly eyes and comforting embrace and me, emptier than I ever thought possible—hug tightly while I cry.

"Let's close up the house now," he whispers. "I'm taking you back and I'll stay with you awhile."

I look up again. *My gosh, he's just like Dad, trying hard not to cry.*

Chapter 13

"*This* is your list?" the judge says so loud I'm sure his secretary heard him.

"Well, I, um, I thought I'd ask for everything, and then maybe I could get some of it?"

"There's enough electronic equipment here for a mission to the moon!"

I can't help but snicker. Now I know some of this is an act. The judge is always trying to make me laugh.

"*Two synthesizers?* I have no idea what a forty-channel mixing board is, but I do know what $4,300 is. Let's see ... two speakers, amplifier, subwoofer, CD player ... what's this about a personal computer?"

"I can play music, feed it into a PC program, and it will print a score automatically. Is that awesome or what? And Judge, I'll use it to help with homework." *Yeah, he's thinking it over,* I think, *but I'm guessing he's never been near a personal computer in his life.* My list took three weeks of research. *I'll be lucky to get half of it.*

"Well, I'll see what I can do," he announces as he sticks the list in his middle drawer.

"That's it?"

His grin is followed by a handshake and a pat on my back. Our meeting in his chambers is over. On the way out of the courthouse, I'm wondering what he'll do to figure this out.

* * * * *

"Before we watch the movie, maybe we should talk about your list of musical equipment," the judge says. "You remember that list from last week, don't you? The equipment that will cost the entire state budget of Texas for a month?"

Not only is he always making me laugh, he's especially funny when he jokes but keeps a straight face. It's been more than a week since the meeting in his chambers and he hasn't once mentioned the list. Once again, when I'm over for dinner and a movie in the big house he lives in by himself, he's sprung a surprise.

"I had a little chat with your music teacher, Mr. Reynolds. I must say, it was very enlightening. He raved about your skills as a percussionist and mentioned a solo you did last fall. But he mostly talked about your talents as a composer. Mr. Reynolds said what you're doing is off the charts, with bare-bones equipment, no less, and worthy of what an exceptional college student might do, even someone at Juilliard."

"Juilliard?"

"That's what he said," the judge replies. "We reviewed every item on your list in some detail. He expressed a great deal of surprise and admiration at your, uh, at your ambition."

"I'm glad he didn't say balls," I tell him. We both laugh, the judge even more heartily than me.

"Mr. Reynolds said what you could do with this equipment will likely be sensational. He told me he thinks you're the most exceptional student he's seen in twenty years of teaching. He also thinks you're a very fine young man and praised you for teaching some of the middle school students. Well, Mr. Fowler, I've never heard this type of praise for anyone about anything. I must say, I knew you had talent, but now I think you're in a different league. Mr. Reynolds thinks you're headed for the big leagues."

Wow. All I know is I love music. I know I'm good, but I had no idea how good. My head is spinning as all this sinks in.

"Bobby, we're going to stretch this out over a few months. If you make good use of the equipment we buy initially, the trust will purchase every item on your list."

"Yes, yes, yes!" I'm out of the chair, shouting and leaping with both arms raised high. The judge is shaking his head and grinning, a little sedately, considering how I'm jumping all around the room. When I settle down, he pats the cushion next to him with that subtle half-smile of his. I sit close. We're ready for popcorn and a movie. I'm about to hit the remote when he looks right at me.

"And don't you get a big head," he says sternly, followed by a large hand mussing my hair.

Later, at home in bed, I still can't get that big smile off my face.

Chapter 14

Birthday breakfast at the Ramada Sunday buffet is over. I'm stuffed, and the bill has been paid. I assume the judge and I are leaving, but he's sitting there leaning toward me with his hands folded tightly, his stare so intense he's making me nervous.

"Your foster mother called yesterday," he begins. "Care to tell me what happened?"

I freeze. Not a sound comes out of my mouth.

"Mrs. Robles told me you wouldn't touch the cake she baked, wouldn't accept her birthday card and gift, and were almost hysterical. And how many times did you slam the door to your room?"

My tongue is paralyzed.

"Bobby, I know how upset you are. Mrs. Robles is upset too. She's trying hard to care for you. You know that, don't you?"

I can't make anything work.

"Can you and I talk, or are you going to become, how do you say it, wicked upset?"

His attempt at humor doesn't help one bit. All I can manage is the slightest nod as I start to slouch down in the booth.

"Yes, we can talk?"

"Yes, sir," I croak. I've never seen the judge like this. My face is so hot it feels like it's on fire.

"She knows she's not your mother and she's not trying to replace her," he goes on. "Mrs. Robles took in a girl several years ago. She knows how difficult it is and how much love and commitment it takes. She understands as well as I do how hurt and scared and alone you are. Bobby, she's trying hard to provide a home and support and structure,

53

and if you let her, some love too. She cares for you, but right now she's quite upset and concerned with your behavior, and it's more than this one instance."

"She yells at me and she drinks!"

The judge frowns and I immediately regret sounding like a whiny little kid.

"There's a lot of strain on Mrs. Robles, and this isn't easy for her either. She and I talked about her drinking, and I do not have any concerns. I also found out she gets after you when you're disrespectful, which is exactly what she should be doing. I told Mrs. Robles it's okay for you to spend time at your father's house, especially now that you have that new equipment, but you have to be respectful to Mrs. Robles to continue that privilege. Bobby, I have to see things going a lot better between you and your foster mother, even to the point where you let her into your life, or—"

I think I know where this is going as he stares me down. I've never seen the judge so totally scary.

"Or what?" I ask, my words coming out in a squeak.

"If this just isn't working, it might be best if we place you in another foster home, this time a two-parent home. We will try to find a home in Dunston, but there are no guarantees."

My drums. How would I play my drums? How would I work on my music? I wouldn't see the Judge anymore, and I'd lose my friends.

I slouch further down into the booth. If I go any lower, all he'll see are my eyes.

"I want you to be happy, but I also have to know you're in a safe and loving home where you can flourish," he continues. "I'm your legal guardian and your friend, and I care for you very, very much. I know you don't want to be in a foster home, but that is your lot in life and you can't change that. I'm sorry for all the bad things that happened, but they did happen and now you have to help us out. So, do you think you can make this work?"

The oddest thought flashes into my brain: I'm only fourteen, but the next words out of my mouth will determine where my life goes for a long, long time. "I guess so."

"Guess so or definitely yes?"

My gosh, he's tough!

"Yes, sir, I promise I will try hard to make this work," I reply.

He relaxes back against his seat with a satisfied little smile, not victorious like he's gloating, just approving. Or maybe relieved. "Good. Well, I have a little surprise for today," he says. "Why don't we head out to the car?"

That's it? It's over, just like that? He was so tough and scary, I thought our entire day was ruined, maybe even our friendship.

Last night was dinner and a movie and a sleepover at his house. When he gave me a birthday card and fifty dollars, I cried and told him I didn't want to celebrate my birthday. He insisted I take the money. When I told him Mom died just after last year's birthday, we hugged for a long time. I thought everything was okay when we left for breakfast. What a scare!

"So where to? Austin?" I ask as we buckle our old-fashioned seat belts.

"Nope. We're going in the other direction, to Ivie Reservoir," he says. "It's a beautiful place. We can explore and take pictures of the dam, and I brought along a picnic lunch."

It turns out to be more than seventy miles away, northwest of Brady, he says. It will be an opportunity to see some pretty Texas scenery, he explains. The judge doesn't talk much while driving, leaving me to my thoughts. Endless expanses of wide-open, flat farmland and ranches and a couple tiny towns drift by. My thoughts wander back to the day Dad took me to Mason Air Force Base, just after we moved here. The base has a runway for a squadron of Air National Guard fighters, a bunch of huge, white dish antennas, and lots of security.

I met his new boss, General Cantwell, his commanding officer in Bosnia and now his good friend and commander of the air base. I remember he came to our house a few times. The general took us up in a small plane and let Dad take the controls. We flew right over Dunston and we saw our house. Way off in the distance was a large lake. "Ivie Reservoir, a great place for fishing and picnics. You should go there sometime," I remember General Cantwell saying.

Dad and I never did.

So much has happened in the past year. One year ago, I was in Hingham celebrating my thirteenth birthday with a huge party. Three months later, it was just Dad and me in that plane flying over my new home and my new life in Texas. Now Dad's gone, I'm in a car with the judge, and I live in a foster home.

A wave of sadness sweeps over me. It hurts more because Mom died one year ago today. I turn to look out the window so he won't see my eyes filling with tears.

The judge looks over and rubs my shoulder.

Bait, it says on a little red neon sign in one window, Miller Lite in another. We've pulled into an almost-deserted, rustic service center at the top of a low hill. Before us is the enormous expanse of Ivie Reservoir, snaking way up a now-submerged river. A map in a glass case shows we're looking at just one of two arms of the reservoir.

Following a gently sloping, gravely trail, the judge leads the way through short, scrubby trees all the way down to a small cluster of picnic tables close to the shore. Other than two boats with guys fishing way off in the distance, we appear to be alone. It's just us and the bright sun, the huge cloudless sky, and this big lake, so blue it's almost electric.

A hot wind sweeping over the low hills surrounding us is whipping up whitecaps, driving them to splash against a rocky outcropping jutting out from the gravel shore. Off go my sneakers so I can dangle my feet over the edge, letting the spray tingle against bare feet and legs. My face and arms are already hot from the midday sun.

The judge stands motionless a few feet away, his plaid shirt and slacks flapping in the breeze. Uncharacteristically, he ignores his white hair blowing around with each gust. Instead, he seems to be communing with the natural beauty of our surroundings.

After a long, deep breath, as if he's trying to draw into his being the very essence of this place, the judge slowly and awkwardly eases himself down close to me. When he gives me an expectant look and pats the flat rock right next to him, I oblige and sit so close we're almost touching. I'm grateful he's still my friend. I feel safe.

We remain quiet and peaceful for a few minutes. The judge drapes his arm over my shoulder. "Bobby, you are a very special young man," he says, still gazing out over the lake. "I know how hurt and scared you are, and I know it's hard to be in a foster home, but you are a survivor and you do it better than most. You have a lot of courage, and you are the most wonderful and special young man I have ever met."

I squint when a gust whipping over the water makes my eyes water.

"Every day I give thanks I can be part of your life and maybe provide a little friendship and support," he continues with a few vigorous rubs of my back.

A powerful swell of emotion begins to build, a confusing swirl which I don't understand. Still entranced by the sun glistening with a million sparkles off the wind-tossed water, it surges through me like electricity.

And just like that, everything becomes clear, as if my eyes are sharper. In an instant, everything is different. Right here and right now, I know I'm going to make it. I know it with a certainty I've never felt before. I'm going to try hard in school, I'm going to excel with my music, and maybe it's not fair being in a foster home, but I will keep my promise to be respectful and nice to Mrs. Robles. Tonight, I'll tell her I'm sorry, and I'll thank her for taking me in.

The judge and Mrs. Robles are here for me, but now I feel strong and I feel powerful and there's hope. There's hope! I stand up and scream into the wind, *"I'm going to make it!"*

Chapter 15

Legs and arms flapping wildly, a long, loud *banzai* echoing around the patio, here comes Danny sailing over my head after a long, running start, followed by a huge splash a good fifteen feet from the edge of the pool. Chloe and I laugh as much as cheer as his head bobs up through sun-sparkling water. Arms raised high in victory, a fierce scream announces another world record. As usual, Chloe has no interest in joining our little contest and is content to lie on the float or splash around in the shallow end of the pool.

The days of summer are passing at a sluggish pace, the August heat so heavy and oppressive it's as though time itself has slowed. If not inside escaping the heat, we splash and laugh and talk or just lie around the pool for hours. Even the judge comes over, always in the relative coolness of the evening, although for the judge, wading around in the shallow end with his white, skinny legs seems to be his idea of swimming. Mrs. Robles, on the other hand, surprised us by swimming like a fish.

"Hey, I'm hungry. Let's go eat!" Danny shouts.

"Is there ever one minute you're not thinking about food?" Chloe fires back.

"Only when I'm thinking about girls," he yells back and splashes wildly at her. Screeching, Chloe hastily climbs up the ladder to towel off and escape inside for lunch.

"Danny and I were talking about you on the way over," Chloe says as she pulls out a kitchen chair.

"Do I want to hear this?"

"We were saying that once you figured out how to use all that new equipment, you went totally nuts," Danny says. "Man, you're doing everything, like your second dance CD, that baroque stuff and far out stuff, even those jazz tracks. It's like all this music is pouring out of you and you can't control it."

"I'll say I can't control it," I holler back and stick my finger in my mouth. Hurling noises complete the image as they crack up at my idiotic humor. But it's true. All this music is pouring out of me and like Danny said, I can't control it. Every day there are new sounds in my head that I can't wait to try on my synthesizers. It works the other way too. I experiment with my synthesizers and discover new sounds that I eagerly incorporate into my compositions.

"What really blows my mind is that you're better than ever on drums," he adds. "You spend hours composing and remixing, but what you're doing on drums is sick. Man, how do you do it all? Are you rolling on drugs or what?"

"No!" I shriek as I badly imitate a severe nervous tic. We all crack up again.

Plowing through the sandwiches Mrs. Robles made, we're quiet for a few minutes when Danny sits back with a heavy sigh. "Crap, next week it's back to jail."

"Oh, stop it," Chloe prisses. "Sophomore year will be a blast."

Danny doesn't look too convinced. "I guess," he mumbles.

"It will be a blast if I hook up with some hot boy when we go back," I tell my friends. "Wouldn't that be great?"

A quick, nervous glance passes between them.

"I just hope this goes okay," Danny says, his eyes darting to Chloe.

"What's the matter? It shouldn't be a big deal," I reply. "Everyone knows, so it won't be this huge surprise."

"Just be careful," Chloe says with a pat on my arm. "You'll be the first out gay kid at a school where there are just two types of students: football players and everyone who worships them."

"And in case you haven't noticed, this is a conservative town," Danny adds.

"You're my best friend, and I want you to be safe," says Chloe with another pat.

My thoughts drift. Day and night, I dream of going out on a date and he holds me tight and we kiss. That's what I want: a boyfriend.

Someone like Kyle Faulkner.

IT'S THE GAY KID

Chapter 16

Mr. Bentley pauses and stares hard at me when he gets to my name during attendance.

"Well, Mr. Fowler, I see you've been assigned to my class," my sophomore English teacher says in a slow, measured cadence. "Now remove that earring."

"Sir, excuse me?"

"I said, remove that earring," he snaps. "Only homosexuals wear jewelry, and I will not have anyone looking like a homosexual in my classroom."

"But, sir, the dress code doesn't prohibit earrings for boys, and other boys wear jewelry."

"Only homosexuals flaunt their perverted lifestyles," he says, pointing right at me. "One more time: remove that earring."

"Mr. Bentley, I'm not trying to flaunt anything … sir."

My teacher rises slowly and deliberately out of his seat, never taking his eyes off me.

"It is quite well known around town that you announced you are gay. Isn't that so, Mr. Fowler?"

"Yes, sir," I gulp.

"Are you going to sit there and tell me and this classroom full of decent Christian boys and girls that you are a … homosexual?" he asks, drawing out each syllable to make sure everyone in the classroom understands exactly how disgusting being gay is.

"Yes, sir, I'm gay."

Mr. Bentley's eyes widen; he sucks his breath in. An older man with long gray hair worn straight back, tall and so thin his cheekbones stick out, he wears a really lame cowboy string tie fastened with a piece of jewelry that's mostly a large, blue-green stone. I think it looks weird.

Mr. Bentley slowly paces over to the windows. Long, bony hands spread wide on the windowsill, jaw set tight, he's just standing there, staring out at nothing. Everyone in the room holds their breath as Mr. Bentley slowly turns and glares at me. I gulp hard.

"Young man, homosexuality is sinful in the eyes of the Lord," he proclaims ever louder, gesturing with his right hand like those crackpot ministers on TV. "It is an abomination, and everyone knows the radical homosexual agenda will mean the downfall of Christian civilization. Now, Bobby, I know you are only fourteen. I believe you are confused and impressionable. Just admit before God that you made a foolish mistake."

Mr. Bentley has reached the head of my aisle. With each slow, deliberate, menacing step, I slouch down in my seat. But how can I say I'm not gay? Am I supposed to announce it was a big mistake and all of a sudden I'm straight?

"I'm gay, Mr. Bentley. I'm not confused and I did not make a mistake."

Mr. Bentley points right at me. "My patience has run out. Admit your mistake before your classmates and the Lord. Homosexuality is a choice, and you've made a choice that is wicked in the eyes of God Almighty!" he thunders, cracking his fist into his left hand with a smack so violent I jump. But the growing heat of my anger is just too strong—

"I'm gay, got it?"

Face turning red, eyes bulging with shock, Mr. Bentley stretches a long, thin finger toward the door. "Leave this classroom at once!"

"Is this for real?"

"Out, now!"

My hands shake as I jam books and note paper into my backpack. Other than my heart pounding, not one sound intrudes in Mr. Bentley's classroom. Even worse, Kyle is sitting right in front of me, watching the most awful humiliation of my life. Everyone stares as I start down the aisle, squeezing against a desk to avoid my teacher towering over me with glowing, angry eyes.

"Hey, faggot, serves you right."

I know who it is without looking but do anyway, a quick reflex glance over my shoulder toward the windows. It's all I need to see Jason's angry, challenging face.

The second I click the door shut, the classroom explodes with excited voices, quickly silenced by an angry bellow from Mr. Bentley. I can't believe this is happening. *Kicked out of my first class because I'm gay? Now what? Where am I supposed to go?*

"I must say, you've caused a bit of a stir around here, teachers as well as students," Mr. Lessard informs me. He's imposing behind his huge desk, staring me down through gold-rimmed glasses, rapidly tapping a pen on his blotter. He's the tallest person in school, other than one senior who plays basketball, and he's big. Everyone calls him Godzilla. Guys swear that flames come out of his mouth when they're in his office getting yelled at. "So what did you do to get kicked out of Mr. Bentley's class?" he asks, leaning back in his leather chair.

"He told me to get rid of the earring because it looks gay and he doesn't want any gay people in his classroom with good Christian boys and girls, and when I said I am gay he got really upset and started saying all this Bible stuff and how wicked it is and gays are going to destroy civilization and they'll be an earthquake in Dunston because of the radical homosexual agenda and my choosing to be gay and I'm sinful in the eyes of God Almighty and he told me to get out of his class when I refused to say I'm confused and admit being gay was all a big mistake … what do I do now?"

Mr. Lessard grimaces and kneads his forehead and the bald part of his head with his fingertips, finishing with a loud sigh.

"All right, you report back to Mr. Bentley's class tomorrow. For the rest of this period … just go sit in the waiting area for your next class," he says with a wave of his hand. Stunned and confused, I don't move. "You're dismissed," he snaps.

That's it? No "I'm sorry this caused you so much trouble," or "I apologize for Mr. Bentley's behavior"? Well, didn't this year start off just great. What will Mr. Bentley do when I show up tomorrow, throw me to the lions?

"What happened?" Chloe screeches before she's even in her seat at lunch. "It's all over school you got kicked out of Mr. Bentley's class." She's loud and excited, drawing attention, which I totally don't want right now.

"Mr. Bentley kicked me out when I refused to say being gay was a mistake." I'm still so upset I'm toying with my food. Chloe listens with amazement and growing anger as I relate my scary confrontation with Mr. Bentley and my visit with Mr. Lessard.

"Total jerks," she fumes. "Wait till I tell Mom and Dad."

"Mr. Bentley looked like Moses parting the Red Sea when he ordered me out." I'm badly imitating Charlton Heston's outstretched arm and ferocious look when the two of us burst into laughter.

"Thanks for sticking with me, Chloe."

She gently holds my hand.

"Homo lover." I turn around to see an upperclass guy continuing past our table without looking back after firing those words at her.

Chloe crinkles her nose and sticks her tongue out. "He's a jerk," she whispers.

"One kid called me a queer this morning. That's twice now. Oh, and Jason; that's three." I'm crinkling my napkin into a ball and I slam it on my tray. "This really sucks."

"I don't blame you for being upset."

"Now everyone's calling me the gay kid. I'm not Bobby Fowler, I'm the gay kid."

The jerk who said "homo lover" to Chloe comes back and deliberately jostles my seat.

"Hey, leave us alone!" Chloe complains, but he ignores her and continues down the crowded aisle. Students nearby are watching and whispering.

"Mom and Dad are worried about you," she says. "Last spring, this Christian group took control of the school board. You should have seen how upset my mother and father were when they banned a whole bunch of books from the school library. My father even called the superintendent to complain."

"And this has what to do with me?"

Chloe rolls her eyes. "They don't like gays. My father said some of the books were banned because they had gay characters."

I don't know what this means, but it doesn't sound good. Before school started, I didn't think being gay would be a big deal. I only thought about meeting up with a hot guy. It's all I've thought about.

* * * * *

Four days of school and twice in Mr. Lessard's office. When Madeleine intercepted me in the lobby, I knew why right away. Once again, Mr. Lessard is drilling me with the same direct, unblinking stare and rapidly tapping his pen on the blotter.

"Are you aware of the AIDS rumors racing through school?" he begins.

"Yes, sir, my friend Danny told me."

"It's not only students and parents. The school board is especially concerned. My phone has been ringing off the hook. Is there anything you want to tell me?" he asks.

"No, sir."

"Young man, this is not a game," he says, his voice rising with anger. "If necessary, I will call your legal guardian. Now, are there any health issues we should know about?"

"No, sir; none, and I already talked to the judge. He said to call if you want him to meet with you."

"Well … I will, should that become necessary," he says, clearing his throat a couple times. "Bobby, there are rumors racing around taking on a life of their own," he continues, "and these people are unduly concerned. I know what HIV is, but to be safe, I checked with a physician at the hospital. It's spread mainly through sexual contact or blood transfusions or sharing needles. I highly doubt you're engaging in any of those activities, and I can't imagine you're posing a risk to anyone. Nonetheless, we need to know if you have a potentially communicable disease."

"Sir, I'm not even sure what AIDS or HIV is," I reply.

"You're not HIV positive?"

"No! I don't have anything! Why is everyone picking on me?"

"You will not raise your voice in my office like that again. You may go back to class now."

"But why is this all my fault?" I ask, angry tears burning my eyes.

Mr. Lessard grimly stares out the window for a few moments. "Look, these rumors and these upset people, especially the school board—maybe it wasn't such a good idea to be so openly gay. Personally, I don't care, but I have to deal with these people. Now, please return to your class. I promise I will put an end to these rumors by the end of the day."

It still isn't fair. It's just not fair.

Chapter 17

How lucky that Kyle Faulkner sits right in front of me. I can't help looking at his athletic neck and his perfect hair. Everything about him is perfect—beautiful lips, bronzed skin, all those muscles. Even his voice is perfect. Kyle Faulkner is a total dreamboat. He has to be the most gorgeous boy who ever lived. What if he turned around and asked if I want to hang out, or what if he—

"Hey, faggot, what are you staring at?" Kyle says, challenging me.

"Uh, nothing. I wasn't staring at you, honest."

Shit! Everyone's looking at me. He's turned back around and he's really pissed, judging from his hunched-over shoulders. *Why did you have to do that? I still love you anyway. You're so gorgeous, so perfect. I love you.*

At least lunch with Danny and Chloe will be cool. But just as I near our usual table, Chloe screeches when I go flying. With a splat and a clatter of my tray, I'm on the on the cold tile floor right in the middle of the cafeteria. Everyone's laughing.

"Hey, faggot. Serves you right for staring at me."

Kyle! He looks over to his friends for approval. I'm scrambling to clean up the mess on the floor with hands shaking from shock and embarrassment. I can't get out of here fast enough.

How could he be so mean? He's been as nasty as Jason and Josh, and now he's hassling me. I bet his jerk friends put him up to it.

School sucks. Every day it's "Hey, queer" or "Hey, fag" from some of the students, and to most of the rest, I'm the gay kid. A few besides Danny and Chloe are friendly and some just don't seem to care. But some of the boys, including a few of the football players, are scary. I try not to use the boys' room because a couple guys messed with me two days ago, but I can't hold it in all day. Now with Kyle being a jerk, I don't even want to go to school.

Still, he's so beautiful, so athletic, so cool. When I see him in the hallways, I get so nervous I turn away to avoid being near him. It's torture when he sits in front of me. I dream that he wraps his arms around me and holds me tight. I dream about hanging around with him after school and doing cool things together. What if he came over and we swam in the pool? What if we were naked? What if he swam right up to me and—

I can't stand it, I just can't stand it. I can't get him out of my mind. I think about him sitting behind him in class, in band, on the bus, at night so bad I can't sleep. Kyle Faulkner is driving me crazy.

"Jeez, when did you do that?" Danny asks when we meet up on Sunday afternoon.

"This morning with some clippers. Is this cool or what?"

"You're asking for trouble. You're going to school tomorrow with a mohawk?"

"Hey, too bad if anyone doesn't like it," I reply. "My foster mother was upset and I told her to mind her own business."

"Come on, man, you're just going to get more trouble."

"Hey, this is me. I've taken three weeks of crap and I should be able to do what I want."

Danny's shaking his head. "Oh, I don't know about this. I hope school goes okay tomorrow."

"Yeah, well I'm fed up with all the shit I'm taking. I'm doing my own thing, and screw anyone that doesn't like it."

* * * * *

"Well, Mr. Fowler, I see you take pride in being a homosexual pervert," Mr. Bentley says after giving me a dirty look. He's doing something at his desk with a yellow highlighter, glancing at me every two seconds.

Here he comes, his eyes trying to burn holes in me as he makes his way down the aisle.

"Young man, God will punish you, but it's not too late if you accept Jesus Christ as your savior and vow to end your deviant ways. Here, read this, where I highlighted," he says, holding out an instantly recognizable book.

"You want me to read the Bible?"

"Mr. Fowler, you are going to learn that you and your kind are morally disordered and that if you don't repent and change your ways, you are consigning your soul to eternal damnation. Now read!"

"But, sir, isn't the Bible supposed to be taught in church and not in school?"

Mr. Bentley holds up his hand just like a preacher. "Our nation and our laws are based on Christian traditions and this good book. God's law is the law. Now, Mr. Fowler, my patience is over and you will read that passage, understand? Maybe it wasn't such a good idea to expose all of these Christian boys and girls to your perverted lifestyle and your radical agenda," he says, leaning forward and inching the book closer to my nose.

"I don't think I have a perverted lifestyle, sir, and I know I don't have an agenda."

"Read, now!"

"Sir, I'm not reading the Bible in school."

"One last time, then I start handing out detentions. Now read and maybe you will be cured of this evil," he says, shaking the Bible right in front of me.

"That's not fair! You can't give me a detention for not reading the Bible."

"I just did, Mr. Fowler, five detentions to be exact. You choose to flaunt your perverted lifestyle in front of this entire school, and you will be punished."

"Five detentions? That's not fair. I'm not reading your stupid Bible!"

Eyes wide in horror, Mr. Bentley's face turns red, almost like it's going to explode. A little vein is throbbing on his forehead like some space creature. "Ten detentions!"

The only sound in the classroom is the scrape of my chair as I stand and hurriedly gather my books together.

"You sit down!" he hollers.

I ignore him and start for the door down the other aisle, still stuffing books into my backpack.

"Where do you think you're going?" he bellows. "You get back here and sit down right now."

I don't even look back.

"You come back—" The slam of the door, so loud it echoes like a cannon shot in the empty hallway, blocks him out. Hardly able to see straight, I storm down the hallway with absolutely no idea where I'm going, kicking a locker along the way so hard it hurts my foot.

I know, I'll see Mr. Lessard. This time he'll fire that jerk.

"What is it now?" he snaps.

"He's trying to make me read the Bible and said I'm evil and perverted and if I don't read where he highlighted, God will punish me and *it's just not fair.*"

"Maybe you should try to calm down," he says. "Who has you so upset this time?"

"Mr. Bentley," I tell him, his name coming out like a bullet. I'm so angry I'm shaking.

"So what are you doing out of class?" he asks.

"I left."

Mr. Lessard, oddly calm, leans forward. "Did Mr. Bentley give you permission to leave his classroom?"

"No, sir."

Mr. Lessard leans way back in his chair and steeples his fingers together. "So you simply decided to walk out on your teacher."

"I guess so, but it's not fair. Why don't you understand? Why aren't you yelling at Mr. Bentley?"

"Young man, you are this close to getting detention."

"He gave me ten detentions because I wouldn't read the Bible," I complain, my face even hotter and my eyes tearing as I realize this is going nowhere.

Mr. Lessard rocks forward, almost over his desk, and points right at me. "If one of my most respected and senior teachers gave you detention, it's for a good reason and you have to take your punishment, understand? That will be all, and may I suggest you get a more normal haircut?"

"This isn't fair!"

"I said that will be all."

"This isn't fair! That guy's a jerk. This isn't legal, and if my father was here, he'd kick his butt and yours too for letting him get away with this, and what kind of school system do you think you're running here …"

I've run out of steam and I have no idea how long I was standing and yelling. Mr. Lessard, his hands clasped in front of him, is completely expressionless. Now what?

* * * * *

The judge is just coming out of the principal's office.

"Mr. Lessard has rescinded your suspension," he says, talking to me in what I call the "judge voice." He can be stern, formal, all business, and he can turn it on and off like a switch. I usually get the judge voice when he's ticked off or when he's giving me a lecture. Scowling, hands on hips, I'd say he's really ticked. "You still have to take all your detentions …"

"Ten detentions? Why do I get any?"

"You slammed the door on your teacher and you screamed at your principal, that's why," he fumes. He points to Mr. Lessard's door. "Now you get in there and apologize to Mr. Lessard and take your punishment, and mister, you'd better be very thankful it isn't worse. And is it too much to ask that you get a more normal haircut?"

Ten detentions. Even the judge let me down. Well screw him, and I don't care if he likes my haircut or not.

Chapter 18

"Come on, guys, let's get tough!"

What a total dreamboat. Even when Kyle is yelling at our football team from the sidelines, he's so totally cute, especially the way he holds his helmet by his knee and looks so cool. How I'd like to be standing beside him. How I'd love to have him put his arm around me. From my seat in the second row just behind the Warriors bench, I have a perfect view of his athletic butt. My heart almost stopped when I realized I could see his jockstrap through those stretchy, white football pants.

Chloe came to the game with me, but despite neither of us having mentioned Kyle, I'll bet anything she's just drooling. "I can't believe we're getting beat by these guys," she grumbles.

"Maybe they'll put Kyle in," I tell her, picturing how totally awesome it would be to see Kyle lead our team to victory over the Brady Bulldogs.

"Yeah, you'd like that," she cracks.

A groan goes up from the huge crowd when our guy running with the ball gets slammed to the ground after just a few steps—again. A few angry shouts drift down from people way up in the stands.

It's our third game of the season, and I've been to both previous home games. Imagine that—me at a football game. I had no idea how exciting these Friday nights could be, but there's only one reason I'm here, and he's standing on the sidelines fifteen feet in front of me.

"Come on!" Chloe screams. A pass thrown by Eric Walker, our senior quarterback, sails right off the field and into the hands of a coach on the other team. The player who was supposed to catch the ball throws his hands up in the air. Our head coach, a really loud, scary guy, is urgently motioning Eric off the field.

"What the hell do you think you're doing? You get your head in the game right now, you hear me?" he screams so angrily his words come out strangled. To emphasize the point, he slams his clipboard to the ground so hard it bounces. I'm very glad I'm not Eric Walker right now.

"Let's go, Warriors!" Chloe chants and claps her hands. I pick it up. In seconds, most of the students are on their feet, screaming and clapping for our team to beat those nasty Brady Bulldogs. To our left, the 100-strong Warrior Pride Marching Band begins blasting out our fight song. Now I'm sorry I didn't sign up this year.

"Why is Brady such a big deal?" I ask Chloe as I look around Walker Field, so crowded all six thousand seats are full and people are standing along the fence.

A girl in front of me turns around with a look of disbelief. "Are you for real?" she says.

"What?" I ask with a shrug.

She and her friends giggle and shake their heads. One of them turns around. "Brady's our biggest rival," she says. "My boyfriend—that's him, number 45—said every game is all-out war."

"Aren't they a lot smaller than us?" Chloe asks. The girl rolls her eyes.

"They're just twenty-five miles up the road," she says as if, isn't it obvious? I guess in Texas, twenty-five miles is nothing.

"Look, we're one of the biggest football schools in central Texas," another girl patiently explains. "We're not supposed to be down thirteen points to these … losers."

Another big groan rolls through the stadium. Eric has thrown the ball right into the hands of a Brady player. On the other side of the field, hundreds of fans from Brady scream and jump up and down as their guy races into the end zone. We're now down by twenty points.

"Come on, Coach, take him out!" a man yells from high up in the stands.

"We're never going to win now," Chloe whines.

I glance at the clock on the scoreboard: 8:14 left in the game.

"Faulkner, warm up," the coach screams, even though Kyle is only ten feet away.

"Chloe, Kyle's going to play!" I screech at her.

"I can't believe Coach is taking Eric out," the girl in front of me says with a shake of her head.

"Well, he's totally messing up," Chloe tells her.

She turns around and looks at us like we're total idiots. She points toward the scoreboard.

"Are you a retard or something? His name is on the stadium, his father's the president of the booster club, and he's the richest man in town."

"And the most arrogant," one of her friends says under her breath.

Chloe sits back in a huff, but I don't care about Dan Walker Field or Eric Walker or his arrogant father. My thoughts, my eyes, my ears are tuned to Kyle throwing long tosses to a teammate.

Another urgent and very loud groan rumbles around the stadium. Kyle looks toward the field to see what's happening.

"What's going on?" I ask Chloe.

"Eric dropped the ball and then one of our guys fell on it," she explains.

"Faulkner!" the coach screams. Fastening his helmet, Kyle trots up to him. The coach grabs Kyle's face mask. I can't hear what he's saying, but my heart leaps when Kyle dashes onto the field. He passes Eric trudging toward the sideline; neither says a word or even glances at the other. Head down, Eric slams his helmet to the ground and slumps onto the bench with a towel covering his head. Not one teammate comes near him.

"Go Kyle! Go Kyle!" I'm screaming and jumping up and down as we hear "Number 5, Kyle Faulkner, now playing quarterback," boom over the PA, until Chloe jabs my leg hard with an elbow. I sit quickly when I realize everyone within thirty feet is staring at me.

"Sorry, I can't help it. That boy is *so* hot," I whisper to Chloe.

"I'll say," she replies for everyone to hear.

First play, Kyle hands the ball to a guy who runs into a wall of Brady players. Second play, the same guy runs toward the left and gets buried before he can get five feet. Kyle spends an extra long time in the huddle.

My hero bends over this guy in the middle, takes the ball, and looks to his right. Kyle darts to his left when he sees one of those big, mean Brady guys coming after him. He heaves the ball way down the sideline and one of our guys catches it! He's running, he's running, he bangs a Brady player out of the way, our players are jumping up and down, the crowd's screaming, I'm screaming ... he dives into the end zone! Chloe flings her arms around me and we jump up and down together, hollering hysterically.

"He's so hot," I tell Chloe, just about out of breath.

"Who?" she asks, still rhythmically clapping to our fight song.

"Kyle," I shoot back like it's totally obvious. "Oh, what I wouldn't do for a date with him."

Seven seconds to go, down by six points, the clock ticking away, our team twenty-five yards from the end zone, the entire stadium is in an uproar. For a moment it becomes quieter when Kyle bends over the guy in front of him and shouts these weird calls that quarterbacks do, followed by hut, hut, or something like that.

Kyle gives the ball to this guy who runs with it a lot—no! Kyle still has the ball and he's running the other way. He avoids a Brady guy, ducks under another Brady guy, and launches the ball. It sails high up into the humid night air in slow motion, so high it almost disappears into the blackness above the stadium lights. It falls in a long path down toward the far corner of the end zone—one of our guys is there! We're going to win, we're going to win!

"No!" I scream. Six thousand Dunston fans do the same, a huge, ugly, terrible roar of choking disbelief. The guy in the end zone dropped the ball. It was in his hands and he fumbled it and it bounced pathetically in front of him. The Brady players are jumping and leaping and screaming and running crazy all over the field and piling onto one another, their fans are going totally lunatic, the Bulldog Band is playing a victory number while I, as well as every single Warriors fan, remain standing here numb with shock.

Kyle is on his knees, his head bowed, not moving. Poor Kyle. How I'd like to go out there and hold him and tell him everything's going to be okay and that he's my hero and it's that stupid player's fault.

"One and three," one of the girls in front of us says. "We were supposed to do really well this year."

"Losers," one of her friends sniffs.

"Why didn't they play Kyle Faulkner right from the start?" one of the others wonders. None of her friends answers as they file out toward the stairs.

"Chloe, I'm going to wait here for a few minutes," I tell her. Completely bummed, she only nods and squeezes past me.

The guy who dropped the ball, the same guy who took Kyle's first pass and ran all the way for a score, is on his knees bawling his eyes out. Now helmetless, Kyle trudges to the end zone, gets down on one knee, and starts talking to the guy. His hand is on the back of the guy's neck so he must be saying something nice. I'm in awe.

"Faulkner, over here," screams our coach, who never seems to talk like a normal person. Kyle obediently trots back to the bench.

"Son, this is your team now," I hear him say. "You just don't accept losing, do you?"

"No, sir," my hero replies.

"Well, I'll tell you something else. That was a wonderful team-building gesture, you helping Richie like that."

Kyle only nods and joins his teammates filing toward the corner exit like a group of doomed prisoners. All sweaty, dressed in those pads and tight pants, his helmet hanging down, he looks so hot and so muscular and so perfect. On impulse, I race down the steps and dash toward the corner where the players are making their way toward the locker room. Along the fence, at least two dozen grade school and middle school boys are shouting at the players for autographs. Every player but Kyle ignores them.

"Next game … when we win, okay, guys?" he says to the throng of kids. He doesn't notice me, and then he's gone.

I've already made up my mind. I'm going to every Warriors football game, away games too, even if I have to hitchhike. Kyle Faulkner is the most wonderful and beautiful boy I've ever seen, and now he's a hero. My hero.

* * * * *

Three times now. Why don't they leave me alone? I wasn't even staring at Kyle, and this time Josh tripped me in the cafeteria.

I've run into the boys' room just down the corridor to clean up. I'm relieved only two freshmen are in here, but I'm totally bummed to find spaghetti sauce on my shirt.

"Hey, faggot!"

I'm terrified to see Jason storming in with Dustin, Josh, and Kyle right behind. One glare from Jason is all it takes for the two freshmen to scram.

"What the fuck are you doing in here?" Jason screams right in my face. I'm backing up and bump into the wall.

"I'm just trying to clean up. Please let me go."

Kyle shoulders him aside. "I heard what you said about me at the game."

"I didn't say anything about you, honest." I'm surrounded. Escaping is out of the question.

"You think I'm a hot stud, that's what I heard. And what are you going to do for a date with me?"

My heart pounding, my breaths fast and ragged, I can't talk, I can't even move.

"You look like a sick freak," Dustin says. "You even dress like a queer."

"Let's beat the shit out of him and teach him a lesson," Jason growls. Kyle ignores him.

"Come on, pal, what do you want to do with me?" They lean in closer. "I don't want a freak queer staring at me all the time and talking queer shit about me. And now you're going to pay, right, guys?" Kyle glances at his friends for approval. Looking like wild dogs going after prey, they don't respond. Kyle grabs my shirt with both hands. Lightning fast, Jason's on me.

"Let me go, let me go!" I scream.

"One more sound, asshole, and I beat the shit out of you for real, got it?" Jason snarls in my ear.

"Get him by the ankles," Kyle tells Jason.

I'm squirming with all my might as Kyle and Jason get me upside down. Kyle's hands are around my ankles so tight it hurts.

"Hey, the little queer hardly weighs anything at all," Kyle says to idiotic laughter from his friends. Now I'm humiliated as well as scared out of my mind. Dustin slams open a stall door with a bang. I squirm with frantic strength when I see what they're planning. It's no use.

"No, please, Kyle, I'm sorry, please don't, I'm sorry. Let me go!" He's got me right over the toilet. Cold water touches my head. My head hits the bottom of the toilet bowl hard. Hold it, hold it, don't breathe.

"Hey, maybe he'll turn the water purple," I hear Josh say. I'm thrashing violently, still holding my breath but just barely.

"Hey, he *is* turning the water purple!" Jason shouts, as the grape Kool-Aid coloring must be coming out of my hair.

I'm dumped in a heap onto the floor, gagging and whimpering.

"Hey, faggot, you cry like a fucking girl. Leave my friend alone or next time your ass is mine," a very red-faced Jason screams right in my face.

"Hey, we'd better get out of here," Dustin says. All four blast through the door laughing and high-fiving.

I want to die.

Chapter 19

My head hurts. It hurts so bad it feels like it's being squeezed in a vise. I feel sick to my stomach. The nurse is talking, but it's hard to make out what she's saying. Someone just came in. I think she said she called an ambulance.

"What happened?" It's a man's voice. It sounds like Mr. Lessard. I'm shielding my eyes from the light. I'm going to be sick again.

"He said he was tripped on the stairwell and hit his head. Here, sit up and lean over," says the nurse with an arm behind my back and a plastic tub under my chin while I dry heave.

"Is it serious?" Mr. Lessard asks.

"He has significant symptoms of a concussion, which is always serious," the nurse tells—I don't remember who she's talking to. "There, there, just lie back now," she says. Sitting up made me feel even worse. My heads hurts so bad I want to bang it against the wall.

"He said he had a headache, and an hour later his vision blurred and his ears were ringing. When he came in, he couldn't remember his name or the day and he vomited. It's at least a level two, but we won't know until he's examined at the hospital."

"Can you tell me what happened?" asks Mr. Lessard from right above me.

"Tripped … me," I moan.

"Did he say someone tripped him?" a voice says.

"Mr. Lessard, he's very confused right now and he has a severe headache. Maybe you should wait a few days," another voice answers.

* * * * *

"I want to know exactly what happened." Once again staring me down from behind his desk, Mr. Lessard makes every trip to his office feel like an inquisition.

"I can't remember a thing."

"You told the nurse you were tripped on a stairwell and fell. You don't remember?" he asks.

"No, sir. Dr. Murkowski told me it's quite common not to be able to remember anything after a concussion. I don't even remember going to school."

It's so odd. I remember absolutely nothing from that day last week except having a screaming headache in the ER. I have the creepiest feeling I knew what happened, but now I can't find that memory. It was there and now it's gone.

"Is that all?"

"I'm getting harassed and called names all the time."

Mr. Lessard throws his hands up. "Well, what did you expect? You flaunt being gay and wear the most outlandish outfits, and I don't even know what to call your haircut, and students are going to react. If there's harassment, it's my job to be concerned. I will do my best, but young man, you are making it very, very difficult."

"Some of them are being mean."

"Then maybe you shouldn't be so gay," he patiently explains. "Try to fit in a little better and act more normal. You may return to your class now. And, Bobby, if there's any more harassment, I want to hear about it, understand?"

"Yes, sir."

Yeah, right, like he's going to do anything about it. He'd be happy if I wasn't even in his school.

"You still can't remember *anything?*" Chloe is nestling into one of the bean bag chairs downstairs in my recording studio. I'm pacing back and forth, still worked up after telling her about my visit to Mr. Lessard's office this afternoon.

"Not a thing. It's like the entire day never happened."

"I can't believe Mr. Lessard actually told you not to be too gay. What an idiot," she sputters.

"Hey, I'll just do my own thing and he can go screw."

Chloe is deep in thought for a few moments. "Mom thinks you're doing this rebellion thing big time."

"What rebellion thing?" I snap at her.

"She said most teenage boys go through this big rebellion thing sooner or later. She said it's even more understandable with you. Mom tried to tell me girls do too, but I got mad at her and she left the room in a huff."

"I'm not doing any rebellion thing. It's the adults who are screwed up. They screw up everything."

"Hey, I told her she's crazy. Look, this is just as a friend, but maybe you should tone down the colored hair and some of the wilder outfits ..."

"I'm just being me!" I shriek. "Don't you understand?"

Chloe's eyes go wide with shock. I never, ever yell at her. I instantly hate myself.

"I'm really sorry, Chloe. I know you're trying to help and I shouldn't have yelled at you."

"Jeez, you're really stressed out," she says, more amazed than upset.

I crash down into the other bean bag chair right next to her. "I'm just tired of all this shit. I'm tired of taking shit for being gay, and then I have to watch those stupid football players get away with murder. Jason was so hung over Monday morning, he fell asleep in algebra and nothing happened. One of the other guys didn't even take the biology test, and nothing happened to him either. Sometimes I think there are separate rules for them."

"Or no rules. It pisses me off too," she says. "Look, I know you want to be as gay as, well, whatever. Just be careful, okay? You know how upset I was when I heard they took you in the ambulance."

"Thanks. It's just hard." I sit back in the chair with a scrunch and stew.

Chloe's biting her nails. "Did you see Kyle today?" she asks.

"I tried not to, but he had to make things ten times worse by wearing that stretchy white tank top."

"Just be careful," Chloe says.

"If he catches me peeking at him again, he'll get really upset, and there's no telling what he and his friends will do."

"Now that he's the big football hero, he's flaunting his body all the time and he gets away with it. What a jerk."

Kyle won his first game Friday night right here at home. Chloe and I went. We yelled and screamed and cheered as our team won big. The crowd and the band and the whole scene were incredible. Kyle was incredible. When the game was over, he was the only player who signed autographs for the crowd of boys lined up at the fence after the game. Maybe it's just as well that he didn't notice me standing nearby.

"Kyle has the most incredible body I've ever seen," I tell my friend, leaning back and looking at the ceiling. "Jason's really built and Josh and Dustin are adorable, but there's something special about Kyle, don't you think?"

"Every girl's in love with Kyle and his—"

I'm at the edge of the pool, dangling my feet in the water. Kyle appears at the sliding glass door leading out to the patio. He's so hot in his tiny Speedo. "Hi, mind if I join you?" he says. Kyle the Sex God sits right next to me, so close our legs and shoulders are touching. His heavily muscled legs look huge next to mine. "I'm sorry I was mean to you. Can I make it up with a kiss?" I'm barely breathing as he puts his arm around me to hold me tight—

"Are you completely zoned out?"

"What?" I gasp, bolting upright.

"Come on, Bobby, you haven't heard a word I said," Chloe says.

"I've been listening."

"Yeah, right. You were thinking about Kyle, that's what you were doing. You were! I know you were." *How do girls know these things? Sometimes I think they read minds.* "You were having a fantasy about Kyle Faulkner. You're blushing, so admit it." She *is* reading my mind. "Come on, Bobby, you and I never have any secrets."

"Okay, okay. I try not to look at him but it's hard. He's so totally perfect. I think about him all the time—"

"You have a crush on Kyle," she says.

"Do not."

"Do too."

"Do not!"

Chloe bolts right off the bean bag. "Yes, you do," she shouts. "I can see it in your face. You can't hide it from me, Robert Fowler. You think about him all the time? That's called having a crush on someone." My face sure feels hot. "How can you have a crush on someone who's being mean to you?" she says, pacing in front of me.

"I don't know."

Chloe growls, clenches her fists, and settles back into the bean bag. If I had told her about what happened in the boys' room, that girl might actually beat me up, but there's no way she or anyone else is going to find out.

Chloe sighs and turns over to look right at me. "Listen, I guess if you're going to have a crush on someone, Kyle Faulkner is the dreamiest boy I've ever seen," she says. "Just be careful, okay?"

"I'm trying."

"Come on, Bobby, he's the big football hero, and he's pissed and his friends are even more pissed … but don't worry, it'll be our little secret," she giggles.

"I can't stop thinking about him," I sigh. "He's so perfect and so, oh, I don't know, he's the most beautiful boy I've ever seen. Is there one girl at school that doesn't want a date with him?"

Chloe doesn't answer. She doesn't have to. Every girl in school wants Kyle.

Chapter 20

I'm trapped. I'm panting in shallow breaths. The burning in my legs is killing me. I can't move anything, not my arms, not my legs, not any part of my body because I'm jammed so tight into my locker. A tiny amount of light seeps in from four narrow vents.

I don't know how long I've been in here, but it must be eight or nine hours, maybe more. It was Jason and another football player, some jerk named Reece, I think. I can still hear Jason's hateful words: "That's for being a queer freak, asshole." They laughed and congratulated themselves all the way down the hallway.

To think I was happy, having just finished a great band practice and a senior drummer actually asked for help with reading, and now I might die, I might die for real. Tears stream down my face, but I can't lift my arms to wipe them away. I'm terrified I'll suffocate in here. I pray again. *Please God, please help me. I don't want to die. Please—*

What's that noise? Way up the corridor. It's a floor-polishing machine.

"Help, help, help, I'm in here. Somebody help."

The sound grows louder with agonizing slowness until it's right outside my locker. The whine of his machine alternates as the janitor sweeps it back and forth across the floor. How bizarre—I'm admiring his ability to keep perfect tempo with a cleaning machine while I'm trapped in here.

"Help, I'm in here, let me out, please help me. Help!" I'm screaming and struggling mightily, trying to free one hand, one leg, so I can bang on the door. It's no use. I'm stuck so tight I can't move at all.

The whining of the floor polisher recedes, little by little. I'm going to die.

"Help. Please come back, get me out of here. Help me," I wail, followed by sobs. I'm in here for the night and they'll find me dead in the morning or maybe days later when they smell something bad. I don't want to die. I am going to die. I wonder if I'll get into heaven if I don't forgive Jason and his friend.

Finally, way down the corridor, the sound of the polishing machine stops. It's eerily silent except for my soft weeping.

What was that? Something made a slapping noise against the lockers. There it is again. It must be the janitor whipping the long electric cord back through the corridor.

"Help, help, I'm in here."

Nothing.

"Get me out of here. Help! I'm in here."

Just silence for an eternity.

"Is someone there?" comes a voice from further down the corridor.

"I'm in here, I'm in here. Get me out of here."

"Hello? Is someone there?" The voice is closer.

"In here, in here. Get me out!"

"Oh no, not again. What locker?"

"I'm in 960. Get me out of here!"

Keys jingle, followed by the metallic rasp of a key sliding into the lock, a sound more welcome than anything I have ever heard. With a loud clatter and a rush of cool air, the door flings open. Bright fluorescent lights blind me as I tumble out, followed by an awkward splat on the cold tile. Pain stabs at my elbow where I landed on it.

Standing over me is Eddie the janitor, an older guy with a ratty cowboy hat and a plaid shirt stretched by a belly so fat it looks like it will burst. Not only is he not moving a finger to help, he's watching me with a stupid grin.

"Hey, I know who you are," he announces, still grinning like this is a big joke. "You're the first this year. We had two last year. I rescued them myself," he exclaims with idiotic pride. "What did you do?"

"I didn't do anything." Sharp, deep pains stab through knotted muscles in my legs. My elbow hurts even more.

Trying to get to my feet, unsteady and shaky, I make a desperate grab for my locker door to steady myself. The pain in my legs is so intense it's making me woozy.

"You okay, boy?"

"Yeah, I just want to get home." It's only adding to my humiliation that I've been crying.

"Well, good luck, boy. Try not to get caught again," he says, cackling as he walks away. I must have been the funniest thing this dolt has ever seen.

The corridor now looks ten times longer than usual as I begin to shuffle toward the lobby. I'm having a hard time walking through school and I have to bike seven miles?

But there's no way I'm calling Mrs. Robles or the judge. I've had enough humiliation. They're on my case big time anyway.

A loud yelp echoes through the empty lobby as I plop onto the floor and land right on my sore elbow. Knotted and throbbing, my legs are screaming not to go one step further. *Come on, Bobby-dude, just get home,* I silently scream at myself. *Get on your feet and get to the bike rack and get going. Seven miles, do it.*

I happen to glance up at the lobby clock: 9:05. That can't be right. I was sure it was early morning. Still, I was trapped in there for more than five hours.

I've plopped down on the side of the road like a bag of potatoes, my legs refusing to go one foot further after trying to pedal up this pathetic excuse for a hill. A pickup truck went by awhile ago but didn't stop. I'm two miles from home, I'm cold and I'm miserable and I hurt. I've been sitting here for quite a while, dreaming that Kyle will come by and comfort me and carry me home, his sturdy arms wrapped around me, his muscular chest nestling my head. He kisses me to make me feel better. I tell him I'm sorry I was sneaking peeks at him. He holds me tighter and kisses me again.

Down there, headlights coming from town! The glare blinds me as the car gets closer. Almost upon me, blue lights and strobes flash on the roof. After braking hard to a stop, the passenger window rolls down to reveal a nice-looking, really young police officer. He's craning to get a look.

"Are you Bobby Fowler?"

"Yes, sir."

"You were reported missing," he says. "Are you running away?"

"No, sir, I'm trying to get home. I hurt my legs real bad."

He climbs out, walks around the cruiser, and kneels down. "Hey there, partner, can you get up and walk?" he asks. He's friendly and concerned and not self-important like some of the other townie cops. Albrecht, it says on his blue ID tag.

"I don't think so. My legs hurt really bad. I tried to make it home, but my legs just gave out."

"Now don't you worry. Everything's going to be all right. Sit tight for a minute while I call in. Say, boy, that's some serious haircut you got going there."

He's nice and he's blond and so good-looking it almost seems worthwhile to get stuck here. Even his comment about my hair sounded more amused than insulting. At one point while checking in, the radio crackles "Memorial Hospital." I don't want to go the hospital. I just want to get home and crawl in bed.

"Well there, partner, we're fixin' to have you checked out. Say, do you know my cousin, Helen Albrecht?"

"Yes, sir. I'm in concert band with her. She's really nice," I reply as he reaches down to pick me up. I'm very gently eased into the back seat. My bike goes into the trunk, punctuated by the slam of the lid shaking the car. Minutes later, my first-ever ride in a police cruiser ends at the ER entrance of Memorial Hospital.

"I remember you," the doctor announces as he appears through the curtains in the ER's small screened-off area. "You're the boy with the concussion," he says while he scans my chart.

I remember him too. His name is Dr. Murkowski, and he was kind and concerned when I was here last month. After examining my elbow and telling me it's only bruised and to use ice, he begins poking around my legs. I jerk and grimace when he hits tender spots.

"So, do you want to tell me what happened?"

"I can't. I'll get in worse trouble."

He squeezes and prods around a little more. My entire body jerks violently and I cry out and jerk hard when he hits one particularly painful clump of muscles.

"Sorry. Hmm … leg cramps. From the two cases I saw last year, I bet you were locked in your locker." He smiles when I look surprised. "And let me guess something else. That concussion wasn't an accident, was it?"

"I don't know. I can't remember a thing."

"I guess we'll never know for sure." He scribbles some notes on a form and looks up. "You're the boy who came out as gay, aren't you?"

Not wanting more trouble, I don't answer.

Dr. Murkowski puts his hand on my shoulder. "Bobby, I know you are. And believe me, I admire you for the courage it took to come out and say you're gay at such a young age, especially in this town."

I'm so surprised I just stare at him.

"Just as your doctor and a friend? You might tone it down a little. I know what you're doing, and I know how angry and hurt you are. But here's where it gets tough. You're going to call so much attention to yourself that you'll get into some real trouble. I know the judge quite well, and I heard about how you lost your mother and father and moved here from Massachusetts."

It's very late, I'm exhausted, and I still hurt something awful. I've been humiliated and frightened out of my mind, and now the last thing I want to do is think about Mom and Dad seeing me here. I bite my lip, willing the tears away.

"And where are you living now?"

"I'm living with Mrs. Robles. It's my foster home." I can't help it when a few sobs escape.

This nice doctor reaches around and rubs my back, a completely unexpected gesture. When I quickly get myself under control, he cups my jaw firmly with both hands.

"Bobby, look at me," he says, staring straight into my teary eyes with intimidating intensity. "You're a very courageous boy. I'm also quite sure you are very hurt and very angry. I don't want to see you back here injured even worse. Maybe just tone it down a little for your own sake, okay?"

Overpowered, I nod yes.

"Your elbow and your legs will be fine," he says. "A hot bath will help, and I'm giving you a muscle relaxant."

"You mean I'll be okay?"

He relaxes into a comforting smile. "I'm afraid you're going to be completely perfect. Officer Albrecht will give you a ride home. He's quite concerned about you."

I get a pat on my shoulder and a little envelope of pills. Soon, I'm on my way home. I'm grateful for the kindness of Officer Albrecht and Dr. Murkowski, but still, it's a night that hurts. It hurts a lot.

Chapter 21

Don't look, don't look, don't look.

I would have to run into Kyle on my way to band practice. If I turn around and walk back down the corridor, he'll think I'm an idiot.

"Hey, um, look, can I talk to you for a sec?" he asks. I nod okay, surprised that he's talking to me. Worse, I'm instantly nervous to be talking face-to-face with the most beautiful boy in the world. He's looking at the floor and shifting from foot to foot.

"Helen told me you had to go to the hospital and, um, I wanted—"

"Hey, QB, what's up?" It's a group of football players, at least a half dozen. Kyle is more than startled—he looks caught.

"Hey, what's up, guys?" he says as he tries to be cool and pretend we were never talking.

"We're going for pizza at Hartwick's. You coming?" asks this guy Colt, a short, blond, aggressive senior with big arms.

Kyle tells them he'll join them and the group walks by, ignoring me as though I was invisible. I guess that's better than hassling me. But just down the hallway, I overhear Colt say something to Kyle. "You and the gay kid friends now?"

"Dude," Kyle snorts, "I was telling him he looks like a freak."

They continue down the corridor with Kyle laughing and elbowing Colt. How can anyone that perfectly gorgeous be such a total jerk?

"You've been kicked out of concert band?" Chloe is reacting so loudly Danny jumps and students nearby interrupt their lunches to look.

"They said I couldn't appropriately represent the school at the Christmas concert."

"You're only their best musician. How could Mr. Reynolds let them get away with that crap?" Chloe demands.

"It was the school board. Mr. Reynolds came right out and told me he wasn't happy about it but there was nothing he could do."

"Stupid jerks," Danny sputters while stuffing his mouth with noodles his mom made.

"Mr. Reynolds said I could re-apply for band next semester. Can you believe that, I have to *re-apply?*"

"So will you?" Danny asks.

"No way. They can go fuck themselves. Fuck the concert band and fuck this stupid school and fuck the fucking school committee. I'm tired of this shit."

It's humiliating to tell Danny and Chloe, but it will be even worse when everyone in the band finds out and it gets all over school. The gay kid got kicked out, that's what everyone will say, just like when I got kicked out of Mr. Bentley's class. Well, fuck them. I will never do anything in music for this school again, ever.

"Gee, you got rid of the color," Danny says with his mouth full.

"And you're letting your hair grow out," Chloe adds, reaching across to lightly brush my hair with the tips of her fingers. "The school committee shouldn't get away with this. Can't you ask the judge to do something?"

"Yeah, right," I sputter. "He's been on my case about my hair, my clothes, even my attitude. Mrs. Robles is just as bad." Danny and Chloe exchange an uncomfortable look.

"Hey, gotta go," says Danny, nodding toward the clock and already up.

"Off to work on your science fair project?"

"Yeah, I'm about to achieve nuclear fusion," he says, and to my relief cracks a smile. Chloe picks up her tray and nods good-bye with a half-smile and a tweak of her eyebrows. I bet anything she'll try to talk me into rejoining the band after Christmas break. I just know she will. Well, I'm not going to, not after—

"Hey."

Oh no, it's Josh. More shit.

"Look, I'm not here to beat up on you." He says nothing more and just stands there on the other side of the table waiting for me to say something. I'm too scared to move, let alone think of something to say.

"You know my girlfriend Helen? She plays flute in the band," he says, shifting uneasily on his feet and looking over his shoulder.

"Yeah, she's really nice," I reply. This is a trap. Kyle and Jason and Dustin are ready to spring another trick, this one likely worse than the others. I glance to my left, then to my right, and not spotting them, look over my shoulder.

"Dude, would you just chill? I'm supposed ... I just wanted to let you know what Helen said."

"Helen?" I ask dumbly.

"She said you're the best musician in the band," he mumbles and looks down at the floor. "She's upset you were kicked out, and she was really upset her cousin Billy had to take you to the hospital. I guess I am too," he says even more inaudibly. Then he leaves.

Did I just dream this? Kyle's friend Josh, a totally hot boy who's been really mean, said something nice.

It must have been Helen. Josh started to say *I'm supposed to,* so it *was* Helen. I hope I get to see her before school gets out.

Still ten minutes before Spanish lab, time enough to work on my special lyrics. I fish around in my backpack and find the secret page that no one will ever see. It doesn't take long to lose myself in the images that steam right off the page I'm holding in front of me.

"Hey, look, it's the little fag."

That nasty comment instantly pops me back to reality. I peer over the top of the page to see three football players standing on the other side of the table.

"Hey, what's the little fag writing?" the tallest one sneers. It's Eric Walker, the senior quarterback who got benched. He's also an arrogant jerk. Lightning quick, he reaches across the table to rip the page right out of my hand before I can stuff it into my backpack.

"Give me that! Please, give that back. It's personal."

"What have we here, a little poem?" he smirks. "It's about ... what the heck is this?"

Why did I have to write "Perfect quarterback, wet dream boy, perfect ass, perfect boy" in the first line?

"Please give that back," I plead, my desperation growing into near panic as Eric holds on to the paper and continues to read. In moments, his face darkens.

"Eric, give that back, you don't understand."

"Let me see it," one of the others says. His lips contorted into a vicious sneer, Eric waves his friend off and stares hard at me.

"Don't understand? You think I don't understand?" he snarls. "I understand you're one sick piece of homo shit. Come on, guys."

Eric storms off, leading his confused friends to join several other football players and their girlfriends on the other side of the cafeteria. He announces something I can't hear and angrily waves his arms, pointing back toward me. Eric's friends crowd around to read along with him. One boy looks up. It's hard to tell if he can't believe what he's reading or if he's disgusted. Probably both, but it doesn't matter because I'm out of here.

I'm walking as fast as I can to return my tray and I don't look back. I think I'm going to throw up.

* * * * *

"If you give me names, I will call them in here and we'll get to the bottom of this," Mr. Lessard informs me.

"It was Eric Walker. He ripped the lyrics right out of my hands and let all his friends read them, and now I'm in big trouble."

"Madeleine, I need to see Eric Walker, right now, please," he snaps into the intercom. "So why will those lyrics get you into big trouble?"

"They were about the football team," I mumble, hoping he won't ask for details. Chloe calmed me down after school when I became totally hysterical and talked me into ratting, telling me Mr. Lessard will pressure Eric into admitting what he did. This better go okay.

After a few uncomfortable minutes, Eric is shown in. I can't believe how smooth and smug this guy acts, so extra polite, sucking up to Mr. Lessard. When he glances at me, however, his eyes glint with anger.

"Eric, Bobby told me you took something of his, some lyrics. Is that true?" asks Mr. Lessard.

"Oh, no, sir, I sure didn't take anything of his."

"Bobby said you did, at lunch yesterday. Eric, I'm asking you again, you didn't take a page of lyrics? Bobby said it's personal and he's very upset."

"Sir, I didn't take anything," he replies, perfectly imitating the fake politeness of the Beaver's nemesis, Eddie Haskell. "I think he's upset because I called him something I shouldn't have." He looks at me with fake sincerity. "I'm sorry I called you a queer. It won't happen again," he adds for Mr. Lessard's benefit. The principal stares hard at him.

"I can have your locker searched."

"Mr. Lessard, honest, sir, I don't have anything of Bobby's. I'll open my locker for you or you can look through my backpack," he says.

Gosh, this guy lies well and I get it now. He passed them off to someone else. He lied about taking them, but he's telling the truth about not having anything of mine. I'm totally screwed.

"You'd better be telling me the truth," continues Mr. Lessard. "You're in enough trouble as it is, and if you've been lying to me, you'll be in more trouble than you can imagine. All right, you may go now."

Eric catches my eye as he gets up. He smiles, a victorious, smug little smile for having lied his way out of Mr. Lessard's office. There's something else in his eyes though, something threatening. *I'm going to get you,* they're saying.

"I'm sorry, but I can't search the entire school," says Mr. Lessard after Eric closes the door. "Why are you so upset about these particular lyrics?"

What am I supposed to say? He'll react really well if I tell him I wrote some really explicit physical descriptions of the quarterback, Kyle Faulkner, and, oh yes, some really hot scenes with him and me.

"I'm sorry, it's very personal. Thank you anyway."

Mr. Lessard stares very intently for a few moments before letting me go.

I have just one thought as Madeleine writes out my excuse slip—*I'm totally screwed.*

* * * * *

Only echoes greet my hurried footsteps through the empty school hallway. A few cars and pickups were in the student lot when I came in, but now, late Saturday afternoon, it's so quiet I suspect I'm the only one in here.

My science fair project complete, I'm eager to get home. Chloe's older sister is taking me and Chloe and Danny out for pizza and a movie. I'm grateful we're still friends. I called her last night and she cried—well, I guess I did too—when I thanked her for her friendship and told her how much she means to me. Yesterday after school, I told Danny as well but he just shrugged and said, "Hey, man, no problem." Such a straight boy.

"Hey look, it's the fag. Where do you think you're going?"

Eric! I didn't even hear him and two of his friends coming around the corner.

"Home," is all I can manage, as hardly any air comes out of my lungs.

"Yeah, you think? So you actually went to the principal and told him I took your fucking sick music?"

I can't get my mouth to work.

"Asshole, I asked you a question."

"I'm sorry, I was really scared," I answer, my voice trembling. "I didn't want to take more shit. I'm sorry, Eric, I'm really sorry. Come on, you didn't get into trouble."

"Listen, you sick fuck, you were writing perverted shit about the quarterback and totally embarrassed me in front of all my friends. *You humiliated me*," he snarls, baring his teeth like a dog.

He thinks the lyrics were about him! If I tell him the truth, I'm still in trouble and then he'll tell Kyle—oh God, I'm fucked. All three are menacing and crowding in closer. Even if I turn and run, they'll catch me before I get three feet.

"Hey, let's take him to the locker room," says DJ, a huge guy with no neck who's as mean-looking as he is dumb. Eric grabs my arm so tight it hurts.

"You're coming with us," he growls. "You messed with the wrong guy."

"Eric, I'm sorry, let me go, please ..."

"Shut the fuck up," Eric barks as he and his two friends roughly drag me down the corridor toward the locker room.

"Let me go, let me go, I'm sorry ..."

It becomes horrifyingly clear that calling for help is useless. I have an awful feeling, a sick feeling, as Eric flings the locker room door open so hard it hits with a bang and bounces back into him, making him even angrier. This is no longer just the locker room; it's now a dark, evil, terrifying hole so frightening I couldn't scream if I tried.

All I can hear is the thumping of my heart almost pounding out of my chest as they drag me toward the shower room.

AT DEATH'S DOOR

Chapter 22

beep … beep … beep … beep …

What's that beeping?

beep … beep … beep …

Pain. Awful pain. Why can't I move my jaw? What's happening?

"Oh my God. Janice, he's awake. Janice, come quick!"

Everything hurts. What's the matter with me? Two nurses—what are they doing here?

"Page Doctor Murkowski," one shouts.

The other leans closer. "You had a close call," she says.

Where am I? What's stuck in my mouth? What's going on? What's happening?

"Easy, easy, don't try to talk and don't struggle. Shh-shh-shh. It's okay," she says.

"I can't believe he woke up," someone says out in the hallway.

"I can't believe he's still alive," another answers.

Are they talking about me? Oh, please, someone make the pain go away. Help me!

"Doctor, he woke up barely two minutes ago."

A doctor appears over me. He shines a very small flashlight in my eye. It hurts. He points it away and shines it in my eye again several times.

"Bobby, I'm Dr. Murkowski. Blink if you understand me."

I do, but only my right eyelid moves. I can't see out of my left eye. Something's there. Is it a bandage? What's happening?

"You're in the hospital," he says. "You were hurt at school and you've been out for a while."

Hospital? The pain's awful. *What's in my mouth?*

He's studying me.

"Bobby, blink twice if you're in a lot of pain."

I do and he orders one of the nurses to bring fifteen cc's of something.

"Right now!" he shouts.

Please make the pain go away. Hurry!

"We're giving you something for the pain, and you'll sleep, probably for quite a few hours." He's leaving. *Don't leave me alone!* He turns around at the doorway to study me again for several moments. "You're one strong and determined boy, that's all I can say."

Dr. Murkowski. Now I remember him. *I'm in the hospital!*

* * * * *

"There, there, you're on your own, young man." Dr. Murkowski is patting me on my shoulder as I gag and gasp after taking that awful breathing tube out. "You're making *great* progress." I like Dr. Murkowski. I feel safe when he comes in.

Something must have caught his eye. He's looking toward the doorway. I can't see because of the bandage over my left eye where they operated, part of the same huge, uncomfortable bandage that covers most of my head, including where they drilled through the back of my skull. It still makes me shudder just thinking about a drill going into my head.

"Would you clean up his chin?" he asks the nurse. He leans closer. "A few more of your friends from school are here. I told them they could visit for a few minutes."

I try to ask who, but nothing in my body is working. Mrs. Robles was here awhile ago. She cried, although she tried hard not to. Danny and Chloe were here. I think.

Dr. Murkowski is smirking. It's an odd smile, just the slightest upturn of his lips. "Kyle Faulkner's waiting outside with some of his friends."

Kyle Faulkner? Here? I try to push up in the bed. I almost scream from the pain. The pain is *everywhere.*

"Easy, easy," he says, patting my right arm just above where the IV needle is taped to the back of my hand. "Don't try to move around too much and don't try to talk. That will come in a few days when the swelling goes down. I'll check on you right after lunch."

Dr. Murkowski is talking to someone just outside. I struggle to hear what he's saying through a haze of drugs and painkillers.

"That was just the breathing tube coming out," I hear him say. "Frankly, he's doing amazingly well, considering the extent and severity of his injuries."

"Is it okay to see him?" a boy asks.

"Oh, yes. When I told him you were coming, it seemed to perk him right up. Keep your voices very soft, and limit your visit to fifteen minutes."

"He's not going to die, is he?" a girl asks.

Dr. Murkowski doesn't reply for a few moments. Every muscle in my body tenses. "I know that Mr. Lessard told you he was right at death's door, but this kid's a fighter, and he has an excellent chance of recovering."

I hear nothing more after that. *At death's door?* It's sinking in how close I came to dying, for real. Death's door. Something cold settles through me, so cold it gives me goose bumps. I almost died. Even though he said I'm going to make it, I plead with God to let me live and to get better.

A girl walks in. It's Helen. I'm so glad to see her, but at the foot of the bed, she gasps and puts her hand to her mouth. *How bad am I? Is my face missing?* A wave of fear floods through me, so intense I feel sick.

Josh and Dustin follow. Their eyes are wide with shock, and Dustin sucks his breath in. Kyle is the last one in. Why are they here to see me after they've been so mean? That's odd—Kyle isn't reacting at all. No one has said a word. Certainly not me, not with my mouth and throat so swollen it doesn't matter if my broken jaw is wired shut.

Helen holds up a little bouquet. I can't talk and I'm starting to cry. She looks flustered and doesn't say anything and doesn't know what to do with the flowers. Kyle is right next to me. He leans down close to my face. "See, I told you I'd be back."

I feel tears going down my cheek and hear myself making small whimpering noises. Eyes glistening, biting his lip, I think Kyle's trying not to cry too. Kyle?

Watching all this from the foot of the bed—and maybe to divert their attention—Dustin investigates one of four IV bags trickling drugs and fluids into my left arm. The one he's studying is connected to a small machine on the night stand, which in turn is attached to a red button taped to my left hand.

"Morphine," he says with a visible shiver. He can't seem to look me in the eye. I glance at Helen, now held tightly by Josh. Her eyes are wet too.

"Hey, dude, how ya doin'?" Josh chirps way too loudly. It makes my head hurt.

How am I doing? He can't be serious. I'm in pain and I can't talk and my head's been drilled and they're pumping me full of drugs and I can hardly move. That question is so ridiculous it's—it's actually funny. I can't laugh, but I can move my mouth just slightly enough for a little smile.

"Way to go, dude," deadpans Dustin, prompting Kyle to stifle a laugh into his fist and Josh to blush. Everyone seems more relaxed, as if they all just let their breath out.

"Does it hurt a lot?" Josh asks. "I mean, we heard you weren't going to make—" He freezes with a look of horror.

Kyle jumps in. "Uh, he means we heard you got pretty banged up."

"And the doctor said it's amazing how well you're recovering," Helen quickly adds.

I'm scared deep down. I found out from Mrs. Robles I wasn't just "out" for a while, I was in a coma from Saturday afternoon until early Monday evening. They did brain surgery thirty minutes after I got to the ER. Since then, they've operated on my broken collar bone, my broken jaw, my shattered left leg, and my bashed-in left eye, and they've done about a hundred tests, all in three days. Then I overhear Dr. Murkowski saying I was close to dying. I can't take any more.

"Can you talk?" Kyle asks, bending down close. The gentleness of his voice and the concern in his face calms me down a little.

I'm trying, I'm really trying to answer him. All that comes out is an oddly high-pitched moan.

Kyle gently grasps my right hand. "Hey, if you can't talk, squeeze my hand," he whispers close to my ear.

My right hand is trembling as I try to close it.

"Son of a bitch," Dustin says under his breath.

"Hey, he can't talk," Kyle announces to his friends lined up at the foot of the bed.

"Maybe we should tell him what's been happening," Dustin says, his eyes meeting mine just for an instant. Kyle leans forward again, awkwardly unclasping his hand from mine.

"Sunday there was a TV truck from Austin outside the hospital, and Monday there were two right outside school," he says. "They interviewed some kids near the main entrance. Dude, you made the news."

"The TV station in Austin is calling it a gay bashing," Dustin explains.

"And they're still looking for suspects," Josh adds. "Everyone's talking about it and trying to figure out who did it."

"And guess what else?" Kyle adds, now louder and more excited. "The governor ordered the Texas Rangers and the state crime lab to help out the local cops. Imagine that? The governor!"

The judge—who Mrs. Robles said called his old buddy, the governor—told me two nights ago what happened as gently as he could. An unknown number of boys, at least two but likely more, beat me up pretty good in the boys' shower room at school. He said they hit me with something but they don't know with what.

"The police grilled Kyle and Jason for three hours Saturday night," Dustin goes on. "The police thought they did it, I mean at first. I mean, they didn't, but they thought they did."

I look up to see Kyle shrugging his shoulders.

"Jason and I were lifting weights at school around the same time you were … uh, the police found out it wasn't us, so they let us go. It was no big deal."

"The cops told Kyle you said one word in the ER," says Dustin. "You said Kyle's name. That's all you said, and then you must've conked out." I'm trying to remember saying his name in the ER, but I remember nothing, not the ER, not being in school on Saturday, not anything else that day, and little of the week before it.

Kyle looks up to give Dustin a look that could kill. Now I feel bad. Kyle's wicked uncomfortable that I said his name. But why would I say his name in the ER?

I notice Helen nudging Josh. "Tell him about Friday night," she urges in a whisper.

"We're going to a candlelight vigil against violence and intolerance Friday night," he mumbles, more looking at the floor than at me. "Helen's church, you know, the Lutheran church—they're putting it on."

"And Kyle and Dustin and Jason are going too," Helen adds in an unmistakable tone.

The pain is getting to the point that I can't stand it anymore. My head is throbbing and the light is too bright. I need more morphine. I squeeze the button in my left hand and hear myself moaning very softly. I feel a tear on my cheek.

Fingers rub my right arm with just the lightest touch. I open my eye to see Helen leaning down, so upset her eyes are teary and her brow is creased.

"You're going to get better, and you're going to be okay. Just remember, you'll never be alone. I've been praying for you every day," she says, her voice cracking. Helen wipes a tear off my cheek, and the next thing I know, she's rushing out the door. Josh, lips pressed grimly together, nodding slightly, follows her out without a word.

"Hey, um, I hope you, ah, you know, get better," Dustin mumbles. He's usually loud and a big flirt and never at a loss for words. Head down, he hurries out.

That leaves Kyle, hanging back with his head against the wall. His eyelids are pressed tightly together and his face is creased in pain. Tears are just visible and he's biting his lip, trying to control himself just like when he came in and I started to cry.

"Hang in there," he says in a strained voice, not really looking at me. In a flash, he's gone.

I can hardly believe it. Kyle Faulkner and Josh and Helen and Dustin were right here in my room, and Kyle was getting emotional. I'm trying to remember every minute of it, but I'm feeling loopy and very sleepy. *Kyle was here, Kyle …*

Chapter 23

"I thought you might like this."

The judge breezes in holding a large Sonic cup with a cover and a straw. He smirks as he hands it to me. Reaching for it, I wince from a sharp stab from my four broken ribs.

"Go easy drinking this. I know your jaw and ribs hurt."

It's a thick, creamy chocolate shake, my best gift since I've been in here. Oh God, this tastes good, even though sucking on the straw makes my wired-shut jaw hurt. Not only that, but my sutured lips and my sewn-up gums where teeth got knocked out are still sore. Even my punctured eardrum aches. The cold of the shake feels good, though.

To pace myself, I put it down and scribble on my pad. Other than single words, it's easier writing on a pad of paper. At least the painful swelling and the sting of the surgical incision under my jaw have eased.

WHAT DAY IS IT?

"Tuesday, just after 7:00 PM. It's your tenth day in Memorial."

All I can tell on my own are the shift changes, daylight and darkness outside my window, and meals coming in—wonderful liquid meals through a straw. Other than that, it's all a blur.

"Dr. Murkowski shared with me how extremely pleased he is with your progress," the judge goes on. "I heard you were up on your feet again and doing some walking," he says while I take a few more slurps of irresistible chocolate.

"Hurt."

"Bad?" he asks.

I answer with a shrug of my uninjured right shoulder. Yes, it hurt, but mostly I was scared of how quickly I became exhausted.

"What hurt today? Ribs? Shoulder?"

I scrawl on the pad and hold it up: EVERYTHING

Broken ribs, broken collar bone, or it can be my whiplashed neck or my broken jaw or my badly swollen groin where they kicked me. Sometimes it's my left side where my lung collapsed. My right eye, the eye I see out of, is still tender from a really bad shiner. My mangled, broken left thigh, covered with a removable cast, throbs. It still hurts to pee because of a damaged kidney, although not as bad as it had been. The nurses are happy I stopped peeing blood. So am I. And was I ever glad when they took that awful catheter out yesterday morning. Strangely, my head aches something awful, but it doesn't cause intense pain.

I demanded to know what was wrong with my head. The doctor looked at the judge and Mrs. Robles, and the judge shook his head to tell me. That's when I found out I have a badly fractured skull near my temple, and damage not only to my eye socket but my eye as well. And then there's the back of my head. I tensed when he hesitated and said it was more than a serious concussion. Dr. Murkowski said my skull was fractured so badly, there's a possibility of lasting brain damage. He performed emergency surgery because of swelling in my brain. He was gentle and hopeful, but after they left, I cried. I'm so scared.

This morning on my feet, everything hurt, especially my left leg and my shoulder. I guess my ribs and groin too. I started crying. I hate it when I do that. At least I took some steps and I felt good about that. Exhausted and dizzy and scared of how weak I am, but afterward I was glad I tried.

The judge reaches for my empty cup when I make those raspy noises through the straw a few too many times.

"Well, my boy, it seems you liked the shake," he says with a grin. "So, would you like some good news?" I nod that I would. "I guess I'll steal Dr. Murkowski's thunder, but apparently your kidney is quite happy where it is and is healing just fine. So is your right testis."

It really is good news. I manage a smile, as much as I can, but so much else is wrong, I'm scared if I'll ever be right. I'm scared of more surgeries and hurting and those awful bandage changes and heaven knows how much brain damage there is and they don't think I'll ever see again with my left eye. I lost it after Dr. Singh told me about my eye.

I cried myself to sleep that night. The judge stayed the whole night. *Take it one day at a time,* he constantly reminds me.

The judge folds his hands together and his look changes. As only he can do, his serious, almost tough look scares me that they're scheduling another surgery.

"The three boys are out on bail."

"No! They can't let them out, they can't!" I mumble, making my jaw hurt something awful.

He sits forward and reaches to squeeze my right knee. "I know you're frightened. No one's going to hurt you, but if it will make you feel better, I will hire a security detail to guard your room."

I told Dr. Murkowski that one of them is planning to sneak into my room and kill me. Dr. Murkowski said my fears are understandable and ordered some pills—tranquilizers or anti-anxiety or something like that. I'm still scared, especially at night. It takes a few moments to figure out what to do.

I scribble on my pad and hold up printing made shaky by the IV still going into the back of my hand: NO GUARDS.

The judge relaxes and eases back into the chair. It was only yesterday afternoon when I heard the news—

"Bobby, Bobby, you're never going to believe it," Chloe shouts as she's hardly in the room. My foster mother, sitting near the foot of the bed, nearly jumps out of her chair.

Danny, eyes wild with excitement, is right behind her.

"At least eight cops stormed into school and arrested Eric Walker and two other kids—"

"Right out of class!" Chloe shrieks. "Oh, hi, Mrs. Robles."

"Eric Walker? Franklin Walker's boy?" she asks.

"Yes, ma'am, that's him, and they took them out in *handcuffs*," Chloe tells her.

"They handcuffed them right in the corridor," Danny goes on, now pacing rapidly at the foot of my bed. "The whole school is completely freaking out."

Mrs. Robles shakes a finger at me. "See, dear, I told you the police would catch them. I told you, didn't I?"

Danny prods Chloe. "Tell him the rumor," he whispers.

Chloe pulls up a chair right next to me and gently takes my hand.

"Some kids are saying Eric boasted about what they did and that a student tipped off the police," she says in a quiet, please-don't-get-upset voice.

"Everyone's trying to guess who snitched," Danny adds.

I hold up my note pad. WHO ELSE?

"Larry Bissell and that stupid big kid, DJ," Danny says. "Fucking football players ... oh, I'm really sorry, Mrs. Robles."

It's the first time I've ever heard Danny use the F-word. Mrs. Robles scowls but says nothing.

"They're in jail now," Chloe says with a pat on my hand. "You can rest easy."

"Those boys are going to pay. God will see to that," Mrs. Robles says, her angry pronouncement spit out with the faith of a true believer.

Eric Walker. What is it about that name? Something is terrifying about that name, but it's just out of reach, almost like a horrible, screaming nightmare you know you just had but can't quite remember it. Eric, Larry, and DJ. So that's who did this to me. How could those creeps do that? How could they hurt me like that?

"That's very brave of you," the judge says, interrupting my daydreaming. "Dr. Murkowski and I are making sure—"

"Oh, I'm sorry, sir."

We both look up to see who just barged in. It's Kyle!

"That's quite all right," the judge says. "Are you looking for Bobby Fowler?"

"Yes, sir, but I can come back later."

"No, no, no, please come in. I have to leave now anyway. And you are?"

"Sir, I'm Kyle Faulkner. I'm the one who found Bobby in the shower room."

The judge bolts right out of his chair and extends his hand. "Of course, you're Frank's boy," he says. "Well, my boy, both Bobby and I are deeply indebted to you."

It was *Kyle* who found me? I never thought to ask, and no one told me. I also never told the judge about my crush on Kyle or the mean things he and his friends did, only that some jocks were harassing me. He heard about Jason, though.

"Just don't tire him out or make him talk too much," the judge tells Kyle.

"Oh, not at all, sir. I sure won't," he replies with the politeness and respect that was such a surprise when I first moved here.

After the judge says his good-byes, Kyle reaches for the chair the judge was in and slides it back two or three feet, apparently uncomfortable sitting too close. Amazingly, this is Kyle's third visit. He, Josh, Helen, and Dustin surprised me with a visit Friday evening. Dustin blurted out that it was Helen's doing, a surprise because I figured of all the people that would be too upset to come back, it would be Helen. On Sunday after church, she came back dragging Josh along. I know they were all here earlier last week but can't recall too much about that visit.

"You ... found ... me?" I ask.

Instead of answering, Kyle is looking right through me. His blank, unsettling stare continues for quite a few moments.

"Are ... you ... oh ... kay?" I ask him.

"Yeah," he answers, his eyes focusing on me from wherever. "Look, I stopped in—"

"*Time for bed,*" announces Janice, today's no-nonsense nurse, in her usual booming voice. She starts her usual routine by arranging the pillows on my bed. "You can stay, hon, but you have to move out of the way," she informs Kyle. "Okay, hon, let me get my arm under here and you tuck your arm there and then we're going to swing you up this way. You know the drill."

"Ow, ow, ow, please, Janice, it hurts, it hurts, *ow!*" I'm grimacing as I'm swung into bed. Janice, who's actually my favorite, ignores my carrying on and expertly arranges the pillows behind my head, which is still covered by an enormous bandage running down across my left eye. My shoulder and ribs hurt a lot.

"There, is that okay, hon? Do you want the bed higher?"

"No," I squeak through pain.

"I'll be bringing your nighttime pills in a little while," she says, oblivious to my sniffling. "Hey, hon, I heard you did really good today," she adds.

"You did?"

"With all the injuries you have, just being on your feet is pretty impressive."

Feeling a little better, my attention shifts to Kyle before Janice is even out the door. He has that intensely peculiar, wide-eyed look of one who's watching someone in pain, a mix of shock and fear and I-don't-know-what-to-do. I've seen it with Mrs. Robles, Danny, Chloe, even the judge. Kyle is up and backing away from me.

"I'm sorry, I've come at a bad time."

"No! Please ... don't ... go," I say so loud a stab of pain radiates through my jaw and up into my left ear.

"Maybe you should get some rest."

"Please?" I say with through wire-clenched teeth. When I pat the bed, he relents, pulling his chair closer to sit. He sinks his forehead down onto balled-up fists.

"I stopped in ..." he begins, breathing harder. "I guess ... I wanted ..."

His fists are so tight I can see white in his knuckles. Swallowing hard, he tries again, talking very softly. "I'm sorry," he says, his face a battle between control and pain. "I'm sorry we messed with you like we did. Helen tried to warn me," he says, his voice so low I can hardly hear.

"Helen?" I ask, pronouncing her name, like everything I try to say, as if someone has stuck a tongue depressor in my mouth.

"She said everyone takes their cues from me." He's hesitating and can't make eye contact. "Some of this might be my fault," he mumbles.

His fault? I'm stunned, watching him sit here saying he's sorry for all the crap he gave me, but my gosh, he thinks he's to blame for what happened?

"You have no idea how bad I feel you got hurt like ... like this," he continues with his head down again.

A million thoughts race through my mind. The instincts of my heart, however, become instantly, absolutely clear. I scribble on my pad with frantic, sloppy strokes, and hold up the words that cover the entire page:

NOT YOUR FAULT!!!

I know with complete certainty there's no room in my heart for hating the Kyle Faulkner now sitting next to my bed, the Kyle who teared up when he first visited. I extend my hand over the side of the bed and open it. Surprised, he accepts my invitation by lightly grasping my hand. I grip his as firmly as I can with an IV needle still stuck in the back of my hand. We exchange one strong shake.

I scribble again and hold it up right in front of his face.

I ALREADY FORGAVE YOU

I watch his shoulders slump as he closes his eyes and lets out a huge, noisy breath. "I gotta go," he says to the floor so quietly I almost missed it.

And just like that, he's gone.

Light from the little TV flickers about the room, but I hear nothing and see nothing. Unlike most nights when my brain is so wired it seems like 4 million thoughts and fears are crackling inside all at once, I think only of Kyle. He was here. Kyle Faulkner was right here, sitting next to my bed, shaking my hand and saying he's sorry. He was actually becoming emotional. He must have a good heart to come here and say he's sorry. And something else: it took a lot of courage.

I'm still thinking about how different the Kyle who came into my room tonight was from the mean, scary Kyle of a couple weeks ago, when I feel the drowsiness overtaking over me. I wonder if I'll dream …

Chapter 24

I wish Mom was here.

I wish Dad could come home and get me out of here.

I'm tired of all the pain. I'm trapped here. Some Christmas this is. It sucks more than I can bear. Fuck this, I'm too tired to care anymore.

Why did they have to hurt me so bad? Why did this happen to me?

Tears stream down my face, but I'm too tired to wipe them off. I want to go to sleep and never wake up. I've been crying since after supper and I can't stop.

I was crying an hour ago when a nurse came in. "There, there, everything's going to be okay," she said, but nothing's going to be okay. She squeezed my arm and tried to be encouraging, telling me the nurses can't believe how well I'm doing and I'll be out of here in a few more weeks. And then what? My life is over. I can't do any more. I'll never play my drums again, or ride my bike, or see out of my left eye. What's the use?

"Hi. Is it okay if we come in?"

I slowly open my eye at the sound of that soft, sweet voice. Helen stops abruptly at the foot of my bed. Her hand flies to her mouth. Josh, holding a large gift, nearly bumps into her. I look away, not wanting gifts and not wanting to see anyone. I feel so tired it's like my whole body has sunk way down into the bed. I can't even lift my head up.

Helen edges to the right side of my bed, the side where I can see better. Yeah, my left eye's gone, just another way I got fucked. Helen leans down to gently brush the tears off my cheek. I can't stop weeping.

"Oh, Bobby, I'm so sorry you have to be in the hospital on Christmas night. It's almost eight. I hope we're not too late."

"Hey, how ya doin'?" Josh asks. Helen rolls her eyes.

"Fine," I squeak through sniffles.

"You're looking a lot better," Helen says. "I really mean it. Most of the black around your eye is gone. There's almost no swelling in your face that I can see."

"What difference does it make?" I sniffle.

With the softest touch, she rubs the back of my hand, now free of the IV.

"We brought a gift for you. It's from both of us. Josh, why don't you open it for Bobby?"

Josh rips off the extra-large red bow, tears into the shiny gold paper, and reaches in to pull out a teddy bear decked out with a Christmasy bow tie and a Santa cap. He's standing there holding the bear with a goofy grin.

"Thanks, Helen, thanks, Josh," I tell them, forcing myself to be polite, slurring my words because my jaw is still wired tight. Helen plops the bear onto my bed right next to me. I'm too tired to knock it on the floor.

"I'm sorry you're feeling so down, but guess what, there's one more surprise," she says. Her eyes are sparkling and she's grinning like I'm going to be extra surprised. I just want to get this over with. I want to be left alone.

Josh, who's been more interested in the cards and flowers and foil balloons on the shelf over by the window, nods toward the door. Not wanting to see anyone else or be surprised, I close my eye and try to turn my head the other way.

"I'd like you to meet Jeffrey," Helen says to whoever just came in.

The chair slides on the floor close to me.

"Hey, dude, looks like you'll have more company tonight than I will."

I know that voice! It's Kyle, here to see me. I turn to look at him.

"Helen wasn't messing with you, you know," Kyle says. "You look a lot better. Man, it must suck to be in here, but you'll be out of here before you know it."

Unlike Josh, who so uncomfortable he's staying on the other side of the room, Kyle is leaning in close. "Nice gift," he says, nudging Jeffrey the bear closer to me. "It will bring you good luck." Kyle flashes one of his dimpled smiles, so perfect, so full of even white teeth, and so cute and adorable I think he should be on the cover of *Tiger Beat*. I can hardly breathe.

"Did you have lots of company?" Helen asks, startling me out of my thoughts.

"Yeah," I reply. "Danny and his folks, Chloe and her mom, Mrs. Robles, Judge, Mr. Huntington from Boston, General Cantwell …"

"Who?" asks Kyle.

"Dad's boss at Air Base."

"Gee, you're talking a lot better," Helen remarks. "Does your jaw still hurt?" I shake my head slightly from side to side. I still talk slowly and a lot of words still come out funny. Chloe is the hardest. She teases me when I try to say her name, which comes out "Cho-ee."

"Oh yeah … Mr. and Mrs. Lessard."

Josh's head jerks up from across the room.

"Godzilla? *He was here?*"

"Yeah, after supper."

Helen's just as surprised. And inquisitive.

"What did he say?" she asks. "Come on, you've got to tell us!"

"He said he's sorry. He was very upset."

Looks of surprise flash among the three of them. They are no more surprised than I was.

We carry on talking about anything and everything. They're doing most of the talking, about tonight's record cold, down to zero, they said, and the big basketball game with Fredericksburg, where Josh scored eighteen points and made the winning basket with two seconds left. Over in the corner, Josh pantomimes shooting a basket. We talk about how long my jaw stays wired shut and am I going to have more surgeries and when will I get out, and, for some reason, what we got for Christmas when we were little kids. I think it's cute when Josh says Kyle's favorite was a teddy bear that he took everywhere, even to stores and restaurants. Kyle's rolling his eyes and blushing. I tell them I got a toy drum set when I was five. Then I tell them I walked all the way to the end of the hallway this morning. Well, it impressed me.

It dawns on me how they happened to come here tonight. This was Helen's idea. She got Josh to come out on Christmas night in the freezing cold, and she called Kyle and asked him to come too. I bet it was more than ask. During a lull, I catch her eye.

"Thanks, Helen,"

She smiles, more with her eyes. She knows I figured it out and leans across the bed, softly brushes my cheek, and gives me another kiss, just a peck, but this time right on my lips. It's the first time a girl, or anyone, has ever kissed me on the lips. I'm glad it was Helen.

"If anyone has the strength and courage to overcome this, it's you," she says.

Courage? I'm scared and I want to give up. I know there will be more surgeries. I can't walk without a walker. Lots of stuff hurts and some hurts a lot, and I'm scared of how bad some of the injuries are, especially my eye and my leg. I'll need serious dental surgery and plastic surgery and more leg surgery and staples taken out and who knows what else. I'm stuck in here and have no choice about what to eat or when to get up or anything. It's Christmas and I hurt and I miss Mom and Dad.

"Josh and I still pray for you every night," she says, softly squeezing my arm.

"Merry Christmas, everyone!" a nurse bellows loud enough to make everyone jump.

Phyllis, tonight's night nurse and the oldest nurse by far, marches into the room holding a tiny Dixie cup with my pills.

"My, my, isn't that just the nicest gift," she says with a glance at Jeffrey, but I can't tell if she's serious or if she's being sarcastic, which is most of the time. "If you think you're sleeping with someone named Jeffrey, I'll tell on you," she says wickedly. She gets after everyone and doesn't care if anyone likes it or not. She makes me laugh and I like her a lot.

Phyllis makes notes on my chart, checks the one remaining IV bag and the connections, and hands me my pills. It's all part of the bedtime routine. She's very gentle when she rearranges my pillows and cranks the bed down.

"So, are you going to be racing up and down the hallway tomorrow?" she asks with an evil smirk.

"On roller blades."

"And I'll be on my skateboard chasing you."

Everyone laughs, an overly loud, overly long laugh. It makes my jaw ache, but I don't care.

"Merry Christmas, everyone," she says at the doorway, not caring that it's now two hours past visiting hours.

Josh taps his wristwatch. They're leaving, and I don't want them to go. Helen is only half out of her chair when she stops with an odd look.

"Josh, honey, why don't you and Kyle go along? I'm going to stay with Bobby until he falls asleep."

"Helen," I start to protest.

She leans down and runs her fingers back and forth on my good shoulder. "It's not right for you to be all alone on Christmas night. I'm going to stay right with you, and when you're asleep, I'll just give Josh a call."

"We can stay too," her boyfriend offers. Kyle quickly agrees.

"Thanks, guys, but Bobby's not going to fall asleep with three people watching him. You go ahead. I'll be fine."

"Thanks, Helen," I tell her through overwhelming tiredness. She smiles sweetly and fusses with my blanket, pulling it up nice and snug under my chin and smoothing it out.

"Try to sleep," she says. "Everything's going to be okay, and I'll be right here with you. And remember ..." she says with a tracing of gentle fingers on my face that feels so soft and soothing, "God is watching over you and He is with you. He's with all of us tonight."

Kyle is watching from the foot of the bed. Unlike his other visits, he's calm, which I think is odd because he's been so tense and emotional.

"Merry Christmas," he says with a nod, and just like that, he's gone.

Josh, who's been pacing over by the windows, pulls up a chair right next to Helen. When he sits, his head is slumped way down. He runs his fingers roughly through his hair.

"I have something I want to say, but it's not easy." He pauses and breathes hard through his mouth. "Look, I know you're never going to forgive me," he begins in a strong, clear voice, "but I'm sorry for what we did to you, and I'm more sorry than you know that you got hurt so bad. Helen and I pray every night for you to get better." It comes out like he's been practicing it.

I glance at Helen's face as she rubs his back. It's full of pride and love, and now I know. She didn't tell or even ask Josh to do this. She left him alone to figure it out himself.

I reach over to the side table for my yellow pad and pencil, scribble a message, and fold it twice before handing it to him. Neither of us says a word as Josh gets up to leave with just a nod. I think he'll be relieved and maybe surprised, as Kyle was, when he opens it. Helen will be pleased too.

It's been about twenty minutes since they left. Helen got up to look out the window and watch the few flakes of snow that we can see swirling about. In spite of bone-deep tiredness, I'm so wound up I can't sleep.

"The meaning of tonight just came to me," Helen says, still gazing out the window. She turns around with a dreamy look. When she paces across the room and sits at my bedside, her face has a glow to it, as if she's just seen an angel.

"God brought us to be with you when you needed someone the most. God gave me and Josh and Kyle a very special gift tonight, the gift of giving," she says, clasping her hands around mine. "Tonight has made me happier than all of today's gifts put together."

Very drowsy now, I say a silent prayer, asking God to bless Helen and Josh and Kyle. Their visit was my best Christmas gift ever.

Chapter 25

Too tired to concentrate, my biology book lies unopened on my desk. I'm not having much success trying to massage the deep ache out of my leg. I idly gaze around study hall. Jason is sprawled in his seat over by the window with his hands behind his head, staring blankly at the warm April clouds and drizzle. Everyone else is hunched over their desks, concentrating on homework, or at least pretending to. Their lives are just going along, happily passing through high school with sports and dating and parties.

The four months since the—I still can't say any words about what happened that day—those four months seem like four years. I try to remember that Saturday, but I can't remember a thing. Mrs. Robles told me I went to school to work on a science fair project. I don't remember even having a science fair project.

The psychologist keeps telling me it's important to talk about what happened, but I can't. The two times I tried, I became hysterical. He also told me to focus on getting better and moving forward, but then I found out those assholes used a baseball bat. I got hit on my collarbone and near my eye and the worst one was in the back of my head, but it's just words because I have no memory of it. All I know are the results. I still don't know how my left thigh got turned into hamburger, or how my thigh bone was broken. Neither does Dr. Murkowski, but he said it wasn't from getting hit with the bat.

I've been daydreaming about things that have happened over the past few months. Thirty-eight awful days in the hospital. Oh, the big sendoff party by the entire staff was pretty cool. But then came two more weeks of painful rehab in the building right next door. It was worse than being in the hospital.

I finally went home, but every week brought more therapy and counseling and pain and exhausting travel and loneliness and feeling violated. I'm afraid every night. Sometimes for no reason I start weeping.

There were a few nice surprises. Last month, the judge and Mrs. Robles brought me up to my house. They told me I was getting an early birthday gift. Then they led me downstairs to unveil a gigantic new set of drums, with black lacquer shells, double bass drums, and cymbals and toms all over the place. When I sat behind the set, I was too hurt and stiff to do much other than tap on the snare drum. I still can't play well, but I started practicing this week, mostly to get Danny off my back. Sometimes when I can't play like I used to, I sit there and cry.

It's no use even trying to study my biology assignment. Once again, my thoughts wander back to the hospital.

* * * * *

Dr. Murkowski, with Mrs. Robles and the judge right behind, breeze into my room. I know just from his look that this is big. Dr. Murkowski is leaning against the side of the bed, towering over me in my chair made only partly comfy by pillows.

"So, how are we doing today?" he asks. "Bobby, we need to talk," he says without waiting. "We're here to discuss your treatment plan."

"You're going to be so excited, dear," Mrs. Robles says.

Yeah, right. "Treatment plan" is code for surgeries. It's now four weeks in Memorial and I want to go home. Even worse, I know what one of the surgeries will be. Eyes already teary, I'm gripping my chair, waiting for Dr. Murkowski to give me the bad news.

"Relax, everything's going to be fine," the judge says. Mrs. Robles, aware she's sitting so close our knees are almost touching, inches her chair back. She'll do anything to avoid hitting my leg, remembering how I screamed when she accidentally knocked a book onto the infected part of my left leg. At least the infection is almost gone.

"I'll tell you exactly what I told Dr. Murkowski," the judge says. "I told him to arrange for the best care and treatment anywhere, just as if you were his own son and money was no object. So, my boy, you're going to be doing some traveling. First class, I might add."

"I don't care about first class. I want to go home."

Dr. Murkowski ignores me and opens a red folder. "Let's get started, shall we?" he says, all business as usual when the judge or Mrs. Robles are here. "First up is a trip to Los Angeles. As soon as you can travel, you're going to the UCLA Eye and Ear Center to see one of the foremost eye specialists in the world."

"Isn't that wonderful, dear?" asks Mrs. Robles. "You're going to Hollywood!"

Just great. I get to see another hospital. And what's the use anyway? They said I probably won't see out of that eye.

"Listen to me," Dr. Murkowski continues. "I forwarded MRIs and other diagnostics and I've talked with the doctor several times. He's an acquaintance of mine, the best there is. Now, no one's making any promises, but he believes he has a good chance of saving the vision in that eye."

"He can save my eye?"

I'm half-listening as Dr. Murkowski nods his head and drones on: more MRI scans of my brain, this time by a specialist in Austin, and then surgery at some world-famous facial reconstruction clinic in Houston I never heard of. I'll have dental work at a clinic in Austin later in the spring, and plastic surgery by some guy Dr. Murkowski knows in Dallas.

"And one more trip, the sooner the better," he says. "You'll be going to the National Center for Sports Medicine in Boulder, Colorado."

"Sports medicine?"

"That's right," Dr. Murkowski says. "They'll examine the damaged muscles in your left thigh, and if all goes well, they'll prescribe treatments, physical therapy, and strengthening and stretching exercises."

"But my leg's totally messed up."

"They've seen these injuries before, especially in contact sports. If more surgery is indicated, it should be routine and we can do it right here."

"You're not … you're not going to cut my leg off?"

"Cut your leg off?" the doctor scoffs. "Where'd you get that idea? I'm not saying this will be easy or that your leg will heal quickly, but if you work hard and get the right treatments, we'll get that leg almost back to normal."

"You mean, I'll be able to walk?"

"More than just walk. In a year, two at the most, your leg should look and function very close to normal. You'll just have a scar."

My eye tightly closed, I feel a tear silently slipping down my cheek. I'm trying hard not to cry. I always try hard not to cry in front of Dr. Murkowski.

"So that's what's been bothering you," Mrs. Robles says. "You've been scared of losing your leg, haven't you? Where'd you get that silly idea?"

"Young man, that leg is yours to keep," the doctor states with great finality.

* * * * *

"Just try to relax. One more bandage and then we'll have a look. You doing okay?"

I don't nod back because the eye surgeon is using scissors. This doctor, unexpectedly young and good-looking and so nice I liked him right away, operated yesterday. The judge is across the room, silent, head down, I think praying. Mrs. Robles was so nervous she said she'd wait in the lobby. I'm so tense and tight I'm almost vibrating. Here it goes, I can feel the last bandage being peeled off.

"No! It's just shapes."

"Relax, relax," the doctor says. "Remember, I told you it will take a day or two for your vision to clear up. Now just lean in here ..."

The doctor has me look into one machine and then another, science fiction laser measuring equipment. I see blurry rings and a fuzzy red dot in the middle. Aside from going "Mmm" a couple of times, he hasn't said a word. He slides out from the other side of the machine.

"Everything looks normal. Bobby, the operation was a complete success. With a corrective lens, there's no reason we can't get you to 20/20."

"You mean?"

"Congratulations," he chuckles. "You're going to see out of that eye, and with a contact lens, it should be as good as your right eye."

"Yes!" I shout with my good right arm raised high.

I hear nothing else except the unmistakable sound of soft weeping from across the room. It's the first time I've heard the judge cry during this entire ordeal.

Chapter 26

"Of course it went well," Chloe shrieks at her usual ear-splitting volume when she thinks I asked something stupid.

"Everyone stared," I tell Chloe and Danny at my kitchen table. We jump when a too-close lightning strike rattles the house as an early March thunderstorm roars through town. "I know what everyone was thinking," I continue. "'There goes the gay kid, the kid who got beat up. The kid with the awful-looking face and the scars and the bad limp.' I thought this week would never end."

"I don't know, I thought everyone was pretty cool," Danny remarks with his head in the fridge. Scrounging for snacks is something he'd never think of doing if Mrs. Robles wasn't out doing her Saturday afternoon shopping.

"And I saw lots of your friends and teachers asking how you were getting along," Chloe adds. "Even some of the football players."

Danny breaks out in an impish grin. "I bet your foster mother was glad you went back to school."

"Yeah, that's for sure."

Both Danny and Chloe grin, but it's not a joke. Mrs. Robles was okay and did a lot to help me, but then I'd hear her on the phone complaining to her friends and relatives that she didn't expect this and how hard it's been. Sometimes I just wanted to cry or scream. She's even drinking more but acts like everything's normal when the judge comes over.

"So when's the plastic surgery?" Danny asks.

"Early May," I mumble. I don't even react to his goofy grin when he holds up a plate of leftover pecan pie.

"You don't look all that bad," he says as he hands me a serving.

Instead of digging in, I'm slumping over the table. "Especially compared with how you looked before you went to Houston." Chloe glares at him. How I looked before Houston is something we never talk about. I couldn't even look in a mirror before the reconstructive surgery. The first time I did, in the rehab hospital, I cried so much they had to give me a sedative. I refused to see anyone for two days.

"You look tired," Chloe says with a mouthful.

Stretching my left leg out, I grimace as damaged muscles ache and cramp. "Maybe nine weeks was too soon, but I was crawling up the wall so bad I had to go back, even if I looked and felt like crap."

"Yeah, but you were able to go back," Danny tells me. "I thought some of those injuries were going to be like, forever. Now look at you. You had awesome news with those brain scans—"

"And all of your surgeries went well," Chloe breaks in.

"And even your leg is getting stronger," Danny says.

"Yeah, but I limp and my left shoulder still doesn't work right and I still have these stupid scars."

Chloe's tapping her finger against her temple.

"Mom said it's all in your head. No one sees the scars under your jaw or the back of your head. Mom said if you feel good about yourself, no one will notice." Her eyes, though, are fixed on the angry scars on my left temple and around my eye. I look down, upset and sad. Chloe's stare is the real truth.

"How can I feel good about myself after …" Tears start to well in my eyes, something that happens out of the blue far too often. It's more than the scars. I can't say or even think the words that describe what happened to me in that shower room. I'm so terrified of getting near a shower I take sponge baths instead. I got permission to quit gym class because I blacked out the first time I walked down the corridor to the locker room.

"A few months, man, give it a few months," Danny says. "Have the plastic surgery and the dental surgery, and by the time you start junior year, you'll be good as new. And don't forget …" I look up to see him pointing at me. "You're still Bobby Fowler. Everything that makes you you is still there. You're still Bobby Fowler," he adds, louder and more insistent.

Chloe's talking now, but I'm not listening. They just don't get it: I'm *not* the same. I don't know what I am or who I am. I'm scared and I'm sad all the time and I still hurt and I'm not the same.

"… what's up with Kyle?" snaps me back to my friends. Chloe's drumming on the table waiting for me to answer. "Come on, Bobby, what's up with Kyle? Sometimes when you walk by him when he's with his football buddies, he pretends he doesn't see you."

"Who knows? I thought we might be friends, maybe even hang out," I tell her. "Most of the time he says hi. Then when he's with a group of guys, he ignores me."

"He's a jerk," Chloe snorts.

"And a stuck-up jock," Danny adds.

"He's been okay, just not—"

Chloe's eyes flash. "Don't apologize for him!"

"I'm not. He's actually been okay most of the time, except there was this one time when he was weird."

Chloe leans forward. "Weird? Like what?"

"I was waiting for the bus, and Kyle was across the driveway in the parking lot. When I looked up, he was staring at me. I thought it was strange, the way he was just staring. Other than that, he's been … remote."

Chloe makes a face. "I don't know about staring at you, but we've both seen him ignoring you. He's a stuck-up jock, just like Danny said. Sexier than ever, if you know what I mean, but still just a stuck-up jock." Chloe's folded arms and fierce gaze are meant as a challenge.

"Don't worry. I'm over him. Yes, he's beyond good-looking and he's more muscular than ever, but I – am – over – him."

Chloe shrugs.

"At least he's not nasty, not like some of those jerks at school." She stops short and takes her dish to the sink.

"Not like what jerks? Come on, Chloe, not like what jerks?" She's so flustered Danny answers.

"She, um, she overheard some girls saying stuff like, that's what fags deserve, and it just proves that God punishes homosexuals, stupid crap like that."

"Just ignore those ignorant jerks," Chloe says. You're better off ignoring stupid, ignorant people like them."

"How can I ignore them? It's the world I live in."

Chapter 27

"Kyle was in the ICU? He saved my life?"

What Helen just said is totally blowing me away. Kyle was right beside me in the ICU when I was in a coma and they thought I wasn't going to make it. I miraculously woke up late that afternoon.

"He called that night and told me about it," she says, grabbing at a napkin blowing off our picnic table in Sandy Gulch Park. "I've never heard Kyle so shaken up. So was I, after he told me how bad it was."

I was surprised but grateful when Helen called to invite me on a picnic for just the two of us in the town's prettiest park, just west of downtown. Now I know why we're here.

"But what was he doing there?" I ask, squinting in the bright March sunlight despite a baseball cap and sunglasses to protect my still-sensitive eye.

"Kyle was called down to Mr. Lessard's office Monday morning when you were still in a coma. Everyone was worried you were going to …"

She hesitates and looks to me for cues. I don't want to hear it.

"I'm sorry," she sighs. "I didn't mean to make you feel weird."

"It's okay, Helen." She's still hesitant. "You can tell me what happened."

"Well, the way Kyle told me, Mr. Lessard figured if you didn't say his name in the ER to report him to the police, it must have been because you wanted him to be there."

"But Kyle and his friends were really messing with me. I don't know why I'd say his name, and he'd never in a million years want to see me."

Helen doesn't miss a beat. "Mr. Lessard can be very persuasive."

"So he goes to the ICU, then what?" I ask her. "What did he do to save my life?"

"No one knows. He's never told me or anyone, even Josh. But he was so shaken up when he left the hospital he couldn't go back to school." Helen reaches across the table to hold my hand. "I guess it was really bad. Kyle said your face was really swollen and badly discolored. He broke down when he said how bad ... I'm sorry. I remember the first time I saw you, and that was three days later."

"And I never even knew he was sitting right beside me," I marvel.

"I haven't gotten to the good part," she says without a trace of a smile. Helen leans forward across the table. "Remember the first time we went to see you?"

"I remember a little of it. I was pretty much out of it."

"I'll say. You were on morphine. Well, anyway, Dr. Murkowski talked to us outside your room. Kyle almost turned white when Dr. Murkowski said he overheard him in the ICU talking to you. Then he said to Kyle, and I remember his exact words, 'That's the second time you may have saved that boy's life.' I thought to myself, *what did he do?*"

"Kyle saved my life," I repeat in numb disbelief.

"And when we went into your room, Kyle said something like, 'I told you I'd come back.' I remember because I thought it was odd." Helen waits for me to absorb all this. "He's never said a word about what he did, even when I bugged him about it," she continues. "He went on and on about how badly injured you were and all the bandages and equipment and how scared he was that the heart rate monitor ..." Helen catches herself with a gasp.

I think I know where this is going, but wait for Helen to finish.

Helen looks down, biting her lip. "He was scared it would flat line right in front of him," she reluctantly admits. "I'm sorry, I've said things I shouldn't have," she sighs. Helen reaches again for my hand and squeezes tight.

Flat line. Why now I don't know, but those two words drive home like nothing else how close I came to not waking up. I came *this* close to—I still don't want to say the word or even think it. A cold shiver violently shakes my shoulders. The very idea of coming so close still haunts me.

Helen goes on, saying she's telling me about one of her closest friends because she wants me to know there's so much goodness in Kyle. I'm half-listening. Kyle was right there, sitting right beside me when I was in a coma. Kyle did something to save my life.

Will I ever find out what happened?

* * * * *

My daydreaming slowly evaporates. I find myself back in study hall, thinking about my one final thank-you note. Mrs. Robles said I should write some thank-you notes to all the people who were special. I did, although it took two weeks, and everyone seemed to appreciate them. Helen even surprised me with a long hug, as did Chloe and the judge, of course.

This last note is for Kyle. I just don't know what to say or how to even give it to him. Certainly not in school. I told Helen I'd stop by his house. She was almost hysterical and told me that going to his house was absolutely not a good idea. Oh, I know, I'll ask Helen to give it to him.

So how to thank Kyle? What Helen told me last month about Kyle going to the ICU triggers a thought. I bury my head close to my desk and begin to print.

> Dear Kyle,
>
> I'm sorry I didn't write before now but I didn't know what I wanted to say. I'm writing to thank you for the hospital visits and the encouragement, especially the visit on Christmas night. That was special. I know you were in the ICU when they thought I wasn't going to wake up. I was in a coma so I don't remember anything. Dr. Murkowski said you saved my life. I hope someday you can tell me about it. You were also the one who found me and called the ambulance. Thank you, but it doesn't seem enough.
>
> One time, you came to see me in the hospital to tell me you were sorry. It took a lot of courage, courage which I didn't have because I should have said I'm sorry too. I did look at you every chance I could get because you are the best-looking boy in Texas. That's just a compliment. I did say things I shouldn't have and

it made you feel awkward and upset and I am truly sorry. I hope we can just be friends.

Sincerely,

Bobby

I wonder if I'll ever hear from him.

Chapter 28

The trim, well-built, older man, his face deeply tanned and lined, his gray hair cut so short there's almost none on the sides, sits so ramrod straight in my desk chair it's as though he's at attention sitting down. He's checking me out, especially my damaged left leg with the long, angry scar up the middle, plain to see because I'm sitting on my bed wearing workout shorts. When he came in, he introduced himself as Colonel Holbrook.

"How's your leg, son?"

"I guess okay, sir," I reply. "I was doing some stretching exercises when you came in. I have to stretch every day and do strengthening exercises three times a week."

Colonel Holbrook rubs tanned, leathery, hard-working hands together.

"I heard how hard you've been working at rehab. The judge said you were first in line when they were handing out guts."

I nod and note the odd phrase. He shifts uneasily.

"I'm here because someone wants to talk to you, and it's someone you might not want to see." He wipes his brow, although I didn't notice any sweat. "It's my grandson. He's waiting outside and he wants to apologize in person. I guess I'm running interference," he says with a cackle that's missing the slightest trace of humor.

"If it's Eric or Larry or DJ, no way. I can't see them, *I can't.*"

"Easy, son, he isn't one of those screw-ups. I thought you knew. My grandson is Jason Towne."

Jason! Stunned, I'm back in my locker, wedged in tight and fighting off panic while Jason walks away laughing. I'm in the boys' room with his angry, red face two inches from mine, screaming nasty things at me. I remember all those awful things he did to me.

"Jason knew you'd be upset, and that's why I came to ask. Well, son, I'm sorry, and so is my grandson, but I can see you're upset. Maybe it's best if we leave you alone." Colonel Holbrook rises from the chair, stiff and formal. "I really am sorry about everything that happened, especially what my grandson did," he says, starting toward the door.

"Wait!"

Can I do this? Can I actually talk to Jason face-to-face?

"He can come in," I tell him.

Colonel Holbrook nods and marches out through the kitchen and the living room. I hear him shout from the front porch; the slam of a car door quickly follows.

A figure appears in my doorway, someone I never in a million years imagined would be in my house, except maybe to kidnap me and leave me in Oklahoma with no clothes and no money. This has to be a dream, a really weird dream.

His eyes are darting every which way. His shorts are dirty and he's holding a ratty baseball cap, but at least he's wearing a clean T-shirt, with the lower part dangling loosely because his chest is so big. I nod toward the desk chair. "Do you want to sit?"

"Uh, no, that's okay," he says in low, slow drawl with a nervous catch to it.

I'm waiting him out.

"I guess I'm the last person you expected to see." I nod my head ever so slightly. "Maybe I'd better sit." When he does, only the very edge of his butt is on the chair. Slumped over, elbows on legs, he's kneading his cap like Play-Doh.

"I heard Larry's testimony. I heard everything they did to you."

"You went to the trial?"

He nods. "Helen needed a ride, so when I dropped her off at the courthouse, I decided to go too."

"Helen was there?"

"She actually skipped school, if you can believe that. Kyle said her mom called last night and he had to go over to her house 'cause of Josh being at the A.A.U. tournament. Helen was so upset she threw up. She said to tell you she'll stop over later with some homemade cookies."

I'm watching his eyes darting toward my leg every few seconds. He knows I caught him looking.

"Your leg, is your leg going to be okay? I mean, I seen you limping around school."

I shrug my shoulders. "Maybe in a year, maybe two." I have this awful, sick, angry feeling when I think about what Eric did, which I heard about after Larry testified yesterday. How could anyone jump way up in the air and land on someone's leg wearing heavy boots, not once but twice? "I'm in the WWF," he shouted as he smashed my leg and broke my thigh bone. The last thing I want to do is start crying in front of Jason.

I didn't mention that I'll have yet another operation in two weeks, or the painful therapy, or the endless hours of painful stretching and strengthening exercises. I don't know if I'll ever walk without a limp or pedal a bike or hike on a beach.

Looking up, Jason starts to say something but puts his head way back down. He's trying to squeeze his baseball cap into a pill.

"Look, I'm not expecting you to forgive me. I look back …" Jason gulps so hard I can hear it. "I look back at the things we—I—did, the things I did to you and the awful things I said to you. Can I tell you what my grandpa told me?" I nod again, but he isn't looking at me. I tell him okay.

"I told him what a shit I've been and how we ganged up on you. It wasn't easy, but I told him everything. Grandpa was so pissed I thought he was going to whale my ass. Maybe he should have. Then he said, 'Jason, you want to join the army and serve your country, just like me and just like your father and his father. When you're on that line defending our country, it's people like Bobby you're supposed to protect, the people that can't protect themselves and the people you swore an oath to defend. That's the real honor in serving your country.'" Jason's head is sinking lower and lower.

"That's where I let my dad, my grandpa, and myself down, but most of all, I let you down," he says, his voice low and shaky. "I guess I'm here to say I'm sorry, but I wouldn't blame you a bit if you told me to fuck off."

My mind whirling, I can't think of a reply, and I wait. He's looking at the scars around my eye and temple.

"Doc Murkowski testified about every injury. Oh, shit," he says, his head sinking into his hands. Jason takes a deep breath to continue. "Doc said he was amazed you didn't … I mean, I'm sorry they hurt you so bad."

"Hurt me so bad? Would it have been okay if they had hurt me just a little, like you did?" I ask, my temper rising with each word. Jason reacts like he's been shot.

"No," he whispers. "I'm sorry." Wincing, Jason puts his head down into his hands. "I wish it hadn't been me doing those things. I know I can never make it up to you, but I'm ashamed I hurt you and I'm sorry."

We're both sitting here, Jason with his head down when I don't say anything at first, and me—well as for me, I don't even know what I'm thinking.

"I know you're pissed, but I had to apologize in person," he goes on as he gets up. "Don't worry, I'll never give you any shit again."

His grandfather is talking with Mrs. Robles out in the living room. I think Jason's still with them. On impulse, I hurry out there as fast as my sore leg will take me.

"Jason!"

Three faces jerk up in surprise. Jason is outright startled, maybe scared I'm really going to let him have it.

"I accept your apology," I tell him. "You just have to give me some time." I extend my hand.

Eyes big and in disbelieving slow motion, he extends his. We shake hands firmly, looking each other in the eye. Nothing else is said.

"You're letting that boy get away with murder. I would have kicked him out, that's what I would have done," Mrs. Robles says after the front door closes.

"A long time ago, my grandmother told me it's not good to live with hate in your heart. He said he was truly sorry, so I figured I should forgive him."

Mrs. Robles stops with an odd look. "That's a very Christian thing for you to say. I'm proud of you," she says, her face breaking out in a smile. She follows with a hug. Another totally weird day in my life. Wait till Chloe hears about this!

Chapter 29

After slamming his chair into the table, Danny furiously paces back and forth in Chloe's kitchen.

"Not one day in jail? *Not one?*" he hollers. "You've got to be kidding me. How can they do that after all you've been through? You've got to be freakin' kidding me!"

I can't answer. If I open my mouth, it will be either out-of-control screaming and swearing or crying in angry frustration. Chloe, on the other hand, is simply speechless. I thought for sure she'd be the one screeching.

Danny resorts to stewing over by the sink. The only sound is the muted ticking of Chloe's Felix the Cat clock.

"It's so unfair," he starts in again, pacing even faster this time. "None of them gets a day in jail. How could they let them off like that?"

Here come the tears. I can't help it. When Judge Roberts announced the sentences this morning, Eric was all smiles. Then he shook hands with each of the high-priced lawyers his father hired like he had just won. I was so upset I told Mrs. Robles I wasn't going back to school. I hid in my room, completely stunned.

"I'm really sorry, Bobby," Chloe says, reaching across the table to squeeze my hand.

"I thought they were going to be punished," I barely whisper as a tear streaks my cheek. *"I wanted them to pay for what they did!"*

"Ten years in jail and all of it suspended," Danny mutters.

"Well, they did get 2,000 hours of community service and ten years probation," Chloe says. "And the $2,000 fines," she adds.

"Big freaking deal," Danny answers while I wipe my eyes hard on the back of my hands. "So they clean up the park, pick up litter in their little orange jumpsuits, and pay some stupid fine. For what they did, they should be in jail forever."

"Larry got even less," I tell them. "He had made a deal by turning state's evidence, and it turns out they didn't even need him to testify."

Chloe squishes her eyes shut, I think remembering that during the trial, an expert from the state crime lab testified that they found microscopic bits of bone embedded in DJ's baseball bat. Bone from my head. Just the thought brings more tears.

"What a screwed-up town," Danny spits, pacing back and forth a few times before settling against the counter. "I'm gonna call that idiot judge and tell him his sentences suck."

My breaths are coming in fast, deep gasps.

"All that pain ... *it's just not fair!*" I'm sick way deep down. It's hard to believe or understand how they could do this to me.

"I'm sorry, Bobby," Chloe says. But it's not enough.

"The judge warned me that first offenders get off lightly," I tell her, "especially since this was unpremeditated, but no jail at all? *None?*"

We're quiet again. I'm biting my lip, trying not to completely break down. The clock is ticking louder now. I've always thought it was the coolest thing, a 1950s collectible, according to her mom, but right now I want to rip the tail right off Felix and stomp that fucking clock into 10 million little pieces.

Chloe reaches across the table with both hands to hold mine. "You've still got your music," she says.

"What's the use?" I snap, getting up from the table as much in frustration as to get the circulation going in my leg. It's been two weeks since my last operation. I'm still pacing with a limp, another gift from Eric.

"Come on, Bobby, you're always going to have your music," Chloe says.

"You're playing your drums and you're getting better every day," Danny chimes in.

My best friends are trying to be positive. The judge tried it, and I said something really nasty about Texas justice. All he said was that I need to move forward with my life. "What life is that?" I asked him.

"I just want to go to sleep and never wake up from this nightmare," I wail.

Overwhelmed, Chloe sighs. Danny's another matter. He's not going to let go.

"You're not giving up," he shouts. "I know this sucks big time, but you – are – not – giving – up."

I'm easing my butt against the countertop opposite Danny, but I can't look at him.

"Do something with music like you've always done," he says.

"Yeah, right. What's the use?" I say more to myself.

"Come on, Bobby, it's like when your father died. You need to get into your music to get healthy up here," he explains, tapping his head.

"And here," Chloe adds, patting her heart.

"Why don't you do something extra special?" Danny asks.

"What do you mean, extra special?" Chloe says when I don't answer.

"I don't know, just something really special. Come on, Bobby, you're the best. Get your mind off this shit and write … oh, I don't know, write an opera."

"An *opera?*" Chloe shouts.

"Well, whatever," he snaps. Come on, man, get your head into your music. Like I said, do something really special."

"Yeah, we'll see," I tell him, having no intention of writing an opera or anything else. And if I know Danny, he won't let up on me all summer, just like he won't let up about practicing on my drums. Well, screw him.

Nothing matters anymore.

Nothing matters.

REQUIEM PER SOGNO INFRANTI

Chapter 30

"Jeez, you look like you're going to piss your pants."

"Good thing I'm wearing a black tux," I tell Danny. He grins at my joke. I'm not about to tell him I'm so nervous I've been to the boys' room three times.

Danny's eyes dart all over the band room. It's filled with musicians, forty-one to be exact, all dressed in black tuxes and white gowns. Over by the windows, a small group of cello players talks quietly about the score one of them is holding up. It's my score, the composition I entered into tonight's district music competition.

"Boy, the place is jam-packed," Danny says. "I've never seen the Heinie so full."

"The Heinie." That's what every student and everyone in town calls the school's huge auditorium, the Heinrich Center for the Performing Arts, a gift from some wealthy old guy back in the '60s. With an enormous stage for theatre productions and almost two thousand seats, it's gigantic, and no high school I know of has anything like it. I guess that's why the districts are held here every year.

Danny slaps at my shoulder. "Would you just chill?"

"Oh, this better go okay," I moan.

"Jeez, of course it will," he says. "Hey, wait till the curtain opens and everyone goes totally spastic when they see a symphony orchestra on stage," he says, so excited and loud several musicians look up.

"String orchestra," I remind him for the hundredth time.

"Yeah, yeah. No brass, no percussion ..."

Danny's head jerks when the second of three rock groups begins playing a wild, thrashing number so loud we can feel it as well as hear it. With the stage entrance just across the hallway, it's plenty loud.

"Renegade," he scoffs. "They're from Lampasas and they suck. Hey, I gotta get back. Sirius Rising is next."

Danny wishes me good luck and dashes back to cheer for Dunston's own alternative rock band. It's too bad the guys in the band turned into jerks. Their CD sold maybe a few hundred copies and made them think they're king shit, plus two of them are wicked cute and they know it. Worse, the other two showed up at school this week with colored punk haircuts much like mine last year, but they're straight and cool, so it's okay.

With Danny gone, I'm alone with my thoughts. As the final entry in tonight's competition, all these musicians and I will be called only after the stage crew clears all the amps and drums and mikes and gets the stage set up for the orchestra. The waiting is unbearable. In just minutes, I have to walk out onto that huge stage in front of all those people and conduct an orchestra for the first time, an orchestra that includes thirty-seven music majors and four professors of music.

Oh crap, I have to pee again.

The band room is empty and eerily quiet. The musicians are now lined up in the wings. I'm pacing in a tight circle, limping around on my bad left leg. Crescendos, the starting tempo, dynamics, solo breaks, and so many other details are whirling through my mind, I'm nearing panic. A voice from the doorway nearly startles me right out of my skin. "Bobby, relax, you're going to do fine." It's Tim, my friend from Austin and tonight's concert master.

"Thanks. I guess I'm a little nervous."

"Of course you are," he says, throwing a muscular arm around my shoulder. "It's a big audience and it's a competition. But just remember, you put all your emotional and creative energy into a magnificent piece of music. Every one of us is excited to be a part of this."

"I'm just as nervous about conducting you guys."

"Well, don't be. We're all experienced musicians and we'll come together just fine. Bobby, take control and *conduct!* Now, I want you to go out there and believe in yourself and give it your very best."

"Thanks, Tim, and thanks so much for coming up here. It's such an honor."

"I'm sure I shall look back upon tonight and think the honor is all mine," Tim says, wrapping his arms around me in a tight, reassuring hug. "Now go kick some ass."

At the doorway, Tim looks back. "Hey, gay boy, you look pretty hot in that tux." Before disappearing down the corridor, he winks and gives me a thumbs-up.

Although I'm still nervous, Tim's advice is reverberating in my head: *take control and conduct.*

"Just go out there and do it!" I command myself in the empty room. I'm ready. But at the faint sound of several tuning notes from the pipe organ, a sharp stab of panic pierces right into my gut. I silently pray for the hundredth time: *Please, God, please make this go okay.*

Halfway up the steps leading to the wings of the stage, I spot Kyle and Josh standing by the main curtain ropes. Josh is parting the curtain just enough to peer out at the huge crowd. I think both must be here as stage hands. *How cool, I'm going to conduct with Kyle watching from close up!*

Still unnoticed, I've inched my way to the top of the stairs, close enough to overhear them talking. "Look, I'm all sweat," Josh says with a swipe of his brow.

"Twelve minutes to clear the stage and get everything set up … are we good or what?" Kyle says. "Man, I still can't believe the Heinie is this packed. Look, there's people standing all over the place."

"Yeah, for a high school music competition," Josh sniffs, like it's the highest rating on the dork scale.

Still unaware I'm at the top of the stairs, both continue scanning the hall, now loud with a uniform buzz of impatient chatter.

"Can you believe this?" Josh asks with a nod back toward the stage. "One minute those punks are jumping all over the stage like total idiots, the next minute, it's like the fucking Vienna Philharmonic." Kyle shrieks and doubles over laughing.

"A symphony orchestra," Josh wonders in disbelief. "Some kid's got brass balls to do this." Sensing I'm behind them, Josh looks back.

"Hey, what's up with the fancy tux? Are you in this group?"

"Actually, I'm the conductor," I tell him.

"No way. You're the conductor? *Of these guys?*"

"Yeah, I entered a composition."

"Wow, no fooling," Josh says.

Near where they're standing is a spot where I can view the entire stage. The orchestra members, with the exception of two who are dashing about placing music on stands, sit quietly and patiently. The orchestra is precisely arranged in a classical crescent. The organ, a touring organ with real pipes, sits in a gap directly in front of the conductor's podium.

It looks even better than I imagined. The fancy music stands, the musicians in tuxes and gowns, the highly polished woods of the string instruments gleaming under the bright stage lights, create a stunning appearance. No wonder Kyle and Josh are impressed.

"So where'd these guys come from?" Kyle asks.

"You'll find out after the performance."

"Come on, man, what's with the big mystery?" Josh snaps. "None of us even knew you were the final contestant. It just said, 'Student from DHS.' What's up with that?"

"Drama," I tell him with a shrug. It will be just like Danny said. The curtain will open and the audience will be blown away when they see a forty-one-piece orchestra on stage. Then I make my grand entrance. This should be totally awesome—as long as I don't trip or pass out.

But Josh just shrugs his shoulders. Kyle's face remains a complete blank, so I guess he doesn't get it either.

"Well, whatever, good luck. We'll be rooting for you," Josh says with a firm handshake. Kyle follows with a quick nod and a tentative shake.

Mr. Lessard, decked out in a tux as tonight's MC, is tapping his mike in the middle of the stage. He signals that he's going out front to announce me. This is it!

Chapter 31

"Ladies and gentlemen," Mr. Lessard's voice booms out to the hall for the fourth time, finally quieting the crowd, "our final contestant is a fifteen-year-old junior from our very own Dunston High School. He's our third composition contestant, and once again, let me explain that he will be graded on the composition, not the skill of the performance. This composition is entitled …" Mr. Lessard pauses and adjusts his glasses while holding his notes up closer. "Uh, let's see, it's entitled … *Requiem per Sogno Infranti*."

Purr? Sog-no? Could he butcher the pronunciation any worse?

"Please welcome our final contestant, Mr. Robert Fowler."

Kyle hauls on the ropes to open the heavy curtain. The murmurs of the crowd, which quickly grow in volume, and even a few gasps, fill the Heinie when the orchestra comes into view. Moments later, dozens of camera flashes strobe the hall.

I glance back at Kyle and briefly make eye contact, pleading with him for even the slightest bit of encouragement. His face remains blank.

And so, to polite applause, I limp out under the hot glare of the stage lights and the anonymous faces of all those people staring at me. From high up the balcony, two blinding white beams track me to center stage. I feel like I'm floating in a dream.

I bow to the judges seated at a table immediately in front of the stage. To my surprise, the applause not only continues but grows louder. I'm taking a second bow when I get it. This isn't just because of the orchestra; they're applauding because I survived and I walked out here. A tense hush grips the hall when I tap my conductor's baton on the music stand.

"Bobby." It's Tim whispering. "You've already won over the audience. Let's give them a show tonight," he grins with another wink.

I nod back, just a slight dip of my head, and take a deep breath. "Just do it," I rasp under my breath. The orchestra members are ready, their faces watching and waiting for me, their bows and instruments poised to begin.

Three slight ticks of the baton count out the slow tempo. The organ begins whispering low notes, accompanied by soft plucking on the basses. When the strings fill in, they create a rich, textured sound, playing the beautiful, lyrical melody that popped into my head one day in chemistry class. It went around and around, and that afternoon I went home and wrote it down.

We rehearsed in the band room, minus the organ, of course. It went okay but this—this is even more beautiful than what I heard in my mind. My baton begins tracing sweeping arcs through the air as the strings soar and glide.

I can't help stealing one quick peek at Kyle, who's watching from the recesses of the wings. He's looking right at me. I quickly look down but I can't help a second peek. He's not just looking at me, he's staring at me with intense, light-gray eyes.

Scared of losing my place in the score, and trying to block him out, I turn my attention to the cellos on the other side of the orchestra.

This is Tim's solo. His head and his entire body bobs and weaves and wills his violin to produce music so dramatic, it's beyond anything I've ever imagined. My baton is down by my side as I watch in dumb disbelief. Tim is unleashing waves of power and emotion through that thin, wooden bow.

The orchestra resumes without me. I panic for an instant until I find my place in the score. I resume conducting, only now I'm *conducting*. Power surges through me. My baton becomes a lightning rod for all of the energy coming out of me. This music—sad, mournful music when I wrote it—now shouts, "I survived! I'm here!"

I can't help it. I sneak a peek, the briefest of glances. It's enough, though. Kyle is still standing with Josh, just staring—at me.

Here it comes. From a brief pause, the orchestra cracks into a crescendo of bold, commanding strings. It's so startling, so unexpected, and so loud coming from musicians without a single amplifier, I'm imagining the force of the orchestra blowing my hair and tails backwards.

Forty-one musicians pour on the power and intensity. The musicians are playing with so much passion, their hair flops this way and that in unison. Gradually the music quiets and slows until only Tim's final solo is left.

The last haunting, impossibly high note of Tim's violin fades away. It's over, just like that. And then—

Nothing.

I don't hear any applause. I don't hear a single rustle or a cough or a sound coming from the hall or from Mr. Lessard or the judges or from the stage crew standing totally still in the wings. Nothing, not even an echo.

My body jerks in a quick bow to the judges. I'm rushing to get off this stage on my gimpy leg right toward Kyle and Josh. I'm trying not to cry but my eyes are filling with tears anyway. I blew it in front of two thousand people. These musicians came all the way up here to watch me be humiliated. Why did I do classical? I hardly notice when a few people clap just as I storm into the wings.

I'm looking to Kyle and Josh for something, anything, but they say nothing. They're just staring at me, almost as if they're in shock. I'm wiping tears on the sleeves of my tux when, as if someone threw a switch, the crowd bursts into a wild roar. The people I can see from inside the wings are on their feet, clapping wildly, shouting, whistling, whooping.

"Dude, what are you waiting for?" Josh shouts over the noise. When I hesitate, he twirls me around and pushes me right out onto the stage. How it's possible I'll never know, but when the audience sees me, the applause grows louder.

"Ladies and gentlemen, please," Mr. Lessard pleads.

"Why's he bothering?" Josh laughs as Mr. Lessard once again tries to quiet the crowd.

"He actually thinks he can get them to stop. They're still going!" Kyle hollers back.

"Come on, get out there," Josh shouts at me. This time he grabs my arm and escorts me halfway out onto the stage for my third curtain call. I take a bow, the orchestra takes bows, and then Tim and I, with both arms raised high, bow together. When the applause seems to quiet somewhat, one part of the hall gets noisier, and soon everyone's into it again.

An especially loud Texas cowboy whoop ya-ha's from the wings. It's Kyle, pumping his fist high in the air.

"Bobby!" a girl shrieks from right in front of the stage. Blinded by the flash of her camera, it takes a few moments to make out Helen squinting for another shot.

This is not a dream!

"Ladies and gentlemen," Mr. Lessard announces, finally getting the crowd settled down and into their seats after three curtain calls. "That was truly a magnificent performance. Our contestant, Bobby Fowler, has asked me to introduce the orchestra. I must say that all of us here at Dunston High School, as well as the organizers of tonight's event, are not only extremely pleased but quite surprised to have some special musicians with us tonight.

"First, let's have a great big heart-of-Texas welcome for the members of the University of Texas Symphony Orchestra who came all the way up here."

"Holy shit," Josh exclaims while another big round of applause shakes the Heinie. Kyle is about to clap, but his hands are frozen halfway. He's staring at me with a look of total shock.

Mr. Lessard continues. "Playing first violin is a special guest. A graduate of Brady High School, a professor of music composition and the artistic director of the University of Texas Symphony Orchestra, please welcome Dr. Timothy Welsh."

"You did it, you did it!" Tim whoops the moment I'm inside the band room doorway. "Oh my God, you did it. It was a complete success. All of us are totally blown away!" He's so loud and excited and so over-the-top, I'm almost laughing.

"Thanks, but I was blown away by your sol—" Not another sound comes out as Tim crushes me in a tight hug.

"Congratulations, Bobby. I'm so very, very proud of you," he whispers.

Standing in the doorway is a tall, older man with perfect white hair, an immaculate black suit, and a disbelieving smile.

"Well, my boy," the judge says, approaching to shake hands, "I'm completely at a loss for words." The judge, who's never at a loss for words, follows his handshake with a hug and a few pats on my back. His eyes light up when I introduce him to Tim.

"Quite a remarkable young man, isn't he?" Tim asks the judge, but before he can answer, Tim turns to me with a smirk. "You thought you bombed, didn't you?"

"Well, yeah! No one clapped or did anything. I was *so* upset."

"Don't you understand?" Tim says. "Something truly special happened out on that stage tonight, something magical and totally beyond anything the audience was prepared for. Bobby, those people didn't applaud at first because they were in shock."

"I even saw a woman in the audience with tears in her eyes," the judge says.

I'm on total overload. Only now is it starting to sink in that something extraordinary happened tonight.

"Tim was a big part of this," I tell the judge. "He got everyone up here, and he's so talented, he elevates the play of everyone around him."

"Thank you," Tim replies with an arm around my shoulder, "but this is about that amazing composition you wrote and your conducting. You took control, and all that emotion was just pouring out of you. We picked up on it." Tim scans the musicians scattered around the band room packing and changing. A faraway look narrows his eyes. "They're excellent musicians, every one of them, but I don't think they've ever played more passionately than they did tonight. It was one of those rare nights of musical magic."

"Hey, Bobby." It's Josh leaning in from the doorway. "They're going to announce the winners." I tense and suck my breath in.

"Come on, my boy. You're going to be fine," the judge says, his large hands squeezing my shoulders.

Before I can follow him down the corridor, Tim grasps my arm to hold me back. His eyes are oddly intense. "Does this ease some of the pain?" he asks.

With all the pressure and excitement, it's something I haven't thought about. Maybe he isn't expecting an answer. Tim kisses my forehead, wraps a comforting arm around my shoulder, and leads me back to the stage entrance—and my moment of truth.

"In third place for composition, with a score of 79.10," Mr. Lessard announces, "from Llano High School, Janet Willingham, for her folk song, 'The Spirit of Enchanted Rock.'"

"In second place with a score of 82.25 ..."

Mr. Lessard pauses while a stage assistant hands him the trophy.

"From Dunston High School …"

I'm praying hard.

"Carl Armstrong …"

"Yes, yes, yes!"

Chapter 32

"So, are your feet back on the ground?" asks Helen, who surprised us by joining me, Danny, and Chloe for lunch.

"It's still hard to believe," I tell her.

"I was surprised when the head judge announced you got the highest score ever for a student from our school," she says. "But when he said you got the highest score *ever* in District 6 competition, I was like, oh my gosh!"

"So what did you do when he said they were awarding the highest score in the history of music competitions in the state of Texas?" Danny asks.

"Probably the same as you guys," Helen answers. "Didn't you hear me hollering?" she asks me.

"Too many people were yelling backstage," I say.

"Ninety-nine point nine zero," Danny says. "Highest score ever," he sighs, shaking his head. Danny's eyes slowly meet mine. He jabs his finger at me. "And would you stop with all this modest crap? It was all you, got it? You thought this up, you wrote it, you conducted … it was you!" Now he's shouting.

Startled by Danny's outburst, Helen's eyes grow big. Danny quickly settles down.

"It's all we've heard about," he tells Helen. "How he lucked out to get the orchestra up here, how talented Tim is, how good the musicians are, how tight they played … he won't stop. Jeez, it was a composition contest and he wrote it."

"And you willed that orchestra to play like they did," Chloe adds.

Helen's thoughts are elsewhere for a few moments. "So, how *did* you get that orchestra up here? Everyone's been asking."

Chloe, cupping her hands over her mouth, explodes with laughter. "Boy, this is going to be good," she says, but when she turns toward me, the grin turns into a challenging smirk. "Go ahead, tell her the story. The *whole* story."

Chloe will tell Helen everything I leave out, and she'll make it sound ten times worse. My face already feels hot.

"Well," I begin, "this past August, I was working at this club in Austin, Club Réalité"

"What do you mean, you were working at a club in Austin?" Helen breaks in.

"I was the DJ."

Helen's considering this. She looks as if I just told her I work after school flying passenger jets. "You're a DJ?" she asks.

"DJ?" Danny bellows. "Not only is he the best DJ in the country, he's recording his own dance music. Here—" Danny pulls his backpack to his lap. After fishing around, he pulls out one of my CDs.

"What's this?" Helen asks as she studies the simple white cover with nothing but "AXIS II" in bold red letters.

"Read what it says on the other side, under the song list," Chloe tells her.

Helen's squinting at the small print. "Let's see, it says, 'All tracks produced and recorded at The Recording Studio, Dunston, Texas. Copyright 1996, Worlds End Records.' Huh, I didn't know there's a recording studio in town."

Danny and Chloe snicker.

"It's Bobby's studio. It's really cool," Chloe says.

Danny sits back in his seat with his hands behind his head, looking extremely pleased.

"Worlds End Records is Bobby's record label. He owns the record company," he tells Helen.

Helen, however, appears dazed.

"He owns a record company?" is all she can say.

"You can have that," Danny goes on. "He's already finished Axis III, and he's doing lots of other stuff like jazz and baroque, and this really weird stuff—"

"Avant-garde," I snap. Danny and I glare at each other before we crack up and smack a high-five. It's been a running joke for two years.

Chloe throws her hands up. "*So anyway,* tell her what happened!" she says.

"So I won this big DJ contest at the club last summer, and they wanted me back. They wanted me to DJ every week but, you know, I'm fifteen and I don't drive and it's a long way from here, so that was kind of tough, but I went back in September—well, I'm supposed to go back next month as well, and I'm supposed—"

"Bobby!" Chloe screeches.

"Oh, sorry. I ran into this really nice guy at the club. Actually, he kind of ran into me, you know, 'cause it's kind of a gay club—well, it's an all-gay club, and he was telling me how much he likes my music." Chloe's giving me the eye. "Well, to make a long story short, instead of staying at the hotel, I ended up at his townhouse."

"And guess where Mr. Fowler slept," Chloe asks with a wicked grin.

Helen doesn't get it, until, after a few more seconds, her eyes get wider and wider and she blushes. Chloe's grin is even more evil.

"So, are you all freaked out?"

"Uh, no, I mean, I don't think so," Helen says as she fidgets with her hands. "I mean, maybe a little. I shouldn't be concerned about other … okay, this is freaking me out." Her face is so red it's glowing.

Chloe leans forward like she's sharing a secret. "So was I," she giggles.

Danny's rolling his eyes. "Would you just get this over with?"

"Hey, he's a really nice guy and is he *hot,*" I'm explaining to Helen. "You saw him, Tim Welsh, the concert master and the director of the symphony. Oh, come on, Helen, I know he's wicked old, but thirty-one isn't bad, and he works out and nothing happened, well, not too much, because he remembered me from being in the news last year and it was just that one time. We're friends, that's all."

Helen has given up trying to speak.

"Anyway," I continue, "we spent most of the time talking music, and when I told him I was writing something for the district music competition, he asked to see it. So I sent it. I guess he and his students liked it a lot, because he called a couple weeks later, and a whole bunch of them volunteered to help me out. And that's how I got them up here."

"Hey, babe."

"Oh, hi, Josh. Hi, Kyle," Helen says, relieved to see the two standing behind her with their lunch trays. After Josh gives Helen a quick peck on the cheek, neither he nor Kyle makes a move to join us.

"Hey, man, everyone's talking about you," Josh starts. "How'd you get those guys up here?"

"Here we go again," Danny moans.

Chloe stifles a laugh so hard she snorts.

"Puppy, I'll tell you later," Helen giggles. "Maybe a lot later, like after graduation."

"After graduation? Come on, babe, what's the big deal?" Josh asks.

"Trust me on this one, okay?" his girlfriend answers.

Josh is thinking about this and doesn't look too happy. We make eye contact. "So what's that foreign title mean?" he asks. "Requiem something?"

"It's Latin, isn't it?" Helen wants to know.

"No, it's Italian, and it's pronounced—"

"*Requiem per Sogno Infranti,*" Kyle cuts in, the words slipping off his tongue as if he grew up in Italy. Dumbfounded, I stare at him. "Hey," Kyle says in his best Texas straight-boy twang when I stare a little too long, "dreams can come true, you know."

"So what's it mean?" asks Helen, who, like Josh, doesn't seem the least bit surprised that Kyle speaks Italian.

I hesitate. Danny, looking down at his tray, answers for me.

"It means Requiem for Shattered Dreams."

Those four words hang over the table in uneasy silence. No one's looking at me, not even Chloe. I flash back to that awful time in the hospital, just a couple days after I came out of my coma, when I first realized how badly I was injured. I'm biting my upper lip and squeezing my eyes tight to shut out the pain, when warm and caring hands gently rub mine.

"God loves you and He has a plan for you," Helen says. "Trust in Him. Your dreams are going to come true, Bobby, I just feel it."

Josh and Kyle are fidgeting.

"Hey, gotta go," Josh says.

"I thought you guys were eating with us," Helen says.

"Uh, sorry, the guys are waiting for us," Kyle mutters, and with Josh's "See ya, babe," they take off.

"Bobby, I'm sorry," Helen says.

"It's okay, I understand."

It's not just that I'm still the only out gay kid in school. Kyle and Josh are star athletes. They're really good-looking and both, especially Kyle, have "it," that special sex appeal that draws the attention of every girl in school. In Kyle's case, it's also every woman in town. They hang around with the other jocks and cool kids. How well I understand.

Chapter 33

The front door swings open. Instead of Helen or her parents greeting me, Kyle is in the doorway.

"What are you doing here?" he gasps, so surprised he lurches backward.

"I was invited. Didn't they tell you I was coming?"

"I just got—"

"There you are! Come in, come in and make yourself at home." This must be Helen's mother. "I'm so glad you're here. Oh, how lovely. Aren't these flowers just the most thoughtful gift. Oh, thank you so much," she gushes with a quick hug. "Kyle, aren't these flowers beautiful?"

"Yes, ma'am," he mumbles before escaping down the cellar stairs.

"Oh, poor you, what happened to your leg?" she asks, watching me scuff through the entryway with a crutch jammed under my left arm.

"I'm having an operation right after Christmas. I have some calcium deposits where I injured my thigh."

"Oh, Bobby, you poor dear."

I don't think Mrs. Albrecht has any idea what calcium deposits are, but it's no big deal because right away I like her. She's Helen, just old. Same wavy, perfect blond hair, slightly taller, bubbly, and all that syrupy politeness is genuine, home-spun Texas hospitality. I feel welcome here.

After meeting Helen's older sister Kate, who's back home from college for the holidays, and her cousin Billy, the nice local cop who found me by of the side of the road that time, I'm wondering if it will be weird with Kyle here. Helen told me he's almost lived here since they were little, so it's not surprising he's here for Sunday dinner. He sure didn't react well. Not hateful or angry, just weird, like he was uncomfortable.

Helen's mom calls us to dinner. The feast they've laid out looks like Thanksgiving. Mr. Albrecht—tall, balding, surprisingly out of shape, loud and a little pompous but still an okay guy— parades in with a platter piled pyramid-high with Texas barbecue. Steaming dishes of candied sweet potato, green bean casserole and a gut-busting array of other dishes jam almost every inch of the table. The basket of hot, buttery country biscuits set right in front of me smells so yummy, I have to force myself not to grab one and stuff the whole thing in my mouth.

"We're so glad you came," Mrs. Albrecht says after grace. "Helen's told us so much about you."

"And just think," Mr. Albrecht jumps in, "not one but two boys at our table brought home state titles. Not many schools have even one state champion."

"We're mighty proud of you boys," adds Mrs. Albrecht.

"Thanks," Kyle says. "It's a dream come true to win state."

"I hear about you all over town," Mrs. Albrecht says to Kyle with a sly, sideways smirk. "You're all the gals talk about down at Theresa's Salon, if you know what I mean." Kyle blushes when Helen and Kate giggle. Mrs. Albrecht's comments, however, seem to have gone right over her husband's head.

"Hon, this is Texas," he says.

"Here comes the football-is-religion speech," Billy leans over and whispers.

"High school football is a religion in this town. We talk football, we live football, breathe football, and eat Warriors football all year long. Winning state means everything in this town. Kyle will be a hero around these parts till the day he dies."

Kyle's fidgeting. "Come on, Mr. Albrecht, you know I got lucky."

"Kyle," he says, all fatherly, "you inspired that team and you led that team all year long, and when you refused to lose, you kicked their behinds. That's what Coach Grady told the Boosters, you refuse to lose. And don't forget, it was you who got that team down near the goal line with those pinpoint passes, and it was you, young fella, who had the sense to pick that ball up and stuff it into the end zone."

"What happened?" I ask Mr. Albrecht. All I know is that a week ago, we won the state championship game in Dallas by three points.

The town, and I mean the entire town, went spastic for the whole of last week.

Mr. Albrecht gives me a strange look.

"I was at the music finals in San Antonio," I explain. He nods.

"Last play of the game, clock's ticking down, no timeouts, ball's on the two-yard line," he says. "Our halfback takes the ball, gets smacked at the line of scrimmage, and he fumbles. The ball takes a miraculous bounce right back to Kyle. He picks it up, sprints left toward the far corner, gets tackled, and stretches out with all his might. The ball lands maybe two inches over the goal line, and we go home as champions." Beaming with pride and admiration, Mr. Albrecht points right at Kyle. "That makes you a hero in my book."

"Everyone in town sure thinks so," Helen's sister says. "You got your own car in the parade."

"Yeah, I saw the parade," I tell them.

"They interviewed him on TV twice," Kate says to me.

"And they gave him the game ball at the banquet," Helen adds.

"And he won the MVP trophy and we put an MVP sign on his front lawn," Josh says to me.

"And don't forget the interviews with the state newsletters and all those recruiters camped outside your house," Mr. Albrecht concludes.

"After all that, you must be a god in school," Billy jokes.

"As if he wasn't already," Helen snickers.

"Okay, enough!" Kyle laughs, his face reddening.

"Now don't you let it go to your head," Helen's mom playfully scolds.

"I'll see to that," Helen says. She isn't joking.

"Poor Bobby, we invite you over and then we completely ignore you," Mrs. Albrecht says. "Why don't you tell us about winning the state music competition?"

"Well, the state finals were in San Antonio in this awesome concert hall, but like I said, it was on the same day as the big game in Dallas. It went well and the crowd really liked my composition. I got a 99.95. Oh, and first prize was this really awesome Waterford crystal bowl."

"You must be so proud. You must be a big deal in school too," Mrs. Albrecht says.

A look flashes between Kyle and Josh. They know how brief my moment of fame and popularity was, like maybe two days tops, and that was after the performance in the Heinie. With all the football madness around here, hardly anyone even noticed I brought home the state title. Chloe said it was as though I had won the state chess tournament. Worse, both she and Danny heard that some kids were upset a gay kid won the state title because it would make the town look bad.

"We're sorry we couldn't see your performance," Mrs. Albrecht continues, "but with Helen cheerleading and Kyle playing ..."

"That's okay, ma'am. I understand."

"Were there a lot of folks from town down there?" Mr. Albrecht inquires.

"Uh, no, not really, sir. I think six went. Yeah, six."

For a few awkward moments Mr. Albrecht considers that I took first place in the state contest in front of a handful of supporters from my hometown.

"Well, son, at least you won and no one can ever take that away from you. You should have been here when Helen came home from the competition at school."

"I've never seen Helen so excited. She went on and on about your performance and that long ovation and your wonderful score," Mrs. Albrecht says.

"It wasn't just me," Helen laughs. She turns to Josh. "I could hear you two from out in the audience."

"Hey, I was just going with the flow," he explains with a grin.

"Kyle, what did you think?" Mrs. Albrecht asks.

Kyle actually stops demolishing his monster plate of seconds to consider this for a few moments. I'm expecting a few mumbled words of grudging praise.

"It was the most incredible music I ever heard. There was this really loud part—right out of the blue—that was so powerful it gave me goose bumps. I've never heard anything like it. The whole thing was just totally beyond awesome. But it was how he looked at the orchestra, like, intense, you know, totally focused. He just took control of that orchestra, and those guys were all from college! Oh, man, it was amazing."

We're quiet for a bit, the easy kind of quiet when everyone resumes eating or is thinking up something else to talk about. Except me. I'm quiet because I'm in shock.

Kyle is once again focused on inhaling staggering amounts of food, but there is an odd tension I've felt it ever since I walked in the door. He avoids looking right at me, but every now and then I catch him glancing at me, and he quickly looks away.

"What's the matter, pumpkin?" Mr. Albrecht asks Helen.

She's just staring at her plate. "Look, I'm really happy for Kyle and all the guys on the football team," she tells her father, "but why didn't they do more for Bobby?"

"Helen, Bobby's picture was in the paper and they wrote a nice article," Mrs. Albrecht answers.

"I know, Mom, but at school all they did was introduce him at the rally. Mr. Lessard made a little speech and shook his hand and that was it. I don't know … it just doesn't seem right."

Everyone watches and waits for Helen to play this out. "If Bobby won the state music competition," she goes on, "shouldn't they have done something special? It's just not right. Daddy, he got the highest score in *history*."

"I know, pumpkin, I know."

"Bobby said he's having an operation right after Christmas," says Mrs. Albrecht, flustered by a scene at the dinner table. "What did you say it was for?"

"Calcium deposits in my thigh," I tell her, but my attention is drawn back to Mr. Albrecht. He nods grimly.

"We'll come see you in the hospital when you're up for company," Helen says, but Mr. Albrecht didn't even hear her. Instead, he's studying me.

"You know, son, after all you've been through, you look pretty darned good. Amazing, actually. How many operations did it take?"

It's not that I can't believe he'd ask a question like that in front of everyone, it's just that I can't think about that right now. The dining room silence becomes tense and heavy, weighing down on me to say something, anything. Helen comes to my rescue. "Daddy, maybe Bobby doesn't want to talk about that." She bolts right out of her chair. "Who wants pie?"

Helen and I stay in the kitchen after Kyle, Josh, Billy, and Kate blast outside to play touch football. Balanced on one leg, leaning on the counter, I'm helping with the dishes.

"That night in the Heinie," she says with her hands in soapy dishwater, "I noticed something about you. Even Josh said something."

Our eyes meet. "You smiled and laughed. I could see it in your eyes. I hadn't seen you smile in a long, long time."

Almost a year out of my life lost, a year I still don't want to even think about. To this day, I can't think or say the words for what they did to me; I can't even say the name of the room it happened in. A whole year has gone by and I still take baths. But after the music contest, things seem different, at least a little.

"It felt good to laugh."

THE CLUB

Chapter 34

"Bobby, come quick. You gotta see this guy. He's the hottest boy I've ever seen! *Come on!*"

Here we go again. Every night, Zack discovers at least one boy so hot I just have to check him out. Tall, thin (anorexic is more like it, but I'm trying to be kind), a few stubborn pimples blaring against pale skin, my friend Zack the club kid usually prowls Club Réalité for the hottest boys instead of looking for a real boyfriend.

"Hurry up, this guy's *incredible*," Zack shouts over the ear-ringing music. He's jerking on my arm so hard I almost stumble down the steps of my DJ booth.

Still clutching me in a tight grip, Zack elbows through the crowd jamming the dance floor of Austin's biggest gay club. For an August Saturday night before the college kids come back, it's unusually crowded.

Growing more desperate, Zack searches both bars and the video lounge. Finally, we're back in the middle of the dance floor. Just as I thought.

"Sorry, Zack, another false alarm."

"Girlfriend, he's here and I'm going to find him," he says, cupping his hand over my ear so I can hear. "You'll see."

Poor Zack. I bet he's so strung out on drugs he hallucinated tonight's calendar boy. Last month, it was a big-name porn star. I wish once and for all he'd take my advice and get off the hardcore drugs. Maybe a little X is okay, but what he and his friends take is scary.

Tonight is all-ages night (which is code for under twenty-one) and the crowd is pulsing to the pounding beat of a hot trance mix. A few boys are shirtless, their bodies beaded with sweat, their drug-glazed eyes gazing inwardly into private little trance worlds. Above us, a burst of strobes freezes everyone into rapid stop-action motions.

The energy on the dance floor is so compelling that Zack begins dancing. I'd like to join him, but I have to use the restroom and get back to the booth. Zack grabs my arm as I turn to leave.

"The music's awesome," he shouts.

I nod back with a smile. Except for quiet interludes, the music is so loud that shouting is useless, unless it's right in the other guy's ear.

"One of your tracks?" he asks, this time shouting so loud in my ear it hurts.

"Yeah," I yell back with a thumbs-up, in case he's too messed up to lip-read. Despite the drugs, I take it as a huge compliment when Zack and his friends tell me the crowd's jamming because of the high-energy tunes I'm mixing, especially if it's a track from one of my CDs. With the possible exception of club drugs, the one thing they know best is dance music. He and his friends can recite the hits of every major DJ and sing the lyrics of almost every track.

"Where's your friends?" Zack asks.

"Next time."

Zack responds with a narcotic smile and continues his robotic dancing. Danny and Chloe have been here twice this summer, each time chaperoned by Danny's oldest sister. She, like my two friends, thinks this is the coolest place in Texas. And Chloe and Danny hit it off with Zack, especially after he taught them his best dance steps.

For two years, Danny has been handing out my CDs to a small but growing cult following at school. But even with my music floating around, hardly anyone knows I've been deejaying here every two weeks this summer, and otherwise every month or two since I won last summer's DJ contest. No surprise there. Gay dance music in a gay club is the last thing that would be a hit with the jock culture at Dunston High School. Well, whatever. When I'm mixing hot tracks and the crowd's really into it, I'm one happy teenager.

The restroom is crowded with boys smoking and primping and admiring themselves in the mirrors. Some peer in closely, squinting this way and that, worrying about real or imagined complexion flaws. Each is aware he's being checked out by the guys waiting in line in the doorway.

I'm at the sink washing up. Unlike everyone else, I'm not pleased when I check myself in the mirror. Even with makeup, the scars around my eye and temple are way too noticeable. Maybe it's the harsh fluorescent lights. Screw it, it will have to do.

Just as I'm turning to shoot a wad of paper towel into the trash can, a boy barrels out of the stall behind me and clips my arm.

"Maybe you could say excu—*Kyle?*"

I'm not on drugs and I'm not hallucinating. It really is Kyle Faulkner, here in a gay club in Austin. He recoils and gasps, so shocked his eyes are bugging out of his head.

Oh, I'm not shocked. I'm merely having a heart attack.

"What are you doing here?" he cries out, but before I can make my mouth work, he says, "Hey, I gotta get going." I holler after him as he bulls his way through the doorway crowd.

"Kyle, wait!"

He doesn't even look back.

Every boy stops what they're doing to watch our little soap opera. Without a word from me, those in the doorway part like the Red Sea so I can chase after Kyle. "Don't let that one get away," one boy hollers as I race out the door.

"Come on, Kyle, wait up."

He jerks to a stop so abruptly I almost bump him.

"Look, I came with some friends for the music," he says. "They just left and I really have to get going."

"Hey, I just knew you straight boys liked dance music. Guess what? I'm the DJ."

"You? You're the DJ? Awesome. Okay, see ya."

"Bobby! Bobby!" The shout is coming from somewhere out on the dance floor. Semaphoring above the crowd is a skinny, pale arm that can only belong to one person.

"That asshole," Kyle snarls when he recognizes Zack. "That jerk's been following me all around and won't take no for an answer. If he comes near me, I'm gonna knock his lights out," he says as Zack claws his way through the packed-tight dancers.

Not good, not good. Zack will get hurt and the manager will call the cops.

"Kyle, follow me!"

He isn't even listening. Zack is just seconds from getting decked.

"Let me show you my DJ booth. *Please!*" With a tug on his arm, I'm pointing toward the open door to the booth just to our left. Kyle stares at me for a few frantic moments.

"Yeah, whatever."

It's all I need to hurdle the three steps in one leap. Kyle, however, is not exactly hustling.

"Come on!" I screech like a little girl with my arm windmilling him to hurry. Kyle, always Mr. Cool, smirks as he trudges up the steps and edges past me. Sure enough, one second after I bang the door shut, Zack catches up and begins pounding away.

"Come on, man. Let me in," he screeches. "He's the hot guy I was telling you about. *Come on!*" I get myself tightly wedged against the door so I can crack it open.

"Zack, listen to me. This is a personal friend. *Stop pushing the door, Zack!* Look, I have to talk to him in private, okay?"

"Just a few seconds. Come on, just a few seconds. Let me in so I can talk to him."

"Zack, will you do this for me, please?" He's craning every which way to get a look inside. *"Zack, please!"*

"Fine. Thanks so much, girlfriend," he says, spitting out each word like snake venom. Zack tries once more to peer inside. He gives me a dirty sneer before stomping away.

That little drama over, I turn back to find Kyle staring uneasily at Richard, my overweight and very gay assistant DJ. He, in turn, is staring back at Kyle. I'm relieved Richard doesn't put up a fuss when I tell him I need some time alone. As he maneuvers around Kyle in the cramped space, they eyeball each other, Kyle recoiling at Richard's tattoos and piercings, spiky black hair, glitter, and makeup; Richard in shock that anyone could possibly be that hot—and in the DJ booth with me.

With my assistant gone, Kyle looks around. "You really *are* the DJ," he says.

I nod with a smile and lean down close to the turntable to inspect the track now playing. It will run another two minutes. Kyle is watching every move I make.

"Hey, I saw a few girls dancing. They knew I was checking them out," he says with a flex of his chest. I resist the urge to tell him that straight-boy crap is not allowed in gay clubs.

"Lots of girls and even straight couples come here," I explain.

Kyle nose crinkles in disbelief.

"They do? To a gay club?"

"Yeah, but only cool straight couples. They have fun; there aren't any fights; gay clubs have the best music; and best of all, girls don't get bothered by obnoxious, drunken straight boys."

Kyle's reacting as if he's adding it up. I'm still trying to figure out how Kyle and his friends got to a gay club in the first place.

"So did you and your friends get to dance?" I ask.

"What? Dance? Oh, yeah … a little."

I'm wondering why I didn't see him out on the dance floor as he continues looking over the equipment. He's especially interested in the dual turntables and the impressive, five-foot-wide array of slide controls and knobs.

"It's called a mixing board," I explain, hoping he doesn't pick up on the nervous catch in my voice.

That boy is so spectacular I can hardly talk. His stretchy, black sleeveless shows off every single muscle fiber in that breathtaking bod. It makes his arms look even bigger, as if those arms needed to look any bigger. Tanned, flawless skin, the white shell necklace stretched tight around his husky neck, tight jeans that show off his athletic butt—it's what I call the Kyle Faulkner look. And it's not just all those muscles. He has the cutest nose, perfect ears, and light gray eyes so devastating it's hard to look at him. *Boy, it sure is hot in here.*

With a start, I realize the track now playing on the first turntable is almost finished. After scrambling to put the headphones on and easing the needle onto the vinyl spinning on the second turntable, it only takes seconds to synchronize both channels and switch to the new track. The crowd cheers and sings along when a popular new Cher track booms out of the speakers.

"Is the music hot or what?" I shout over the music.

"Yeah, it's incredible," Kyle shouts back.

"Your friends had to leave?"

"Yeah, and I'm just leaving too."

"Hey, listen, before you go, why don't you do the next mix?"

"Look, I really gotta get going," he says, leaning closer so I can hear.

"Come on, Kyle, I bet you're dying to know how it's done."

"Dude, I wouldn't even know where to start."

"It's easy. I'll show you how."

"No way. I'll screw up and everyone will hear it."

"Don't worry, I'll make it foolproof. Here, put these on."

Kyle hesitates before reaching for the bulky headphones I'm holding out. Once he adjusts the fit, his face lights up.

"Hey, is that the next song?"

I nod that it is.

"Take off one headphone," I tell him, accompanied by a pantomime. Kyle can now hear the track we're about to mix in one ear, and the track playing out on the dance floor in the other. The beats are out of sync, quickly corrected by a few taps on the queuing lever on Kyle's turntable, slowing the speed until the two beats precisely match.

"Okay, you're going to slowly increase the volume—this slide here—and move it up to seven." He nods back. "Here we go."

At my signal, Kyle advances the volume control. The intro segment of the new track, designed solely for mixing, slowly merges with the music out on the floor. When Kyle hits seven on the volume slide and the vocals on his track kick in, I slide the volume on my turntable to zero. The mix was flawless. I hold my hand up, palm toward him. He smiles and slaps a high-five.

"So that's why you have two turntables," he says. "You get two going, sync them up, and then you change the volumes. Hey, I did a mix!"

"See, you're a DJ already."

For good measure, I press a button, which swooshes clouds of stage smoke onto the dance floor from two nozzles in the ceiling. Deafening music, great energy on the dance floor, flashes of club lights stabbing through the haze of smoke, red laser bursts showering a million bright sparkles off the crystal ball, the scene down below is amazing. Kyle is mesmerized. So am I—watching him.

He isn't saying much. He's not leaving either. Kyle is mostly watching the crowd, but the couple times we made eye contact, he tensed and looked away. *How could he still be that uptight about gays? He came to a gay club, didn't he?*

Chapter 35

One o'clock, closing time. The manager is very picky about ending on time for all-ages nights. The mellow track I put on to bring the crowd down fades to a soft piano part. Just like that, it's over. I'm on the mike when the house lights come up.

"This is your DJ, Bobby Fowler. I hope you liked the music. Good night, everyone!" It's my signature sign off. I wave as the crowd applauds. A few kids shout for more, but already most of my faithful fans are streaming toward the exits. Zack, thank God, is nowhere to be seen.

Kyle's watching me power down all the equipment. He's watching me very closely.

"Well, I guess that's it," I tell him. "I hope it was as good as you were expecting. Oh, here, my new CD, Axis IV. And if you want the others, just let me know."

Kyle mumbles a thank-you and just stands there.

When I finish stacking the records under the deck, he's *still* just standing around. I'm completely confused as to what he's waiting for.

"What are you doing?" he asks when I reach under the table for my backpack.

"I'm calling a cab and crashing at the hotel. I'm not supposed to be alone on the streets at night. Part of the deal, you know?"

"You have a reservation?"

"Nope, but they're not busy until school starts. Besides, they know me."

Kyle's about to say something but catches himself. That's it, I'm leaving.

"Okay, I'd better get—"

"I can give you a ride back."

Kyle is offering me a ride? *Just the two of us?*

"You sure it's no trouble?"

"Nah, it's stupid to stay in a hotel when I'm going back," he says.

"Cool. Where's your car?"

"On San Jacinto, maybe five or six blocks from here."

So Kyle and I, the unlikeliest pair in history to walk out of a gay club, find ourselves on the busy sidewalk of Sixth Street, Austin's main drag for music and nightlife.

"Wow, still hot and steamy," I remark.

"Mmm."

Okay, that went well. I'd talk sports but there's just a teensy chance he might not watch men's gymnastics the same way I do. I don't know enough about football to talk with a star quarterback, and I can't talk girl stuff because I probably sound like a girl.

As usual, gay guys are out and about on this part of the street. I get a kick watching heads turn as we stroll by. Kyle pretends not to notice, but I bet the cruisy stares are making him even more uptight. Are the guys walking by wondering if I'm his date? I overheard one older guy say, "He must be into cute little twinks." Yeah, that would be the day.

"I was going to eat at this really cool place. Hungry?" I ask to break our uneasy, block-long silence.

Kyle's thinking it over, and I know exactly what's going on in his head: Is he going to be seen eating with the gay kid? Let's see, he's seventeen, he's an athlete—

"Yeah, starved."

He doesn't notice my grin.

It's about two more blocks to our destination. As we stroll along in silence, my thoughts wander.

Kyle and I never really talk. It's like we live in two different worlds. A few of the athletes and really good-looking guys are friendly, however. Even Josh and Jason say hi all the time, although I suspect neither is really comfortable with my being gay.

At least Kyle didn't turn into a total jerk after winning state last December. The outright adulation is still going on, in town as well as at school. I only wish he'd stop boasting about all his dates and all that stupid straight-boy talk about scoring last weekend and the "she wants it" shit. It's all he talks about. He did it again, right in my booth, when he was talking about checking out the girls, and he flexed his chest and gave me that stupid I'm-so-hot smirk. Give me a break.

"Just how far is this place?" Kyle's impatient question jars me back to busy, steamy Sixth Street.

"There." I'm pointing to the next door down the block. Brightly lit, noisy, always busy, a red neon sign in a window announces we've arrived at Ma Brown's.

We're hardly in the door when a very large black woman with enormous hoop earrings and a white apron lights up with a smile brighter than her sign. "Bobby, honey!" she shrieks. Yes, Ma Brown is a real person, and she's pointing right at me. "Is that hunk jes for me?" she shrieks above the din of the restaurant.

"Yes, ma'am. He's all yours!"

Ma Brown holds both arms out, bends a bit backwards, looks to the heavens, and screeches, "Thank the Lord!" so loud everyone looks. "Ah's gonna be rockin' and rollin' tonight," she proclaims. People nearby are laughing so hard they're rocking back and forth. I'm almost doubled over, and not just because this is vintage Ma Brown. Kyle, caught dead-center stage, is blushing.

I spot an empty booth way down in the corner, but Kyle motions us toward two just-vacated stools. Hopping on a seat, he quickly buries himself in a menu. I'm more amused than irritated when I realize the seating arrangement means we won't have to sit facing each other. Just as well. He's so hot tonight he's making me nervous.

Kyle sneers when he sees our waiter, a skinny, heavily tattooed punk with at least a dozen piercings. After we place our orders, I sense Kyle wants to say something but is too uptight to make eye contact.

"Did you know Danny's been handing out my CDs at school and using Internet file sharing?" I ask, trying something to break the ice.

Before Kyle can answer, a burst of raucous laughter to our immediate left signals we're about to be honored with a command performance from none other than Ma Brown.

After she leans in for a peck on the cheek, her attention shifts to Kyle. Standing in front of us with hands on her ample hips, she starts with a very obvious once-over.

"Oh, baby, you and me gonna be doin' some coochie-coochie tonight," she says in a high, singsong voice. I can't help it and crack up. I'm laughing so hard I'm rocking back and forth on the stool. Others around us are enjoying the show as well. Kyle's not—he's blushing worse than ever.

"Mmm, mmm, mmm," she concludes with a long, admiring look up and down Kyle's jacked physique before moving on to the next victim.

Kyle's face is now scarlet. I'm sure he's unhappy at being singled out in front of everyone, and especially with the suggestion that he'll be doing some coochie-coochie. If only he knew what else I've heard coming out of that woman's mouth.

We're quiet for a bit, but I feel eyes on me. Kyle isn't exactly looking right at me. He's pretending to look straight ahead at a woman making chocolate shakes, but I still feel eyes on me. He looks right at me only when I turn to give him an inquiring stare.

"Your hair is longer," he says, inspecting my head from front to back.

I nod yes, just a slight tic of my head.

"I don't want people to see the scars," I tell him.

"I'm sorry," he replies, his voice a sad whisper. "But it looks really good that way," he says, his face brightening. "You're really blond." He's pointing and his hand is almost up to my ear. Is he going to touch my hair?

"My hair looks okay?"

"Oh, yeah," he says. "I wish my hair was floppy like that." Kyle quickly withdraws his hand to his lap, where he kneads his napkin into a tight ball.

The waiter brings my usual big breakfast. Kyle's ready to plow into his enormous roast chicken dinner even before the plate hits the counter. He digs in, but he's oddly tense. I don't want him to feel awkward after saying something nice to me.

"Ma Brown is like that with everyone she likes."

"Wonderful," he says under his breath, not taking his eyes off his plate.

"I'm sorry about Zack. You know, he's really not a bad guy, but, man, did he have a thing for you."

Did I just imagine I was talking? Not responding in the slightest way, Kyle continues to demolish his dinner. Incredible amounts of food are disappearing into his mouth. I don't think that boy is actually eating, like physically putting food in his mouth. I think the food is beaming in.

But still, he's so tense he's making me tense. Every now and then

I catch him glancing at me out of the corner of his eye, so quick it's more like a nervous twitch. Sitting next to a hot boy like him, I'm the one who should be nervous. I hope the ride home won't be as weird as eating with him.

Chapter 36

"Well, you have a thing for me, don't you?" Kyle says without so much as a glance at me. Instead, he's totally focused on his cherry pie.

My face is getting hot. My tongue is becoming so thick I'm not sure I can talk.

"I—I—I'm gay; you're straight. I really don't have a thing for you, honest."

I wince, realizing how lame that came out. Kyle's only reaction, however, is to slam the last of his chocolate shake.

"All set?" he asks. No making a face, no smirking, no nothing. Kyle eyes the check on the edge of the counter. I grab it.

"I just got paid," I explain.

Back outside in the hot, sticky air, we march toward the lot where Kyle parked his car. As we walk along, I'm puzzled that Kyle didn't come with a date. Kyle always has a date. Girls line up ten deep just for a chance at a date.

Maybe he did come with a date. Maybe they had a fight and his friends drove her home. That's it! That's why he's by himself, and that's why he was so upset when he bumped into me. And then he gets stuck with a gay boy.

We continue our walk, away from the lights and clubs and crowds. I think back to last spring, when Helen and I happened to be talking about how sweet and concerned Kyle was during those hospital visits. That's the real Kyle, she'd said, the Kyle she knew when they were kids. She went on to say that not only is he generous and caring, he's gentle, even sensitive. Helen said she thinks Kyle puts on an act for his friends and teammates, especially Mr. Macho, Jason. He's the only one Kyle really looks up to, she added.

The feeling comes over me that this is important. But what did she mean when she said, "the real Kyle"? The real Kyle and what, the Kyle of a thousand girlfriends, the Kyle who hassled me so bad? I just don't get it. Why does he have to show off and prove how macho he is when he's such a terrific person? It has to be that stupid, caveman jock culture.

The lot that Kyle parked in is small, squeezed in between two buildings. It's also empty. When we pass through the gate, however, I gasp when I see what was hidden behind the signs covering the chain-link fence.

"Whatcha think?" Kyle asks with a grin.

"Holy shit. I get to ride on your motorcycle?"

"Ever been on one before?" I shake my head no while running my fingers over the stitching in the black leather seat. Kyle holds out a pair of goggles. "Here, put these on. This baby's really fast, so you'll have to hold on tight," he says as he swings his leg over the bike with the effortless grace of an athlete.

I'm trying to figure out how to get on. I realize I have to hold on to his shoulder. *I can't actually touch Kyle, can I?* He turns to look at me.

"Are you going to get on?"

Without hesitating, I grab on to him and awkwardly lift myself onto the smaller, slightly raised rear seat. It's so tight I'm almost touching Kyle's body.

"What do I hold on to?" I ask.

Kyle just sits there, not moving a muscle.

"Kyle, what am I supposed to hold on to?"

"Um … just … just hold on to those hand grips down by the side."

The engine starts with a deep growl so powerful and percussive I jump. Before Kyle heads out to the street, though, he almost completely twists around.

"My friends didn't want anyone to know we went to a … you know."

"A gay club?"

"Are you cool with that?" he asks.

"Fine. If you're that uptight, I won't say a word."

I'm holding on to those hand grips for life itself as we ease out of the lot. Once out in the street, however, Kyle guns the engine with another alarming, showing-off roar. We rocket down the street so fast, the force mashes my back into the padding of the low chrome backrest. Maybe this wasn't such a good idea.

At the end of the block, Kyle brakes so hard for a red light, I squish right into him. "Sorry," he says. The light changes, and he guns it again, accelerating so fast I scream like a girl and grab his arms.

"Sorry, I thought I was going to fall off," I shout over the engine roar.

"Is this baby jacked or what?" he hollers back.

"Yeah, but I don't want to land in the road."

"I'll take it easy."

It takes awhile for the lights and suburbs of Austin to fall behind. Soon we're zooming up and down the dark hills of central Texas toward home.

"Whatcha think?" he shouts back over the howl of the wind on a long straightaway.

"It's wicked awesome." We're going fast, very, very fast, but I have to admit, it's exhilarating. "Are we going over a hundred?"

"A hundred? We're doing sixty-five."

"Is that all?"

"Deer," he says. "They're all over the place. My dad said if I hit one, they'll have to scrape me off the road."

I'm impressed. Kyle was showing off back in Austin, but he's actually being responsible on the open road. On the other hand, what would it be like to cruise home at a hundred miles per hour?

Miles of gently hilly, wide-open ranch country pass by in a blur. Except for a glance at the quarter moon winking at us from low in the sky, I scarcely pay attention to the scenery. All I see is the thick, light brown hair, the muscular back, the ballsy shoulders, the deeply tanned, perfectly smooth skin of this Greek god astride his hot steed.

I dream of Kyle holding me tight, his hands exploring every inch of my body, his lips and tongue caressing mine, his hot breath setting my naked body on fire. I desperately want to press against him and massage his perfectly sculpted chest and tightly ridged abs. I want to run my fingers through his hair and kiss his neck and ears and every inch of him. I want to feel his hot lips pressed against mine.

I can't stand this any longer.

Maybe if I tell him my arm's asleep and I might fall off, I could put my arms around him. That's it! I'll tell him my arm fell asleep. Then I'll reach around and hold him tight. What if he was riding naked? What if I was too? There's no one around, so both of us could take our clothes off. I could put my hands all over him. I'd kiss and lick every inch of that gorgeous body. I could even reach around and stroke—

Idiot! Now he'll feel this hard-on. Bobby-dude, you stupid idiot.

We've passed Llano. We'll be home in less than an hour. Can I really do this?

Do it, do it, do it.

Oh, he'll get mad and then he'll make me walk home.

Just do it!

Oh God, this better go okay.

"Kyle, my arm's asleep. Can I hold on to you so I don't fall off?"

"Yeah. Hold on real tight. If you fall off, my dad will blame me."

I have to scrunch forward tightly against him to release one hand so I don't blow right off the bike. Kyle lifts his arm when I snake my hand around his chest. Now the other arm. I have my arms around him! My heart is jackhammering so hard he has to feel it.

I can't believe I'm doing this. I squeeze in tighter, my body conforming to his perfect form. He hasn't reacted other than to press his arms in tighter, locking my arms to his sides.

I imagine Kyle kissing me when he drops me off. He asks if he can see my bedroom and says he's too tired to go—

What was that? The engine just coughed and sputtered.

There it is again.

With one final, hacking bang, the engine quits. We're gliding and slowing toward the side of the highway. The only sound is the wind—and Kyle's anger.

"What the heck is going on?" he roars, braking hard to a stop on the shoulder. Scared of his temper, I immediately hop off and watch as he punches the starter a couple times. The engine obediently turns over but won't start.

"What the *fuck?*" he bellows. Kyle swings off the bike and stands over it with a stare that might melt it. He controls himself enough to remove the gas cap and peer into the tank.

"I don't believe this. We're out of gas. Jesus Christ!"

"Can you call someone?"

"Yeah, let me try." Kyle violently fishes around in both of his saddle bags.

"Just great. I forgot my cell phone." He throws his head way back. "Great, this is just fucking great."

"Let me try mine." He shakes his head when I flick the cover down. "No luck. There's no signal out here."

We're on a dusty county road, a shortcut, he said, to the northeast part of town where I live. There's nothing around but open country. We passed a ranch, but it's miles back. The few lights dimly visible way up ahead can't be within walking distance. No traffic, no houses, no cell phone signal. We could be out here for hours.

I'm slowly backpedaling. I've seen Kyle lose his well-known temper and was on the receiving end once or twice. He's pacing and he's still fuming and we're stranded out here. It would have been different if it was a girl on the back of his bike.

Maybe it would be better if I plop down a couple of fence posts up the road.

Minutes slowly tick by. Aside from Kyle—quiet this whole time and sitting cross-legged next to his bike—my only company is the steady, buzz-saw droning of insects in the fields. It's amazing how loud they are.

Even the moon slinked beneath the horizon when I wasn't looking. Out here in the middle of ranch country, the horizon is miles away in every direction, especially heading up the road. The enormous expanse of stars twinkling against the pitch-black sky would fill me with awe on any other night, but now I'm left wondering when we'll get back home.

I can't stop thinking about Kyle. Old Kyle, new Kyle. Sweet, gentle Kyle and scorecard-keeping, party-boy, macho Kyle. I just can't get him out of my mind.

Chapter 37

"Kyle, I need to talk to you." I've plopped down onto the shoulder right in front of him, sitting Indian-style.

"What's up?"

"At the diner, you asked if I had a thing for you and I said no. That's mostly true, but … maybe not a hundred percent true."

His head jerks back.

"Look, Kyle, it's not what you think. You *are* physically gifted, and any gay boy in his right mind would be crazy not to check you out. Look at you. You're athletic, you're really good-looking, you lift weights … I could give you a gay-boy description of you from head to toe, but you'd be embarrassed and think I was hitting on you. I'm not."

Kyle rolls his eyes.

"Oh, come on, Kyle, I'm not, honest. You're straight, I'm gay. Maybe this is weird for you, but finding another guy is the only way I'll ever be really happy."

Kyle squishes his face.

"Look, I know you're not comfortable with two guys being together. I just think … I just think I'm drawn to you in some way."

"You're *drawn* to me?"

I'm wincing at how that sounded.

"Well, not like that. There's a Kyle I see underneath that incredible physique you've been blessed with. It's the really sweet guy who visited me in the hospital. It's the guy who's caring and generous and full of fun. That's the Kyle I see deep down, and that's what I'm drawn to. I just don't want you to think it's a sex hang-up thing, because it's not."

"Are you setting me up for something?"

"No, really, I'm trying to explain where I'm coming from. I was trying to tell you I think you're an incredibly nice guy."

"Hey, I think I'm a nice guy," he says.

"And you saved my life not once but twice. And that Christmas when you were there for me, and those other times as well. I guess what I wanted to tell you is maybe someday you might really need someone. Maybe you'll be desperate. I'll be there for you, and that's a promise. When you really need someone, I promise you, I'll be there for you."

Kyle's face is a complete blank.

"That's cool," he says.

"Look, I know we're not friends because I'm gay and I'm not part of the jock crowd, but who knows? Maybe someday you and I will be friends. Maybe we can even hang out and do stuff together."

"You're going to hang out with me and my friends?"

"Oh, great," I moan as my head sinks into my hands.

"Hey, look, I didn't mean ..."

But he did mean it. The unathletic gay kid who hangs with the computer geeks and science-fiction kids hanging around with Kyle's A-list friends? I get up and trudge away, only ... only I stop and turn back. I don't know what's making me do this. It's like my feet are in control of my brain.

Kyle cocks his head when I stand in front of him.

"There's something else," I tell him.

"Hey, look, I'm sorry about—"

"I understand. What I was going to say is I think you cover up the real Kyle with another Kyle."

"Like I'm some space alien underneath?"

I ignore his wise-ass remark.

"That nice Kyle isn't always what I see. There's another Kyle, the Kyle you want everyone to see, you know, the one who hangs around with the jock crowd and the pretty people, the one who gets invites to all the best parties, the Kyle who flaunts looking good—"

"What?"

"Sorry, I didn't mean it like that, but why do you have to work so hard at this Kyle image? Why do you have to be anything else other than who you really are? You're such an amazing, wonderful person without all that macho stuff."

Kyle's eyes are big with amazement.

"Look, dude, I'm just me, got it?" he bellows, his face turning red, his

eyes blazing. He jabs his finger at me. *"And for your information, my life is none of your fucking business. Got it?"*

It hits like a cannon blast. The horror of realizing how pissed he is, and how totally I went over the line, quickly sinks in. I stutter a quick apology.

A sick feeling burns in my stomach as I traipse a few fence posts further up the road. Plopping down onto a patch of dusty scrub grass, pulling my knees up close, hiding my head in my arms, I want to curl up and die. I made a complete fool of myself and messed up one of the best nights of my life. I was actually talking to him. I had my arms around him, and now he's really pissed. Let alone kissing any friendship good-bye forever, he's going to be mad at me for the rest of my life. Why can't I take Chloe's advice just once and keep my mouth shut?

It's been almost an hour, and Kyle hasn't said a word. Actually, I looked over there and he was watching me. He must be seriously teed off.

I'm on my feet, yawning and stretching. All but a couple of the brightest stars are gone, washed out by the grayish-blue of early dawn and a feathering of dim, rosy light on the horizon. It will still take a long time for the sun to come up, but when it does, it will get hot. Real hot.

"Hey, you okay?"

My head jerks up when I hear him right behind me.

"You startled me."

He's fidgeting with his hands and gulps so hard it requires quite a physical effort.

"You don't have sit all alone," he says.

"I'm really sorry. I made a total fool of myself."

"Hey, we're cool," he says. "I, uh, I feel bad about all the stuff that happened to you. I thought, uh, maybe, would it be okay if I gave you ..." Kyle stops when I point past him. Far up the road, which is now a barely visible dark strip stretching for miles toward home, a distant gleam of lights has caught my eye. Kyle turns to follow my point.

"There's a car coming!" I holler.

Instead of whooping and hollering, Kyle sighs and his shoulders sag. He tramps back to his bike with his head down. *What did I do?*

The lights disappear in the washboard of gentle hills for what seems like an eternity, making me fear that the car has turned off somewhere.

I'm relieved each time they re-appear on the crest of the next hill. It seems to take forever for the car to get to the flat section we're on.

At last, the headlights appear just down the road. As they come closer, they reveal they're attached to an ancient pickup truck, now slowing as it draws closer. Dusty and rattling, its red paint chipped and dull, its fenders rusted and loose, this old wreck should have gone to the junkyard years ago.

The truck slows to a halt in a cloud of dust and a scary metallic screech from worn-out brakes. Inside are two Mexican-Americans, both wearing clean straw hats and immaculate, pressed white shirts. *Of course. It's Sunday morning.*

The one on the far side, young with a sharp, dark face and a thin, menacing mustache, doesn't look at me, but with the slightest shake of his head, appears annoyed that they stopped to help two gringos. The other—shorter, much older, his round face deeply sun-creased— impassively watches us from the driver's seat.

"*Hola!*" I say as I edge closer. The old man nods a wary greeting.

"*¿Por favor?*" I continue in Spanish, hoping I remember enough from my two years in language lab not to say something stupid. "Señor, we are isolation here. Could you please sell us a small gas? This is all I have left," I explain, holding up a twenty. He breaks out in a broad, nearly toothless smile, creasing his face even more.

"*Si,*" he replies. "So, *muchacho,* you ran out of gas," he says with a chuckle.

The old man somewhat painfully eases himself out of the cab, reaches behind the seat, and produces a long, plastic tube and a small gas can. With well-practiced steps, the can is filled in less than a minute. The other guy, still slouched in the cab smoking a cigarillo, hasn't said a word, utterly unconcerned that we're stuck out here in the middle of nowhere.

Once Kyle has carefully trickled our lifesaving gas into the tank, he holds out the empty can for the old man.

"*Gracias, señor,*" he says in a straight-boy, Texas drawl so deep it sounds like country-boy talk with a Spanish accent.

"*Bueno,*" the man replies with another toothless smile that would be scary if he wasn't so nice.

"Thank you very much, *señor,*" I continue in somewhat halting Spanish. "You are very kind to stop and help me and my friend. We are tired and want to go home." I knew it. From Kyle's slightly inquisitive look, I'm guessing not much of his two years of Spanish stuck. "My rich gringo friend should learn to take care of his motor bicycle better, but he doesn't want to get his pretty hands dirty."

The old man snorts a laugh as he climbs back into the cab. Kyle's face remains a complete blank as I hold up the twenty. The old man eyes it for a few moments.

"*Amigo,* save your money for college and go home," he says in English. "You look like you need some sleep." The truck coughs and shudders to life with an alarming cloud of dirty white smoke.

"*Gracias, señor, muchas gracias.*" He gives a brief wave as the pickup lurches forward and grinds and rattles its way down the dusty road. Filled with gratitude and respect for the old man, I raise my arm high to wave a final goodbye.

Now for the scary part. Kyle is already on his bike.

"All set?" he asks.

"You mean I'm not walking home?"

He nods to get on. Not wanting to keep him waiting for even one more second, I grip his shoulder and hop on. I haven't the slightest thought of putting my arms around him or anything. I just want to go home and crawl into bed.

We're underway for only a few minutes when I look back to see the sun just above the horizon, its reddish glow the sign of another scorching, humid day. What could have been one of the best nights of my life is almost over.

Despite being exhausted, sleep is not coming easily. Thrashing all over my bed, I'm alternating between replaying tonight's events and feeling sick about how I blew it.

I bolt upright with a start. There was something about getting on his motorcycle in the parking lot; he hesitated when I asked what I should hold on to. Maybe he just didn't hear me. *But what if—?*

Forget it. I need sleep.

"Holy shit!" What did he want when he came up behind me? He was talking about giving me something. "Did Kyle want to give me a hug?" I say aloud to my bedroom.

Bobby-dude, get real.

Forget Kyle. Just forget about Kyle Faulkner, just forget ...

THE TUTOR

Chapter 38

"Mr. Evans was yelling at *Kyle?*"

Chloe's grinning back at me. Knowing I'd be shocked, she calmly unwraps her Big Mac and takes a dinosaur-sized bite. A few students at nearby tables, sharing the shade and relative coolness under one of our high school's century-old live oaks, briefly interrupt their lunches at the mention of Kyle's name.

"That's what I heard," she replies with a mouthful. "Mr. Evans was so angry, he slammed his desk drawer."

"Wait a minute. Mr. Evans never yells. I've heard him cut kids to shreds so bad they almost pee their pants, and he doesn't even raise his voice. So how'd you hear this?"

"Tom Travis. He told me this morning."

"Come on, Chloe, tell me what happened."

"Tom went back to his locker after band practice yesterday," Chloe says. "Mr. Evans was yelling so loud he could hear him down the hallway. Tom said he hung around when he heard Kyle's name."

"I wonder why Mr. Evans was that upset."

"How about not studying and flunking tests? And get this: Mr. Evans told Kyle, 'You're more interested in looking good and going to all the cool parties than getting good grades.' That's exactly the way Tom heard it. Want to hear the big one?"

I'm eagerly nodding that I do.

"Tom swears he heard Mr. Evans tell Kyle he's going to flunk him. If Kyle flunks history, you know what that means," she says with that evil grin of hers.

"No more football," I answer, in awe at the thought that our team's star quarterback might get kicked off the team. Chloe, never one to have sympathy for "stuck-up jocks," as she puts it, leans back into her seat with a supremely satisfied look. "But that doesn't make any sense," I go on. "You know those football players get away with murder. Like that big kid, Ryan. He didn't even take his physics quiz last week and he got a passing grade. And how many times has Jason come in hung over and fallen asleep in class, and nothing happens? Mr. Evans flunking Kyle? Not a chance."

"You tell Kyle that. Mr. Evans *promised* Kyle he'll flunk him if he doesn't get his act together."

"You know, Kyle was in a wicked bad mood when he came in this morning. Jason was busting him about Myra Rose … oh, shit!"

Chloe's hands fly to her mouth as she tries not to laugh out loud.

"I heard Kyle has to use a tutor for history, and you know who that is," she says.

I lean forward to whisper.

"Kyle's type." Chloe almost chokes. "Myra's the smartest girl in school and she's nice enough, but jeez, couldn't she get some better glasses and clothes and wash her hair?"

"You're a history tutor," Chloe says.

"It's just me and Myra, and we're supposed to tutor freshmen and sophomores."

"Maybe Kyle will ask you," Chloe says with an even more evil grin.

"Yeah, right. That'll be the day. Well, we'll see what happens in tomorrow morning's history class."

"All right, everybody, quiz tomorrow on Chapter 17," Mr. Evans hollers over the usual end-of-period rush out the door. "Bobby, I need to see you for a minute."

"Sir?"

"Bobby, I'll cut right to the chase," Mr. Evans says when the room clears. "You and everyone else know Kyle's using a tutor." I nod. "It's not working out, and in all fairness to Kyle, it's not his fault. I strongly urged him to use a tutor until the final." Mr. Evans doesn't have to say another word. "So, do you want to give it a shot?" he asks. "It's only for two weeks."

I'm hesitating.

"Look," he continues, "I know there's a little tension between you two, and I told Kyle he'd better get over these gay hang-ups of his if he wants to keep playing football."

How can I do this? Ever since that disaster coming home from the club, I try not to think about him. And he practically avoids me. Tutoring Kyle will be weird.

"Kyle's under a lot of pressure," Mr. Evans continues. "You know he hurt his knee. He didn't play well the last two games with college scouts watching, plus his grades are slipping. You don't have to do this, but Kyle could use a little help right now. Come on, Bobby, you can do this."

"Okay, I'll give it a try. When should I start?"

"Work that out with him. Just remember the quiz tomorrow. If he flunks even one quiz or doesn't get a C-plus on the final, he flunks the course."

"I guess we should start right away."

"And just so you know, Kyle wants to keep this among the three of us," Mr. Evans says.

"Like Myra was a secret?"

Mr. Evans grins.

"I know she told just about everyone in school. I'm sure every girl in school would love to be Kyle's tutor." His grin is bigger and unmistakable. "This whole thing is up to you. You're in the driver's seat."

It's so quiet in Mr. Evans's room that when the clock hand advances to six, the tick echoes through the room. *Kyle gets ten minutes and then I'm—*

How about that, he's right on time. My eyes instantly zoom in on his stretchy gray athletic shorts and the bulge between his legs. Not only is his package eye-poppingly obvious, it's jouncing around with each step. Did he walk through the corridors with just those shorts and no jock? God help me.

Mr. Cool saunters to the desk next to mine, chucks his history text and a notebook down with a thump, scrapes the chair back, and plops down in a slouch. He hasn't said a word.

"I thought we'd spend part of the hour preparing for tomorrow's quiz," I tell him.

Kyle shrugs with a "who cares?" look.

"Let's just do the work, okay?"

"That's what I was planning on doing," I snap. What did he think we were going to do? Any more of this attitude shit and I'm out of here.

"He aced yesterday's quiz?" Chloe shrieks at her locker.

"Yeah, and you should have seen the look on him when Mr. Evans told the entire class he got every question right. And then I saw Jason giving him the brown nose." I'm rotating my closed fist over my nose.

"Kyle owes you one, that's for sure. Are you guys getting along better?"

"Better than I expected. I mean, the first two sessions went well. We went through the text and he wrote notes, and believe it or not, he asked intelligent questions. Kyle's no dumb jock, that's for sure. Then at the end of each session, we set the time for the next one, and he leaves."

Chloe jabs a finger at me.

"He's a jerk."

"Maybe he's still upset with me."

"He's still a jerk and even more so because you're helping him," Chloe says.

"Sometimes I wonder what's eating him. He does his usual Mr. Cool act, but underneath he seems uptight and tense."

"So he's an uptight, tense jerk."

The insistent shrill of the bell signals the end of our hallway discussion. As usual, Chloe has the final say.

Chapter 39

"Here," I whisper, tapping Kyle on the shoulder when Mr. Evans isn't looking. Glancing all around to see if anyone's watching, he snatches the note I'm holding out and hides it under his desk.

> *Kyle,*
> *I'm glad you got another A yesterday. Unfortunately last night I got soaked and cold in the rain and hurt my leg so I can't bike back and forth to school anymore. Can we meet during lunch or can you give me rides?*

Kyle's hunched over scribbling a note. Let's see what he's giving me

> *Sorry, I'm busy at lunch and I can't arrange a ride. Maybe you can get a ride? Are we still on for 6:30?*

He's busy at lunch? Yeah, eating with his friends. And he can't give me a ride? I don't get that. His dad picked him up last night, so what's the big deal? He usually rides his motorcycle—oh, so that's it. He doesn't want anyone seeing me on the back of his bike.

> *Thank you for your concern. If we can't meet during school, we can't continue our sessions. Good luck with the last two quizzes and the final.*

> *Bobby*

P.S.: Maybe you could study at my place instead. No one will ever see you there and I promise not to make you uncomfortable.

He's holding the note under his desk again. I can just see the little wheels and gears spinning in his head. Kyle whips around when Mr. Evans writes on the blackboard.

"You promise?" he whispers. I scribble in my notebook and hold it up: ABSOLUTELY.

Light the candles on the table. Light the candles around the pool. Check the time again—twenty minutes to six. Make sure my textbook and notebook and pencils are perfectly lined up on the table. Fluff and arrange the pillows again. Nineteen minutes. *Kyle Faulkner is coming here, he's coming to my house!* Maybe I'd better go inside and put some clothes on—

"Oh, shit! What are you doing here?" I screech. Kyle is in the sliding glass doorway, so startled by my scream, he jerks backward.

"The door was open, and I thought I was supposed to come in," he stammers.

"You were, but you're early. Just give me a minute to get dressed."

Shit, shit, shit! I promised not to make him feel uncomfortable, and he's here three seconds and finds me naked on the patio. Shit!

I return to find him gazing over the pool from the edge of the patio. It's obvious from the unusual long and narrow shape and the two swim lanes marked to NCAA standards that this is one serious lap pool. Maybe he wants to jump in and try it out. Not only is Kyle a football star, he's by far the best swimmer on the swim team. The rich get richer.

I walk right up beside him.

"Hey, I'm sorry about—"

"Is this twenty-five yards?" he interrupts.

"Uh, no, it's twenty-five meters. My dad had it put in the summer we moved here. He was on the Harvard swim team."

"Hmm," is his only reaction.

Kyle directs his attention back to the patio, coolly surveying everything: the stainless steel barbeque island reflecting the rays of the late-day sun; the large glazed planters overflowing with flowering plants and small trees; the teak chaise lounges, comfy with thick, inviting cushions; and finally, the large, glass-topped patio table and cushioned chairs with colorful pillows, perfectly arranged. If he's impressed, he's not showing it, unlike everyone else who comes out here.

"What's that?" he asks, strolling toward the large, boxy shape nestled close to the house. He lifts the thick vinyl cover. "A hot tub!" He's sniffing the steam billowing from hot, crystal-clear water, which I scented with a splash of tropical fragrance. "This place is amazing," he says as he slowly scans the patio from one end to the other.

"My dad hired an architect to design it when we moved here. It came out so good it was featured in a homes and gardens magazine." Kyle nods and I motion toward the table. "I thought we'd study outside."

"No problem," he says, craning to get a look at the strings of tiny white lights running along the ribs of the umbrella.

"Look, I'm sorry you got caught in the rain," he says when we get seated. "I should have asked if you needed a ride, but my dad ... I'm sorry."

"Your dad?"

"My mom and dad aren't too cool about, you know, about ..."

"Me?"

"I think it's anything or anyone gay," he says.

"They don't know you're studying with me?"

"Something like that," Kyle mutters.

"Okay, I'm cool," I tell him, pleased he apologized and equally pleased I sounded cool. "It's no big deal, but I can't bike for a couple of days. You can see it's quite a distance from here to school. Seven point fourteen miles, to be exact."

Kyle squishes his nose. I roll my eyes and sigh. I couldn't have sounded any more like a complete dork if I tried.

"Are you naked on the patio when your folks are around?" Kyle asks.

"My folks?"

"Yeah. Are they out?"

"They're not here."

"Will they be back soon?"

Kyle thinks Mrs. Robles lives here and that she's my real mother! That's right, he only met her at the hospital and never visited me at home, so he thinks this is where I live. I'm hesitating and find myself holding my breath. Why is it so hard to tell him?

"My mom's dead," I reply, my voice already shaky. "Mrs. Robles, the woman you met at the hospital, she's my foster mother. My mom died three years ago in Boston when she got run down by a drunk driver. We moved here three months later."

Kyle rolls his head back, closes his eyes, and lets out a soft, anguished moan.

"I'm really sorry. I had no idea," says the gentle, caring Kyle who came to see me in the hospital, not Kyle the Jerk who's been avoiding me these last two months. "And your dad?" he asks.

Dad? He still doesn't get it. I'll start sobbing like a little kid if I tell him everything. I can't cry in front of Kyle, I just can't.

"He's away," I explain while grabbing the textbook and fumbling through the pages. "Let's just get through this, okay?"

Chapter 40

The scrape of Kyle's wrought iron chair on the fieldstone signals the end of our second session at my place. It went as well as the first—no attitude, no mention of our trip back from the club, just studying.

"Do you have to rush off?" I ask.

"Yeah, why?"

"I was going to jump in the hot tub. I bet you're dying to try it out."

Kyle freezes. His history text is suspended halfway into his backpack.

"I promised my father I'd get the car home."

"It's relaxing and healing. I know you hurt your knee."

"Yeah, it's my MCL," he says, sounding more sad than bitter.

"Bad?"

"Nah, not enough for an operation. But just my luck, the scouts are watching and I'm off balance when I throw. It's my fault we lost two games."

"The hot tub will help."

He's thinking this over. "Maybe for a few minutes."

My entire body surges with electric anticipation at the thought of Kyle stripping down.

"I have some gym shorts you can put on," I tell him, heating up even more just thinking about Kyle Faulkner in a pair of wet, clingy gym shorts.

"That's okay. I brought a swimsuit."

"Cool. Let me get some towels."

Racing inside, I flip on the CD player, which is all set up to pipe soft, classical guitar music through the outside speakers. Then the dash to the couch to pick up the two fluffy white towels I left just in case. Before going back outside, however, I decide, what the heck. I'm so excited stripping down to my orange racer swimsuit that I trip and land flat on my face.

I'm not even through the sliding door when the breath is sucked right out of me. Kyle is casually leaning against the hot tub, wearing a tiny black competition swimsuit smaller than mine. With his hands bracing him from behind, the hard, knotty muscles in the back of his arms pop right out. His suit rides low on his hips, so low I can see most of the creases that curve from his hips down to his groin. I don't understand how he could swim at a meet and not have that suit fall off. Maybe it does!

The second he sees me in the doorway, he hops off the tub with a gasp, scaring me that I made a mistake wearing this swimsuit. Neither of us speaks as we face each other. It's taking all my willpower not to stare at anything other than his eyes.

"I'll get the tub ready," I tell him, but so little air comes out of my mouth, the words squeak out. The pouch of my suit is straining so bad it's hard to walk.

"Give me a hand?" I squeak while I tug at the bulky cover and try to hide behind it at the same time. My hands shake as we fold the cover back and ease it over the side. After it's carefully tucked away, I vault right into the water so he won't see the front of my little orange suit explode. I take a quick peek at Kyle's swimsuit. My eyes almost pop when I zero in on the pouch. *Is there a banana stuffed in there?*

When I motion him to the corner opposite me, Kyle hurdles over the side and jumps in, only to launch himself right back up with a violent splash.

"Wow, hot," he says. This time Kyle eases his body into the 106-degree water. With the touch of a button, the entire tub erupts in a foaming boil from dozens of jets, half of them under and around where Kyle has settled in my usual spot.

I sink down too, almost to my jaw, with my head resting on the black rubber pad behind me. Eyes half closed, I try to focus on relaxing things—the calming music, all those heated jets soothing and massaging every part of me—anything but the pouch of Kyle's tiny swimsuit or his magnificent chest or … *oh, God, this is harder than I thought.*

"Try sinking down to your neck," I tell him.

"Oh, man, this feels good. Mmm, it's so relaxing." Kyle leans his head back onto the headrest and dreamily soaks in the relaxing heat.

"You look really good," he says.

"Thanks. So do you."

"Mind if I sit over there?" He's nodding to a spot right next to me. I pat the top of the spa next to me.

"I'm really glad we're studying together," he says. We're sitting so close we're touching. Our eyes meet. We don't look away as his hand slips across my back and pulls me into his impressive chest.

"You've added more muscle," I tell him.

"So have you. What do you have stuffed in that swimsuit?" he asks. "Man, are you packing or what?" I don't answer as his hand begins to reach—

"You really think my knee will feel better tomorrow?"

"*What?* I mean, yeah, definitely," I reply, focusing on Kyle sitting in the far corner. We're quiet for a bit as my heart rate gradually slows from something like five hundred.

"You use this a lot?" he asks.

"Almost every day unless the weather's really bad. When I was healing or had a tough physical therapy session, I'd be in here at least twice a day."

"I'm sorry. I didn't mean to bring up, you know ..."

Kyle shifts and his leg touches mine. When he leaves it there, I shift mine. We're quiet for a few minutes.

"I'm getting a little dizzy," he says. I glance at the outdoor clock on the side of the house.

"You're overheating. Fifteen minutes is long enough at 106 degrees," I tell him as I swing over the side to get out. "Before you leave, would you like to see my recording studio?"

"It's here?"

"Yeah. Want to see it?"

"I can't stay long."

"No problem. This will just take a minute."

We quickly finish drying off. I throw on my shorts, but Kyle seems content to follow me through the house and down the cellar stairs wearing nothing but his wet Speedo. He comments that none of his friends except Helen has a basement.

"Holy shit!"

Kyle gawks at the electronic equipment on the left side, equipment that now includes a used but still-workable DJ deck; three synthesizers; amplifiers; a work table covered with a mess of CDs and half-completed scores; and, beside my PC, more electronic equipment stacked on shelves. He studies the whole setup but doesn't ask questions. Instead, Kyle shifts his attention to my drums on the opposite side. The double bass drums with shiny black lacquer shells, five toms, and gleaming brass cymbals would be an impressive set for a big-name rock group.

"This looks expensive," he says.

"Oh, on the north side of five grand."

"Five grand?" He's thinking this over as he lightly taps on a mounted tom. "So what are you waiting for?"

"You want me to play?"

"Yeah. Show me what you've got."

Once I get seated on my padded stool, Kyle decides that he'll stand just to my left, hovering over my hi-hat, unlike everyone else who watches from the front. I'm slouched over, trying to force my breathing to slow down and my hands to stop shaking. With that magnificent bod hovering right over me, all the blood in my body has gone to another intense woody. Luckily it's not too obvious through my bulky khaki shorts.

"Are you okay?" he asks.

"Uh ... yeah ... I was just trying to figure out how to start." It sounds dumb, but Kyle nods that he understands.

"What's that for?" he asks when he sees me twirling my sticks at arm's length like airplane propellers.

"Just loosening up," I reply. "I start on these two cymbals. It's called a hi-hat and they clap together with the foot pedal, like this. This is the snare drum, this is a crash cymbal, these are double bass drums ... sorry, maybe I should just start."

I launch into my standard solo, now improved after a year of recovering and another year of improvising and practicing. I'm so tight, and my dick is aching so bad, I've never played worse, frustrating because I want this to be my best ever. Little by little, though, my wrists loosen and I settle into a groove. Two-thirds of the way through, I'm on fire. The cellar is filled with a wall of sound from my high-speed drumming and cymbal crashes.

At the end, rapid hits on the bass drums thunder like the grand finale of Fourth of July fireworks. Five extra-loud crashes on the cymbals and bass drums end my solo.

"That was my Buddy Rich ending," I tell him, panting just a bit.

Kyle's staring blankly with this odd combination of surprise and a disbelieving grin, a look I've seen before when people hear me for the first time.

"Was that okay?"

He snaps out of it with a visible start.

"Okay? That was unbelievable. Helen said you were good, but I had no idea anyone could play like that."

"Thanks. My newest dance track isn't finished yet, but would you like to hear it?"

"Yeah. You really use all that equipment?" Kyle asks.

"Yeah, all of it. I do everything down here, like the composition I entered last year, jazz and classical, dance music … hold on a sec, let me get everything powered up."

The room begins to vibrate to the thumping beat of my newest track.

"He's so beautiful … so, so beautiful … beautiful … beautiful … beautiful …"

I turn it off a minute later, wondering if Kyle will figure out who the "he" is.

"Unbelievable," he murmurs as I shut everything down. Kyle's on the bottom step when he takes one final look at my drums and recording studio equipment. He's shaking his head going up the stairs.

And I know what I'm going to do the minute he leaves.

Chapter 41

"I told Helen I heard you do a drum solo," Kyle's telling me the next night just as I turn on the hot tub jets. "She wants to know, when does she get to hear you play?"

"Wait a minute. You told me these sessions were just between me and you," I tell him while sinking down into the relaxing, steaming water.

Kyle looks down with a sheepish grin.

"Helen figured if I was getting all A's and I wasn't studying with Myra, I had to be studying with you. Nothing gets by Helen. Don't you know that by now?"

My turn to grin. He could be talking about Chloe. It has to be a girl thing.

"Are you entering the music competition this year?" he asks.

"The contest? No, not really. How could I ever top last year?"

"Yeah, well, we were kind of thinking that maybe you should take that big set of drums to the contest and beat the crap out of them on stage. Dude, no one else will have a chance!" Kyle the football player shouts with a fist pump.

Kyle wants me to enter the contest? *Kyle?* Ah, I bet Helen thought this up and got Kyle to ask. Very clever, Helen, very clever. Still—

"Come on, do it."

"All right, you talked me into it, but only on one condition."

"What's that?"

"You have to watch from the wings."

The hint of a smile, just enough, escapes Kyle's famous cool.

We're quiet for a few minutes. Kyle has sunk low into the water with his eyes closed, relaxing in the powerful jets. It's now or never. I just have to tell him. It's all I've thought about last night and all day long.

"Kyle?"

His eyes slowly open halfway.

"Are you all right?" he asks.

I'm having trouble getting the words out. I lean my head back on the foam rubber headrest and stare up at the earliest stars.

"I need to tell you something. It has to stay between you and me."

"Sure, whatever," he says.

"I mean it, Kyle. No one else can know about this or bad things will happen to me. Really bad things."

"All right, all right."

"You know I told you my dad was away?"

"Yeah, what about it?"

"He is, but he's never coming back."

"Like, he's all freaked out because you're gay?"

I sit upright and give him a hard stare.

"No, it's more like I'm all freaked out because he's dead."

At first nothing registers, but Kyle's head slowly sinks into his hands with a groan. "Shit," he says to himself, regretting, I'm sure, his wise-ass remark. "Hey, look, I'm really sorry," he says.

"No problem." I force a cough, which does nothing to clear the shakiness out of my voice. "A few months after my mom died, my dad told me he had taken a job at an air force base in Texas. I thought it was crazy, but now I think my dad had to get away." I take a deep, shaky breath. "The patio, the pool ... I think Dad did it partly for me."

Trying not to become emotional, I tell Kyle everything: Dad's last mission overseas, Mr. Huntington's scary visit, that awful day the judge told me Dad was dead, my foster home, the trust, everything. Kyle now knows how I get to use this house and where my drums and equipment came from.

"Mrs. Robles and I get along pretty good now, and I help her out a lot, but I spend lots of time here. Last summer, Chloe and Danny and I even slept here a few times. I do some chores around here, and the judge thought it would be educational for me to learn how to run a house and pay the bills."

"Jesus Christ, my mom's always yelling at me for not keeping my room clean, and you're running a house." Kyle cocks his head. "I don't get it. You said bad things will happen."

"This state agency, Child Protective Services … if they find out I'm spending most of my time here instead of down the street, they could put me in a new foster home. It could be far away, and I'll have to leave all my friends and my drums and the recording studio behind. They could make me move right in the middle of senior year."

Kyle takes a few moments to digest it all.

"You mean, it's like your parents are away for the weekend, only it's forever?" When I don't answer, Kyle continues. "Dude, every kid in school could only dream about something like this."

"I guess. But sometimes when I feel sad or something bad happens, I come up here and there's no one to talk to. Mrs. Robles tries hard, but it's not like having my mom. It's the same when something good happens. It's just an empty house," I sigh. "Sometimes I just want to lean on someone's shoulder." I stand up to get out. If I keep going, I'll get emotional.

"So why are you telling me all this?" Kyle asks as he swings his legs over the edge of the tub.

"I guess I needed to tell someone."

"Like, you want to lean on my shoulder?"

Kyle's question stops me cold. *Is he offering?* I decide he isn't. If I tell him I want a hug, he'll be mad at me all over again.

"I just had to tell someone, that's all."

Kyle's staring at me with an unreadable expression.

"Tomorrow night's our last session," I tell him, but instead of leaving, he's drilling me with a penetrating stare. "I have to study physics now."

His eyes hold mine for a few more unsettling moments.

"Yeah, see you tomorrow night," he says, nearly whispering.

All day I was obsessed with telling him. Now he thinks I'm an emotional little gay kid. The minute he leaves, he won't give me a second thought. *Nice going, Bobby-dude.*

Chapter 42

Kyle is toweling off over by the hot tub. Our final tutoring session is over. No more studying with Kyle out on the patio, no more jumping in the hot tub with him, no more seeing him at the front door wearing just those stretchy gray athletic shorts that show everything. Kyle will get dressed, he'll go out the front door, and that will be the last time I'll ever see him here.

"Hey, Kyle, come sit here," I holler to him as I stand over a cushy patio chair.

"I gotta get going."

"Please?" I ask with a few pats of the cushion. "It's just for a few minutes."

"Am I getting a haircut?" he asks with a grin as he saunters over. He lowers himself into the chair wearing nothing but his Speedo.

"Just relax. I'm going to do what Helen told me you'd like."

Kyle's head whips around.

"You're going to do *what?*"

"Helen said you wouldn't ask on your own."

"*What are you going to do?*" he shouts, almost in a panic. He knows exactly what I'm going to do.

"Relax. It's just a light, therapeutic massage. Helen really liked it. And besides, I'm an expert, especially after all that physical therapy."

"Yeah, but..."

"It will help with lifting and football and everything."

"Oh, man, I don't know about this," he says.

"Kyle, I *promise* this will be totally professional."

"I really have to get the car home." Kyle's halfway out of the chair when I push down on his shoulders. There was a time when he would have decked me for touching him like that, but he stiffly settles back. And besides, he came on his motorcycle.

"Look, will you please give this a try for one minute? If it sucks or you're too uncomfortable, then just leave."

"Yeah, whatever," he mutters. "This better be quick."

At least two minutes go by and nothing has happened.

"Nice massage, dude. I don't feel a thing," he says.

"Sorry," I reply. My voice is trembling so bad I can hardly talk. "I guess I'm a little nervous." Kyle reacts with just the hint of a grin.

I take a deep breath and press my fingertips firmly into the back of his head. My thumbs press hardest right under the base of his skull, where the neck muscle attachments are tightest. Kyle's so uptight his neck feels like straps of iron.

"Try to relax. Breathe in and out slowly. Here, I'll do it with you." I lean close to his ear, breathing in and out through my mouth, slowing each breath just like I was taught. I inhale, he inhales.

"Keep your eyes closed," I whisper, remembering how soothing and relaxing my therapist's gentle voice was. "That's it; focus only on your breathing. In slowly … out slowly. Feel the tension flowing out of your body," I murmur. "Every part of you is relaxing. You're sinking into the chair."

Kyle's shoulders sag. He exhales a noisy, deep breath.

"Think of being at the ocean," I whisper. "The sun is warm on your shoulders. There's a gentle breeze. You're totally relaxing. You can hear the surf and smell the salt air."

"I've never been to the ocean."

I resist the urge to scream.

"Relax. Just close your eyes and relax." This time, he takes an exceptionally deep breath and lets it out completely. Every muscle in his neck is softening.

My fingers work all over his scalp. His light brown hair is thick, yet soft and silky to the touch. I'm alternating working his scalp with pressure and then lightly with my fingernails, tracing little circles all over. I remember being surprised at how good it felt to have someone dig into my scalp.

In the middle of his massage, it occurs to me that I really am keeping this completely professional. I'm pleased with myself, and maybe a little relieved too.

"Oh, that feels good. What's that nice smell?" he asks in dreamy tones when I knead a bit of ointment into his neck and shoulders.

"Tiger Balm. It's some oriental massage stuff." I hear nothing but a couple of soft moans.

After a few more minutes of working his scalp, I move around front. My fingers press firmly against his forehead and temples.

"Trigger points," I whisper. I switch to tracing my fingers over his face with the softest touch. Even his ears get a light massage.

"You're totally relaxed," I whisper one final time as my fingers trace over his skin so lightly, they're hardly touching. "Keep your eyes closed and breathe slowly and deeply. Take your time, and when you're ready to get up, do it slowly. And then you'll be really hungry."

On the steps, I look back. Other than his chest rising and falling in slow motion, he hasn't moved a muscle.

"Hey, that was incredible," he says a few minutes later. I'm busy at the stove and don't turn around.

"Could you bring those placemats and table settings outside?" I ask while I concentrate on cooking.

"I really have to get home."

"You're wicked hungry, aren't you? I make a killer omelet, and it's almost ready, so just stay five more minutes, okay?" My answer is the clinking of silverware.

Out on the patio, lit only by the warm glow of candles, Kyle watches me slide half of a gigantic omelet and a steaming pile of golden brown breakfast potatoes onto his plate. He doesn't hesitate to dig in.

"Wow, this is really good," he says. "Is cooking omelets a gay thing?"

"Yeah, Kyle, you're eating a gay omelet!"

Kyle takes the joke and lights up in a brilliant smile.

It doesn't take him long to wolf down his meal. And now it's over. It's time for Kyle to leave for good.

At the front door, Kyle hesitates, like he wants to say something.

"Thanks for the tutoring," he mumbles, almost robot-like. His eyes don't leave mine.

"No problem. I hope you ace the final."

He's still staring.

"Hey, um …" Kyle gulps hard. He reaches for my upper arm. When he touches me, his hand is shaking. "I couldn't stop thinking about all those things you told me about, you know, like losing your mom and leaving your home, and your dad …" He's gently squeezing and rubbing my arm but doesn't finish his thought. "I'm really sorry." His voice sounds shaky.

I'm just about to ask if I can get a hug when he whirls out the door and hustles onto his Harley. He doesn't look back or even wave when he roars down the deserted country road toward town.

Mrs. Robles went to bed two hours ago. I'm still awake, tossing all over my bed. I can't stop thinking about Kyle. Scenes replay in my mind in a crazed, nonstop parade: Kyle in his tiny swimsuit; Kyle almost naked at the front door with his huge package jouncing around; or flashing one of his famous movie star smiles when I told him he was eating a gay omelet. And most amazing, Kyle telling me he couldn't stop thinking about me and gently rubbing my arm, so softly and yet so unexpectedly, I could hardly breathe.

After that awful night in August, I thought he was out of my mind forever. Now I can't stop thinking about him. Again.

Chapter 43

"Helen was in the hot tub? Did you see pussy?" Danny, who's been stuffing his face with microwave pizza his mom left for us, is almost halfway out of the chair.

"Would you chill out? She was wearing a swimsuit … a cute little two-piece number, and boy, did she look hot," I add just to torment my friend. I guess it does. He's biting the back of his hand and making little high-pitched sounds.

I was telling Danny that Helen asked if she and Josh were going to get an invite to use the hot tub. When they came over last night, Kyle was with them. He was acting totally innocent, but I knew he had talked Helen into asking.

"I wish I had been there," Danny sighs. "She's the most supremely awesome girl in the entire school. Well, you made out, gay boy. You had Josh to look at."

"Yeah, right. He shows up wearing those stupid board shorts. I just don't get it, Danny. Josh is one of the hottest guys in the entire school, and he wears about ten acres of fabric. Why do they even call them swimsuits?" I don't think Danny heard a word I said. "They're coming back next weekend. Want to join us?"

"For real?"

He screeches with both arms raised high when I tell him it is.

"So, guess what?" I ask Danny as he nukes another pizza. "Remember I told you Kyle asked me to do a drum solo in the music competition?"

"Yeah, you're going to, right?"

"Yep, and guess what else happened. Mr. Reynolds asked me to come back to the concert band and help start up a jazz band."

"It's about time you went back," Danny says while munching on his pizza.

"Get real. I told him I'd think about it, but there's no way."

"What do you mean, no way? You've got that big set of drums sitting in your cellar and no one hears you. So you played for Kyle."

"And Josh and Helen," I remind him.

"Okay, you played for Kyle and Josh and Helen. Big deal."

"Once they kicked me out, that was it for me."

Danny's quiet while I blab about the competition. It's when he gets up and paces that I know something's bothering him.

"We need to talk about the concert band," he says.

"Oh, come on, Danny, fuck the concert band!" Danny recoils as if he had just been slapped, and I instantly regret it. "Danny, I'm sorry. So what about the concert band?"

"Nothing. Just forget it."

"Look, I'm sorry I jumped down your throat. Come on, please tell me about the concert band." Danny resumes pacing, now even more rapidly.

"Well, for starters," he says, talking so loud he's almost shouting, "you were never kicked out of the band. They told you not to play the Christmas concert, remember? *You* decided you were never going back. Hey, I don't blame you, but that was almost two years ago."

"I can't go back. It was totally humiliating."

Danny throws his hands in the air.

"So that's it, to save face," he hollers with his finger jabbing right in my face. "I'm going to say it," he says, back to pacing like he's on speed. "Maybe it's time to grow up a little. I know how pissed and hurt you were. We all were, but dude, get over it. You've got so much to offer, and this will be good for you. And wouldn't it be great if you taught some of the younger kids how to play drums? Come on, Bobby, you love helping kids. Jeez, all you do is play your drums for an audience of one. Well, think about playing that big set of drums in a jazz competition. Look, man, I'm your best friend. Get your gay ass back in the band."

Heat rushes into my head like a volcano about to explode. "Grow up a little" wasn't quite what I wanted to hear. But as my best friend plops into his chair and rips an angry bite out of his pizza, what he said slowly sinks in. I snicker just thinking about that last comment.

"Get your gay ass back in the band? Is that what you just said?"

My snickering is turning into outright laughter. Danny picks up on it. Laughing, he jumps out of his chair and points right at me.

"No, gay boy, I said grow the fuck up." Shrieks of laughter fill the kitchen.

"Okay, homeboy, you win." I'm laughing so hard I can barely talk. "I'm going to get my gay ass back in the band!"

"Bobby, wait up!" A voice pierces through the noisy crowds of kids lined up at the endless yellow line of school buses. Helen is almost out of breath when she catches up to me. "Welcome back to the band!"

"How did you find out? I only told Mr. Reynolds about ten minutes ago."

"I saw him on the way out. He really thinks a lot of you for coming back." Helen gently grasps my arm. "I do too." Helen's smile vanishes. "Bobby, there's something I have to tell you."

"No problem."

"It's about Kyle."

"Can you believe he aced the final?"

I'm picturing the scene this afternoon when Mr. Evans handed out the test results, and announced to the class that Kyle got a ninety-five. Kyle raised both arms and let out a whoop, and the whole class applauded. Oh, and the look of shock on Jason's face was priceless.

"Bobby, you were really nice to help," Helen answers, oddly not smiling. "I know he appreciates it …"

"But …?"

Clasping her books tightly with both arms, biting her lip, Helen looks pained.

"Oh, I might as well just come out with it. Josh and I had dinner at his house yesterday. Josh spilled the beans, and Kyle's parents found out he wasn't in a study group, he was studying with you … at your house." Helen pauses. "And to make this totally messed up, they know Kyle was in the hot tub with you."

"With the gay kid."

"I'm really sorry," she says. "Mrs. Faulkner has some issues with gays. She's a really nice person, but she has some very strict religious beliefs. She was doing the upset parent thing and really letting Kyle have it. It wasn't the first time, either."

"Not the first time? What do you mean?"

"Josh and I were talking about the big scene after you came out,"

Helen explains. "Mrs. Faulkner found out Kyle sat next to you and helped you in gym. She called the school and demanded that Kyle be moved. So anyway, Kyle's grounded for two weeks, and he's not to see you or speak to you, ever."

I'm digesting this and I swallow hard. Being grounded after coming home with a ninety-five on his history final because he studied with a kid who happens to be gay?

"So, for me, Kyle no longer exists," I tell Helen.

"I'm really sorry," she says. "So is Kyle. He said to tell you how much he appreciates all your help. If he flunked history, he'd be off the team."

I'm reeling so bad I'm almost unsteady on my feet. I thought at last we could be friends. I feel bad for Kyle too.

"Some of this is my fault," I say.

"How's that?"

"I suggested studying at my place when I couldn't ride my bike for a few days. And I'd be lying if I said it wasn't a thrill to have Kyle at my house. And now he's in trouble because of me."

"No, Bobby," Helen says with just the lightest touch of her hand on my arm. "Kyle wanted me to tell you that it's not your fault. And please don't be upset with Josh. He feels awful about this," she says.

"Tell Josh it's okay. And tell Kyle … tell him I understand."

Helen dashes off to catch her ride with Josh. I half-stumble across the parking lot in a daze. I'm unlocking my bike when I recall something Mr. Evans said a few weeks ago in history, something about snatching defeat from the jaws of victory. Yeah, that pretty much sums it up.

WILL YOU DJ FOR US?

Chapter 44

"Mrs. Robles took your key?" Chloe shrieks while I angrily pace in front of my drums.

"I have to ask every time I come up here. Can you believe that shit?"

"So you had to *beg* your foster mother for the key to come up here today."

"You haven't heard the worst part," I tell her. "I have to keep a log. I come up to play my drums, I record it in a log; I come up to compose, it's in the log; I come up to use the PC, even for homework, it's in the log. Does that suck or what?" I'm twirling a pair of drumsticks at arm's length like an angry airplane propeller.

"Yeah, it's gross. What brought all this on?"

"Another new agent from Child Protective Services, so of course we just had to go through the whole routine—my chores, my grades, my summer lawn-mowing job, how much time I'm spending up here, my physical condition, my psychologist …"

"You're not still scared about being sent to a new foster home, are you?" she asks.

"I guess not. I mean, it's only four months to graduation."

"So what's with the key and the log book?"

"It's not the agent; the judge thought this one up," I tell her.

"The *judge?*"

"He said he wanted to prove that my time here is for specific activities."

"That sucks. I'm really sorry, Bobby," Chloe says.

"I'm just sick of all this crap. Why can't they leave me alone?"

Chloe's deep in thought while I swipe at the dust on the base of one of my music trophies lined up on a shelf. District Music Competition, 1997, it says on the plaque, and in larger letters, "First Place, Performance," for last fall's drum solo.

"So what are you going to do?" she asks.

"I guess I'll have to keep the stupid log," I tell her as my drumsticks sail through the air and clatter against the far wall.

"Gee, you're really stressed," she says.

"I'm sorry. I'm okay."

"Oh, yeah, I can see that," she says with a snort. "I'm concerned about you."

"I'll be fine," I say as I plop next to her on the couch.

"I know, but with all the pressure from the agency."

"And those stupid jerks at school."

"What jerks? Did something happen?" she asks.

"You know the group that won the right to have a prayer club at school? Well, this afternoon they had their first meeting. Guess what one of their prayers was about?" Chloe shrugs. "I found out they made a big deal about the part of the Bible they use as proof that being gay is sinful. I'm probably one of the reasons they wanted their stupid club in the first place."

Chloe gently rubs my arm. "I'm sorry," she says. "I'm still concerned. You're as stressed out and uptight as I've seen you in a long time."

I don't answer my best friend. What am I supposed to say?

"Hey, why don't we send out for pizza?" she asks. "Food is always good when you're upset."

I just shake my head and chuckle. Food is always good when *Chloe* is upset. Come to think of it, for Chloe, just like Danny, anytime is a good time for food.

* * * * *

"That's him. That's the fag I was telling you about."

Those hateful words are just loud enough for me to hear over the hallway bustle and noise between classes. I whip around to spot two punks—freshmen, no less. A few kids squawk as I elbow my way against the flow of the corridor crowds. It doesn't take long to get right in the face of the kid who looks guiltiest.

"Watch your mouth, asshole!" I shout.

He and his jerk friend play macho and glare at me before slipping away into the corridor crowd.

My next class, senior English literature, is the next door down the hallway. I'm so steamed I'm not aware of anything or anyone in the room as I storm to my desk. My books slam to the desk with a loud whap.

"Hey, man, what happened?"

I look up to see Josh hovering over my desk. "Nothing."

"You were screaming at those two kids."

"Just some asshole punks giving me the usual homophobic—"

"All right, take your seats," our teacher bellows. "Josh, we don't have all day here."

My senior English lit teacher is none other than Mr. Bentley, the homophobic, ultra-religious jerk who gave me such a hard time my sophomore year. Last August, when I reported to class on the first day and found Mr. Bentley looking down his nose at me, I wondered if I was just supremely unlucky or if God was angry with me. Since then, he's only made a couple anti-gay remarks, and I bit my tongue. Mostly he's just formal and cold. Not hostile, not nasty, just formal. Then he makes a big show of being friendly when he talks to someone else, especially if it's a guy. It gets me royally teed off, and even more so when I think about the unfair shit he did to me two years ago.

"Okay, class, you'd better be caught up in your reading assignment for *Moby Dick*," he says, sounding like a pompous jerk as usual. "Now, who can tell me what Melville was describing in—"

Kyle's slouched in his seat right in front of me, idly tapping a pen on his notebook and gazing out the window. Not long after our history tutoring last fall, his grades went right back downhill. Maybe he's daydreaming about Kathy, a really nice girl—petite, reddish-brown hair, so good looking she's stunning, never shy about speaking her mind—who became his first steady girlfriend just before Christmas. I'm happy for both of them. Or maybe Kyle's reliving the titanic upset of the football team in the second round of the playoffs, throwing the school and the entire town into a funk that lasted for weeks. Or it could be he's stressing about college. He didn't play all that well because of his knee. When the scouts stopped visiting, his dreams of a football scholarship vanished, or so I heard.

"Mr. Fowler. Mr. Fowler!"

"Sir?"

Mr. Bentley is slapping his long wooden pointer into the palm of his hand.

"Would it be too much to ask that you pay attention? We were discussing the scene at the Spouter Inn where Melville describes Ishmael and Queequeg sharing a bed. Maybe that arrangement was acceptable in the nineteenth century, but it's certainly not appropriate today. Then again, you probably think it's just normal," he sneers.

I'm too stunned to respond.

"Michelle," he says, turning his attention to a girl up front, "if Melville was describing a contemporary scene, wouldn't you as a Christian think he was deliberately trying to provoke us by the vile and repugnant notion of two men sharing a bed?"

My hardcover copy of Melville's novel slams onto the top of my desk with a crack so loud Kyle jumps.

"What did you just say?"

At first startled but quickly reddening with anger, my English teacher stalks down the aisle with his pointer held upright like a knight's lance.

"If you have a comment," he says, "you will raise your hand and wait to be called on. Otherwise, I will not tolerate that type of outburst in my classroom, understand?"

My eyes are fixed on his pointer. He's swinging it down. He's swinging it down, right at ...

"Mr. Fowler, I asked you a question. It was not rhetorical. Mr. Fowler, are you just going to sit there? You either answer me—"

Let me go! I'm sorry, let me go! They're holding me against the wall. A fist slams into my stomach. I'm gagging, trying to puke. The pain is awful.

"*What's the matter with you? Oh my God! What's happening to him?*"

An awful metallic taste fills my mouth. A warm trickle is coming from my nose and the pain is making me nauseous.

"*Someone help him. Will someone get him up off the floor?*"

Please don't hit me any more ...

"*Does anyone know what to do?*"

I'm sorry, I'm sorry, just let me go. Please don't hit me any more ... my collarbone ...

"*I think he's having a grand mal.*"

"*Someone get the nurse!*"

I don't want to die ...

"*Bobby, Bobby! Can you hear me? Oh, shit, someone get the nurse. Get the nurse!*"

Please, God, please make them stop.

"*Bobby, what's the matter? Bobby? Oh, God, what's the matter with him?*"

"*He's having a seizure. Helen, help me.*"

"*No, don't touch him!*"

Stop, stop, make them stop.

"*Well, are you happy now, Mr. Bentley? Haven't you fucking done enough?*"

"*Mr. Lessard, Bobby's having a seizure.*"

"*Oh, dear God. Everyone out of the classroom. Now!*"

I'm going to die ...

Chapter 45

"Hi, Frank. How's he doing?"

"Physically he's fine, but he's pretty shaken up. I gave him a sedative. He was a bit groggy when I last checked."

"So what the hell happened? Everyone was saying he had a grand mal."

"Actually, Joe, it wasn't a seizure. It might have looked that way, but he wasn't seizing."

"So what was it?"

"I'm quite sure he has PTSD, although I've scheduled an MRI and some other tests to be absolutely sure there's nothing else going on."

"PTSD? What the hell is that?"

"Post-traumatic stress disorder. It's like when soldiers came home from Desert Storm and for months and years after, they relived the awful things they saw—you know, like body parts blown around and friends getting killed right next to them. It's called flashbacks, although that's just one of many symptoms."

"So, Bobby was seeing things … oh my God!"

"Joe, it was worse than that. He was there. He was right back in that shower room with those three boys punching and kicking him and taking swings at him with the baseball bat."

"Jesus Christ, Frank!"

"This episode was unusually severe. Two years—it's a wonder it took so long."

"The poor kid. What an awful thing to go through."

"I hear him stirring. You can go in now. I've got your other patient next door."

A very tall, very large, balding man parts the curtain in the ER exam room. I know who it is anyway. I recognized his voice and Dr. Murkowski's when they were talking just outside.

"How are you feeling?" Mr. Lessard asks.

"Okay, I guess."

"I know you're groggy, but do you remember anything?"

"I vaguely remember voices, people screaming and crying," I reply. "They seemed far away."

"Some of the students said you were attacked. Do you—oh, hello, Judge, Mrs. Robles."

"Bobby, me boy." The judge brushes right past Mr. Lessard. Mrs. Robles stops at the foot of the bed and puts her hand to her mouth.

"I knew it. I just knew those awful head injuries were going to cause …" My foster mother turns away and begins silently weeping into her hands. The judge lightly touches her shoulder.

"There, there, Merelda, I know this is hard for you." It takes a few moments for her to calm down.

"Are you okay, dear?" she asks, dabbing at teary eyes with a tissue.

I nod that I am.

"Why don't you check in at the nurse's desk?" the judge asks her. "I believe you have to sign some consent forms." The judge leans in closer after Mrs. Robles disappears through the curtains. "Her daughter died of a brain aneurism. This is difficult for her. Joe, I'm sorry, I didn't mean to be ignoring you," he says to Mr. Lessard.

"I quite understand," he replies with a firm, two-handed handshake. "Look, Frank told me there's nothing physically wrong with Bobby, so I'm going to leave you folks alone. I'm sure he'll fill you in with all the details as soon as he's done next door." Mr. Lessard leans right over my gurney. "I'm very sorry this happened. Right now, just focus on getting back on your feet."

"Yes, sir," I mumble.

The judge leans in close with one of those intense stares of his. Not accusing, not mean, just intense.

"Was it PTSD?" he whispers.

"How did you know?"

"Just a guess," he says. He excuses himself to check on my foster mum.

"There you are! What happened? Are you all right?" A woman's frantic cries are coming from the exam room right next to this one, separated only by a curtain.

"Mom, calm down. I'm fine."

That's Kyle's voice!

"Mrs. Faulkner, Kyle's a little shaken up but physically he's fine," explains Doctor Murkowski. "Your son had a very frightening flashback. It's a clear symptom of PTSD." Doctor Murkowski explains the symptoms of post-traumatic stress disorder. I check off more than half of them.

"I told you not to quit those counseling sessions," his mom says.

"Mom, I'm fine," Kyle replies.

"Mrs. Faulkner," says Doctor Murkowski, "these symptoms can last years, and Kyle's won't just continue, they very likely will get worse. I'll set up an appointment with our resident psychologist to schedule a program for counseling and therapy."

"How did this happen, and why now?" Mrs. Faulkner asks.

"Kyle was reliving the incident at the high school when he found Bobby Fowler in the shower room. Apparently it was triggered when Bobby had a severe flashback at school today."

I hear nothing for a few moments.

"I just knew that boy would be more trouble," she says in a low voice, almost like she's clenching her teeth. I'm getting so drowsy I don't have the energy to get upset. I just want to sleep.

"Mmm, yummy, still warm."

Helen's face brightens in a sunshiny smile while I stuff the rest of a home-baked chocolate-chip cookie in my mouth.

"So this is where you live," she says, glancing all around my cramped bedroom. She smiles ever so slightly when her gaze lingers a little too long on my poster of a shirtless Brad Pitt. I realize it's not just Chloe I have a common interest with.

"Pretty neat, huh? I get two homes to live in."

"Now I see why you spend so much time up there ... oh, not that there's anything wrong with your foster home."

"No problem. I'm mostly allowed up there to work on music and use the hot tub and pool for exercise and therapy. It's demanding, but I manage."

Helen gets my little joke. "Did you hear the big news at school?" she asks.

"Mr. Bentley got fired?"

"Don't you wish. The police came and questioned him. Bobby, the news was all over school that he attacked you."

"No way! Did he go to jail?"

"No, nothing happened," she answers, "but he was shaken up, I'll say that. He didn't even give Jason detention … oh, you probably didn't hear that part." I shake my head no. "When you were on the floor and everyone was like, weirding out, Jason got right in Mr. Bentley's face and screamed at him … he used the F-word," she adds in a whisper.

"Jason?"

Helen nods.

"So what did Mr. Bentley do to … spook me?"

"Will you be okay if I tell you? I mean, you won't …"

"I hope not. Helen, I feel safe with you here." She relaxes and relates everything that happened, right up to the point where I was curled up in a ball on the floor next to a desk I tipped over, making odd, high-pitched noises, as she put it. Her eyes are glistening and she's biting her lip.

"I'm sorry …" she says, nearly whimpering.

"I can't remember any of it," I answer with a shrug. Neither of us knows quite what to say for a few awkward moments.

"So what happened to Kyle?" I ask.

"Kyle? Oh, it was so scary," she says. "After the EMTs took you out on a stretcher, I noticed Kyle standing off to the side like a statue. I asked him if he was all right a couple times, and he didn't answer. Bobby, he was looking right through me." Helen's wringing her hands. "Shit, the whole thing was so scary. First you, then Kyle."

"Did Kyle go in the ambulance?"

"No, Josh took him. When Kyle came to, he started crying. That shook me up even more, watching Kyle crying right in the middle of the classroom. The nurse came running back and said she thought he was okay but told us we should have him checked out at the hospital. I don't know which was scarier, what was happening to Kyle, or Josh racing to Memorial on two wheels."

"I heard Kyle and his mom in the exam room right next to mine."

"They made us stay in the waiting room," Helen continues. "He was only there for a couple hours."

"Is he okay?"

"Huh," she snorts. "Just before I came over, I called, and you know Kyle—it's like nothing ever happened."

"Yeah, that sounds like him. Doctor Murkowski told his mom he'll need counseling and therapy or his symptoms will get worse. You know there's lots of symptoms, don't you?"

"Not really. I never even heard of post-traumatic ... post-traumatic ...?"

"Stress disorder. Trouble concentrating, depressed emotions, trouble sleeping."

"You know, Kyle has bouts of not sleeping well, and he told me—oh, I think last spring—he'd be doing homework and he'd have trouble concentrating on what he was reading."

A light bulb just went off.

"What?" she asks.

"Are Kyle's grades slipping because he can't focus on his homework?"

Helen thinks on that for a moment.

"I never thought of that. You mean, this post-traumatic thing can affect you like that?"

"Absolutely," I reply. "I couldn't concentrate at all when I first went back to school. Poor Kyle. Maybe it's not his fault, you know, about his grades."

Helen's quiet for a few moments. "When will they make you go back to school?"

"Tomorrow," I tell her. "But maybe I can milk another day out of this."

"Yeah," she laughs, "until you start climbing the walls."

I'm tense for a few moments, thinking about my first day going back to school.

"What's the matter?" she asks.

When I put my head down in my hands, Helen gets up and sits right beside me on the edge of the bed. A comforting hand gently rubs my back.

"I feel like a freak," I tell her. "When I go back, everyone's going to be thinking, there goes the kid who had a seizure, the gay kid. It will be just like two years ago."

"Come on, Bobby, it won't be like that."

"And it's not just that. Those flashbacks ... I can't take another one of those. I *do* remember, little bits and pieces, just flashes ... horrible things," I wail. "Doctor Murkowski said there'll be more, and I don't know when the next one will hit. I don't even know what the triggers are!"

Helen slides closer and puts her arms around me as I sniffle and wipe my eyes. It's all I need to let go. She holds me tightly and gently rocks me back and forth, just like a mom, while I sob quiet tears on her shoulder. Her hand grips the back of my head—and the scars.

"Oh, I'm sorry," she says, jerking her hand away as if she had touched a hot stove.

"It's okay," I sniffle. "Here, feel right here." Her fingers find where my middle finger is pressing in. "That's where they drilled. The other scars are where they put my head back together."

"Oh, Bobby, I'm so sorry," she says, her eyes wet with tears. Helen squeezes me so hard her fingers dig into my back. "Jason told me you're a warrior," she says with a sniffle. "That's quite the compliment, coming from him."

"This is the Jason I know?"

"Yeah, imagine that. Jason's changing. He's really upset about what happened. I asked him if he wanted to come over, and he said he would, but he thought he'd be the last person you'd want to see. Maybe sometime."

And I do something that I never in a million years thought I'd do—

"Tell Jason, the next time you come over..."

Chapter 46

The hallway is flooded with the usual crush of students between classes. Someone taps my shoulder. I whip around to see Josh towering over me, all six feet three inches of him.

"I need talk to you … in private," he says. "You want to blow study hall?"

"No problem. Where to?"

"Let's go to the caf."

It's a long walk, almost the length of the school through corridors quickly emptying when the bells ring. Along the way, I have the most awful thought that he's upset with me for scaring the crap out of everyone in class, or maybe he's upset because of what happened to Kyle.

"How's Mr. Ramirez?" he asks.

"Oh, not bad. He's right out of college, but he's cool and he doesn't take any grief."

Josh grunts that he understands. When I returned to school yesterday, Mr. Lessard told me I had been reassigned to Mr. Ramirez's English lit class. It was my good luck in more ways than one. I don't have to face Mr. Bentley again, and Mr. Ramirez is young and he's hot.

"You know about the big party Beth Sandman's planning?" Josh asks as we pop through the doors of the cafeteria, empty of even the kitchen ladies. Everyone knows Beth Sandman, a cheerleader and one of the most popular girls in the senior class.

"Of course. I always get invites to Beth's parties."

Josh ignores my sarcasm.

"We were thinking maybe it would be cool if you went to her party and deejayed."

"You were *what?*"

"We were thinking you could deejay. Everyone will be there, and they'll get to hear your music. You could even hand out your CDs. So what do you think? Will you deejay for us?"

"Is this a joke?"

"No. We just thought you might have some fun, and everyone would get to hear your music. Why?"

"Because Beth's in that prayer group that sure has it in for anyone remotely gay, and never once in *four years* did I get an invite to one of her parties, and now you want me to go so I can *work?*"

"Hey, take it easy," he says, alarmed at how worked up I am. "We just wanted to do something nice for you."

"Nice? Nice? How can you call this nice? All the shit I've been taking and now I get *more shit …*"

"Come on, it's not like that. Beth's really cool—"

"Yeah, I can see she's really cool with gays."

"It's not like that. Come on, we just thought you'd have fun deejaying—"

"Fun? Working? *What the fuck, Josh?* You get the gay kid to your party with all the pretty people who shit on me, and now I can take even more shit? Well, fuck this! Just fuck this whole fucking deal! I can't fucking believe you want to torment me more. How can you do this to me? I've fucking had enough, I've had it, I've fucking had it and I can't fucking take any more of this fucking shit. I've fucking had it …"

Frozen in place, wild-eyed, not twitching a muscle, Josh is very, very quiet. I screamed at him for—I don't know for how long—and I think I was mostly incoherent. I stopped in mid-scream when I realized I had become so out of control and upset, I was in tears. Now I've added humiliation to my nuclear meltdown.

The cafeteria door crashes open with a bang as I charge outside.

"I can't take any more!" I scream into the chill of a gray, gloomy February day. I'm blasting across the back parking lot so pissed I actually can't see straight. Upset with myself, especially because I started crying, I want to get as far away from Josh and school as I possibly can. I'm across the service road, onto the grass, and where I'm going, I don't know and I don't care.

I'm tearing across a baseball field. I'm over the lines on the far side and onto another field.

And with every upset, angry step, and every whiff of raw breeze cooling me down, it's sinking in that I screamed at Josh something awful. Maybe he was trying to do something nice, even if it was a stupid idea. I bet he and Helen thought this up. Shit, I really screamed at him. It wasn't hollering, it wasn't yelling or shouting—it was all-out, throat-busting, out-of-control, bursting-into-tears, friendship-ending screaming. It was like I was blasting swears at him with a flamethrower. I had a total meltdown. At Josh.

Oh, fuck me.

"Bobby?" The voice coming from behind me, soft and tentative, belongs to Josh. "Hey, you all right?"

I'm sitting on the cold ground with my head down on my knees, so upset with myself I can't bring myself to talk to him or even look at him. Josh eases himself down, arranging himself right beside me with long arms and rangy, muscular legs.

"Hey, look, I'm sorry I triggered you off. You didn't have a, a …?"

I'm squeezing my eyes tight and I shake my head no. "I'm sorry, Josh. I'm so sorry." My eyes are tearing up, despite trying to hold everything in. "I yelled at the one guy who's been kind to me. I'm sorry, Josh, I'm sorry," I say again, sniffling and unable to hold back the tears.

"Jeez, it's freezing out here," he says, watching me shiver out here in the cold. I hear a shuffle behind me as he stands up. A heavy leather jacket is gently placed over my shoulders like a cape. Josh kneels on one knee next to me.

"Can you get up?" he asks.

I nod that I can. Feeling totally stupid about what happened, and now even worse because I got so emotional, I wipe my eyes hard and slowly get to my feet. I can't look at him.

"Are you okay?" he asks.

I'm trying to tell him I'm fine, but instead I burst into tears.

"I just can't take any more. I'm sorry I'm losing it," I sob. "I wanted to make it through this year and just get out of here, but I've got nothing left; there's just nothing left. It must be my fault."

"Shit," he says under his breath. "It's not your fault, you understand?" he barks. Running a hand through curly blond hair, Josh paces back and forth. "It's not your fault," he repeats, his words insistent and angry. And then Josh does the unexpected. He wraps his arms around me, pulling me close. I feel his hand mussing my hair on the back of my head. Fingers rub over the scars and jerk away, just like Helen did.

"I'm sorry," he says in an oddly strained voice.

I look up to see Josh grimacing with his eyes shut tight.

"It's just not fair," he whispers.

"Hey, guys, is everything okay?"

Josh jolts away. Somehow, Mr. Ramirez has tracked us down.

"Mr. Ramirez, Bobby got really upset and needed to cool off," Josh tells him. Mr. Ramirez takes his time looking me over.

"Bobby, is everything all right?" he asks.

"Yeah, I guess so. I got real upset at Josh, and I feel like a total idiot."

"Look, you had every reason to go off the deep end," Josh says. "The stress on you must be unbelievable. Mr. Ramirez, Bobby's been under too much pressure, and he kind of lost it. I'm going to take him home."

I'm rubbing eyes that must be so raw; I don't want to be seen back at school. Mr. Ramirez is considering Josh's offer.

"Josh, tell Madeleine, and then get your car and we'll both take him home." Josh is hesitating. "I'll make sure Bobby's all right. Go ahead, we'll meet you by the cafeteria. Go!"

With Josh pumping long legs back toward school, it's only now I realize that I had walked across three sports fields to a point about as far from the main school building as you can get. It's just Mr. Ramirez and me, with Josh's brown leather coat hanging to my knees, out here in the February chill.

"Sometimes things can get overwhelming," Mr. Ramirez says. He nods toward the main building. As we begin the long walk back, a strong arm wraps around my shoulders and pulls me close.

"Listen to me, *amigo muy especial*," he says close to my ear. "You are a hero to every gay person in school, and the whole town for that matter. You know that, don't you?" I shake my head no. "Well, you are. Two freshman boys are going to come out to their parents and friends this week, and it's because you are their inspiration. You, Bobby, are their hero."

"Me?"

"Yes, you. There are other gay boys and girls at Dunston High School. Some of them don't know it yet, some do and aren't out, but every one of them knows who Bobby Fowler is. There are people in town afraid to come out, but they know who Bobby Fowler is. They see you out and proud of who you are. They see you stand up for yourself and what you believe in. Bobby, I'm gay. I wish just once in my life I could have half the courage you show every day."

Mr. Ramirez's arm remains around my shoulder as we head back. Just when I thought the stress was going to crush me, I'm caught by Josh, who could have and should have beaten the shit out of me, and now by Mr. Ramirez, who has given me comfort and hope in a way that Josh and Helen and Chloe and all the rest can never fully understand.

Chapter 47

"Helen, Bobby Fowler's here," Mrs. Albrecht hollers down the cellar stairway. "Hon, why don't you go right on down and make yourself at home," she says with a bright, cheery smile.

Unlike my usual machine-gun clatter going down stairs, my steps are slow and tentative. From the cars and two pickup trucks parked out front, I know it's not just Helen and Josh waiting for me, it's all of them. And another thing I figured out: Helen set this up because of what happened after school yesterday, just one day after what Danny calls "The Texas Chernobyl."

Helen had asked me to meet her in the lobby right after school. When she showed up, Beth Sandman was tagging along. They wanted to explain about the prayer group, Helen told me.

Beth said she went to one meeting of the new Christian club when a friend asked her to go. She quit after she saw what "traditional family values" really meant, and especially when she heard that not only did her views not reflect the true word of God, her views wouldn't be allowed. Beth told me she heard what happened with Josh the day before and said she was sorry I was upset at her. When I asked Beth if that meant she was still asking me to deejay at her party, she said she only wanted to tell me the real story and how bad she felt. I walked away with a new level of respect for Beth but said nothing about deejaying at her party.

At the bottom of the stairs, I'm even more wary as I encounter eight pairs of eyes focused on me. Kyle, Josh, Jason, and Dustin—the Four Amigos—are waiting for me with their girlfriends in what looks to be a finished rec room. Josh, always friendly, jumps up off the couch he was squeezed onto with Helen, Jason, and Jason's girlfriend, Chrissy.

"Hey, man, come on in. We're not going to bite," he says. "Here, have a seat." Josh pulls out a tall stool with a round swivel seat and a low backrest. It's one of four arranged in front of an impressive curved bar, complete with an overhead rack of glassware, a sink, and a Coors Light neon sign hanging on the wall. Taking up most of the far end of the room is a pool table with a long green lampshade suspended low from the ceiling.

"Bobby! You're limping," Helen says.

"Yeah, I pushed a little too hard in the gym a couple days ago."

"Is this the leg—" Helen's hand flies to her mouth.

"I'm fine," I tell her as I remove my backpack and hop onto the stool. "When my leg hurts like this, it usually goes away in a few days."

"So you've been hurting—"

"Nothing I haven't had before," I tell her. The group sitting on the other side of the coffee table is studying me, making me feel like this is an inquisition, missing only the bright light.

"I guess I'm supposed to start," Jason says with a nervous look toward Helen. "Look, we're all upset about all the crap that's been going on. You know, those punk kids you yelled at, and that awful flashback, and you being so upset and all. And all of us, especially me, we're sorry about all the shit that happened since you got here, and we're proud of how you hung in there. So," he says with a nod to his friends on each side, "we decided that the Four Amigos are going to *destroy* any assholes that give you any more shit." With a whap of his thick fist in the other hand, it's Mr. Macho at his most macho.

"Yeah, man," says Josh, "we feel real bad about all the pressure on you. Jeez, I don't know about these guys, but I couldn't have made it if I went through what you did after losing my folks."

They know about Mom and Dad? I throw Kyle a look.

"Hey, I'm sorry," he says, gulping hard, "but I thought it was time these guys knew what really happened. I'm sorry. I hope you're not upset."

"Bobby," Helen chimes in before I can tell Kyle it's not a problem, "Chloe told me how upset you've been about the state agency, and now on top of that, you've been in pain."

"No wonder you fucking cracked," Jason mutters, more to himself while biting a fingernail. Helen frowns, I'm guessing because Jason's language isn't welcome in the Albrecht household.

"We're trying to help and we're trying to change," Helen says. "All of us. I'm sorry this took so long, and maybe it's way too late, but to me, you're not the Gay Kid anymore. Bobby, you're a very talented and really nice guy who happens to be gay."

"Thanks, Helen. I didn't think I'd ever hear that."

"You're up again," Josh signals to Jason.

Jason gulps, gets up off the coach, stuffs his hands in his pockets, and begins pacing.

"Look, I don't want you to get upset," he says. He swallows again, this time even louder. "I told these guys I figured out why I was so angry at you for being gay." Jason has stopped less than an arm's length from me. He nervously runs a hand through his blond hair. "Don't get upset, okay? I, uh, I told them I thought anyone who was gay was nothing but a little fairy."

"You think I'm a little fairy?"

"No! Not anymore. I mean, I thought guys who were gay were little sissies and didn't have any guts and couldn't throw a football. Not real boys, you know? Maybe you can't throw a football, but I watched you fight back from those awful injuries and go through rehab like an Army Ranger. One of the trainers at the downtown gym told me you lift weights as intense as anyone. And I know you practiced through pain to play your drums again. Yeah, I'll say. Some of the shit you were doing in that contest, like when you were playing like crazy and holding one stick in the air, that was just sick, man.

"And then Kyle was telling us how you were hurting from losing your folks and moving here and taking all sorts of shit from us, especially from me, and you have to take it all alone." Jason hesitates, his brow creased, his lips clamped together. "I don't know how you ever hung in there, I just don't," he whispers. He returns to the couch, and his girlfriend Chrissy rubs his back. Shorter than Helen, cute and freckled, Chrissy is shy and talks almost in a whisper.

"Jason said you've got more courage than all of us put together," she says in her usual sweet way.

"Thanks, man," I say to Jason.

Not a sound can be heard for several long moments.

"Is this a *quid pro quo*?" I finally ask. They're all looking at one another and shrugging their shoulders. "Sorry, judge talk. Is this a deal?

I deejay, you guys watch my back?" This time Helen gets up off the couch and paces right next to me. She gently rubs my back.

"Bobby, what they're trying to say is that with or without you deejaying for Beth, we all want to protect you from getting bullied anymore just because you're gay." Helen surprises me with a light, sweet kiss on my cheek.

It's utterly silent as I try to figure out what to do. I suppose I could tell them all to go screw. Even after I recovered, they all looked the other way when someone gave me shit, at least until now. Jason or Dustin or even Kyle would call me the Gay Kid behind my back once in a while, and some of the shit they did still hurts.

But as I scan their faces, I'm not so sure. Kyle looks concerned. It's the Kyle who didn't get really pissed the night I made a complete fool of myself, the Kyle who visited me when I needed it the most. Then there's Josh. How could he be so nice after what I did? Kyle told me Josh is the nicest guy he ever knew.

And Helen has to be one of the most wonderful girls I've ever known. With her looks and goody-goody talk and too-perfect smile, it would be easy to think she's fake, but Helen is anything but. Mrs. Robles said Helen's Christian values are what they're supposed to be. And then there's Jason, who had the guts to come to my house that time and tell me he was sorry, and now, what a surprise! Kathy? Dustin and his girlfriend of the moment? They've been the quietest. Maybe it's time for a leap of faith.

The tension is peaking as they wait for me to make up my mind. It's so quiet the buzzing of the neon sign behind me sounds like a bedroom mosquito right in my ear. It's when Helen casts a worried look at Josh—and he responds by holding her hand tightly—that I know what to do with complete certainty. I bolt right off the stool.

"I'm going to need two four-plug receptacles, 120 volts, GFI, total of 70 amps," I announce in a loud rush of words. "I'll need a long table and a lot of help to bring my amps and speakers, my deejay deck, mixing board, and all my other equipment to wherever and get it all set up."

I'm wound up and pacing in front of the bar and talking ever louder and more rapidly.

"Two of the speakers will be suspended from the ceiling, and everything will have to be cabled. I'll rent a lighting system and I'll need help installing it. Someone will have to help with electrical supply, Danny and Chloe get invites or it's no deal, and just exactly where is this?" I'm so hyped up, I'm almost shouting. No one answers for a few moments.

"Uh … it's at Beth's house … they have a basement," Dustin mumbles.

"Great. We're going to put the lighting system along the sides. I'll get a smoke machine and some strobes and lasers, but maybe the room's too low for a ball. I'll need to control all the lighting from my central console. And by the way," I add even louder, "I have rules or it's no deal: no fighting, no weapons, no requests for heavy metal or country or any of that crap, no throwing up on the dance floor, and no anti-gay anything," I count off on my fingers. "Oh, and what are the hours?"

Again, no one answers. All of them, the Four Amigos and their girlfriends, sit motionless, just staring back, some with their mouths open as if they're in shock. Josh looks to his left and then to his right for help. No one makes eye contact with him.

"Well, maybe we can do eight to eleven-thirty?" Josh asks in a small, meek voice.

I stare back in amazement, wondering if he could possibly be joking.

Flustered, Josh looks to Helen, who shrugs her shoulders.

"Well, we could do less if that's too much," Josh says, now looking to Jason for help. He shrugs *his* shoulders. "Like eleven," Josh continues. "We could do eleven. You just tell us what you want to do."

"*Eleven? Eleven?* You want to *end* at *eleven?*"

Josh, now even more flustered, whips around when Kyle bursts out laughing.

"What's the joke? What did I do wrong?" Josh asks Kyle, who's now laughing so hard he's slapping his knee and doubling over.

"You doofus," Kyle yells back, "he wants to *start* at eleven."

"Look, let's start at eight thirty or nine," I suggest. "Maybe we'll go to two or three, or I'll go all night if that's what you want. I don't care how many hours I spin, as long as everyone's having a good time … and there's a lot of hot guys there," I add with a grin.

"Oh, I don't think you need to worry about a lot of hot guys at this party," Kathy answers with a sly smirk.

"Oh yeah, I almost forgot the final rule," I tell her. "Hot guys, no shirts." Kathy shrieks with laughter. Helen and Chrissy stretch across Josh and Jason to exchange a high five. But Kyle's giving me an odd look. I can't quite figure it out until I remember Kyle stripping to his swimsuit last fall. Kyle *loves* showing off that body. He jumps up off the arm of the chair.

"Guys, you have no idea what you're in for," he says, so excited he's waving his arms. "You're all going to get *blown away*. This guy's making his own dance music, and it's hotter than anything you've ever heard!"

"How do you know so much about his dance music?" Dustin asks in a suspicious tone. Kyle glances at me to bail him out.

"Danny gave Kyle two of my CDs," I explain.

"CDs? What CDs?" Jason asks.

"He's been making his own dance CDs," Josh replies. "They're all over school. Dude, where ya been?"

I reach for my backpack and dump ten CDs onto the coffee table with a plastic clatter.

"Here, I brought two complete sets of my dance music. Help yourself, and if anyone wants more, just ask."

Jason is the first to reach into the pile. He holds a CD up close to study the cover.

"Axis four? You made this?" he asks.

Josh rips the CD out of Jason's hands and points to the bottom of the cover liner on the back.

"You see this, Worlds End Records? That's Bobby's record label. Not only did he make the CD, he owns the record company."

"*He what?* The gay kid owns … oh, shit." Jason grimaces when he realizes what he just said.

"Jason, it's okay," I tell him. "I even call myself the gay kid sometimes." I offer a handshake. "Can we just be friends?" Nodding his head, Jason stands to grasp my hand.

"Yeah, friends. I guess there's a lot I never knew about you. Holy shit, your own record label."

Kyle is still so worked up he's pacing in front of the coffee table.

"You guys better listen to me," he says. "This is going to be major. It will be like the music contest, only you can dance to it. Every one of you guys is going to get *totally blown away!*"

"Look, Kyle's exaggerating, but I promise to play my hottest, high-energy dance music," I tell them. "I play pretty loud, too … uh, make that really, really loud. Will we get in trouble with the police?

"Oh, I really don't think so," Kathy replies.

"Why's that?"

"Beth's father is the chief of police."

Chapter 48

School's just out, and Mr. Ramirez is standing to greet me in his homeroom. Next to him are two nervous twelve-year-olds.

"Bobby, this is Eddie and this is Jimmy."

"Hey guys, what's up?" I nod toward them. Neither extends a hand or says hello.

"Bobby, these boys have something to tell you." He looks at the two like an approving mother hen when neither makes a move. "Go ahead, you can do this," he says to them. "I know it's hard. Just take your time."

The one who was introduced as Eddie, the taller one, skinny like most kids his age, black hair cut short with a little lift in front, nervously fidgets with his hands. Several tense moments go by.

"I'm gay," he blurts out.

"I'm gay, too," the other one says.

"What grade are you guys in?" I ask, immediately realizing I just said the dumbest thing of all time to two kids just coming out.

"They're both freshmen," Mr. Ramirez chimes in before I can say something even less supportive. Still, it's hard to believe these two are in high school. Jimmy must be reading my mind.

"I'm fifteen," he says.

"Me too," Eddie adds with a little edge to his voice.

"These are the two boys I was referring to last week," Mr. Ramirez says. "They've told their folks, and it went ... it went pretty well, and now you're the only other person at school who knows. Hey, guys, I'm really, really proud of you."

And I know what to do. I hold my arms out wide to Jimmy, the one closest to me, and embrace him in a tight hug.

"I'm proud of you, too," I tell Eddie as he gets a hug. Both of these kids are adorable, but Jimmy, a little chunkier, with perfect, pale skin, blond hair styled with the same cute haircut, and a look I can only describe as angelic, really does look twelve.

Mr. Ramirez again nods to them to say something.

"We want to thank you," Eddie says.

"You're our hero," Jimmy adds.

"Me? I'm no hero."

"But you're the only out gay kid in school," Eddie explains. "We wouldn't be out if it wasn't for you."

Jimmy's eyes light up.

"We're going to tell our friends this afternoon!"

"Yeah," Eddie says, a lot less confident than his friend.

"Are you two guys, like, together?" I ask.

They both nod and smile. Eddie reaches for Jimmy's hand.

"We've been together for three months," Eddie says. "We do everything together. We even sleep together on weekends."

"Yeah, and his older brother gets really pissed because Eddie gets to sleep with me, and his mom won't let him sleep with his girlfriend," Jimmy says. I have to think about that for a moment. It makes perfect sense, but still, it's a surprise.

"We sing and dance together," Eddie says.

"Like an act?" I ask him.

A worried look passes between them.

"It's okay," says Mr. Ramirez. "He won't bite."

"We made up lyrics to a couple of your trance tracks. I hope you're not upset."

"Come on, guys, that's so totally cool. Hey, maybe this weekend you can come over to my recording studio and sing through my system."

Two pairs of eyes light up. I get a sudden, crazy idea.

"What?" Mr. Ramirez asks.

"It's pretty wild. How would you guys like to …"

"What do you mean, you ordered fabric?" Chloe screeches at her usual megaphone volume. Only a few nearby students eating lunch, apparently recently arrived in Texas, look our way. Danny leans forward to hear my answer.

"I ordered a whole bunch of fabric on the Internet from this supplier of used exhibition materials, half cream-colored and half purple."

Chloe makes a face.

"How'd you ... where ... what is going on with you?"

"I got a lot of help from this guy I told you about, you know, the guy I met in a gay AOL chat room."

"The guy in Boston?" Danny asks.

"Yeah. I told him about the party, and he's been sending suggestions and advice on everything , like lighting, sound system, decorating, glow sticks, stuff like that. He even helped me locate suppliers."

Chloe gives me a squinty-eyed suspicious look. "How are you going to pay for all this?" she asks.

"This must be thousands of dollars," Danny says.

"All that fabric—sixty bucks. Paul located a lighting system guy right in Austin, and he's giving me everything for one fifty. I already have most of the sound system, and the same guy rented me an extra speaker and a bigger amp and a smoke system for another one fifty."

"That's still a lot of money," Chloe says. "Oh, I know. You hit up the judge. You did, didn't you!" I nod, and Chloe beams with that look of supreme satisfaction when "girls just know" everything that boys do or think, even gay boys.

Danny's sitting back with that almost easy-to-miss smirk. He thinks it's entertaining when Chloe figures boys out, unless, of course, it happens to him.

"Why are you making such a big deal of this?" he asks. "Jeez, it's not even your party."

When I respond with a shrug, Chloe lights up and points a finger in my face.

"It's the gay drama thing. I know you, Robert Fowler. You *love* drama!" My face is getting warmer. "Danny, it's just like the music contest. Remember when he put his drums up on a riser and every stage light in the place was pointing right at him?"

Danny ignores her.

"You still haven't said what you're going to do with fabric."

"Well, you'll just have to wait and see for yourself when you and your mystery date show up," I tell him. "You do have a date, don't you?"

Danny hesitates.

"*You don't!*" Chloe screeches.

"I do too," he snaps. "Tomorrow night you'll meet the girl who can't keep her hands off me."

I glance at Chloe, but she's busy chugging milk instead of busting him. After some awkward scenes and hurt feelings, Chloe and I push the dating thing just so far. If Danny was as good with girls as he is at getting all A's, my good-looking friend would have girls lined up at his front door. His only steady lasted all of three weeks, and that was last spring. Sometimes I wonder if he really wants a Cambodian girl to date. Boy, can I relate to not having anyone to date!

"You're nervous, aren't you?" Chloe asks as we stroll back to our lockers for afternoon classes.

I respond with a shrug.

"Don't deny it. I know you are."

Nothing gets by Chloe.

"I play gay dance music. What if they don't like it? What if hardly anyone shows up? What if something goes wrong and the equipment doesn't work? What if—"

"Would you stop? Everything's going to be fine. And besides, Kyle will be there," she says with a coy smirk. I grab Chloe by the elbow, stopping her right in the middle of the crowded corridor as students push past us.

"I don't have fantasies about Kyle, I don't daydream about Kyle, I don't stare at Kyle … he's just not part of my life," I hiss so others won't overhear. "Now get off the Kyle thing, Chloe."

Chloe's eyes grow big. She and I have disagreements, but we never fight. I'll apologize later for barking at her. But ever since our tutoring sessions ended badly last fall and Kyle got in big trouble, Chloe knows I've put him out of my mind once and for all.

This is a first. Helen asked if I needed a ride home from school. So here I am in the back seat of Josh's big, old Ford convertible, with an unusually warm February sun beating down, the custom stereo cranked up with country rock, Josh and Helen rocking side to side, and the wind blowing my hair about wildly.

"How can Kyle and Kathy go to the party if I'm there?" I holler. Helen turns the volume down and exchanges a look with Josh. Even though he's wearing sunglasses, Josh and I make eye contact in the rearview mirror.

"Kyle had Kathy tell his mom about it," he says. "I guess it was okay as long as he's going with Kathy."

"That's cool. I hope enough people show up."

"Enough people?" Helen screeches. "Haven't you heard? Beth said the whole school's talking about it. She's so afraid of everyone crashing the party, she's handing out written invitations. I heard her father is going to station a cop at the end of their road."

Josh snorts. "Yeah, Helen and her friends saw to that."

"And you and Kyle and Jason, for that matter," Helen declares.

"What've you guys been doing?" I ask. This time, Josh half turns around.

"Oh, they're telling everyone you're one of the top DJs in the country, and that you'll be making a 'guest appearance' at Beth's party, complete with lights and a big sound system—"

"Just like a big club," Helen chimes in.

"You're telling everyone I'm a top DJ?"

"That's what they're telling everyone," Josh answers with a grin.

"Oh, great. I'm maybe the thousandth best."

"Come on, Bobby, even Kyle's been raving about your music," Helen says. "He's playing your music nonstop."

"*Kyle?*"

"When he's running, when he's studying, when he goes to bed. He said he'll get a song going through his head over and over, like it's on a loop," Josh explains.

"Holy shit," I murmur to myself.

Helen turns completely around in her seat. "You must be getting excited."

"Yeah, I am. In some ways, this is more exciting than my job in Austin."

"What job in Austin?" Josh asks.

"Didn't I ever tell you?" Helen asks him. "He's a DJ in Austin."

Josh looks up into the rearview mirror, his eyes big with surprise.

"It's called Club Réalité," I tell him. "After I won the DJ contest last summer—Helen, remember I told you about that?—I've been deejaying there every month or so.

"Hey, babe, maybe he really is one of the top DJs in the country," Josh says just as he pulls into Super Ace Foods. "Wait till I tell Jason he's a DJ in Austin!"

"This is going to be the best party ever!" Helen squeals after she and

Josh kiss. She's so excited she almost skips into the store to her part-time job.

"Hey, man, I'm really sorry I can't help tomorrow," Josh says as he roars out of the parking lot with me in the front seat. "I have to work at the 7-Eleven until six."

"No problem. We've got a whole crew and a pickup truck lined up, so we should be all set. Even Jason will be there."

"Hey, Jason's a really good guy. He feels really bad about everything you went through," Josh says. "And you have no idea how blown away he was when he found out about your record label. It's all he talked about for the rest of the week."

The strangest feeling comes over me, like the earth under me is shifting. And it's not just Jason. It's everything that's happened over the last two weeks—the Four Amigos at Helen's, Mr. Ramirez, the party, Eddie and Jimmy, my talk with Beth, on and on.

"Jase is going in the army next August," Josh goes on. "Being an Army Ranger is all he's ever dreamed about. And you know what he said about you? He said, 'That guy's got enough guts to be an Army Ranger.' That has to be the biggest compliment of all time."

Josh's old Ford careens into my driveway in a cloud of dust, braking to a stop so hard I have to brace my hand on the dashboard. I tell him thanks. He nods as I hop out.

I'm halfway to the door when he shouts. He's just sitting there, leaning over the door with long arms draped over the side. I return when it's clear that he has more to say.

"It wasn't just Jason that was blown away," he says, propping his sunglasses on the top of his head.

"What do you mean?"

"Everyone was. When you were at Helen's, you came across like … like you were in total control. It was kind of like Coach Grady at halftime. You were freakin' unbelievable."

"I … I didn't mean—"

"Hey, it wasn't anything bad. It was the way you took charge that surprised us. You've always been sort of quiet and kept your head down, and then—blam! You took total control like none of us has ever heard before. Helen said it was another side of you she's never seen before. Hey, gotta go." Josh backs his car out of the driveway in another giant cloud of dust that mercifully blows toward the other side of the road.

With a plume of dirty exhaust, a chirp from his tires, and a brief wave, he rockets back toward town.

I'm deep in thought about what Josh said as I trudge to my room. It's not often that I learn something about myself.

With a scrape of my chair, I slide behind my desk. As I've done so many times, I stare out at the dry, brown fields of scrub and scattered oaks silhouetted by the late afternoon sun. I sit here just wondering—about who I am, about life, about the things that have happened recently, about what Josh said. Not much time passes before a smile curls my lips. *This is going to be one party that Dunston High School will never forget.*

Chapter 49

The front door swings open to reveal not Beth, but the scowling face of Andy, one of our biggest football players. Danny and his date Emily, a whiny, high-strung, red-haired junior who thinks she's Danny's equal as a computer geek, take a step back.

"You got an invitation?" Andy growls.

Intimidated, maybe thinking he's supposed to produce a written invitation, Danny shakes his head no.

"Well, get lost."

"Hey, Andy," I shout before he can slam the door.

"Bobby? Hey, man, why didn't you say something? Come on, Beth's waiting for you." A 320-pound, blond-haired senior football player I hardly ever speak to because he said something nasty to me sophomore year, Andy is so big he doesn't have a neck. He gives me a friendly, one-of-the-guys smile and extends a meaty hand that engulfs mine.

Beth's living room is already packed and noisy with excited party talk and laughter. Over in the doorway leading to the kitchen, one couple is already going at it with hands all over each other. Not exactly what I wanted to see.

In the hallway, a crew-cut sophomore boy is talking with two flirting, giggling junior girls. It's no mystery how a sophomore scored an invitation to this party. It's not that he's especially athletic or tall or well-built; it's just that this kid is so cute and his sex appeal so high in the stratosphere, he became the favorite of every girl the first day he walked into school. Mine too!

"Bobby!" a girl shrieks. It's Beth, squeezing past the couple making out. "The downstairs—everyone's like, blown away!" she hollers from three feet away. "This is so totally awesome!" she shrieks, so excited she's bouncing up and down.

Whatever is on her breath is almost knocking me out.

"Hey, Beth, you know Danny and Emily—"

"Yeah, hi. Do you want a beer?" she asks me, hardly glancing at my friends. "The guys brought *three kegs*. They're out back in Ryan's pickup."

"No, thanks. I don't drink when I'm working."

"Oh my gosh, this is *incredible!* Hey, everyone, Bobby Fowler's here, *he's here!*" Almost everyone in the living room looks up. I wave, just a slight wiggle of my hand. Most call out friendly, happy greetings, and two couples and a few guys bound over to shake my hand and slap my back and talk about how they can't believe what they found downstairs. Soon, however, most return their attention to their dates or talking with friends.

On a table right next to the door leading to the cellar is the basket I had filled with glow sticks. Not one kid has one on. Country bumpkins!

I grab one, snap it around my neck in a glowing circle of blue, and hand a couple to Danny as we pound down the stairs. On the overhead on the way down is a sign done in fluorescent orange, lit by a black light tacked to the wall. *Club Xtreme,* it announces. It was Danny's idea.

"Oh my God!" Emily shrieks about ten times when the entire cellar comes into view.

Danny grins and nudges me with his elbow.

"Told you she'd flip out."

Everyone flipped out when we finished a few hours earlier. Chief Toby said, "Holy crow! You've turned my basement into a club!" Then he told his wife to take the good china off the shelves after I did a trial run of the sound system.

From the top of the metal support post in the middle of the cellar, long swaths of fabric in alternating purple and cream sweep out in graceful, expanding arcs to the perimeter and then down the walls, creating a dramatic, festive canopy. Each of the three support posts in the middle of the cellar glows with strings of white lights wrapped from top to bottom. Encasing each post is a square column of translucent cream fabric, stapled at the top and bottom to simple wood frames. Club lights and strobes hang from the rafters in two neat rows near the sides. The effect is stunning.

It's a squeeze to get behind the equipment-packed table, which Chief

Toby placed kitty-corner opposite the stairs to create a little DJ booth. Josh and Helen and a few dozen others already down here crowd around when they realize we're about to start. Josh hesitates when I hold out a pair of headphones.

"Come on, put these on," I tell him. Confused, he looks to Helen. "Josh, you can help with the first mix, and then I promise I'll give you back to Helen."

Lighting up with one of his wonderfully goofy smiles, Josh adjusts the fit while both he and Helen squeeze behind the table.

"Are you guys ready?" I ask them.

Josh gives me a thumbs-up, but Helen—so excited she's almost hyperventilating—is clapping her hands rapidly and bouncing up and down.

With the flick of a switch, every overhead light in the cellar goes out, and just as if controlled by a switch, the cellar becomes instantly silent. The needle eases down into the soft vinyl groove …

thump – thump – thump – thump
I just wanna dance
I just wanna dance
I just wanna dance – dance – dance!

The track kicks into deafening high gear, along with every club light and strobe light and the two lasers. In a few moments, the strobes will blind everyone with staccato bursts, and the first shot of stage smoke will billow into the room. Danny already has his sunglasses on, protection against the glare. I reach for mine, a pair of neat white wraps that Chloe picked out just for tonight.

Danny shouts something I can't make out and points toward the stairs. A stampede of kids is actually running and leaping down the cellar steps and pushing their way into the crowd. Danny shouts again. *Wicked cool,* I think.

I motion to Josh to do the first mix. He prods the slide control with little taps, looking to me for approval with each tap.

"You did it!" I holler over the music when the mix is complete. Josh raises a fist high in the air and lets go with a cowboy yee-ha so loud, Helen doubles over laughing.

"Go dance, go dance!" I scream at them. "And here, hand these out." Josh and Helen drift through the crowd, offering glow sticks to everyone and showing them how they snap on. Soon, the cellar is full of neon circles of blues and yellows and reds and greens. Motionless neon circles, that is. It's no big surprise that not one couple is dancing. At the club, it sometimes takes an hour for the first people to get out on the dance floor. Tonight it will just take one brave couple. Like Helen and Josh.

My body twisting, my butt shaking, my headphone cord bouncing wildly as I lip-synch to a hot diva hit, my eyes closed imagining a hot boy holding his hips to mine, I'm dancing up a sweat. I have never felt so alive! The concrete floor under me is spattered with my sweat.

Unlike the club, where the sides are thick with guys watching the action out on the floor, or cruising around, or imagining themselves making out with the hot guy who'll never give them even one look, every person in Beth's cellar is dancing. The energy and the vibe are incredible, but some of these guys dance like cavemen with two left feet.

"This is amazing!" someone shouts. It's Kathy, with Kyle holding her tightly around the waist. "How did you do all this?" she asks.

I shrug with a grin.

"This music makes me want to dance," she says.

"I was scared no one would like the music," I holler back. Kathy leans way over the table.

"Everyone loves it. It's so crowded people are dancing upstairs. You wouldn't believe how far down the road we had to park."

While she's been talking, Kyle's been staring. Not looking, staring. It's so unsettling I'm not sure what to say.

He realizes he's staring when Kathy nudges him and nods toward the dance floor.

"Where'd you get the cool shades?" he shouts. I'm trying to tell him, but Kathy has already grabbed his hand to drag him onto the dance floor. He looks back briefly before they disappear into the shaking, juking, jam-packed crowd of dancers.

Chloe just came in with a girl who she introduced as her cousin Louise from San Antonio. I'm disappointed Chloe doesn't have a real date, but she's out there with large, gold hoop earrings jangling around crazily as she shakes and jams like she does in my cellar. Her cousin, a tall, gangly, lighter-skinned girl with a pleasant, round face, straight black hair, and as quiet as Chloe is loud, is one of those annoying people who dances with their heads bobbing back and forth exactly like a chicken pecking at feed. But Chloe is blissfully unconcerned with her cousin's dancing or what anyone thinks of her own crazed contortions. She's in a little trance world.

A cheer sweeps through the crowd. I'm on my tiptoes, looking all around, but there's no guy making a fool of himself, no girl lifting her blouse. I look to Chloe, questioning with my hands palms up. She leans way over the table.

"We were cheering at the end of that long crescendo," she explains with her hand cupping my ear. "I think everyone's just happy." She rejoins her cousin and shakes and rolls and boogies harder than ever.

I'm admiring Chloe's free spirit and the crowd's high energy when I feel eyes on me. The first one with his shirt off in the now stuffy, sweaty cellar, Kyle is dancing facing the DJ table. He instantly looks away when our eyes lock. No thumbs-up, no signal, nothing.

I watch for a few moments. Except for Eddie and Jimmy, he dances better than anyone else down here, way beyond some of these uptight guys who don't even move their feet. Kyle is grooving with his ass swaying back and forth, his eyes closed in a dancing trance, his arms and his whole body expressive, just like the club kids in Austin. Little trails of sweat streak his arms and chest. As his pants slide lower, I don't see a hint of boxers, just those sharp creases that run from his hips to his groin. It's hard to see from here, but those pants are riding awfully low on his butt. I wonder if …

Maybe I should do the next mix.

Chapter 50

"There's two kids at the door," Josh yells over the sonic thumps of the subwoofer. "I told them to get lost, but they said you invited them."

"They made it!" I screech. Waving and pantomiming to Danny to fill in, he and Emily squeeze through the crowd to get to the DJ booth.

Josh and I encounter a throng of kids on the stairs watching the packed mass of dancers below. I, too, can't resist stopping to watch. The cellar is a sea of heads bobbing and jamming with club lights playing over them like New Year's Eve searchlights in Times Square. A thin fog of stage smoke lights up like lightning in a storm when the strobes fire off rapid bursts. In the tight space of Beth's cellar, this is even cooler than the club. Josh taps my arm to get going.

"These kids look like they're in seventh grade," he gripes when we reach the hallway. "What are they doing here?"

"You'll see."

Josh reaches for the knob and flings the heavy oak door wide open. Taking a step back when they see him in the doorway are none other than Eddie and Jimmy.

"Hey, you guys made it!" I holler. Before either says a word, I'm reaching for Jimmy to give him a tight hug, and quickly follow with one for his boyfriend. Jimmy's under one arm and Eddie's drawn close with the other as I turn back toward Josh.

"Josh, this is Jimmy, this is Eddie. I asked Beth if they could come to hear the music and dance, and she said it was okay. And, guys, you can dance together."

"What the ..." Josh sputters.

"Josh, they're gay and they're a couple."

"How old are you guys? Twelve?"

"Fifteen," they both snap.

Josh gives me a you've-got-to-be-kidding-me look and steps back to let us in. A few kids in the living room notice our little procession and stare. Josh shrugs at one surprised girl when Eddie and Jimmy hold hands.

Like everyone else, they stop near the bottom of the stairs, their eyes lighting up in Christmas-morning wonderment. I try to imagine myself as a freshman coming down these steps to discover a cellar overflowing with older kids, all dancing under the colorful canopy and the lights and strobes and the overpowering beat of a hot diva hit.

Danny, who knew they were coming and knows about the big surprise we have planned for later, exchanges high-fives and shoos them out onto the dance floor. Eddie and Jimmy instantly let loose, their moves uninhibited and expressive, full of energy and joy. I can't stop watching them.

"Look at those two dance!" I shout to Chloe, who's close by. She watches for a moment and leans in close.

"They dance like the kids at the club," she says.

Both are wearing bulky pants worn dangerously low on slim hips and tight sleeveless shirts. Cute haircuts glisten with gel. Even more amazing, both had the colossal balls to use glitter. They're gay, they're proud, and they're letting everyone know it.

Couples nearby stare and talk into each other's ears. I can imagine the comments. *Those two boys are dancing together! They're so young!* I'm loving it. Welcome to the new world, Dunston High School.

Impulsively I decide to join in. Eddie and Jimmy react with shrieks of glee. Another long track is on, an eighteen-minute mix with a quiet interlude in the middle and a long crescendo at the end that will drive this crowd into a jumping, cheering, sweaty frenzy. Danny, at first surprised to see me dancing with the two kids, gives me a thumbs-up. Meanwhile, Emily pouts with arms crossed and a sour expression because she's stuck in the DJ booth. I'll let Danny handle Emily. After all, he reminded me at least four times a day this week that he wanted to help deejay.

"This is totally awesome!" Eddie screeches.

"It's the first time we've ever danced together," Jimmy yells.

"Hey, watch it!" Eddie yelps, stumbling into Jimmy when someone slams his shoulder from behind.

Owen Huckins—Huck for short—a rough, scary redneck with a

foul temper, bad hair, and grease-stained fingernails, confronts them with an angry glare.

"What the fuck you think you're doing?" he screams in Eddie's face. "We don't want any of that fag shit here," he growls, slurring his words through a haze of too many beers.

I tap him on the shoulder. "Come on, Huck, would you just chill out?"

Huck's face contorts in pit bull rage. *"Fuck you, you faggot."*

An instant later, I'm on the floor after this jerk knocks me down with a violent, two-handed shove. I'm trying to get to my feet when Huck reaches down, and it's not to help me up. His fist never reaches me. From behind, someone grabs Huck's arm and twirls him around so hard he almost loses his balance. It's Jason, glaring at this creep, his hand still clenched around Huck's wrist.

"Come on, Huck, why don't you get a beer and leave them alone?" I hear Jason yelling over the pounding music. Couples are gathering around. Huck's eyes bulge and his face gets even redder.

"Those fags were dancing together!" he screams, pointing at Eddie and Jimmy. "We don't want any of that shit here."

"Beth said it was okay, so maybe you should apologize and mind your own business."

Huck is so dumbstruck he's almost strangling trying to talk. "What's up with you, man? You turning into some kinda sick homo lover? *You fucking traitor!*"

"Get your ass outta here," Jason screams back, jabbing a finger within an inch of Huck's nose.

"Jason!" a girl screams.

Huck takes a crazy, off-balance swing and misses, almost stumbling in the process.

"Fight! Fight!" someone yells. Almost faster than my eyes can follow, Jason's fist crashes into Huck's face so hard his head snaps back and his whole body twists around and backward several feet. My drunken attacker crumples to the concrete right next to me with legs and arms splayed every which way. Jason stands over him, glowering with fists clenched, ready for another round, but this jerk is out cold.

To add to the drama, Danny stops the music. I'm still on the floor with an out-cold jerk lying next to me, Eddie and Jimmy cowering against the wall clutching each other, the stairs jammed with spectators, and everyone in the cellar crowding around. It's dead quiet as Jason extends a hand to help me to my feet.

"You okay?" he asks.

"Yeah, I guess."

"Oh my God, oh my God!" Beth slashes her way through the crowd, shrieking with her hands to her face. She's almost in tears, watching her party slip away. "What happened?" she screeches.

Jason points to the heap on the floor, about to be hauled off by a couple of Jason's buddies.

"He was beating up on Bobby 'cause he was dancing with those two kids, and talking all kinds of nasty shit."

"Oh, no, how did he get in here?" she wails. Jason wraps a well-muscled arm around my shoulder.

"If you want to go home, everyone will understand." I look over to Eddie and Jimmy and scan the tight circle of faces. I glance at Jason, still inflated with that tight, ready-to-fight posture, except for a gentle look of concern in his eyes. I check my wristwatch.

"Three more hours. *Let's dance!*"

"Let's hear it for Bobby!" someone shouts. The entire crowd responds with applause and cheers. I suspect it's as much relief that the party will go on as it is cheers for me.

Jason reaches for my T-shirt to adjust it back into position and lightly flicks at some dust on my sleeve, a surprising gesture. Our eyes lock.

"Thanks, Jason, I really owe you one."

He stares hard and squinty for a few moments, shaking his head slowly from side to side.

"Not even close." As Danny cranks up a new track, our hands grip in a tight shake.

"I'm so sorry," Beth cries.

"Beth, I'm fine." I nod toward Eddie and Jimmy. "They're pretty shaken up. Can you take them upstairs for something to eat?" Beth confers with them and leads them past my table like little ducklings. Jimmy stops when I give them a thumbs-up.

"We're going to dance some more," he says defiantly.

"I'm proud of you!" I shout back.

"Are you okay?" Chloe asks, her eyes still big from the excitement. I nod that I am. "I'm proud of you for hanging in there," she says.

"Thanks, Chloe. I didn't want to let Beth and everyone else down, but I really didn't want Eddie and Jimmy to learn the hard way that we're supposed to let creeps like Huck get the best of us." Chloe reaches over to give me a hug.

Helen signals from the dance floor with a nod of her head. Not understanding, I answer with a shrug. She waves like a cop. I'm wanted out on the dance floor.

I holler and wave to Danny. He's not far away, and he and Emily—who's rolling her eyes and shaking her head in a snit once again—slip behind the table to take over.

I'm doing dance steps before I'm even around the end of the table.

"Wow, you can really dance," she says as I try some moves I saw at the club and hope I don't look like an idiot. Helen's looking me over from head to toe.

"You're looking good," she says with an odd smile as we begin dancing.

"Thanks, so are you." Helen ignores my compliment and scans me up and down again with an approving nod of her head.

"That tight T-shirt looks good on you. Those sunglasses are hot ... you seem taller. There's something different about you," she says in my ear.

Before I can think of anything to say, a guy, apparently much taller than me, wraps blond-haired, sweaty arms around my chest and grinds into me from behind. I whip around to find out—Josh! Helen's giggling as she lets go so I can dance at a discreet distance from her hot, shirtless boyfriend. He leans down close to my ear.

"Sandwich time."

"Are we going upstairs to eat?" I ask, but with a sly grin, he nods to someone behind me. I let out a screech when another guy, shirtless as well, presses into me even tighter. Whoever it is, he and Josh press close together. Real close. I'm locked in tight. Close by, Chloe's shrieking and doubled over.

We begin to sway to the beat as one, side to side. I'm giggling out of control, scrunched between two straight boys. Whoever's behind me has a tight grip on my hips and is pressing his crotch into my butt. I'm getting a wicked hard-on. I'm scared Josh and everyone else will see the tent in my pants.

"Put your hands in the air," Josh leans down to tell me. My arms aren't even halfway up when hands from behind grab the bottom of my T-shirt and lift straight up. I shriek as I'm now as shirtless as my two pieces of guy-bread. They press even tighter and sway back and forth in perfect rhythm. Whoever's behind me is holding me tight against what feels like a huge package. If he wasn't straight, I'd swear he had a woody.

Eddie and Jimmy have returned and are watching all of this in wide-eyed shock, astounded that I'm sandwiched out on the dance floor by two shirtless straight guys. Right next to them, Helen, Chloe, her cousin, and even Emily, are just dying.

Josh and the mystery guy (I'm pressed so tight I can't even look behind) do a high-five above my head. My sandwich is quickly over when I'm released, with Josh laughing and reaching for Helen.

"Kyle!" I shriek. He grins and gives my arm a few squeezes. "Where's Kathy?" I shout at him.

"She got sick, and I had to take her home."

"That sucks. I'm glad you came back."

"Hey, gotta find some pussy," he says with a flex of his chest.

"Can I have my shirt back?"

Not answering, Kyle squeezes through the crowd, tucking one end of my T-shirt into the back of his pants.

Chloe's waving me over for an update.

"Kathy went home sick, and now he's on the prowl. Can you believe that? He's going steady! That is the horniest guy in the entire school."

Chloe isn't answering or even looking at me. She's watching Kyle maneuver through the crowd with the unmistakable look of pure desire.

Chapter 51

Few people know what's up when Danny carefully positions two microphone stands on a small riser just to the right of my table. He thumps the mikes with his thumb to make sure we're live. Josh, snaking a power cord behind the riser, is almost in position just to the left of the mini stage with a halogen spotlight. Right in front of me is Andy, our tallest basketball player, patiently waiting with a second spotlight.

Waiting not so patiently inside my cramped DJ space are two performers, one so nervous he's actually shaking, the other eager to hop onto the tiny stage at Danny's signal. Chloe knows exactly what's going on and has positioned herself and her cousin directly in front of the stage.

A new track begins playing. Helen, dwarfed by Josh's six-foot-seven teammate, raises the mike to begin her announcement when I nod and turn down the volume.

"Hey, everybody. Hey, over here. It's me, Helen," she shouts into the mike, waving for everyone's attention. Josh puts two fingers to his mouth and unleashes a whistle loud enough to shatter glass. "We have a treat for you," Helen announces with a glance at me for approval. I give her a thumbs-up.

"And now, on the main stage," she continues, hamming it up like a real emcee, "please welcome our guest performers, Eddie and Jimmy!" Just as Danny shoos the two freshmen onto the two-foot-high riser, the lights held up near the ceiling by Josh and Andy flick on with a harsh, yellowish glare. The music, one of my tunes with catchy lyrics written by our two guest performers, resumes pounding out of the speakers.

Eddie begins singing mechanically into his mike, but Jimmy grabs his mike stand, swings the microphone right up to his mouth, cocks his head back, and blasts away.

Your dancing's a drug
I'm hooked on you
Your dancing's a drug
I'm up in the blue

Helen is almost squeezed into my table as the already jammed-in partygoers crush into our corner. Eddie's loosening up as he and Jimmy add dance steps to their singing, which, I learned when they rehearsed in my studio, is far harder to do than it looks.

The audience responds with an enthusiastic cheer, revving Eddie and Jimmy to new levels of energy.

"Jeez, they're really good!" Danny shouts.

"They've been practicing," I shout back.

Many in the audience begin clapping to the beat. More dance steps follow but with even higher, more inspired energy. Maybe surprised to see a boy band that's really good and it's the two cute little freshmen, the crowd responds with a far louder cheer that explodes through the cellar. When Eddie and Jimmy jump up and down and clap their hands above their heads, everyone joins in.

Our two gay-boy entertainers blaze through the last catchy refrain with frantic energy, singing the melody with perfect pitch, making a connection with their excited audience. When they make it through the last stanza, both raise their arms and laugh and screech in sheer joy. Helen again screams into the mike.

"Let's hear it for Eddie and Jimmy!" But she can't be heard over cheering so loud it's drowning out the sound system. I'm already mixing the next track as Dunston's newest out gay kids take a bow and try to catch their breath. I'm betting those Texas-sized smiles will last the entire weekend.

"Those kids were amazing," Helen shouts while reaching over the table with the microphone. "Are they going to sing again?"

"No, they're leaving." Puzzled, Helen makes a squishy face. "Curfew," I explain. "They're only freshmen." Helen rolls her eyes.

You're so beautiful, you're beautiful ... beautiful ... beautiful ...
Take that, Kyle. Tired, (well, maybe intrigued too) of looking up every five minutes to find him peeking at me, I'm lip-synching the words and pointing right at him, giggling to myself watching his reaction.

From a spot near the stairs, he's staring blankly, his mouth slightly open, his eyes big and unblinking, his feet shuffling as he dances robotically with a junior girl. I'm dancing in place and gradually turn my back to him, slowing my dance steps to a sensual half speed. My butt is swaying back and forth in an outrageous, sexy invitation while I look back over my shoulder with pouty, pursed lips, just like some of the club kids in Austin. My thumb is hooked on the back of my pants, pulling one side lower and lower, to the point where half of my butt is showing.

Kyle has stopped dancing. He's not moving, he's not doing anything other than staring at me with an almost glazed expression. His dancing partner looks up, follows his gaze back to me, and jabs at his shoulder. Not ten seconds later, she leads him up the cellar stairs, leaving me with tonight's big unanswered question: just exactly what is up with him?

The throbbing, sweaty crowd is jammed wall-to-wall, to the point where it has become tight for dancing. During a quick break, right after I hugged and kissed Eddie and Jimmy good-bye, I discovered the upstairs was as crowded as well, some dancing, some talking, mostly couples making out. Then I looked out back. Ryan's pickup was the center of attention for guys and girls drinking and laughing and talking real loud like kids do when they get a major buzz. I even heard a few kids came down from Brady. So much for written invitations.

He's back, this time with another girl, Allison Baumann, a black-haired sophomore who, by universal agreement, is the biggest flirt in school. Allison playfully rolls a strap of her slinky red dress off her shoulders, licks her tongue slowly over lips bright with siren-red lipstick, and smiles devilishly at Kyle. *Oh, the things girls do to straight boys.*

Dancing close together, Allison and Kyle have inched their way from the stairs to a spot directly in front of my turntables. He's cupping his hand over her ear, and whatever he's telling her, it's making her dark eyes sparkle. Kyle crosses his arms over his head with his eyes closed, and I screech as Allison pulls Kyle's pants to the floor. He's four feet from me and he's completely naked. My eyes are fixed on just one part of him, the part that's very red and very big and uncut.

With his dancing partner's arms around his sweat-streaked body, Kyle is rocking his hips back and forth, making his dick—*oh my God, he's getting a woody!*—bob up and down and his low-hanging sack bang back and forth. Eyes closed, his arms extend upward and back over his head, stretching his body into a dazzling, flaunting show of abs and muscles. A very large tent is forming in my pants.

Kyle grimaces as his dick gets harder and redder, to the point where it's no longer flopping. I can hardly breathe. And to make it even weirder, no one seems to mind, certainly not the girls next to him, giggling and rubbing his spectacular arms. Kyle, eyes closed and head tossed back in something like dancing ecstasy, doesn't respond.

We make eye contact for an instant. He's intense, unsmiling, and quickly turns back toward his dancing partner. I watch in a breathless state of sexual shock as his tight, hairless, athletic ass, dotted with tiny droplets of sweat, framed by faint Speedo tan lines, sways back and forth a few feet away. The tent in my pants is so painful and so obvious, I have to lean on my elbows and scrunch way down over the table, hoping no one will notice I'm about to rip a hole in my pants.

It's all over all way too quickly when Kyle holds on to Allison to pull up his pants. Seconds later, they disappear up the stairs.

"Oh my God, oh my God!" Chloe screeches.

"I know! He was right in front of me," I snap at her.

"Kyle was naked! Oh my God, oh my God, oh my God."

"Chloe, will you just relax."

"Why are you leaning over like that? Are you sick?"

"No, I'm fine. Now will you leave me alone?" Chloe's eyes get big and her hand flies to her mouth.

"Did you get a little excited?" she giggles.

Chrissy leans over the table to interrupt. "Kyle gets naked at every party," she explains.

"He *what?*" Chloe and I shout together.

"Every party he goes to, he gets naked," Chrissy says. I groan but Chloe is speechless. "He gets other guys naked, and they play naked boy games like belly-flopping onto pillows and streaking—"

"All right, all right!" I holler.

"Why are you so upset?" Chloe asks.

"Well, what do think? I'm gay, and he's sticking his woody right in my face."

"Oh, shit, I didn't even think of that," Chrissy says. "Wait till I see him."

"Where's Jason?" I ask her to change the subject.

"Huh," she sputters, "he's out back."

"Twenty minutes and then I have to sign off," I tell her, tapping on my wristwatch. She nods that she understands and pushes toward the stairs like she's on a mission.

"I'm really sorry, Bobby," Chloe says. "Do you want me to bring you a soda pop or something?"

"No, I'm fine. Go dance. We're almost done." Chloe gets a peck on the cheek before she spots her cousin nearby.

Kyle and Allison Baumann haven't re-appeared. It's just as well, because I don't think I could take another naked performance. The dance floor is still crowded, which I think is wicked cool for a high school party at this late hour with three kegs out back and everyone making out. And here I was, uptight worrying that not many would show up or they wouldn't like the music. With ten minutes to go, a new mix, a bit softer and a few beats slower, gradually brings the crowd down.

At precisely one o'clock, just as I promised Chief Toby, the music slowly fades to a pretty piano part, and just like that, it's over. And just like the club, I'm on the mike.

"This is your DJ, Bobby Fowler. I hope you liked the music. Good night, everyone!" My friendly sign-off is met with total silence. Not only that, no one's moving, no one's heading for the stairs, no one's clapping, as if time has stopped. To make sure everyone gets the message, I flip the switch for the overhead fluorescents, blinding the cellar with an ugly, whitish glare.

"Let's hear it for our DJ!" a familiar but slurred voice shouts. It's Jason, leaning over the railing, exhorting the crowd. They applaud, gradually building into a prolonged cheer with shouts and Texas whoops. A tidal wave of classmates surges toward my corner, offering hands to shake or congratulations when they can't get close. A beefy arm reaches over the table.

"You're awesome, man," Jason screams. "I'm telling you, right from the heart, you're fucking awesome! I don't care if you're gay, you're a regular—"

With a grin at me, Chrissy grabs Jason and points him in the direction of the stairs.

"Hey, he's awesome, isn't he?" he asks his girlfriend, and follows with an alarming burp.

Chrissy just rolls her eyes and leads him away.

Chapter 52

It's not just eerily quiet down here in Chief Toby's cellar, it's dead. What was an amazing scene two hours ago is now an empty cellar. I glance at my wristwatch. It's ten till three. Despite being totally wiped out, I'm still so wired my body is vibrating. There isn't a sound upstairs, so I guess everyone has either left or passed out.

I was scared when the cops came in thirty minutes ago and cleared everyone out, including all the guys drinking out back. But no one got arrested, and they even drove some guys home or made sure they had rides. After all, these cops were doing the same thing when they were in high school.

When I went upstairs to get something to eat, everyone swarmed around to offer congratulations and tell me how blown away they were and ask how I ever came up with this; a few even said they recognized tracks from my CDs. It was very cool. But Chloe and her cousin and Danny and his date were totally ignored, even though we were hanging around together. I felt bad when they left early.

I came back down to pack my vinyl. It helps me decompress. My pants are still damp with sweat and uncomfortable, so off they go, undies too, kicked into the corner. Pulling an extra pair of pants and a fresh T-shirt from my backpack, I'm thinking about how awesome tonight worked out.

"Quite a night, Bobby-dude," I announce to the deserted cellar.

"Got that right."

So startled I literally jump with a yelp, I whip around to see Kyle, still shirtless, leaning against the railing at the bottom of the stairs.

"Jeez, you startled me," I tell him. "And you're catching me naked *again*," I say while hopping around on one foot with a sneaker snagged in my pants.

Kyle slowly pads toward me, a bit unsteadily, but not just to the front of my table. Kyle continues around the far side and right into the cramped triangular space of my DJ booth. He reaches for the table to steady himself.

"Nice of you to put your pants on," I tell him without a trace of humor.

"I saw you come down here," he mumbles. "I wanted to, um, I guess I need to apologize." Kyle hesitates and fidgets with his hands. "Chrissy kinda reamed my ass out. So did Chloe. I'm sorry. I shouldn't have gotten, you know … naked in front of you. I'm sorry."

A bit angry, I hesitate. *Should I ream his ass out as well?*

"Hey, look, I didn't mean to get you upset," he says. "Maybe I should go."

"That's okay, but I'll feel better if you tell me you liked the music."

"Oh, yeah, that's the other reason I stopped down. My tank top," he says, nodding toward a white tank strewn in the corner. A bit unsteadily, Kyle bends down and almost misses grabbing for it. "Here," he says, removing my T-shirt from the back of his pants.

"And the music?"

"What? Oh yeah, the music was fucking amazing. Better than Austin. Jesus Christ, man, this was ten times better than fucking Austin!" he says, getting loud and saying "fuck" when he almost never does.

"Thanks," I reply, my mood brightening and hoping he doesn't pass out or throw up on my records. "I was afraid Beth's friends wouldn't like dance music."

Kyle reacts by shaking his head in disbelief. He's swaying so much he has to reach out and steady himself on the table again.

"Wouldn't like it? Jesus Christ, dude, it's all anyone talked about. Remember over at Helen's? I *told* them they'd fucking get blown away. No one can even touch you. Jason, Chrissy, all of them, they couldn't fucking believe it," he says, almost shouting. He's looking over my mixing board and turntables and reaches out once again to steady himself against the table before shifting his attention to the canopy stretching across Beth's cellar.

"Man, look at this. How'd you do all this?" he asks, shaking his head.

"I don't know," I say with a shrug. "I like music and I like to deejay."

"Shit, you don't even know what I'm talking about. You pulled this whole thing together. You don't even know how good you are," he scoffs. "Man, just fucking look at this," he says, still looking up in wonderment. "I couldn't even think this stuff up. The whole school, man, the whole fucking school, they're going be talking about this all week. The whole town! Maybe the whole fucking state," he shouts.

"Okay, okay, Kyle. Take it easy." I'm a bit nervous at how drunk he is. I wonder if he's going to topple right over my turntables.

Kyle's looking me over but isn't saying anything.

"What?" I ask.

He's breathing heavier, louder.

"You looked hot tonight," he says, oddly talking almost in a whisper, like little air is coming out. "Like when you were dancing and pretending to sing."

"It's called lip-synching."

"Yeah, that's right! Like in Austin. And those sunglasses, man, that was one hot look," he says. "Helen was talking about you."

"About me? Was she upset when you took my shirt off? I mean, I don't look like—"

"Dude, Helen and Chrissy were saying you look fucking awesome. You're taller; look how your chest and delts and arms have filled out. Fuck, dude, look at those abs," he says, followed by a seismic burp.

"Are you drunk?"

"Huh, no way. I had six beers … or was it eight? I can't remember. Fucking Jason had twenty. Hey, I'll give you a ride. I gotta get going."

"Thanks, but I can't. Chief Toby assigned a cop to take me home," I tell him, upset because I really want to ride home with Kyle.

He's just standing there, not leaving even though he just said he was. A few moments pass, Kyle swaying slightly, and me waiting for him to say good night.

"Hey, I heard you were dancing with the two gay kids," he says.

"Yeah, that's why Huck got so upset. Did you hear their performance?

"Yeah. For little kids, they were incredible. At first everyone was like, you know, two guys holding hands and dancing? And some people freaked when they started kissing. But after that performance, most of the guys were cool. All the girls think they're cute."

"I'm glad it went well, but even I couldn't believe they were kissing on the dance floor."

"Yeah, but when I saw you watching them, you looked upset," he says.

"You were watching me? I thought you left."

"I came back down and stopped on the stairs, just watching the crowd, the lights, you know, the whole scene. You were staring at the two gay kids kissing, and you turned away and wiped your eyes. Were you crying?"

I'm looking down at the floor, remembering Eddie and Jimmy kissing nonstop during a long interlude. When I look up, it's right into Kyle's eyes. He has that concerned look, that really nice guy look. It's making me melt.

"I really am happy for them. But when I was watching them, I was wondering, when do I get a kiss out on the dance floor? When is there a special guy who takes me in his arms and tells me, *I love you?*" My head hanging, I let out a long, sad sigh. "I wonder if my dreams will ever come true."

Kyle remains silent. I can feel his direct stare. I look up just enough to see his hands gripping the sides of his pants. "Remember when we were doing that tutoring thing and we were using the hot tub?" he asks with an odd tremor in his voice. "When I asked you if you wanted to lean on my shoulder and you said no? You did, didn't you?"

Looking at the floor, I nod once, hardly moving.

Without a word, Kyle reaches out and wraps both arms around me in a hug. Holding me lightly at first, Kyle's hold steadily becomes tighter as his arms squeeze me into him like a machine. He presses his cheek against mine and even rubs my back. But just when I get my arms around his thick, shirtless torso, wishing this could go on forever, he jerks away.

"I gotta go," he whispers. Kyle stumbles around the table and hurries toward the stairs without looking back. He doesn't even say good night. Only a minute later, the roar of a car peeling down the road pierces the chilly February night.

My blanket pulled tightly around me, curled up in bed but still wide awake, scenes and images flash in front of me nonstop. Not of everyone dancing under the lights, or how spectacular the cellar looked, or Jason rescuing me, or the crowd cheering for Eddie and Jimmy. All I see is

Kyle. Kyle looking at me every five minutes; sensual, beautiful Kyle moving better than anyone else on the dance floor; Kyle sneaking up on me from behind and pressing me with his crotch into Josh; flaunting his stunning, naked body and that monster, ready-to-explode hard-on; wrapping his arms around me and pressing his cheek against mine. Beautiful, stunning, delicious, dazzling, gorgeous, perfect, sex-god Kyle Faulkner. I can't get him out of my mind. Again. And he said I looked hot!

IT'S *OUR* PROM

Chapter 53

We're hardly out of my driveway when I spot them off in the distance, right over the center of town.

"Hey, look at the searchlights! Where'd those come from?"

Police Corporal David Ochoa, blond-haired despite his Hispanic name, grins as we speed toward downtown Dunston in his black-and-white.

"Chief got those," he says. "Some friend of his in San Angelo is what we heard."

Two searchlights, an unexpected but exciting addition to tonight's big event, sweep and crisscross pale white beams through the Texas sky, still bright with the glow of the setting sun. As we cruise into town, Corporal Ochoa—dispatched by Chief Toby to pick me up—swings onto a dusty, dreary side street. Within minutes, the long, imposing limestone bulk of the National Guard Armory comes into view.

"Wait till you see the front," he says as we make the turn onto Sam Houston Boulevard, one of Dunston's main drags.

"Wow, look at that, a canopy of nothing but lights!"

"The workmen put those up right after you left. Chief said it's the Texas version of a Broadway theater." Corporal Ochoa slows as we approach a vaguely sinister-looking black unmarked cruiser parked opposite the armory. The driver's darkened window rolls down to reveal the handsome, grinning face of Chief of Police Tobias Sandman, who I've called Chief Toby, or just Chief, ever since Beth's party. He surprises me by wearing a white police shirt and a dark blue dress jacket. I've never seen him wear anything other than jeans, a plaid shirt, and suspenders that are stretched out by the beginnings of a pot belly.

"Hey, Chief, the searchlights are awesome!"

"Figured you'd like those," he replies. "I thought the front came out pretty classy too, don't you think?"

"It's incredible!" I'm shouting, hopping out of the cruiser with a thank-you wave to Corporal Ochoa.

"I took a look inside after you left. Hard to believe it's the same old dump," Chief Toby says. "The old dump" is what he jokingly—at least I think he's joking—calls the armory, which sat empty and unused for years. It wasn't quite a dump when I first saw it five weeks ago, but the place sure needed a lot of cleaning, to say nothing of several hundred other tasks to get the building ready.

"Hey, Chief, Dunston's going to have its very own circuit party."

"Circuit party? Is that because of all the electrical equipment?"

My mouth is open trying explain gay circuit parties, but nothing comes out.

"We're detouring traffic," Chief Toby continues. "We don't want traffic jams out front with hundreds of kids milling around."

"I sure hope this goes okay."

"That's what you said the last time. You still starting at 8:00?"

"Yes, sir. Maybe earlier if there's a lot of kids inside."

Chief Toby peers up at me with a stern cop look. "One o'clock, right?" he says.

"One o'clock sharp," I answer, trying not to smirk. The ending time has become somewhat of a joke between us. I wanted 2 AM; Chief Toby said 11 PM. I told him that was so eighth grade, so when he said 11:30, I informed him he had made it to ninth grade. I instantly regretted being such a wise-ass, but Chief Toby burst out laughing. It was when I suggested it was better to have everyone inside dancing instead of outside drinking and getting into trouble that he stared hard for a moment and then settled on one o'clock, the same as for Beth's party.

Tight-lipped and serious, Dunston's popular police chief puts a hand on my arm.

"I'm really sorry about what happened at school," he says, his voice so filled with concern, I'm touched by his simple country goodness.

"Thanks, Chief. I'm glad those kids got caught. And, Chief, you've been totally awesome. Thanks so much for everything."

Dunston's police chief breaks out in a broad grin. "You just go and have fun. Good God, that was quite a scare you gave us this afternoon." Not waiting for me to respond, Chief Toby—who I've come to like a lot as well as respect—gives me a friendly wave, puts his cruiser in gear, and slowly pulls away.

So here I am, standing in front of the fortresslike stone facade of the National Guard Armory, with a half dozen tables right outside the main entrance awaiting a squadron of volunteers to sell tickets and give out wristbands; a festive entrance canopy fashioned from nothing but strings of white lights; a small but growing crowd milling around out front and more streaming down the street; and a trailer with two rotating searchlights parked right in the middle of Sam Houston Boulevard, announcing to the entire town—and to all of central Texas, for that matter—tonight's big event, It's *Our* Prom.

And to think that a month and a half ago, this wasn't even a dream.

Chapter 54

Six weeks earlier

"A date? You have a date for the prom? For real?" Chloe screeches so loud the snare drum she's sitting at resonates with a faint buzz.

"Yeah. I'm going to the prom!"

"Com'ere. You're getting the biggest hug in history." Arms outstretched, Chloe almost jumps around my drums to wrap me in a tight embrace. "I'm so happy for you," she says as she begins to tear up.

"Thanks, Chloe. I can hardly believe it. Please don't cry."

"Then tell me all about your dream date," she says, dabbing at her eyes. "Is he cute? Does he play sports? Where's he from—"

"Okay, okay, it's Matt. Remember I told you I met him last month at the club?"

"Yeah, I do, and you said he's wicked cute."

"Sophomore at Texas, plays soccer, crew cut, lean and muscular … oh, Chloe, he's adorable!" Chloe shrieks and jumps up and down. "And guess what else? He's taking me in a limo!" Chloe lets out a screech worthy of *The Price Is Right*. When she grabs onto me, we both scream and jump up and down together.

"Will you and Matt …" she starts to ask when we calm down.

"Will we what?"

"You know, spend the night together?"

"My foster mom's letting me stay here after the prom. She said, 'Well, I guess you two aren't going to be making babies.'" Chloe's hands fly to her mouth as she gapes with a mix of delight and pretend shock.

"Oh, Bobby, I'm so happy for you. After all you've been through, you deserve this. And I'll tell you one other thing, Robert Fowler. This Matt is the lucky guy."

"Thanks, Chloe," I say as I wrap my arms around her. "I hope you get a date. You deserve it too."

"Thanks, Bobby. Hey, wait till all the kids at school hear about this!"

* * * * *

I can feel it. Something doesn't feel right as I approach the administration counter. Madeleine glances up and immediately looks for something on her desk. I have to announce myself with a fake cough.

"Mr. Lessard said you can go right in," she says, oddly all businesslike.

Mr. Ramirez was also acting like he was nervous when he told me to report to the principal's office.

Mr. Lessard looks up when I peek in. "Hi, Bobby. Please, come in and have a seat," he says, pointing to a chair in front of his desk. "We have to chat," he says, flopping way back in his leather chair with a loud whoosh. "Look, I'm very sorry, but you can't go to the prom with a same-sex date. It's the policy of the school not to allow same-sex couples at school functions, and that includes the prom. You can attend with a girl or you can go alone."

This news is so stunning it takes a few moments to think of something to say. "You mean it just *became* policy."

"Whether it did or not doesn't really matter," he says.

All the air, all the life, is leaking right out of me. I'm collapsing, deflating down into the chair. "Isn't there anything you can do?" I ask, but I know it's a feeble, useless attempt to salvage something out of this.

"My hands are tied, and this is the policy of the school district." Mr. Lessard distracts himself by wiping off his glasses. "Bobby, I can read you like a book. I know you're terribly disappointed and upset. All I can say is I'm truly sorry. I really mean that, but this is the school board's policy and that's that." My principal harshly rubs his fingers up and down his forehead and sighs heavily. "I want you to go back to your class now. I'm expecting your best behavior. I know this isn't what you wanted to hear, but you're almost up to graduation. Sometimes we just have to take disappointment in life."

"Take disappointment? Mr. Lessard, I feel like I've just been screwed."

"Bobby, please, just go back to class. I'm sorry, I really am."

As I drift away from the admin area in a daze, Madeleine calls after me, but it's a distant voice, one that I ignore. Everything seems unreal, as if I'm floating through a very bad dream. And with each step through the corridor and up the stairwell, anger grows, anger that wells up in waves of heat, flushing my face almost to bursting. I'm so angry I'm mumbling to myself.

"My date, the prom, it's all gone. How can they do this? It's not fair. Well, fuck this place. And fuck Mr. Lessard and fuck those stupid fucking right-wing religious assholes on the fucking school committee.

"This place sucks!" I holler, slamming my foot into a locker so hard it hurts my big toe, angering me even more. At the same time, the bells ring.

Almost instantly, the corridor is swamped with students. I elbow my way through, ignoring anyone who squawks when I bump into them. Second period class is with Mr. Evans, but right now all I want to do is scream and throw my books at something, anything.

"Listen up everybody," Mr. Evans intones in his usual mild way to begin an AP history class I suddenly have no interest in. "Open your books to Chapter fifty-six and read the first five pages about the cold war, and be prepared for a discussion. Bobby, please follow me."

Mr. Evans, who could easily be Mr. Ramirez's father, and whose thin frame, sport coat, bow tie, and rimless glasses make him look like a teacher in an English schoolboy movie, is holding the door open. He ticks his head toward the corridor when I put my fingers to my chest and silently mouth, "Me?"

Saying nothing, his expression unreadable, my favorite teacher leads me out into the hallway and halfway down to the next classroom. Mr. Evans unexpectedly leans against a locker and crosses his arms.

"I know you've just been to Mr. Lessard's office," he begins. "I can see it in your face."

The heat of anger instantly wells up with a pressure that feels like I'm about to let go. "It's just not fair."

"I bet you're just about ready to explode, aren't you?" he asks.

My face hotter, my jaw and fists clenched tightly, I don't answer. If I do, screaming anger will come out like a flamethrower.

"I know you are," he continues. "I got a little heated myself in the teacher's lounge when I found out this morning. Bobby, I personally am very sorry about the prom, but you're probably tired of hearing people around here saying they're personally sorry while you get screwed."

That just got my total attention.

"So, listen," he continues, "I want you to promise that you're not going to throw a titanic fit or do something totally stupid. Then you, me, and Jorge Ramirez are going to talk right after school. Can I have your word on it, please?"

I'm still angry and I'm thinking about it, but hearing it come from Mr. Evans, especially saying *please,* clinches it. "Yes, sir. You have my promise."

Just before he opens the door to his classroom, he stops to pat me on the back. "Hang in there," he says. He growls under his breath when we find a full-fledged spitball battle going on.

Mr. Ramirez, stretched out at a front-row desk, waves me in and points to the seat next to him when I poke my head into his homeroom. Mr. Evans is casually leaning against the front of the teacher's sturdy oak desk.

"Bobby, we're just as upset as you are," Mr. Evans begins. "You must feel powerless. I'll bet that's why you're so angry."

"It's just so totally unfair!" I say.

"Yeah, well, we were thinking—"

"Bobby," Mr. Ramirez butts in, "of course it's unfair. What they did is demeaning and it hurts, but don't go off the deep end and yell and scream. Do something meaningful and positive. Maybe one of the important lessons you can take out of this is to turn a negative into a positive."

"It sure seems pretty negative right now," I tell them.

"We understand. Chloe told me about your date," Mr. Evans says.

"Still, there's an opportunity for you," Mr. Ramirez continues.

"Like what?"

A look passes between them. Mr. Ramirez leans toward me. "Bobby, everyone at school heard about Beth Sandman's party last month. Not only was it the talk of the school, it was the talk of the teachers' lounge as well. We heard all about the sound system and the lights and the music. We even heard how you transformed Beth's cellar into a fabulous night club. One of my students told me she stood on the stairs looking at this fantastic scene, and she was in tears. That's how overwhelming and beautiful it was. *You* pulled that off."

"Beth wants another party?"

"No, Bobby, we think you should put on your own prom," Mr. Ramirez says.

"My own prom? Come on, Mr. Ramirez, you can't possibly be serious."

"Not a stuffy, formal prom with tuxes and gowns," Mr. Evans says. "More like a dance party."

"Like what you did for Beth, only bigger," Mr. Ramirez explains. "Everyone will go, believe me, and if you don't believe me, just ask Beth."

"I can't put on a prom. How do you know anyone will come? How could I possibly put on a prom?"

"Bobby," Mr. Evans chimes in before I go off the deep end, "you know how to plan and organize things better than any student I've seen in a long time. Look at how you pulled Beth's party together in under two weeks. This will just be bigger. You can even invite kids from schools all over central Texas."

"Oh, I don't know about this."

"Some of those kids will be gay kids," Mr. Ramirez says. "Shouldn't gay kids be able to come and listen to your music?"

My mind has been whirling with a jumble of thoughts, but what Mr. Ramirez just said catches my attention.

"Hmm, gay kids. A prom that's not a prom but a big dance party," I'm saying to myself. My teachers patiently wait. "Yeah, my own prom, like a protest. This could be way cool. Yeah, let's do it! But wait a minute. Where could I possibly put this on? Certainly not here!"

Mr. Evans lifts himself off the desk.

"Oh, I think we know just the place," he says with a mischievous grin.

Chapter 55

"How about the Stick It in Your Ear Prom?" Danny shouts. His suggestion is good for laughs all around our crowded lunch table.

"I got it," yells another of my friends. "How about the School Committee Sucks Prom?" Crazy, chair-rocking laughter fills our section of the cafeteria.

"Maybe it's just a teensy bit over the top," I suggest.

Danny slams his fist on the table so hard our trays rattle. "That screwed-up school committee better keep their grubby hands off this prom, I'll tell you that much," he says.

"That's right. This is going to be our prom," Chloe tartly replies.

"That's it, that's the name!" I shout at my friends. "It's *Our* Prom. Chloe, you're a genius." Chloe's looking around like she hasn't a clue, but is happy she's a genius.

"That's the name, It's *Our* Prom?" Danny says.

"Yeah, what do you guys think?" I ask everyone.

For a few moments, my friends are silent.

"I think it's just right. In-your-face, but not too offensive," Chloe says. Everyone else is nodding their heads in agreement.

"I just got it!" I screech. "It has a double meaning." I have to explain when my friends react with blank looks. "Look, every gay kid in Texas will get it—it's for us, too. But it's a code, so straight kids won't get scared off thinking it's just a gay dance. Oh, this is just too cool."

"I've never seen you so excited," says Chloe.

"Yeah, now all you've got to do is put it on," Danny says.

"So, it will be bigger than Beth's party," I tell him. "I've got six weeks to get ready. How hard can it be?"

* * * * *

"What's the matter with you?" Chloe asks as I toy with my mac and cheese at lunch. A whole week has gone by since I agreed to put on It's Our Prom. "You've been in this depressed mood ever since you got to school."

"My friend from Boston—remember the guy who made all sorts of suggestions for Beth's party?—he found a friend of a friend who's a circuit party promoter in New York City."

"What's a circuit party?" Danny asks with a mouthful of his mom's oriental noodles.

"Paul, the guy from Boston, told me that they're huge gay dance parties. Guys fly to whatever city's putting them on from all over the country. They're fabulous, with big light and sound systems and thousands of boys. Well, anyway, the guy in New York City's helping me out."

"Awesome," Danny mumbles. "What's he doing?"

"This. He e-mailed it last night." Danny intently reads the first page of the sheaf of papers I pulled out of my notebook.

"It says Master Task List," he informs Chloe. "Is this what you need to put on your prom?" I barely nod. "This is awesome. It's awesome, isn't it?"

"Danny, it's eighteen pages," I tell him.

"So what?" Chloe chimes in. "The judge is renting the National Guard Armory and you've set the date. Won't this list tell you everything else you need to do?"

"It's *eighteen pages*," I moan. "There's no way I can do half this list with only five weeks left." I sigh heavily with my head drooping onto my fists. "It's over. There isn't going to be a prom." It's very quiet at our table through the rest of lunch. On the way out, Chloe makes a detour to the teachers' table.

"This is a wonderful list," says Mr. Evans, looking up from half the eighteen-page list, while Mr. Ramirez leans over his desk, immersed in the other half. "It's exactly what you need to put on your prom."

"Yeah, for next year," I reply.

"Look, I know you're concerned," he says, "but Jorge and I are here to help."

"We're never going to get this done," I mutter. "The company in Austin can't do light and sound systems big enough for the armory."

Mr. Ramirez looks up. He points his finger right at me. "I know you," he says. "You can pull this off. You did Beth's party in less than two weeks. Chief Toby is renting the armory to you for what, one dollar? Don't worry, we'll find the big equipment, and once we do, everything else will fall into place. And like Kevin said, we're here to help."

"Well, well, well, you missed something," Mr. Evans says, holding up a page. "Look here, on the last page. It's a contact name and number for all the big equipment."

"*What?*"

"That's right; we can call them right now."

"You mean I might actually get the big lighting and sound systems?"

"Dude, we're on our way!" says Mr. Evans with an exuberant and totally unexpected fist pump.

"Gee, this might actually work," I tell my teachers. "Hey, Mr. Evans, what did you just call me? Dude?" The three of us crack up. "Hey, for teachers, you guys are pretty cool."

"*For teachers?*"

Two weeks of planning drag by. A totally unexpected visitor is enjoying my hot tub.

"Oh, this feels so good," Kyle says as he sinks down to his neck. Forty water jets churn the steamy water to a bubbly froth. I remain sitting upright, looking at Kyle. "Hey, look, I don't mind your using the hot tub, but I thought you weren't supposed to even look at me under penalty of death."

Kyle's eyes pop open with an angry glare. "I'm almost eighteen and I'll do what I want… Sorry, I didn't mean to snap at you."

"That's okay. I just don't want to get you in trouble."

Kyle ignores that last comment. Instead, he closes his eyes and sinks even lower.

"Helen said you're all stressed out," he says a couple minutes later with his eyes closed.

"I'm doing okay. There's just a lot of pressure and a lot to do in the next three weeks. But I got some incredible news today. You remember Larry Bissell?"

"The kid that turned state's evidence?" he murmurs.

"Yeah, that Larry. His father owns Bissell Construction. The judge hired him as a general contractor. He's going to take over everything that needs to be done to get the armory ready. And guess what else? He's doing it at cost. He told the judge it's the least he could do to make up for what his son did."

"Holy shit," Kyle whispers.

"You haven't heard anything yet. We found a totally awesome lighting system and a humongous sound system from this gay guy's company in Chicago, and at cost, can you believe that?"

"I get Mr. Bissell, but why's this gay guy doing it at cost?"

"He was contacted by an Internet chat room friend of mine, and he found out I'm gay and what happened to me two years ago. He told the judge he'd be glad to help out a gay kid in rural Texas."

Kyle says nothing, but his eyes narrow, as if he's thinking the same thing I'm thinking: do gays watch out for one another like this?

"So are you going to tell me what the big secret is?" I ask Kyle as we towel off.

"You have to promise not to tell anyone. I mean no one. And don't tell anyone I was even here."

"Fine," I reply with a shrug.

"It's just an idea. Can we talk down in your recording studio?"

* * * * *

"No posters?" I ask Danny.

"Get real," he replies as he scrounges in his mom's fridge for snacks. "Look, you said the judge figured out we need to sell eight hundred tickets to break even. So, how do we reach kids in high schools all over central Texas?

"How about if we mail a demo CD to every high school?"

Danny rolls his eyes. "Come on, man, get out of the dark ages. We're going to use the Internet," he says. As he pops a big bowl of homemade noodles in the microwave, Danny once again expresses admiration for our website, ItsOURprom.com. A friend of Mr. Evans at the insurance company in town, a computer guy, just got it up and running. The guy was really impressed with Danny's design help.

"We need a marketing plan," Danny says.

"Marketing plan? Did you just say 'marketing plan'?"

Danny ignores my jibe and puts placemats on the table. "I even came up with a name for it," he continues. I call it 'viral marketing.' Is that cool or what?"

"Danny, it's a dance party, not a disease," I tell him between noisy slurps of steaming oriental noodles.

"Look, we're going to use the Internet to reach kids and create a buzz. We'll do chain e-mails and get into chat rooms 'cause that's where kids are today. They'll reach other kids, and it keeps on going, like a virus … a good virus," he adds.

I always knew Danny was good with computers and the Internet, but viral marketing—oh, I don't know about this. The more I think about it, though, the more sense it makes. Danny's ideas usually do.

"Tomorrow I'm going to put the ticket count up on big poster boards in the lobby," he continues. "Mr. Lessard said okay, just like that."

"Wow. That's like giving the finger to the school committee. What's the latest ticket count?"

"Uh, this noontime it was … twenty-eight," he mumbles.

I close my eyes and groan. "Nine days to go. I'm so totally screwed."

"Maybe everyone's waiting until the last minute. Tonight we'll be hooked up to do orders online, so that should help. Oh, about the ticket inquiries …"

"What about the ticket inquiries?" I ask.

"I got some e-mails asking about the prom from kids as far away as San Antonio," he says, "and from San Angelo, a few from Austin … oh, yeah, there was one from Lawton, Oklahoma."

"Oklahoma? For real?"

"Can you believe that? And one …" He hesitates.

"One what? Come on, Danny, one what?"

"One from Taiwan," he says, grimacing and shrinking back like he did something bad.

"Taiwan? *The country?*"

Danny nods his head yes. I laugh hysterically, but Danny is completely straight-faced. "You're not upset?" he asks.

I'm laughing so hard I'm rocking back and forth in my chair.

"Jeez, I haven't seen you laugh in three weeks," he says.

"Taiwan? I'll be really impressed when we get one from Mars!"

We crack up with insane laughter, the kind of screeching, screaming, side-busting, howling, rocking-in-our-chairs laughter we can't stop. Two of his younger sisters come to investigate. Not understanding why we're laughing, their giggles quickly turn into peals of out-of-control, rolling-on-the-floor laughter.

It's a good five minutes before we escape to Danny's room.

Chapter 56

"We better sell a lot of tickets in the next five days, or I'm royally screwed," I tell Danny as we stroll across the driveway toward the school's main entrance.

"What's going on?" Danny asks with a nod toward the bank of glass doors.

"I don't know. How come there's so many kids in the lobby?"

"He's here," someone says when I yank the door open. The entire lobby instantly quiets, as if someone snapped a switch. I sense a weird vibe, like everyone's tense. No one makes eye contact.

I spot one of my friends from computer lab. With a grim expression, she raises her arm to point up and back toward the concrete-block wall over the main doors. At first, what my eyes see doesn't register. Spray-painted across the entire entryway, in crude, red block letters, is the message NO FAG DANCE IN DUNSTON.

"No," I moan, reeling in shock.

"I'm sorry," someone starts to say when my eyes focus on the wall where Danny and Chloe had taped one of the posters we plastered around school, and what was supposed to be today's ticket count. Every bit of air leaves my body. FAG DANCE is spray-painted in black across the poster, spilling out onto the wall. Only a corner of one of the counter posters remains.

"They can't do this!" Danny cries.

I don't acknowledge him or anyone else. I'm hoping I'll wake up and find this is all a very bad dream. Students congregate around me, trapping me, some saying they're sorry in low, sad voices, like at a funeral. Other voices are angry, and still others buzz about who did it.

I hear them, but it's like words on a TV set I'm not paying attention to. One thought forms, one awful, horrifying thought: It's over. My prom is gone, it's all gone. I swallow hard so I don't throw up.

I'm at my desk. I have no idea how I got here. I don't remember walking through the corridors or up the stairs or into homeroom. More students gather around, but I feel as if I'm in a bubble, that I can't and don't want to acknowledge anyone or talk or do anything.

Kyle comes in, looks around at the crowd gathered at my desk, and then stares at me, like he knows something really big is going on. I don't say anything, because if I do, I'll lose it. Someone tells Kyle what happened. He looks at me, and then back at the kid. "No way!" he says. Another guy tells everyone about the mirrors in the boys' room that were spray-painted. I hear about another cruel message meant just for me: GOD HATES FAGS. I can't tell if Kyle's angry or can't believe it—

"Bobby. Bobby!" Mr. Evans is shaking my shoulder and leaning down close. "We need to go to the principal's office," he says quietly and gently.

I feel numb, like I'm gliding through corridors still crowded with arriving students. Many stare and some say they're sorry or words meant to be encouraging, but I don't answer, and I am not encouraged. *It's over. It's all gone.*

Mr. Lessard is talking to me and Mr. Evans. I mumbled something when I came in, to be polite, but I'm not really listening.

I couldn't go to the school prom, now I can't even do my own prom. It's gone, it's all gone.

Mr. Lessard stops talking in mid-sentence. A hot tear is streaming down my cheek, although I'm not crying.

"Kevin, you stay here with Bobby. I'll be right back," Mr. Lessard says as he bolts out of the office.

"I'm really sorry," Mr. Evans says with a gentle pat on my back. It's not enough. Nothing will ever be enough to make up for this.

"Mr. Lessard, Kevin, can you give us a minute, please?" I recognize Mr. Ramirez's voice in the doorway.

"Kevin, I need to run something by you outside," the principal says to Mr. Evans. The door closes with a soft click.

A chair slides across the carpet, close to me. A hand squeezes my forearm.

"Bobby, this is why we need to put on your prom," Mr. Ramirez says, his voice both firm and quiet. "You understand that, don't you? Now we have to go forward with this more than ever."

I let out one little sob, although I didn't want to, and sniffle a bit too loudly. "I just thought …" I sniffle again. "I thought we were past all this. Now I can't do my own prom. It's all gone." I can't look at Mr. Ramirez. Ashamed of my tears, I'm wiping each eye hard with my knuckles.

"No, it's not all gone. We have to put on this prom. And I'm sorry, but we're never past all this. We're never, ever past shit like this. We really can be happy in our lives, but we've got to be strong because there are ignorant, bigoted people out there. Bobby, you and I have come a long way, and we both have an even longer way to go. Putting on this prom is part of our journey, and it's an important part. Can I tell you why?"

I nod yes, barely moving my head.

"I heard about the incident with Owen Huckins. This is like that, to show everyone we're stronger than they think. It's to show everyone we won't collapse like a house of cards when there's hate like this. And your prom will be a good time, a wonderful time, I promise you. Bobby, you have this talent, through your music and so many other ways, to make people happy. That's what our world needs, to be happier. You can help do that in spite of what happened today. And don't forget, there'll be gay kids coming from all over, and they need this too, maybe as much as you do right now. They're counting on you. Eddie and Jimmy are counting on you. We're not going to back down, you got that?"

"Yes, sir," I whisper.

"I want you to go back to your class, and I want you to focus on your work. I know it will be hard, but most of the students are upset about this. Bobby, they're on your side now. Accept their support! And I want you to keep focused on the prom. That's an order, gay boy, got it?"

It takes a few moments, but I get up slowly. "Yes, sir," I reply. "We're going to do this." Mr. Ramirez nods his approval. "But it seems like all the fun is gone."

"I know you're strong," he says with a pat on my shoulder, "but maybe you're tired of having to be strong all the time, so, Bobby, you can lean on me."

As we leave Mr. Lessard's office, we're surprised to see three cops waiting at the administration counter.

"Last night, three junior-class students vandalized our lobby and one of the boys' rooms," Mr. Lessard begins. A hush descends over the eleven hundred or so students gathered in the Heinie for a special afternoon assembly. Helen, sitting next to me, looks over with a supportive nod and a firm squeeze of my hand. Simmering with all-too-obvious anger, gripping the lectern tightly, Mr. Lessard continues.

"They left hateful graffiti, which I found to be completely unacceptable for students who wish to attend our school. Little did those students know they were recorded by a security camera. Those three students have been suspended from school, and they have been arrested for vandalism. Later today they will be charged with felony hate crimes." This news results in a loud buzz that quickly fills the massive auditorium. Mr. Lessard growls for everyone to be quiet.

"But there is more than just the defacement of our lobby and restrooms. It's the message of intolerance and hate that is totally unacceptable. Those messages and the thoughts behind them have no place whatsoever at Dunston High School," he thunders.

"And now, I am announcing a new policy at Dunston High School. With the full and unqualified support of the superintendent, I am announcing a zero-tolerance policy for acts of discrimination and harassment ..."

While Mr. Lessard drones on, I turn back when Chloe, sitting with Danny in the row behind me, rubs my shoulder.

"I've never seen him so angry," she whispers.

"I've never been so angry," Helen hisses.

Half-listening to Mr. Lessard, I appreciate what he's doing, but the horse is out of the barn, at least for me. I'm just trying to focus on getting the prom ready, as I promised Mr. Ramirez, but all the fun is gone.

Way down on the stage, Mr. Lessard whips off his glasses. "Are there any questions?" he asks in an angry and intimidating way, principal talk that means *I'm done and my question was rhetorical.*

From down below, in about the middle of the auditorium, a boy with short, blond hair stands up and shouts, "I think those assholes should be made to apologize to Bobby Fowler!"

"Go, Jase!" shouts Josh, sitting on my right, as cheers and applause erupt all over the auditorium.

"Jason, I know you're angry, and actually, I hope every other person in here is as upset as you are," says Mr. Lessard, shockingly unruffled at Jason's language. "I promise you, that will be a condition of their return."

Mr. Evans spots me just as he exits the main doors amid a throng of students buzzing about the assembly and eager to get out of school.

"I know you're upset and discouraged," he says. "Jorge told me he talked to you this morning." I'm not sure what he wants me to say, and I don't feel like saying much of anything. He leans close. Josh and Helen and Danny and Chloe lean in too.

"Mr. Lessard never gave the school committee an opportunity to comment on the new policy, especially the inclusion of sexual orientation. I'd say that was pretty courageous on his part. Clever, too."

I nod, mumble some thanks for his support, and team up with Danny for the walk to the parking lot. Right now I don't seem to care much about anything.

Chapter 57

"So when I picked up the phone, I thought it was you," I'm telling Chloe as we back out of my driveway in her mom's car. "It was Dustin."

"Dustin? Dustin Sanchez?" she asks.

"Yeah. He almost never talks to me in school, and he's calling me on the phone. So he said, 'I hope you're hungry, because you're having company, and make sure the hot tub's ready.' Then he hung up."

"Weird. So what happened?" Chloe asks.

"Well, not two minutes after I raced up the road, a car tears into the driveway. And who do I find at the front door? Dustin, Kyle, Josh, and Jason, and Jason's holding a stack of pizzas." Chloe screeches in surprise. "Doesn't this sound like something Helen would cook up?" I ask her. "So anyway, we had pizza and laughed and joked around, and then Kyle got everyone to jump in the hot tub."

"Oh my God! Were they naked?"

"Girl, these are uptight straight boys," I remind her.

"Still, it must have been steamy with those four in the hot tub. And you didn't call me to come over because why?"

"Chloe, they would have been totally distracted by your Polynesian beauty."

Chloe shrieks in mock insult and swats at my arm.

"It was a lot of fun," I continue. "Boy, did Jason and Dustin freak when they saw my recording studio and my drums. They left only because the judge called to tell me to come down to the armory right away."

"You haven't smiled in weeks," she tells me as we head into town.

"I've been concerned about you. And then you walk into school and find all that crap. It's nice to see you smile," she says with a pat on my arm.

"I'm getting excited again, and Chloe, it wasn't just the Four Amigos. I mean, having them come over was fun and a big surprise, but you and Danny and a lot of others have been there for me. It means a lot." Chloe holds out her hand. I clasp it tightly.

We've reached a dark, depressed part of Sam Houston Street, mostly dusty, deserted space except for a couple of used-car lots and a hunting-supply store. Just ahead is our destination, the imposing National Guard Armory and my hastily arranged meeting with the judge. Before we glide to a stop right out front, we pass two huge trailer trucks idling with their flashers on.

With the judge is the contractor, Mr. Bissell, a short, balding guy with a no-nonsense look about him. They're conferring right in the middle of the armory's immense central area.

"Hello, Bobby, Chloe," says the judge. "Did you see what's parked outside?"

"Is it the equipment from Chicago?" I ask him.

"It sure is," says Mr. Bissell. "I'm glad they got here, because there's a lot of work to get this set up."

We spend a good half hour going over decisions that Mr. Bissell needs to begin work, which, I was amazed to hear, begins tonight.

"This place is gigantic!" Chloe squeals when we finish. With the judge and Mr. Bissell huddled a few yards away over some diagrams, Chloe gawks at the armory's interior, looking lost out here on the immense floor that was used for drills a long time ago. A balcony, originally a running track, rings the entire perimeter some twelve feet off the floor. Huge iron girders, painted battleship gray but now chipped and dusty, rise from ground level and go through the balcony to span high above the floor, creating a sense of enormous space. Tall, thin windows, coated with years of grime, rise above the balcony on each side, adding to the impression that we're inside an old, abandoned factory.

"We're sure going to need a lot of fabric," Chloe says.

"I'm not doing fabric."

"Well, what are you going to do?" she asks.

"Nothing."

"What do you mean, nothing? You've got to make this place look fabulous. You're gay!" she shrieks.

"Look, the first time I stepped in here, I knew it should look industrial, like a huge rave. This place is perfect."

Chloe bursts out laughing. "Now your prom is a rave?"

"No, not a rave. Actually, it's the anti-prom. No streamers, no punchbowls, no tuxes or gowns, no stupid Under the Sea theme, no limos, none of that shit," I explain to her. "Come on, Chloe, this is *our* prom."

"That's cool," she says. "I hope we sell a lot of tickets. We're at how many?"

"Around two hundred, but don't forget, Danny's going crazy with this Internet viral marketing thing. And then we're going to have sound and lighting systems that take up two trailer trucks."

Chloe puts her fists on her hips and gives me a look.

"What?" I ask.

"It's that gay drama thing. Robert Fowler, you *love* drama."

"It's Chloe," Mrs. Robles says while handing me the kitchen phone. "You'd better talk to her," she whispers with her hand over the mouthpiece. "She's almost hysterical."

Cradling the phone, I'm wondering how she could possibly become hysterical when we left the armory just thirty minutes ago.

"Chloe, what's the matter?"

"Turn on the radio, turn on the radio!" her voice screams out of the phone so loud I have to hold it away from my ear.

"I don't have a radio." She screeches something incoherent. "What's going on?" I holler into the phone.

"Hold on, let me put my radio up to the phone. Wait till you hear this!"

"So, D-Man, where are you having this big prom that's not really a prom?" says a voice that can only be that of a radio disc jockey.

"At the National Guard Armory in Dunston," says a voice identified only as D-Man. It's the biggest dance party in history, and every high school student in central Texas is invited. Except no freshmen."

"D-Man?" I wonder aloud. "That's Danny!" I shout, but Chloe still has the radio up to her phone.

"This Saturday night, music fans, the cool place to be is Dunston, for It's *Our* Prom. You heard it right here on KANG, bringing you 50,000 watts of music power from San Angelo. So, all you fans out there in KANG music land, if you want a good time, check out this tune our caller sent in. Wowie Howie's says Dunston's gonna be the place to be this Saturday night."

The radio-over-the-telephone begins broadcasting a dance track. I know it well. It's a number I remixed called "Perfect Angel."

"Bobby, can you believe it?" a familiar voice screeches as the music recedes into the background.

"That was Danny!" I shout into the phone.

"Oh my gosh! Oh my gosh!" she screeches over and over.

"I'll call you later," I tell her, hanging up to punch in Danny's number. Of course it's busy. With three sisters, Danny's phone is always busy. Wait till I see him tomorrow.

Two days to go, and I'm watching Danny tacking up today's ticket count in the school lobby. I haven't busted him yet about last night's surprise on the radio.

The first poster board contains a two-foot-tall "3." The next one, to the left, a "2." The third—a zero? A fourth poster?

"One thousand twenty-three?"

Danny just grins back. A small crowd has already gathered around. "Oh my God!" someone says.

"Wait till everyone hears about this," another says.

"So how long did it take to get on the air last night?" I ask him.

"On the air? What do you mean, on the air?"

"Oh, come on, D-Man. KANG in San Angelo."

"I don't know what you're talking about," he replies with a shrug. "I was studying calculus."

Yeah, right. He could have written the calculus text.

* * * * *

Seven hours to show time. The armory is silent, still. Sunshine from the thin side windows stripes the main floor like a giant sundial, their slow movement across the just-polished wood drawing me ever closer to the start of It's *Our* Prom.

A small area, screened off for my DJ booth with fabric left over from Beth's party, sits in the middle of the balcony. The amps and powerful speakers will sound impressive only when tuned to the unique qualities of the armory. It's my final task, but if this doesn't come out right, I'll be the biggest jerk in history. Making my tummy flip-flop even worse, my first try sounds like I'm inside an oil drum.

The silence is interrupted by the crash of a door.

"Bobby, Bobby!" a frantic voice screams.

"Danny, I'm up here," I holler back as I adjust an amp. "What's the matter?"

"The counter, the counter!" he hollers, panicky and almost out of breath.

I rush to the balcony railing.

"What about the counter?"

"It just hit twenty-five hundred!"

"*What?*"

"Two thousand five hundred and nine. And it's going up every minute! I tried to call but I couldn't get through," he starts to explain, but I'm already at the stairs, taking maybe three steps to blast down to the first floor.

The front door crashes open with a bang that startles Corporal Ochoa, munching on a doughnut in his cruiser parked out front.

"Get the Chief, get the Chief!" I scream.

"Easy, easy. What's the big emergency?"

"We sold too many tickets! Please get the Chief. Oh man, he's going to kill me."

Corporal Ochoa nearly spills his coffee as he bolts upright and reaches for the radio microphone. Within seconds, Chief Toby's voice rumbles over the cruiser radio.

"Chief, Bobby Fowler's here—"

"The ticket counter's over 2,500 and climbing," I scream. Corporal Ochoa covers his ear.

"Twenty-five hundred?" the chief says. "Yesterday you told me fifteen hundred."

"Everyone's buying tickets at the last minute. The counter's climbing like a rocket!"

Corporal Ochoa motions with both hands to calm down. A frantic minute goes by before Chief Toby's calming voice returns through the patrol car speaker.

"Okay, Bobby, now let's not panic. Is there any way you can cut off ticket sales?"

"I don't know. The computer guy from the insurance company set it up."

Corporal Ochoa is calmly sipping his coffee with a vaguely amused expression while I force deep breaths to keep from hyperventilating.

"Try calling him," Chief Toby goes on. "Now listen, I need you to calm down and just get ready over there. Is everything else all right?"

"I guess so. I haven't tuned the sound system yet. Sorry, I'm just freaking out. Shit! I've handed out more than fifty comp tickets. Chief, will they all fit?" The cruiser radio is silent for a few moments.

"Yeah, I think so," Chief Toby says. "That old barn's pretty dang big. Now listen up. Contact all your food vendors and give them the new count. Don't worry, they know a big payday. Bobby, we're going to make this work."

"Thanks, Chief. Later …"

"I'm really sorry. This is all my fault," Danny says after listening from the front doorway. "Am I fired?"

"Look, it's not your fault, and you're still the assistant DJ. You heard what the chief said. Can you call Mr. Evans and give him the final count?"

"Oh, crap," he moans, "maybe I shouldn't have called so many radio stations."

With my arm wrapped around my best friend's shoulder, we head back into the hall, where the first food vendors are just setting up.

"I hope this goes okay, or I'm going to look like the biggest loser in history," I tell Danny.

He's still so upset he can't even look at me.

Chapter 58

Thirty-seven thousand watts of sound system power are pumping out dance hits at an ear-splitting volume. It's an hour and a half since we started—fifteen minutes early because so many kids piled into the place—and the dance floor is crowded.

Helen's cousin Billy, standing just inside the curtain that separates both ends of my DJ booth from the rest of the balcony, is trying to tell me something. I wave him closer.

"Chief needs to talk to you," he shouts right in my ear. "Can he come up?"

"Yeah. What's up?"

"You'll see," he says with an odd grin before disappearing through the divider. A minute later, the curtain parts again. In saunters Chief Toby, followed by Billy.

"Everything going okay?" the chief hollers in my ear.

"Yeah. Look downstairs. It's really jammed," I tell him.

"There's a couple hundred kids out front trying to buy tickets. We already sold three hundred cash tickets, and I let in one group that drove down from Oklahoma—"

"Some kids came from Oklahoma?"

"Yeah, four boys from Lawton," Chief Toby replies. "I don't think it's safe to let any more in. It's getting too crowded down there. Look, the balconies are full."

"We sold out?"

The chief nods with a grin.

"We can hear the music pretty loud out front," he says. "The street's blocked off, so we're letting the kids hang around and dance outside."

"Hey, every now and then we hear cheering," Billy shouts. "What's going on?"

He hardly finishes when he and the chief shield their eyes from a brilliant, staccato blast of strobe lights mounted just six feet above us on the gigantic, erector-set lighting structure suspended above the dance floor.

"It happened at Beth's party," I shout back, protected from the strobe attack by my baseball cap. "Someone starts to cheer when the music reaches a crescendo, and then the entire crowd cheers."

Chief Toby reacts with an odd look. Leaning over the railing, he and Billy gaze out over the crowded dance floor. The chief shakes his head in wonderment before exiting through the curtain. Billy follows, but just before he disappears through the curtain, he gives me a thumbs-up and flashes a brilliant, perfect, Albrecht smile. *My gosh, that family has good genes.*

The cheers from the crowd, charged up by Eddie and Jimmy's performance, are just fading when out of the corner of my eye, I catch Kyle and Kathy waving from the curtain. With perfect timing, the trance track now playing eases into a quiet interlude. It has become hot in the armory, and Kyle, like quite a few boys down below, is shirtless.

"This is fabulous," Kathy says with Kyle's arm securely around her waist. "Are you up here all alone?"

"Danny's helping. He's on a pizza run."

The music gradually builds to a crashing, high-energy, uplifting crescendo.

"I don't even know what to say," she says with a hand cupping my ear. "This is almost surreal."

Distracted, I'm half-listening. Once again my eyes have been drawn to a hunky, shirtless boy, his blond hair sticking out from underneath a red baseball cap, his look so hot that he stands out from the crowd jammed onto the opposite balcony. Hunky hot boy is leaning over the railing, dancing in place, and waving both arms exuberantly above his head.

I can't take my eyes off him. Kyle follows my gaze and spots baseball-cap boy. He stares. And keeps on staring. Responding to a nudge from his girlfriend, Kyle points across the hall, says something in Kathy's ear, and follows with a nod in my direction.

"He's hot," I shout with a grin to Kathy.

She looks toward baseball-cap boy before turning back to me. She's nodding her head as if to say, *he sure is.*

"Tim!" I hear Kyle shout. Appearing just inside the black curtain is a guy so good-looking I bolt out of my chair. A bit taller than Kyle, he has sexy, dark blond hair, a white tank top stretched over a long, lean, athletic torso, and blue eyes so icy light they almost glow.

Apparently he and Kyle know each other, because they're eagerly shaking hands and slapping each other on the back. In a few moments, he turns toward me.

His body is tight, tense; his eyes darting around, not making eye contact with me. He hesitates. I wave him closer so I can hear what he has to say. With a darting glance at Kathy, he edges at most a foot toward me, fidgeting with a baseball cap he's holding.

"Are you Bobby Fowler?" he asks in a husky, sexy drawl.

Hardly able to breathe, I nod that I am.

"I'm Tim, Tim McClellan from Brady," he says, still kneading his cap. "I'm sorry I barged in, but I heard all about you. In many ways, you're my hero."

Did I hear that right?

"Tonight I want to ask someone to dance," he goes on. "I've had my eye on him for a long time, but I haven't had the courage to ask him, and I haven't had the courage like you to come out and say …" He gulps, hard. "I'm gay. That's all going to change tonight. Will you help me out?"

"You know Kyle?" I shriek, immediately regretting it. Once again, I've said the dumbest thing possible to a boy just coming out.

"Yeah. We both play football. He kicks our ass every year."

I glance at Kyle. His face is a picture of pure shock. So is Kathy's.

"Hey, I'm no hero, but of course I'll help you out," I say to Tim. "I hope you don't mind my telling you you're totally gorgeous."

Brady's hunkiest football player grins shyly.

"Thanks. His name is Zane, and he's dancing right below. I want to bring him up here and have you introduce us. I mean, he knows me, and I know him … oh, man, I'm just so scared. You're the only other gay kid I know."

When I hold out my arms, he edges back. I suppose he's not used to a boy lining him up for a hug. Once I wrap my arms around him, however, Tim hugs back in a tight, almost frantic embrace.

"Thank you for sharing something so special with me," I tell him. "Everything's going to be fine, so just relax. Where is he?"

"Look, I bought a little laser downstairs. It's really neat." Tim leans dangerously far over the railing to scan the crowd directly below. "There, see him? He's the cutest boy in the entire school."

I stretch over the railing. The bright red dot of laser light zigzags over his dream date. He has short black hair, dark blue jeans, and a stylish long-sleeve shirt made of a shiny, silvery material.

"Tell you what. Let me do the next mix, and then I'll run down myself and bring him up here," I tell Tim. "Can you stand guard with Kyle and Kathy?"

"Yeah. Oh, man, I'm so nervous, I'm going to shit."

Kathy protectively squeezes tighter into her boyfriend. Neither she nor Kyle has said a word, but when I hold out the headphones to Kyle, he lights up like a little kid being handed a surprise gift.

Wow, it's really packed down here. I'm just about under the DJ booth when I spot him bobbing about the dance floor not ten feet away.

He's dancing with a girl. Tim didn't say for sure that he's gay. What if he's really straight and he takes a swing at me? He's turning this way. He has the same cute haircut as Eddie with some gel in it. Tim was right, this kid is wicked cute. *Oh, he's wearing about three neck chains. Gay!*

Zane is confused and surprised when I squeeze in close enough to tap his shoulder. He follows only when I motion again, this time more urgently. We stop at a spot somewhat quieter near the foot of the stairs.

"Hi. I'm Bobby Fowler—"

"*You're Bobby Fowler?*"

"Yeah, why?"

"Because I've heard of you. It's so neat to meet you," he says with a vigorous handshake.

"Likewise. So you're from Brady and your name is Zane, right?"

He cocks his head. "Yeah, how'd you know?"

"Oh, someone told me. Not here with a boyfriend?"

Zane's shoulders slump as if he's deflating. A sad look in his eyes, he shakes his head. "No, no boyfriend," he replies. "I'm the only gay kid in Brady."

"Anyone from school you think is hot?"

"Oh God, yeah! There's this one guy. He's around here somewhere.

He's tall, blond, plays just about every sport, and every girl in school has a total crush on him. What a shame he's straight."

"Zane, someone asked to meet you. He's up in my DJ booth."

"Someone wants to meet me? Is he cute?"

"Nah, I wouldn't exactly say cute," I reply. "More like the most totally gorgeous guy in history. If you don't want him, he's mine."

"Ah, I don't know," Zane says.

"Come on, give yourself a chance. Hey, I think you're wicked cute."

"Oh, come on, Bobby."

"You are! You know, sometimes you have to believe in yourself and make a leap of faith, okay?"

"Yeah, I guess so," Zane replies, not terribly convinced.

I have to shout "coming through" several times to lead him by the hand through the throng jostling on the stairs to get up to the balcony.

"You have to keep your eyes closed when you go into the booth," I tell him as we squeeze between the wall and the kids dancing on the balcony.

To make sure he does, I get behind him and put my hands over his eyes when we get to the curtain divider. Zane, who's almost exactly my height, gropes for the curtain and steps into the surprise of his life.

Tim is waiting in the middle of the booth, looking even hotter wearing his white baseball cap. Kathy has her arm wrapped securely around Kyle. Danny, back at the DJ table and chonking on pizza with the headphones on, stops with a slice almost in his mouth when he sees who's coming through the curtain.

"Okay, Zane. Your mystery man is standing one foot in front of you, and he has something he wants to tell you."

"Hi, Zane. I wanted to meet with you and talk to you," Tim starts somewhat stiffly, as if he rehearsed this. "Until tonight, I never had the courage to be with you. But I've thought about you for a long time. I want to dance with you, and I want hold you, and I'm going to die if I can't kiss you. And tonight, the whole town is going to know that I'm gay. I want it to start with you, if you'll give me a chance." Tim nods for me to take my hands off.

Zane's face instantly transforms into a look of pure shock. He can't seem to get any words out until his face reddens and he turns to me. "How could you do this to me?" he screams. "How could you humiliate me like this? Now the whole school's going think I'm a total loser!" he wails as angry tears begin to flow. Zane angrily lashes out with his arm as he storms toward the curtain.

"Wait, wait!" I yell, lunging to get him in a bear hold. Zane thrashes, but I hold on tight, squeezing even harder. "Zane, listen to me. Listen to me!" His whole body taut with anger, he makes one last, violent jerk before stopping. "Sometimes dreams come true," I yell in his ear. "Tim's gay, got it? This is his coming out and he's scared shitless, and he needs someone to help him through this. And you, Zane, are Tim's fantasy."

Still locked in a tight bear hold, Zane faces Tim when I forcibly turn him around.

"Please give me a chance," Tim pleads. "I want to dance with you and I want to kiss you, and I don't give a shit who sees us. I just want to dance with you, okay?"

Zane relaxes—a little bit, anyway—as I ease up on my grip. Staring into Zane's eyes with a pleading yet nervous look, Tim slowly and gently puts his arms around him. He says something right into Zane's ear. All I hear is, "I'm really scared." I let go completely.

Tim gently kisses Zane, whose eyes are big with shock.

Zane pulls back. "This is for real?" he asks.

Tim places both hands on his dream boy's jaw. He gently kisses him again.

Zane relaxes and wraps first one arm, then the other, around the athletic, perfect boy he's fantasized about, maybe throughout all of high school. I watch in awe. The incredible, impossible dreams of two boys have come true right here in my DJ booth. One of Tim's hands finds the back of Zane's head as they kiss passionately. Tears stream down Zane's cheeks, but instead of angry tears, they're trails of pure joy.

"Okay, go dance, go dance!" I shout at them. First Zane, still teary-eyed, and then Tim give me hugs, but they're the brief, hurried hugs of two guys who can't wait to get downstairs to dance and laugh into each other's eyes, and, if they're bold enough, kiss out on the dance floor.

I'm thinking I've witnessed one of the most beautiful things I've ever seen when I notice Danny mouthing "wow." Kyle still looks like he's in shock. Kathy, however, is shaking his arm.

"Kyle," she shouts. "Kyle!" He snaps out of it. "Let's go downstairs."

"Can't I do a couple more mixes?" he asks.

Kathy's answer is a withering glare.

"Like I said, we're going downstairs," Kyle says as he trudges after his girlfriend. Before he disappears from the booth, I grab his arm.

"You're going to do fine," I tell him.

He gulps, nods, and then he's gone.

Chapter 59

It's close to midnight, time for the last of three live performances. Danny, who has a special track ready to go, leans over the railing toward the front of the hall. He waves back when a friend helping with the live acts signals with his flashlight.

A figure appears on the darkened stage. Danny lowers the volume and snaps a toggle switch, bathing the small, improvised stage and our surprise performer in the bright white light of two spotlights.

"You gotta be kidding me!" he shrieks as I pick up the mike.

"Ladies and gentlemen," I begin, "now performing on the main stage, please welcome, from Dunston High School, the one, the only, Kyle Faulkner," I scream into the mike.

My introduction is greeted by a noise rising up from below that's not so much a cheer as a cry of surprise.

"That's Kyle Faulkner!" Danny screeches. I have to remind him to turn the volume back up.

It really is Kyle Faulkner on stage. I kept it a secret from everyone, even Danny and Chloe, after Kyle paid me that surprise visit a couple weeks ago. He heard I was going to have live performers and asked if he could audition. He even brought a CD. This is Kyle Faulkner we're talking about! He only had to sing a few bars before I signed him up.

Kyle is raising the mike on precisely the right cue. He launches into his number in a voice so strong and clear, and with such true pitch, I was stunned the first time I heard him sing.

"He's lip-synching," Danny snorts.

"No, he's singing live."

"That's live? Wow, he's good. I can't believe it's Kyle!"

We listen spellbound as Kyle continues through the first stanza. Danny slaps his forehead in amazement when he breezes through a difficult high part.

"What language is that?" Danny shouts, still dumbfounded that the school's football star, and still by far the best-looking boy in school, is not only singing on stage in front of thousands, he's really good.

"He's singing in Italian. He's a quarter Sicilian."

"Kyle?"

"Yeah. He said his grandmother taught him to speak Italian when she lived with his family." Watching the audience crush around the stage, I recall Kyle telling me it would be a big surprise, even though he occasionally sings in church. And not only is their football hero singing like a star, he's at his spectacular best, going on stage with no shirt. Marky Mark never looked so good.

It's when Kyle leads into the second stanza that I realize how much stage presence he has, how he connects with the audience. He's even dramatic, stretching one arm out, arching his head back, and holding the mike almost vertically up to his lips during another high part.

During an interlude, Kyle kneels down to touch the stretched-out arms of dozens of girls jammed around the stage.

"Huh, they look like little girls at a Menudo concert," I tell Danny.

"Jealous?"

"Of course not!"

I'm crashing my way down the back stairs before Kyle gets to the last note. Dashing straight from the stage as the cheers die down, sweaty and nearly out of breath, Kyle arrives at the foot of the stairs the same time I do.

"Oh, man, I was so nervous I thought I'd die," he says. "Was that okay?"

"Okay? Kyle, that was amazing," I tell him as I hold the door to the large storage closet we converted into a changing room.

Not ten seconds later, we're interrupted by a knock on the door. The kid who was coordinating the performers sticks his head in. Before he can say a word, he's almost trampled by Kyle's friends and his girlfriend Kathy. She screeches and jumps into his arms. Jason and Chrissy, Josh and Helen, Dustin and his date, and two other couples surround Kyle, all loud and excited. The girls are jumping up and down and squealing about how they can't believe it was Kyle out there.

"Hey!" Kyle shouts when their fawning goes on a little too long. "Bobby gets some of the credit. He remixed the number."

"I told you," Helen says to Josh.

Kathy nudges her boyfriend and whispers something to him.

"Hey, guys, I'll meet you out on the dance floor," he tells his friends. He follows by embracing Kathy and making a show of how passionately he can kiss her. His friends, still chattering and excited, reluctantly file out.

It's only moments later when we're interrupted a second time; an older couple is waiting to see Kyle. Puzzled, Kyle nods to let them in.

"Mom, Dad!" he shouts. "What are you doing here?"

"Mikey told us you were going to perform," his dad says, referring to Kyle's little brother. Mr. Faulkner, his features coarser, his body not in the best shape, still looks a little like Kyle.

"Mikey got us tickets, and we watched from the balcony," his mother, a typically blond-haired Texas woman with sharp, penetrating eyes, says in a high-pitched, nasally voice. "You sang so beautifully. And look, we got it on video," she tells her son while holding up a camcorder. "Well, I see you two lovebirds must be having a good time," she says when Kyle holds Kathy even tighter and gives her a peck.

"You guys aren't upset?" Kyle asks.

His dad responds by holding up a cell phone. "I called Grandmama in New York. She was asleep, but I woke her up. She heard you singing that beautiful Italian song. She heard you, Kyle, and she went to bed in tears, tears of happiness that her grandson would bring her such joy." Kyle's dad gives him a peck on each cheek. Mom, not to be outdone, follows with a hug. Kyle looks like he wants to be somewhere else.

"I'm sure you two just want to dance the night away," his mother trills in a singsong voice.

"Before you go ..." Kyle says as they reach the door, "Mom, Dad, this is Bobby Fowler," he says in a firm, almost defiant voice. "He's the one who put this dance on, and he remixed *Viva per Lei*."

Dad's expression is open and friendly as he approaches with his hand held out. "Thank you for helping my son," he says in a deep Texas drawl.

Kyle's mom, however, remains planted near the door, glaring at Kyle. Her all-American boy has been talking to the gay kid! She turns toward me with a forced half-smile. "How do you do," she says in a flat voice with a slight, cold nod. When Mrs. Faulkner holds out her hand to her husband, her meaning is unmistakable: *we're leaving, now.*

"Ready to dance?" Kyle asks Kathy with yet another kiss. Just before they disappear through the doorway, Dunston's newest singing sensation glances back, a quick but intriguing stare. No nod, no smile, no thank-you, nothing but a brief stare.

I'm trudging back up the balcony stairs wondering if I'll ever figure that boy out.

Chapter 60

"Totally awesome!" someone says.

"Thank you for coming."

An endless stream of prom-goers, couples mostly, but knots of girls and boys in small groups here and there, pours out of the armory's front doors, splitting to flow around me like a stream surging around a boulder.

Some are gay, like the four boys from Oklahoma who engulfed me and squealed like little club kids on ecstasy, and others look and sound like they're gay. A few look around furtively, as if talking to me will confirm to their friends that they're gay. Most, however, just want to find their cars for long drives home or get to Hendricks Drive-In or Sonic or the big party at the sandpit I heard about.

"The kid's a regular little politician," Chief Toby remarks to a county sheriff standing nearby.

"Hey, look who's here!" Dustin, who thinks he's the coolest guy in school (Kyle is, no contest), is practically bouncing out of the armory. He and his date are followed by Jason and Chrissy and a few other couples I know. Shouting loudly, they gather around. Jason is the first to reach for my hand and slap my back.

"I never thought I'd see anything like that," he says. "Where'd you get the searchlights?"

"Chief Toby."

"Hey, what was the final count?" Dustin shouts. He's now close enough for me to see his dilated pupils. Whatever he's on, it's not ecstasy.

"With comps and cash sales at the door, somewhere around 3,200.

Hey, did you guys hear some kids came all the way from Oklahoma?" My very excited classmates gasp, but it's not about Oklahoma.

"Three thousand two hundred?" Jason screeches. "Holy shit!"

As the group reacts with more excited chatter, a meaty hand reaches from behind to grasp my shoulder.

"And you were worried about getting to eight hundred," Chief Toby says in my ear before retreating back to his sheriff buddy.

It's another five minutes before the departing crowd slows to a trickle of stragglers. It's time to pack up.

"There you are," says Mr. Evans, holding a cash lockbox at his side. Shoulders slumping, eyes drooping from fatigue, my favorite teacher still manages a warm smile. "I must say, I've experienced anything like this in my entire life. Congratulations, Bobby," he says with an outstretched hand. "Gee, maybe my ears will stop ringing in a few days."

"Yeah!" a familiar voice roars. It's Mr. Ramirez doing a double fist pump worthy of a football player. Unlike Mr. Evans, Mr. Ramirez wraps me in a quick hug. "It was fabulous!" he screeches in a fabulously gay accent, flicking his wrist for added effect. Mr. Evans shakes his head and chuckles.

"Thanks to you guys," I tell them. "It was your idea in the first place. It was your doing and Danny's, and a whole bunch of people. You guys were awesome."

Mr. Evans is shaking his head.

"Bobby, Bobby, Bobby. This was your show. I know a lot of people helped, but you pulled the whole thing together."

"And the music, too," says Mr. Ramirez. "You put all those tracks together, and I know some of them were yours. I used to go to clubs in Miami, and let me tell you, tonight's music was smoking hot."

My two teachers guide me around while chattering about the music and the crowd and the lights and everything else. Vendors are packing up and lugging tables and supplies to waiting trucks. Dozens of empty water bottles, some squashed, litter the dance floor; trash overflows the barrels placed at both ends. The armory has reverted to its original state, an empty old dump.

We amble over to one of two tables where my big batch of just-arrived CDs were being sold. Only a hand-lettered poster and a cardboard box remain.

"So how'd we do?" I ask Mr. Evans.

"Maybe a hundred left here," he says, leaning down to peer into the carton. "The other table sold out."

It takes a few moments to sink in. "Wait a minute. I brought three hundred complete sets. That's fifteen hundred CDs. There's only a hundred left?"

"Congratulations, Bobby," says Mr. Ramirez. "You just made the Billboard Top Fifty."

"Fourteen hundred ... that's fourteen thousand dollars!"

"There's more," Kevin says with a grin. "Jorge, tell him about the concessions."

"Those kids ate and drank everything in sight. You're going to make maybe twice what we were planning."

"Plus seventy grand in ticket sales, more or less," Mr. Evans says. "Maybe you can donate some of your profits to the school committee," he adds with a wicked smirk.

"Did you see many gay kids?" I ask Mr. Ramirez.

"There must have been thirty or forty in that corner alone," he says, pointing toward the back.

We continue an aimless walk through the main hall, kicking at empties here and there. Mr. Evans and Mr. Ramirez give me updates about the near riot when they ran out of pizza—which I find so funny I burst out laughing—and the long lines at the girls' porta-potties. A few troublemakers were thrown out for drinking, and some guys were warned about giving gay kids a hard time. Our hired bouncers tossed a couple jerks for shoving two boys who were dancing together.

Earlier outside, Chief Toby said there were problems here and there, mostly drugs and drinking. Amazingly, there wasn't a single fight. Overall it was far less than he expected, and nothing like the big rumble after last year's game with Waco. He said he just wants everyone to get back home safely.

I give Mr. Evans and Mr. Ramirez vigorous handshakes before they leave. Two teachers, two friends. Who would have thought?

Chapter 61

The vast interior of the armory is deathly still. The massive lighting system, dark and lifeless. The powerful sound system, which had been blasting out dance hit after dance hit, utterly silent. The dance floor, only an hour ago a surreal scene of thousands dancing under the club lights, now empty and strewn with trash. The vendors, the security guys, the man picking up the lockboxes, Mr. Evans, Mr. Ramirez, Danny, the cops—everyone has left. It's just me sitting up here in this great big old barn, staring at nothing, not quite believing we pulled this off.

And yet, for all the excitement, the power of those hot dance mixes, for all the success, the nice words, people saying they couldn't believe it, the sheer size of the crowd that stunned everyone, including me, a cold sadness is slowly seeping in on what should be the greatest night of my life. It's not from the stress of the last five weeks, or going to bed last night so excited and nervous I couldn't sleep, or the big scare this afternoon. And not even that shit at school. It's just me sitting here all alone. Again.

I envy Eddie and Jimmy and picture them cuddling in bed together. And Tim and Zane, what will their joy be like when they wake up tomorrow?

I sigh deeply. "I'd trade all this for a boyfriend," I mutter aloud. I force myself to get up and head downstairs to the dressing room. I need to change out of this sweaty shirt, which I wiggle out of while trudging down the stairway.

"Oh, sorry!" I screech when I open the dressing room door. Kyle is at the far side of the cramped space, holding on to a pair of jeans.

Otherwise, he's wearing nothing. "What are you doing here?" I ask when he just casually stands there, not only without the slightest trace of embarrassment, but making no move to put his jeans on.

"Aren't you supposed to say, *quite a night, Bobby-dude,* or something like that?"

"I was just thinking that," I joke. I can't help getting a good look at that incredible bod. Not only is he not shy about being caught with nothing on, he grabs his pants in one fist and lets them fall down to his side, a rivet clinking when it hits the floor. Kyle couldn't be any more naked.

"So what *are* you doing here?" I ask, trying not to hyperventilate.

"I forgot I left a change of clothes here," he says. "What are you doing here? It's late."

I nod toward my purple-and-white school gym bag tucked under a card table. "I was just packing up and came down to change my shirt," I tell him, holding it out so he can see how sweaty it is.

"I thought you had a date," he says as he inches closer in small, shuffling steps.

"A date? You mean my date for the school prom? Yeah, right. I got dumped."

"What happened?"

"When I told him about the new school prom rules, he called back and said he didn't want any of this high school drama, and maybe he should date someone more mature. That was the end of my big romance. Well *fuck him.*" I didn't mean it to sound quite so bitter. Well, yes I did. Kyle is now just inches away. He grasps my shoulder.

"I'm really sorry," he says in a whisper, intently staring at me through narrowed eyes.

"Thanks. I guess that's the way it is."

Not only doesn't he let go, his breathing is deeper and noisier. "I thought Beth's party was amazing, but tonight ... I don't even know what to say. Everyone was blown away," he says, absently running his fingers over the solid muscle of his chest with his other hand.

"Kathy liked it too?"

"Yeah, of course. You pulled this off. I don't know how you did it, but you pulled off the most amazing thing that's ever happened in this town."

"Thanks. I had tons of help." I breathe deeply, slowly, letting some of the tension and excitement escape.

Kyle's eyes dart up and down my body in the time it takes to blink. He swallows hard, almost as if his throat has tightened up. The silence is becoming awkward. He's making no move to get dressed and leave.

"Were you upset when Tim and Zane started kissing?" I ask him.

"Up in the DJ booth? Yeah, I guess a little. I thought Tim was this super-cool guy, and he turns out to be gay. I mean, I guess it's okay. Two guys isn't my thing, you know, but if they got together, I guess that's okay. Hey, isn't Kathy hot?"

"Yeah, I'll say. She's really nice, too," I reply, wondering about the odd mention of his girlfriend.

"Kathy was really upset about what happened at school this week. I mean, I was too. Are you okay?"

"Yeah, I'm fine, but right now I just want to get home and get some sleep. Maybe tomorrow it will hit me that we pulled this off." Inching closer, gulping so hard it's like he's trying to swallow a whole apple, Kyle gently places both hands on my upper arms, rubbing gently. His hands tremble just enough so I can feel it.

"I'm really sorry about your date and what happened at school last week," he says in a shaky, near whisper. "I bet you need a hug."

Kyle wants to give me a hug? He's naked!

"Ah, that's okay. I don't want you to feel awkward, you know, me being gay and you being a straight boy. I'll be okay."

"You go home all alone again," he says, an odd strain pinching his voice. "It makes me feel bad. The best I can do is a hug."

"Oh, let me put my sweatshirt on." Kyle doesn't loosen his grip.

"Look, in four years you never once hit on me or anyone. It's just a hug, that's all."

So very naked Kyle wraps his smooth, rock-hard, muscular arms around me. But this is no Josh-like straight-boy hug, or even his hug after Beth's party. This is chest to chest, hips to hips, legs to legs, dick to dick. He even presses his cheek, raspy with the slightest bit of stubble, against mine. And he isn't letting go.

"Someday your dreams will come true," he whispers. He rubs my bare back and neck. He squeezes his arms around me even tighter. His nostrils raggedly wheeze like bellows.

I'm unsure what to do. He's the straightest boy in the entire school, but something about this feels awkward. Maybe he's experimenting like I've heard about in chat rooms. "Straight-but-curious," that's what they call it. On the other hand, this is the only real hug I'll ever get from the most adorable boy who ever lived.

"I just want to find someone special," I whisper back. Not quite believing I'm doing this, my arms press tighter, my hands explore the balls of those muscular shoulders, and sweep across every ripple of perfect skin on that massive, sexy back. This feels so good, so hot …

Chapter 62

"For mercy sakes, they could have taken a better picture," Mrs. Robles sputters at the supper table with a forkful of beans in one hand and the latest issue of the *Dunston Weekly Register* in the other. "Irene Grady, down at the hairdresser, told me everyone in town's been talking about your prom. I wish I hadn't been feeling so poorly that night."

"Go ahead, Mum, read what else it says."

"Let's see, it says, 'Chief of Police Tobias Sandman, who had a ten-member detail on duty for this event, called Bobby Fowler's prom a spectacular success. He told the *Register* that what Bobby Fowler did at 17 years old just to put this event on was remarkable, and even more remarkable was attracting 3,200 well-behaved teenagers, many of whom traveled great distances. Chief Sandman was also quoted as saying that the school committee might want to rethink their policies about gay students.'" Mrs. Robles gives me a look over the top of her reading glasses. "Now there's a slap at the school committee if I ever heard one."

"Yeah, right, as if the school committee is ever going to change their policies."

"A lot of people in town are fed up with their nonsense. Next fall we're going to get some reasonable people in there," she says as she continues reading the article on the next page.

"And I'll be long gone."

Frowning, Mrs. Robles puts the paper down. "Something's wrong. You've been moody all week. Sometimes you act like you're angry. What's wrong, dear?"

"Nothing," I mutter.

"Well, I know what it is. It's that college student," she says, each word spit out like machine gun bullets. "The nerve of that boy, telling you he's taking you to the prom and then just dumping you."

My foster mom is getting worked up, and as far as I'm concerned, it's so over, I don't want to think about it or talk about it. While I toy with the last of my barbecued sirloin, my foster mom picks up the paper and angrily shakes out a crease.

"Boys," she sputters. Mrs. Robles realizes she's getting worked up, puts the paper back down, and reaches out to pat my hand. "I'm really sorry, dear. I know you're hurt. Someday things will change."

"I'm okay," I sigh.

"That boy ought to be ashamed of himself, but that's not the way boys are. I remember when I was seventeen—or was I sixteen?—and this boy, Doug Rheingold ..."

Maybe I should clear the dishes.

* * * * *

"Forty thousand? I cleared forty grand?"

The judge leans way back in his black leather chair, folds his hands on his lap, and does that rapid little rocking thing. "Well, just remember, some of that's from your CD sales. Now, with the taxes you owe the IRS next quarter—"

"Taxes? I'm seventeen."

"Doesn't matter to the government," he shoots back. "You make a profit, you pay taxes. Where was I? Oh, yes, with the police detail bonuses, five hundred each to Mr. Ramirez and Mr. Evans—that's mighty generous of you—and the gifts to Danny and Chloe, you're in the neighborhood of $27,000. There's a lot of people in these parts who would love to make twenty-seven grand in a year. Bobby, on the phone you mentioned a charitable donation. What's this about?"

"It doesn't feel right to put on a prom for twenty dollars a ticket, and then I walk away with all that money when I just wanted to break even. Judge, $27,000! So, here's what I want to do: I'll keep the profit from the CD sales and give the profit from the prom to the Rainbow Hope Program in Austin for troubled gay kids, and some to the Police Benevolent Association."

The judge leans forward over his immense desk. "Bobby, you put this on, and you took the risk. If this affair flopped, it was you and no one else who was going to look bad and take a financial hit. It's okay to reap the reward when you do well."

"It still doesn't feel right. It wasn't even my idea. Mr. Bissell took over all the armory work and did the work at cost. Danny came up with the marketing that really got all those kids here, and the guy in Chicago gave us a great deal—"

"We know all that." The judge sighs and leans way back again. It's lecture time. "Bobby, that's the way it's supposed to work. If you did all that work yourself, would you have been able to put on the prom?"

"I guess not," I mutter.

"You're supposed have other people do things for you. It still has your name on it and you pulled it all together. Bobby, do you know how many MBA students at Harvard Business School would give their right arms to have this real-life experience?" He throws up his hands. "Fine, but just make sure you keep at least half that net profit. You need a car—"

"Danny and I are going to San Angelo to buy a car Wednesday night."

"At last," he says. "Well, congratulations. A boy's first car is always the most special. The Honda Civic you liked so much?" I nod yes. "Well, anyway, you keep at least half that money."

As usual, it's impossible to argue with him.

"How much to the Police Benevolent Association?" he asks to end further discussion.

"Five."

"Five thousand," he says, scribbling on a legal pad. "The chief will be mighty surprised when he opens his mail and finds a check for five thousand dollars. I'd love to be there just to see his reaction."

"The chief was awesome. I owe him a lot."

"When I met up with him Saturday night, he was effusive in his praise for you, young man, as am I."

"You saw him Saturday night? You were *there?*"

"Me boy, of course I was there," he says with a grin and his best Irish accent. "I accepted your invitation. I knew you were stressed and busy, and I didn't want to bother you."

"So what did you do?"

"The chief and I had a look around. We watched that spectacular light show, put in earplugs, and we watched the kids … well, I guess you call it dancing. Bobby, I'm just some old fuddy-duddy. What did you want me to do, dance?" The judge's chamber echoes with raucous laughter.

"Gee, Judge, I would have bought a ticket to watch you dance!" We both share a hearty laugh.

"So what's this you wanted to show me?" he asks, peering at the paper I've been holding in my lap.

"It's an e-mail I got last week," I tell him as I hand it over. When we make eye contact, he knows this is serious.

While the judge sits back and holds it up close, I'm back at my PC that night, reliving the emotions I felt when I read it the first time.

> Dear Bobby Fowler,
> I am 15 yo and I am gay. I live with my folks and my grandma and two brothers. My Mom found out i'm gay a few months ago and told me I'm going to hell. Then she told every relative I have not to talk to me and I have lots of them, they are all my family. I wanted to run away. Mostly I want to die because I cant stand it anymore. Then I snuck off to your dance with a girl from school even if it got me in trouble. It was so awsome I cant describe it. The lights were grate too. I met this boy who was really nice looking and we danced and he kissed me! It was my first kiss and I was in heaven. He told me all about you. Bobby, you made me see it's ok to be gay and that gay people can do neat things. If it wasn't for you I really dont think I'd even be here.
>
> Thank you from your new gay friend,
>
> Brian Hale
> Circle H Ranch
> Eden, Texas

"Since then, I received ten more e-mails and two letters—" I stop when I notice the judge's tightened lips and moist eyes. "I wrote back and told him to hang in there, because there's a better life ahead," I continue. "I told him that God loves him and that he's a good person. I wrote back to everyone." The judge is very quiet. "How I'd like to meet Brian Hale someday," I say to myself.

"You're special," the judge says softly. "They seek you out because they know you're special."

"I want to help gay kids. I think that's one of the things I want to do with my life, Judge, help gay kids." Saying nothing, he nods, appreciating the power of this e-mail from a scared, lonely kid. His secretary bursts in to announce he's late for a hearing. Our time is over.

On my way down the wide stairs to the limestone-paneled lobby, I'm thinking that the real payoff from the prom wasn't so much the eye-popping profit, or giving the finger to the school committee, or the newspaper clippings or all the nice things people said. It was something Mr. Ramirez said. "There'll be gay kids there, and some of them will need this prom as much as you, maybe more."

Brian Hale. That's the real payoff.

"... and it was full of light!"

Chapter 63

"What a jerk," Chloe squawks. "I've seen Kyle walk right by you in the hallway, and he just ignores you. Turn left here," she says, pointing over the dash of the Honda Civic I bought last night in San Angelo.

"Am I doing okay?"

"Yeah, you're fine. When you get a little more experience, you'll drive faster," she says, glancing over her shoulder at the line of vehicles behind me. "Every day he shows up wearing a stretchy muscle shirt or tank top so he can show off how hot he looks," she sputters. "And they let him get away with it! Someone said he used the queer word, and what was he doing flirting with Allison Baumann right in the hallway? Bobby, he's going steady!"

"You're really okay I went with electric blue instead of the silver?"

"Yeah, I told you I like the blue," she replies. "Did you hear he almost punched out some kid this afternoon?"

"Who did?"

"Kyle!"

"No, I didn't hear anything," I tell her. "Do I turn here?"

"Not yet. It happened this afternoon, and Travis, you know, from my French class, he was right there. He said this kid accidentally got pushed into Kyle between classes, so macho boy got real upset and was ready to punch him out, except his friends talked him out of it. Bobby, this was some skinny little sophomore. Then Kyle gloated like he's this big macho stud. That boy is out of control." Chloe points just up ahead. "Do you want to practice parallel parking?"

"Nah, that's all right."

"Sorry, I didn't mean to get you upset," she says.

"Oh, it's not that. Lunch period's almost over. We have to get back."

"Great," she says, rolling her eyes. "So what is going on?"

"Nothing's going on." I look this way and that, check the rearview mirror, glance at the speedometer, check the rearview mirror again, all the while hoping Chloe will find something else to talk about.

She turns around halfway in the seat to look right at me. "Something happened at the prom," she says. "It's the dividing line. Kyle was so friendly before, even going over to your place to practice that song and use the hot tub, and now he's a complete jerk. Why can't you tell me? I *know* something happened."

"Well, he isn't being nasty. Maybe he has some issues."

Chloe makes a face. "Come on, Bobby, you never once held back. Ever. Look, I'm not trying to pry, but it's like, all week long when I ask why Kyle's ignoring you, you clam up. You seem angry, too. He didn't get drunk and beat you up, did he?"

Chloe can be relentless. She'll get this out of me eventually, and she'll get really suspicious if I tell her it's none of her business. And she's right. I've never held back from her, ever. Well, just that one time I was jerking off at the pool and the pool cleaning guy showed up.

My new car bumps off the road into a gas station parking area, coming to a stop next to a display of hunting blinds.

"No, Chloe, he didn't beat me up."

"Oh, no. You hit on him. Is that what happened? *You hit on Kyle?*"

My head drops onto my arms crossed over the steering wheel.

"It's okay," Chloe says, squeezing my arm. "You know I'm here for you."

"I didn't hit on him," I answer in barely a whisper. "It was the other way around."

"It was what? Did you … oh my gosh, oh my gosh! Kyle hit on you? Kyle? Oh my gosh, *oh my gosh!*"

"Look, it's why I can't tell anyone. Chloe, you have to understand, he really is straight, but maybe he's what some of my chat-room friends call 'straight-but-curious.' Like he's experimenting or something. If I tell you what really happened, you won't tell anyone? Promise?"

"Come on, Bobby, everything you and I have ever talked about is between me and you. I promise this won't go anywhere else."

I begin relating what happened almost two weeks ago after the prom, beginning with my startling discovery in the dressing room.

Chloe listens with growing amazement, her eyes getting bigger and her screeching getting louder with each new detail.

"He *wanted* to give me a naked hug."

"Is that why he was so nervous?" she asks.

"I don't know. Maybe he'd been planning it … oh, shit, he planned the whole thing! Chloe, we didn't meet up by accident. Kyle was waiting for me. He wanted me to find him there."

"So what was he doing while he was giving you a naked hug?" she asks.

"Rubbing his hands all over me."

"Jeez, that would've turned me on," Chloe says as she fans herself with her fingers.

"At first it felt awkward … I'm sorry, the whole thing was so hot I couldn't help it. I hugged him tight and got my hands all over him."

"Don't be sorry. You're gay and he set this up."

"There's more," I tell her. "He didn't let go. He was holding me tight, and that's when he got his hands inside my pants and all over my ass, and he started squeezing and rubbing. He was trying to make a joke out of it, like, 'Oh, so that's what gay-boy ass feels like,' or something like that. He was so nervous he could hardly talk. That's when he got a woody."

Chloe's hands fly to her mouth. "That's some experiment," she says.

"It's not like we had sex. So, anyway, he jerked away and said, 'What the fuck are you doing?' He was angry, like he was the one getting groped."

"And then he beat you up?" Chloe asks.

I shake my head no. "He put his pants on as fast as he could and ran out of the dressing room. I heard him scream 'fuck' real loud just before the front door slammed open. I figured he'd be wicked upset at school. Guess I was right."

"Have you talked to him?" she asks.

"That's the thing—he won't even look at me. I tried talking to him. I left him two notes, and he got real angry and tore them up. The second note started with, 'I know you're straight.' Oh, Chloe, he's just completely freaking out, like he's desperate to show everyone he's straight."

"How about talking with Helen? She and Kyle are really close."

"I can't tell her! She'll jump to the wrong conclusion. Then Kyle will freak out even worse, and he'll beat me up for real."

Chloe leans toward me. "Maybe it's not the wrong conclusion."

"Chloe, the guy's straight. He was just experimenting or something."

"He plans the whole thing and tricks you into a naked hug? He runs his fingers all over your ass and gets a woody? What am I missing here?"

"Sex. I'm sure he didn't want sex. Oh," I groan, "I can't believe this happened."

"So you're upset. You seem angry too."

"I'm not angry!"

"I'm sorry, Bobby." Chloe settles back in her seat and lets out a sigh. "I was hoping you'd be happy after the prom," she says.

"Look, I'm sorry I snapped at you. The prom was awesome, and those e-mails and letters are what made it really worthwhile. It's just this whole thing with Kyle has me so freaking upset. He shoves his hard-on in my face at Beth's, and then he gives me a naked hug and gropes me, and it's my fault. Then he goes totally spastic at school. I gotta get away from here, Chloe. I want to get the hell out of Dunston and get on with college."

We pull out of the gas station in silence.

Chapter 64

Helen and I are just setting our trays on a table shaded by one of the school's immense live oaks, escaping the direct sun on a blazing hot day. Dozens of students surround us, happy that it's Friday, eating, gossiping, making weekend plans, boys checking out girls, girls checking out boys. I tried to make excuses this morning when Helen asked if we could eat together, just the two of us, she said. Helen can be very insistent.

"Have you been to the new Wal-Mart?" she asks as she starts picking at her fruit salad.

"Chloe and I are going tomorrow. This afternoon I'm going to the mall so I can get some new workout sneakers. The guys at Sneakerama really know their stuff."

"The Wal-Mart is huge. Lot of excitement for our little town. First the prom, then the Wal-Mart Superstore opens.

"Hard to believe tomorrow will be two whole weeks since the prom."

"That's what I wanted to talk about," she replies, setting her fork down to lean closer. "Can I tell you what happened?"

"Yeah, definitely," I tell her, surprised because I thought this was about Kyle. "Something that happened to you?"

"Oh, yeah," Helen says, her eyes sparkling. "It was magical. Josh and I were dancing the night away, you know, with the lights and your music and everyone having a wonderful time. You played this beautiful song. Josh was looking into my eyes, and I was looking into his. It was like everything disappeared, and it was just the two of us on the dance floor."

"And you guys started making out?"

"Stop it," she giggles. "I started singing along. You know it. It's a song you remixed. 'You are my perfect angel, you make me feel so happy,'" she sings in a high, soft voice.

"Oh, that song is *so* romantic."

"Josh kept looking at me, like he was lost in my eyes, and he leaned over during a quiet part ..." Helen's eyes mist over.

"Come on, Helen."

"I'll remember every word until the day I die. He said, 'Helen, I love you more than I ever thought I could love someone. I don't have the words to tell you how much I love you, but I love you with every piece of my heart.' Then he whispered in my ear, 'I want to be with you forever,' and he followed with the sweetest kiss. I told him I want to be with him forever too. It was magic. And it was your prom and your music and that wonderful song that made it so special." Helen stops to dab at her eyes.

"That's beautiful. I'm really happy for you."

"I know you're not very happy right now," she says, her tone instantly changing from mushy romance to all business. "It's the other reason I wanted to talk to you."

Now we'll talk about Kyle.

"Josh and I are worried about Kyle. I know he's been ignoring you, and he's been like, weird lately. He's having some issues or something, and it's bothering me. Both Josh and I tried talking with him, and he just brushed us off." Helen reaches to softly grasp my hand. "Josh and I are here for you too, you know."

"Thanks, I really appreciate it. I tried talking to him, but that didn't get very far."

"It's not your fault," Helen says. "There's a lot of pressure on Kyle, way too much."

"What do you mean?"

"Look, don't go around telling people this, okay?" I nod that I understand. "Kyle's on the summer swim club, and his times are getting worse. The coach is really on his case, especially about his attitude. Josh heard he might even get kicked off the team."

"He's their best swimmer!"

"He's been on the team since eighth grade. And last week he told me—Bobby, this has to stay between you and me—with his grades and no football scholarship, the best he can do is junior college. Kyle's devastated, and he's scared to tell his parents. You know how they can be, and they're really on his case about his grades and his attitude. I guess Coach Meyer called them a few days ago, and Kyle said his dad went through the roof."

"I heard a rumor he and Kathy are breaking up."

"They broke up Wednesday night. Kathy … well, let's just say it's over."

"Maybe that explains why he's been so weird."

Helen gives me an odd stare and leans even closer. "I've got to tell you something I heard." She hesitates and takes a deep breath. "I know that Kyle met up with you at that club in Austin last summer."

"How'd you hear that?"

"My cousins Anita and Zack live in Austin."

Try as I might to play it cool, the mention of Zack's name zaps me like an electric shock.

"I know Kyle went to the club, and I know he spent quite a bit of time with you in the DJ booth," Helen continues, but now she's wringing her hands, as if she's afraid of where this is going. "And I know you two went home together. Zack was there, and he said he couldn't get near you two. What was Kyle doing alone at a gay club?"

I gulp hard but nothing goes down. "He didn't go alone," I explain, but my voice is already nervous-shaky. "He said he went with some friends to hear the music, and he stayed after they left. I bumped into him and showed him my DJ equipment and let him mix a few tracks. When he found out I was staying at a hotel, he offered me a ride home, that's all." I'm trying to remain totally casual, but nothing gets by Helen. The stare, the tight lips with the slightest hint of a you're-not-fooling-me smile—she's not buying it.

"My cousin Billy was checking up on the armory well after the prom was over, and he saw Kyle go into the dressing room," Helen says, taking another tack so scary I can't move a muscle. "Then Billy saw you go in, and he said you two spent quite a bit of time together. When Kyle left, Billy said he was extremely upset. *Something* happened in there. Since then Kyle's been … I hate to say this, but he's been acting like a jerk, and you've been acting like you're upset."

I tense even more, if that's possible, waiting for Helen to ask if I hit on him. She's wringing her hands and glancing around to see if anyone's listening in. She leans in close. "Bobby … did Kyle hit on you?"

Not only am I almost knocked off my seat, there's no way I can answer. If I say no, she'll know I'm lying. But if I say yes, she'll jump to the wrong conclusion and say something to Kyle. I don't even want to think about what will happen then.

I'm already bolting out of my seat, tray in hand. "I have to get ready for my next class," I mumble. Hurrying away, I glance back. Helen's head is down in her hands.

Chapter 65

I'm gasping for breath, my back pinned against the white van by Kyle's powerful grip, waiting for him to start punching me out right in the middle of the mall parking lot. I've never seen him so pissed. And here I thought all I'd be doing this afternoon was buying sneakers and eating at Peruvian Chicken.

I know Kyle said something really nasty after he crashed into me inside the mall, but did I have to crush his balls?

I'm still waiting. Cringing with my eyes clamped tight, all I hear is heavy breathing.

Hands let go of their grip. Here it comes …

Nothing's happening.

Why's he waiting, just to torment me?

"Go ahead, just do it. Just get it over with!" I scream at him.

But instead of painful blows, gentle hands cushion my jaw. At the exact moment my eyes pop wide open, lips press against mine, lips soft and warm. Every muscle in my body tenses.

Kyle grips harder, pressing his lips into mine, his kissing becoming more urgent, air rushing in and out of his nose in loud, shaky breaths, his body pressing tightly into mine. He pulls back.

"I will *never* hurt you," he says with whispered, intense words.

A hand finds the back of my head, bringing me closer so he can kiss even more passionately.

And just like in the dressing room two weeks ago, I give in, wrapping my arms around him, impulsively kissing back. But somehow, this is different from the prom—this is for real.

His head draws back, his hands fall away.

I wait for more, but nothing happens. I look up and gasp. A tear is about to escape eyelids pressed so tightly together that his brow is creased. A single, anguished sob escapes.

"No," he moans in an odd, high-pitched squeak.

"Kyle?"

"It can't be," he cries, still with his eyes shut tight. A tear leaves a streak on his cheek.

I reach up, but before my hand can touch his cheek, Kyle abruptly turns, walks aimlessly away like a drunk, and repeats through tears, "This can't be happening." He breaks into a stumbling run toward his motorcycle just outside the food court.

And then the truth hits with the force of a lightning bolt. What Chloe realized, and I insisted wasn't possible, is true. Kyle is gay. *Kyle Faulkner is gay.* And he's falling apart right in front of me.

Kyle stumbles to his Harley, places his hands on the black leather seat and slumps over, his head hanging low, his chest heaving violently. I dash after him and scream his name.

I don't make it in time. Flinging himself onto his bike and not looking back as I frantically holler to wait up, Kyle guns his Harley to life with a shattering roar. In moments, he's screaming out of the mall's parking lot so recklessly I'm scared he'll crash. Running a red light, almost colliding with a trailer truck that complains with a smoky screech of brakes and a long, angry blast of its horn, a distant figure in a white tank top roars up Route 87 at fantastic speed. Dazed, all I can do is watch.

A sickening, horrible fear rises from the pit of my stomach. I know what Kyle is going to do. I don't know how I know, I just do.

"Bobby, what the hell happened?"

I whip around to see Danny hanging out of the food court doorway looking wild-eyed.

"Kyle was crying. What happened?" he shouts.

It takes a moment to recover, but when I do, I run to my friend. "Danny, I've got to help him. I've got to help Kyle. He's in trouble!" I scream. All too quickly, I'm becoming a mess of hysterical tears. "Help me, please, Danny. I've got to find Kyle. Please, help me!"

"Okay, take it easy and calm down. What happened? Why was Kyle crying?"

"He's running away. I think he's going to end it. Please, Danny, you've got to help me."

"End it? What do you mean, end it?"

"I don't know where he's going. I've got to find him! Danny, Kyle's running … and I think …" I'm gasping so hard and fast I have to force the words out. "I think he's going to kill himself!"

Danny reacts with a look of horror. He begins pacing like a crazed person with his hands clamped over his head, mumbling, "Oh, no," over and over. Anxious moments seem like minutes.

"I think I know. Hang on a sec, I need paper," he says.

Danny charges into the food court while I pace and wipe tears. Each second of waiting is agony. I'm too scared to even think of what will happen if I don't get to Kyle in time, but I do know what will happen.

Just as I'm praying hard to God to help me find Kyle, the door bangs open. Danny races out waving a piece of note paper.

"I'm pretty sure he'll go to this place at Ivie Reservoir. Guys go there fishing and drinking, and that's where Kyle goes when he wants to be alone. He and I used to go there when we were friends." Danny hands me the note. I'm so upset and my eyes are so filled with tears, I can hardly read his hand-scrawled directions.

"Here," he says, grabbing it and pointing to each direction. "Route 87 up to Brady, follow 87 west at the town square … you got that? Turn north on Farm Road 503 …"

I'm having a hard time concentrating, but the directions seem detailed enough to follow. Danny shouts something about not driving too fast, but I'm already sprinting toward my car.

It's going to be a long, terrifying drive.

Chapter 66

Boat ramp, the metal sign with a bullet hole says. My new car eases onto the concrete ramp well above where it dips steeply into the vast expanse of Ivie Reservoir. A single white pickup with a boat trailer in tow is parked farther up the road. Way off to the left, up one of two long arms of the reservoir, a boat with two guys fishing drifts across a band of water sparkling gold in the low sun.

Otherwise, it's just me—and no sign of Kyle's motorcycle. I'm trying to ignore the sick, panicky thought that I've driven over an hour for nothing. A quick double-check of Danny's directions confirms I'm right where I'm supposed to be.

The final instruction is "Follow right trail." Not finding anything resembling a trail after an anxious, too-quick look around, I decide to park farther up, for some odd reason afraid that my new car will roll into the lake. The sun will set in an hour or so. *If I don't find him soon ... no, I can't let anything happen to Kyle, I can't.*

A feeling of dread reaches near panic when I still can't find the trail. Both sides of the ramp are filled with dense scrub brush and an occasional stunted tree. If anyone saw me, they'd wonder why I'm darting back and forth across the ramp like a crazed person.

Near the lip where the ramp makes its steep descent, a closer look reveals a small parting through the brush. I push through a few feet. It's the head of a path. I let out an enormous breath, clutching my chest in hopes that my heart won't explode.

He's here! Not five feet into the brush, his motorcycle lies tipped on its side. Kyle had pushed his Harley into a thicket of low brush and dumped it. Its right-hand mirror crushed and twisted, the ground glitters with crunchy pieces of glass. Instinctively, I check more closely. A single key on a Warriors key chain still sits in the ignition. With some bizarre sense of concern, maybe to grasp one little piece of order from this overwhelming fear, I slide it out. Kyle will need it, I'm thinking, as I tuck it far down into my pants pocket.

No other sign of Kyle is visible, only this lonely trail gliding at a slanting angle down through the thinning brush to the shoreline, a strip of sand and gravel so narrow that two people would have to walk single file. Up ahead is a gradual, gravelly bend, the far side hidden by scrub. My heart pounding, stomach rebelling, more of the narrow shoreline around the bend comes into view with each step.

A horrible vision appears of what I'll find, a vision of a body floating face-down in the water. Down on my hands and knees, dry heaves rack my body.

I've got to keep going, I scream at myself; I have find him before it's too late. Filled with dread, desperately praying with each step, more of the far side comes into view, only to reveal a long, shallow bay toward a distant point. The long, tiring hike, at least a mile, is filled with fear so overwhelming I again collapse to my knees from another attack of dry heaves.

After at least a twenty-minute trek, a few yards ahead is the end of the trail, a sharp, rocky jut into the upper arm of the reservoir. The shoreline of gravel and pebbly stones, littered here and there with disgusting empties and broken glass, disappears around the other side. I force a few more desperate steps, scuffling across the gravel.

I gasp out loud.

Kyle sits motionless, as if in a trance, his hair mussed, his head lying on arms crossed over drawn-up knees, his butt resting on a low rock outcropping almost over the water. He doesn't move or react in any way, even when I'm almost upon him. All I want to do is give him a hug and tell him I'm here to help.

"Kyle?"

With startling swiftness, he grabs something bright and shiny metallic by his side. My mind screams when I see what it is.

"No!" I shout, backpedaling quickly. "Kyle, please don't, please, Kyle, please!"

"Why did you follow me here?" he asks in a voice cracking with anguish.

"Kyle, I'm sorry. I came to help. Please don't do anything. Please put that down, Kyle. I won't come closer, I promise." I'm upset with myself for weeping already.

"Just go and leave me alone. Go!" he barks. The long-barreled pistol, which looks to be chromed, returns to his side, but his hand rests on top of it, ready to pick it up in an instant. Kyle's head droops to his chest.

Another vision intrudes, more horrible than the first, a vision of blood spurting from a gaping wound on the side of his head as he collapses onto the rocks.

Too unsteady to stand, not for one second thinking about taking off and leaving him to die in this lonely place, I've sunk onto my butt on the stony ground, furiously gulping air, struggling not to heave again, reminding myself that Kyle is still alive not twenty feet from me. He desperately needs me. But he's going pull the trigger to get out of the trap he sees no way out of.

Quietly sobbing, a wave of sadness overwhelms me, a feeling of immense tragedy about to unfold right in front me, and there's nothing I can do to stop it. This isn't TV. This is for real, and I don't know what to say; I don't what to do. I'm trying to calm down to think of something, anything, to say to him.

"Kyle, I know you're scared."

He doesn't respond or so much as twitch. He remains sitting on that rocky point, staring out over the calm waters of Ivie Reservoir.

"Kyle, I know how scared you are. I've been there. Will you please just talk to me?"

Again, nothing. I'm angry with myself because I can't stop weeping, and upset thinking I'm making things worse. It takes precious minutes to force myself to be steady.

"Kyle, please let me talk to you," I gasp. "I'm sorry, I don't know what to do, but I came here for you. Please let me talk to you."

"I'm sorry I hurt you and what I said," he says, his voice cracking. "I can't go back," he says, weeping now. "I fucked everything up anyway. Now please go away, Bobby, just go." He nudges the gun.

"No! Kyle, please don't!" He doesn't move a muscle. "There's something I have to tell you. I only realized it when you kissed me in the parking lot. Please don't freak out on me. I love you. I know you don't believe me, I know you think I'm just saying it, but it's true. Kyle, I love you and I can't lose you. I can't see you end it all here. You've got to listen to me."

He responds by putting his head back down on his knees.

"I can't lose you!" I scream way too loudly. His shoulders heave in quick, rapid motions. I cry again too, but I can't help this boy who means more to me than anyone in the world if I just sit here and cry all night.

"I hit your head against the van," he says in a trembling voice, "where you were hurt …" Choked up, he can't finish. "Just go," he manages to spit out. "*Get away from me!*" he screams with ferocious anger that frightens me.

"I can't leave, Kyle," I wail. "You didn't hurt me, and if you need me to say it, I forgive you. You were hurt and angry. I love you, Kyle. Don't you understand? I really do love you. Please let me help so you don't have to be scared all alone."

Kyle puts his hand on the gun. The instant surge of panic is so fierce I can't move, I can't scream, I can't breathe. But he only nudges it a few inches to move his butt. My heart thumping violently, it takes more precious minutes to calm down, minutes on a clock that's counting down.

"Do you remember when we rode back from Austin and you ran out of gas?" I say to him. "I told you something. Do you remember?" Kyle doesn't move or react. "I said, 'Someday you'll really need someone,' and I told you I'll be there for you. That's now; I'm here for you right now. You can share this burden with me; you can share being scared. We can get through this together if you'll only let me help. Kyle, please, I don't want to lose you."

Nothing. My fear grows more intense, if that's possible. If Kyle pulls that trigger, I won't be able to bear it. Someone will find two bodies, because I won't be able to go on if Kyle goes through with it. I can't let him do it. I can't lose him!

It's been a while, and neither of us has moved, neither of us has spoken, as if we were frozen here by the side of the reservoir, now rapidly darkening into an ominous, frightening twilight.

"Kyle, I have something to tell you. Will you listen?"

His shoulders twitch, the slightest shrug, at least that's what I think he did.

"When I was a little boy, we lived near a lake. One day, my dad took me down to the lake to teach me to swim. There was a little sandy beach and a dock, and Dad waded out to the end, up to his chest in water. He told me to walk to the end of the dock. I did, and I was looking down at that inky-black, scary water, more terrified with each step. When I got to the end, my dad held his arms up. 'Jump, Bobby, jump in,' he said.

I froze. The water looked so black and scary, I couldn't move. My dad said, 'Come on, Bobby, jump in. I'll catch you.'

"I just stood there, frozen in fear. No, it was more than that. It was pure terror. I kept looking at that scary water, and I couldn't do it. But you know what? Eventually I jumped in. I made a leap of faith to overcome my fear. My daddy caught me, and I hardly got wet. Before you know it, I was running off the dock, screaming and laughing.

"Kyle, I'm pleading with you to make a leap of faith. You're not just scared, you're terrified. You feel trapped, but it isn't a trap, and ending everything here isn't the way out. There *is* a way out. I promise you there's a way out, and I'm here to help you find it."

I thought he might move or at least say something after all that. I was hoping he'd get up and hold his arms out, and I'd run to him and hold him and save him. He's just like I was, though, standing at the edge of that dock, frozen in fear, trapped by choices he can't bear. But I can't give up, I can't! He's got to see that there's a way out.

I continue, "At the club, I talked with this older guy. He said he came out a few years ago when he was in his fifties. He has a wife and a son, and he was terrified too. He was so scared he said he couldn't think straight. But he said admitting who you are, and accepting who you really are, is like putting a key in a door and then having the courage to open it. Kyle, he said somehow he found the courage, somehow he made the leap of faith, to turn the key. And when he opened the door, it was into a room ..." I'm sobbing again, squeaking the words out. "He said it was a room full of light. Don't you understand? He had been in darkness all his life and never knew it, pretending everything was okay, trying to live a life he thought everyone expected of him. He said he only deceived himself. He opened the door into a new life, and it was full of light!

"Please, I love you so much. Do you understand? Do you hear my words?" I shout. "I just can't live without you, and I *promise* I won't live without you. I've lost everyone, and I can't lose the only person I've ever loved now. Did you save my life in the hospital so I could lose you now? Please, I'm begging you, make the leap of faith."

His head down on his knees, Kyle remains frozen on this small outcropping jutting into the darkened waters of Ivie Reservoir. "I can't go back," a small, shaky voice says.

"Please, Kyle!"

I'm going to lose him, and there's nothing I can do to stop him. I want to run to him and grab him and kiss him and tell him everything will be okay. I don't, fearing I'll startle him into grabbing the gun and pulling the trigger. So we're at an impasse—Kyle so scared he can't move, and me unable to do anything or say anything to talk him out of it. I clamp my eyes tight, my hands tighter, and mouth silent words of prayer, begging God to give me the words or tell me what to do to save Kyle and let him live. I have never prayed so hard in my life.

Kyle hasn't yet brought himself to end it. He can't seem to bring himself to do anything other than stare at the now-black water. I'm more than scared. This feeling of sadness is overwhelming, knowing that the boy I realized only this afternoon I desperately love, is going to end his life right in front of me, that I'm going to lose him forever, that my life will be so empty it won't be worth living.

No, it can't be like that; it just can't!

I am not going to let that happen. I am not going to let Kyle pull the trigger.

Fuck this!

I'm on my feet. It's now completely dark except for the half moon almost directly overhead.

"Kyle, stand up!" I bark. His head jerks slightly, nothing else. "Kyle, stand up, please," I say, this time gently. "I know you can do this. I'm putting all of my faith in you. You can do this. Just stand up, that's all. Please, Kyle, just do this one last thing, do it for me; it's all I'm asking."

At first, nothing happens, but with a heave of his shoulders so deep it looks like he's inflating, Kyle's head lifts up and his sneakers scuff on the rocky surface. Slowly and almost creaking, surprising for an athlete, Kyle gets to his feet. Facing away from me, his shoulders slumped, Kyle gazes over the now-dark arm of Ivie toward low, treeless hills just barely visible in the moonlight on the far side.

"You need to listen to my voice," I tell him. "Don't think of anything else but my voice. Turn around and look at me. Please, Kyle, this one little step, do this one little thing for me. I know you can do this; I just know you can. Just turn around and look at me."

He's turning around! Maybe out of shame, his head droops onto his chest.

"Kyle, please, you need to look at me. Please, just look into my eyes. *Just look at me!*"

His head jerks up and he does look, straight into my eyes. Even from this distance, maybe fifteen or twenty feet, and with just the soft light of the moon, I can plainly see eyes that are red and puffy—and filled with fear.

"I know you can do this," I plead with him again, our eyes locked as if there's a laser beam linking us. "I know you can make that leap of faith. There's a part of you that doesn't want to give up, a part that knows I love you. Listen to it! Kyle, I want you to move your left foot forward, just one step. Just one little step, that's all I'm asking. Come on, just move your left foot; do it for me. *Don't look away!*" His head snaps back, his eyes focus on mine, looking terrified, but I see something else in his eyes: he's pleading with me to help him.

He hesitates and then … he's moving his foot toward me! One small move, scrunching along the rock, at most the length of his sneaker, but his foot moved. I almost can't believe it. One little step, that's what I asked him to do. But for him, that one little step is something far more—Kyle is choosing to live. He's letting me show the way, but he has to choose which fork in the road to take, and he's choosing to live!

"Kyle, I told you I'm here to help carry part of the load. I'm going to meet you halfway. I'm going to take one step toward you, and you're going to take one step toward me. We're going to get through this together."

I step. So does he.

"Now again," I tell him. We both step, nearly in unison, slow steps, small steps, hardly the length of one foot, but huge steps for both of us.

"Jump off the dock, Kyle. I'm here to catch you," I tell him as I step again and he hesitates. "Please, I'm begging you, come out of that dark and scary place because I love you. I love you with all my heart, Kyle. I love you with every last piece of my being. Please make the leap of faith and meet me halfway."

Carefully, deliberately, I step again. He does too, a small step toward me. It isn't much of a distance separating us, but it might as well be from the earth to the moon. For real, it's a gulf of life and death for both of us. It seems to take forever, me staring at him, willing him forward, refusing to accept losing this incredible, wonderful boy, and Kyle, looking frightened and wild-eyed. It's taking an eternity, but he's following me step for step.

Finally! We're so close I can put my arms around him. He looks shell-shocked.

"When the Book of Kyle is written," I tell him, "the first Chapter will be about courage, because, Kyle, that was the most courageous thing I ever witnessed."

Kyle clamps his eyes shut, creasing his brow, and takes one quick, shaky gulp of air. He begins to sob.

I lunge to wrap my arms around him in a frantic, tight embrace. "You're safe now," I tell him. Kyle grasps onto me just as tightly—no, even tighter—a furious, clawing, grasping, desperate embrace, as if I was all that was preventing him from falling into some abyss of unspeakable horror. "You're safe and it's all over. Just let go. It's okay to let it all out."

In my fast embrace, his head buried on my shoulder, Kyle weeps, his legs so weak he collapses onto me. He wails quietly, but his whole body is so wracked with heaves, he can hardly breathe.

"It's okay to cry, just let it all out," I keep telling him while rubbing his back and running my fingers over his head, trying to soothe this boy who trusted me with his life. Poor Kyle; he came within inches of dying.

"I love you, Kyle. I love you so much," I tell him over and over. "I love you with all my soul."

For a while he just weeps, then he wails loudly. I don't think I've ever seen anyone cry so hard. I comfort him as best I can and cry with him, realizing how close I too came to the unthinkable.

Even after Kyle's cries become deep, heaving breaths, we remain in a tight embrace, rocking slightly, our hands comforting each other, both of us exhausted, both of us drained, both of us bonded together as I never knew two people could be.

Chapter 67

"I never knew anyone could love me so much," he croaks, lifting his head off my shoulder to stare deeply into my eyes.

"I couldn't bear to lose you. I love you, Kyle. I mean it, I love you for real."

"Bobby ..." I'm silently pleading with him to say it. "It feels weird to say it, but I love you too. I think I've been in love with you for a long time." We grasp each other even more tightly. "You just wouldn't let go. Oh, shit, I'm so sorry," he says, grimacing and throwing his head back. "You must have been so scared. I'm sorry for what I put—"

"No!" I shout with my hand flying up to his mouth. "You don't ever have to say you're sorry."

We embrace again, a hot, tight embrace that goes on without end. *How odd,* I'm thinking as we gently rock back and forth, *the boy I've always thought of as the hottest boy I've ever seen is now in my arms, and it isn't some sexual thing; no, this is the most powerful love I've ever known.*

"You saved my life," Kyle says. "You followed me up here and saved my life."

"You saved my life too, remember? Now we're together."

"Maybe that's the way God wants it to be," he whispers. We hug and caress and comfort one another. A wonderfully crazy thought pops into my head.

"Hey, Kyle, you started to do something in the parking lot. Maybe we could try again? This time you might not catch me by surprise."

Kyle relaxes enough to return my grin, just a slight upturn of his mouth.

Holding his hands lightly around my jaw just like in the parking lot, soft lips gently brush mine. I allow myself the amazing pleasure of falling into his embrace. Kyle's hand jerks away when he feels the scars on the back of my head. "I'm sorry," he says.

"It's okay. Go ahead, put your hand back there." He does, touching lightly, pulling back, softly touching again. "You can touch me anywhere, scars and all," I tell him. "I'm all yours, every bit of me, and you'll have to take me just the way I am."

Kyle considers this for a moment, as if touching those scars was something he would never think would be acceptable. When he cups his hand firmly around the back of my head, it feels as if those scars have finally healed, as though by some magic, Kyle's touch has changed me.

We continue to kiss, but lightning fast, it becomes hotter, more intense. We kiss wildly, madly. Kyle is free for the first time to kiss someone he really wants to, and he's letting go completely, consumed, almost frantic. So am I. Nothing else exists, only Kyle's lips against mine, my body uniting with his. Our hands explore every part of each other feverishly, almost harshly, rubbing, gripping, kneading, pulling, stroking, squeezing, our tongues probing and caressing, our bodies entwined tightly. It goes on forever.

Heaven, that's what this feels like. With Kyle's arm wrapped tightly around me, the fingers of his other hand lightly stroke through my hair. I hold him tightly too, softly massaging his neck and head, pressing my cheek against his. Nothing has been said for what seems like hours.

This is not like what I thought it would be like. All I looked at and all I dreamt about these last four years were the looks and the muscles and the killer eyes and the total cool of the most popular boy in school, the boy who would never be mine. This Kyle in my arms is all that, to be sure, but infinitely more. This Kyle is real, the scared-shitless boy who opened his soul to me, the boy caught in a trap who trusted me with his life, the boy who allowed himself to cry on my shoulder and say he loves me. This boy that I love so much had the courage to escape the fear, the deception, the expectations of his parents and his friends—and the whole town, for that matter. This boy in my arms is the very real, humble, gentle Kyle I've always been drawn to. I love him with every part of my soul. I'm never letting go.

"I never knew I could be so scared," he says. "Then a few minutes later, I never knew I could feel so good."

"That's what coming out is. It's terrifying and it's sheer joy, all at the same time. I was so nervous telling Danny and Chloe, I was shaking. After that, it felt so good it was hard to describe."

"I love you," he whispers in my ear. Standing on the narrow, gravel shore of Ivie Reservoir, gently lit by a half moon, we rock back and forth like a couple dancing to a slow love song, tightly embraced, thanking God that we're here, that we're alive. We are so incredibly alive.

"Go ahead, say it," I tell him.

Not understanding, he looks up.

"The magic words. Three words you have to say," I tell him. "It begins, 'I am.'"

It takes a few seconds before the light bulb flicks on. He hesitates.

"Come on, Kyle, this is the payoff. Say it out loud."

Afraid after all, the boy who saw himself as the ultimate straight boy, the jock football hero, clams up.

"After what you've been through, you can do this. We'll say it together, okay?"

Kyle gulps noisily.

"I … am … gay."

He only says it in a whisper. I turn away, my feet landing right at the water's edge. I scream into the night those liberating, joyous words. Kyle joins me.

"Here goes," he says. *"I'm gay!"* he announces to the entire starlit universe, so loud he's bent over backwards. "I can't believe it," he shouts, all excited. "I actually said I'm gay! Oh, man, I can't believe I just said it. I'm gay!" He wraps me in his arms. "It's still scary," he says. "Weird, too."

"But you and me, we'll get through it together. The scary part will go away, I promise."

"There's something else, like this enormous weight's been lifted off me. Everything just feels right. It's like … oh, I can't even explain it."

But I understand. *Oh, God, how I understand.*

"That feeling—*everything's* going to feel right," I tell him. "It's going to feel like everything suddenly fell into place the way it was meant to be. This is your real life, and it's going to feel right. It's going to feel like you're whole."

"I wouldn't even be here if it wasn't for you," he says, squeezing tighter. "Now I'm here and it feels right. And I'm starting to realize just how much I love you." Kyle lifts his head to gaze into my eyes.

"I used to sneak peeks at you and I had no idea why," he says. "I didn't understand what was going on, or maybe I didn't want to. Whatever, I'd find myself looking at you all the time, and not once did I ever think about being gay."

"So what happened in the parking lot?"

Kyle sighs deeply. "I saw this beautiful, wonderful, amazing guy waiting to get punched out, and I couldn't control it any longer. I just had to hold you and kiss you and make it up to you."

"Boy, you sure surprised me."

"It felt so exciting and so good," Kyle says. "That's when it hit me like a shock. Holy shit, it was just like getting hit with a lightning bolt. Wham! It hit me right in the head—I'm gay! I couldn't believe it. I'm gay, for real. I couldn't believe it was actually happening to me."

"I was really scared when you took off," I tell him. "I was almost hysterical, especially when you almost got hit by that truck."

"I'm sorry. I totally panicked. I raced home and took my dad's revolver. I thought that was the only way out." Kyle looks around and finds his dad's shiny, chrome-plated revolver still resting on the rocky point where he left it. Picking it up with great care, he examines it for a few moments, like a scientist discovering a rare mineral.

"I'm alive!" he screams so loud I jump. A distant plop on the moonlit surface is all I hear when the boy who came so close to using his dad's revolver flings it far into the night, never to be found in the depths of Ivie Reservoir.

"Thanks don't seem enough, but thanks, Bobby," he says, squeezing me in a desperate embrace. We continue hugging each other so tightly we're almost one body. Kyle lifts his head to look into my eyes once again. "Can I tell you a secret?" he asks with an odd grin.

"Kyle, we don't have secrets anymore."

"I'd … I'd …" He's hesitating. Actually, I think he's blushing. "Sometimes I'd jack off thinking about you. I'd think about how hot you looked at Beth's party. I'd think about you lip-synching at the club. I'd think about getting you in my arms and holding you tight. Even your blond hair turned me on."

"Well, now when you think about me, you won't have to jack off," I tell him with a big grin. Kyle gets it and grins back. We can't stop looking into each other's eyes.

"Hey, maybe we should head back," I tell him.

He checks his heavy silver wristwatch. "Holy shit, it's after midnight. We've been here for hours."

"So maybe you can come back to my place? You can use the hot tub. Or I could tutor you in history." Kyle laughs, an overly loud, tension-releasing laugh, I bet for the first time in weeks.

"It feels so good to laugh again," he says. "It feels good to be alive!" he screams.

"Yeah, Kyle," I tell him with a sweet kiss, "it's awesome to be alive."

Chapter 68

His expression is unreadable. He's standing over the motorcycle that he hastily dumped in the brush hours ago. He's not angry or upset; he's just standing there looking at it.

"I thought I'd never ride my bike again," he says, his voice soft and full of wonder. Leaning down to check it more carefully, Kyle winces at the damage to the right mirror. "Oh no, someone took the key," he groans. He looks up when I tap him on the shoulder, holding what he's looking for dangling from the Warriors key chain. "You took it?" he asks.

"I figured you'd be wicked upset if you came back and found your bike gone."

Kyle grabs both of my shoulders.

"You knew I'd come back!" He follows with a fierce embrace. "You're amazing," he murmurs, running his fingers through my hair. "Can you help get this up?"

"Yeah, I'm really good at that. Oh, you mean the bike?"

It takes him a moment to react. "Hop on, Bobby-dude," he says, shaking his head and grinning. "I can't wait to get back to your place."

"What should I do about my car?"

"Your car? Oh man, I never even thought about how you got here. Where is it?"

I point further up the narrow parking lot, my shiny new Civic just barely visible in the soft moonlight. "I just bought it Wednesday night and it'll be kind of weird leaving it here. What should we do?"

He's thinking hard. "Can I still go to your place if we go back separately?"

"Yeah. I'll be waiting on the driveway, but my clothes might accidentally fall off."

"Then I'll be naked when I pull in," he grins.

"Maybe I should leave the car here."

We're looking into each other's eyes, holding on to each other tightly, the setting half-moon lighting my driveway in a gentle, romantic glow.

I shrieked when I got to my driveway. Kyle had raced ahead of me so he'd be waiting naked. We kissed madly the second I leaped out of the car. Somehow during that mad embrace, I managed to kick my shorts and undies off.

"Welcome to your new home, Kyle," I tell him with a light brush of my fingers through his hair. "So what would you like, hot tub, eat, or me?"

"All of the above, please," he says, his face lighting up with one of his irresistible smiles. "You have no idea how awesome it is just to look at you."

Once my new car and Kyle's bike are safely in the garage, we stroll into the kitchen with arms tightly wrapped around each other.

"I'm going to make one of my famous omelets. Wanna help?"

"Yeah, I'm really starving," he says. "I haven't eaten since lunch."

Soon, soft classical guitar music floats into the night from outside speakers. It's still warm out, so Kyle gets put to work with place settings and candles for the patio table. He comes back to wrap his arms around me from behind and nuzzle my neck while I tend the stove.

"Is this a gay thing?" he asks.

"Yeah, I told you before, omelets are gay." Shrieks of silly laughter fill the kitchen, laughter that quickly ends when he slaps his forehead.

"Shit! Mom and Dad don't know where I am. They probably have the cops out looking for me." For some screwy reason, this is good for more crazy laughter.

Kyle decides to tell them he and Jason and Josh are camping out, and is relieved when he gets their recorded message. "How about your foster mom?" he asks.

"I called her on the way up and told her I was sleeping over at Danny's," I explain.

Maybe because of the mention of Josh's name, Kyle reveals what happened just before he crashed into me. "Josh was the one who wanted to go to the mall. He said something about buying new sneakers, but when he went into the store, he looked around for like, one minute, and then he walked out. It was weird. He was kind of nervous too."

"Why was he nervous? He's your best friend, isn't he?"

"Maybe not anymore," he replies while I add a banana to the protein shake in the blender. "Josh was asking all sorts of stuff like, have I talked to Kathy, is everything okay; he and Helen are concerned, something's wrong. It was getting on my nerves. Then he mentioned you, and I got upset and started yelling at him."

"Because you were upset with me?"

"No, Bobby, now I know it was because I was scared," he says, hugging me tightly. He sighs heavily. "I'm really sorry. I was a total jerk."

"You were scared, and it's over. It's you and me now," I tell him as he gives me a squeeze.

"I had this feeling Josh was prying," Kyle continues.

"Did he come right out and ask if you're gay?"

"No, I don't think he really knows for sure, but he was going on about how he's here as my friend, and I can count on him no matter what, stuff like that. Then he asked if something happened at the prom, and he looked kind of funny, like he wasn't supposed to ask that. I totally lost it, and screamed at him to stay the fuck away from me and he's no longer my friend, and then I took off. Poor Josh. I was such a shit to my best friend, and he was trying to help."

And now I know what happened. No wonder he lost it when we collided.

It's only a few minutes before we're out on the patio, shoveling down piles of food and slamming protein shakes into empty, rumbling stomachs. Kyle's face is especially soft and beautiful in the glow of the candlelight, more beautiful than I ever remember. There's something about him, something so powerful I want to be with him, I want to be part of him, I need to be one with him. Kyle can't stop looking at me either. We're holding hands when we finish eating.

"Kyle, will you sleep with me tonight?"

"Oh, yeah," he says. "I want you in my arms all night long." He squints ever so slightly. "How did you get to be so beautiful?"

"Me?"

"You're more beautiful than ever. I can't stop looking at you."

"That what I was thinking about you. Is this what falling in love is?"

"It must be. I just can't believe how beautiful you are." Kyle begins to sing in a high, soft voice. "*Tu sei cosi bella. Tanto, tanto, tanto bella. Tu sei quella che ho sempre voluto. Tanta, tanto, tanto bella.*

"It means you're beautiful," he whispers.

My eyes are misting up. Kyle's irresistible, light gray eyes—Chloe calls them bedroom eyes—sparkle in the candlelight.

"Is this heaven?" I ask while we softly caress each other's hands.

"Yeah, it sure feels like it, and you're one of the angels. What?" he asks when I grin.

"Bed," is all I say. The boy who will incredibly climb into bed with me leans over the corner of the table to give me a sweet kiss. My heart is already beating faster.

"I feel gross," he says. He lifts his arm, sniffs, and makes a face. "Can I take a shower?"

"Uh … sure."

"You sure it's okay?"

I nod that it is as our chairs scrape back over the patio fieldstone.

"This is your shower?"

"It was my dad's shower but we both used it," I tell him while fetching a towel from a closet long unopened. I sniff to make sure it's okay.

"Look at this," he says as he surveys the stone-tiled walls. I have both arms around him; I only look at him. "It's so big there's no curtain. And what, three shower nozzles? Look, there's one right above! Holy shit, you must use this for hours."

Clouds of steam billow to the ceiling while Kyle experiments with each of the nozzles. I continue forcing myself to focus only on him. I cannot allow my eyes to see anything but his beautiful, tanned, glowing skin, slick with trails of water. He still doesn't have any body hair, at least that I can see, except for a thick, dark patch of pubes.

"What's wrong?" he asks, wiping water from his eyes. "I was hoping you'd hop in … Bobby, something's wrong."

"If I go in there, will you hold me tight? I mean, really tight?"

"Yeah," he shrugs.

I'm taking small, cautious steps toward the shower, keeping my eyes locked on his. I look at nothing else, just his eyes.

"Hey, it's okay," he says when I bury my head into his neck. Wrapping my arms around him, taking strength from the love of my life, we rock back and forth in the hot, stinging spray.

"What's wrong? Is it me?" I shake my head no on his shoulder and find the courage to lift my head and look into his eyes. "I haven't been in a shower stall or even used those two words in two and a half years. Kyle, I haven't even been in this bathroom until tonight."

"Oh, no," he moans, clutching me tightly. "Shit, I'm such a jerk. Come on, let's get out of here." I shake my head no against the slickness of his chest.

"I have to do this." I look up again. "I need to do this, Kyle. I can do it with you here. There's just one condition."

"What's that?"

"You have to let me wash you."

Kyle relaxes, kisses me all over, and squeezes me hard.

"Here, time for a shampoo," I tell him. But before I can squeeze a gob of shampoo into my palm, Kyle grabs my shoulders.

"You're safe now," he says, staring into my eyes with terrific intensity. He follows with a hug so tight we might have to be pried apart. "You're safe," he whispers again. I gulp hard and nod. Dunston's gay football star leans down while I massage his hair with shampoo left in here long ago.

"Oh, yeah," he moans. "This is just like that massage thing you did last fall when you wanted to get your hands on me."

"I can't believe I did that! I was so nervous I could hardly talk." We both laugh. It helps me relax.

Soap gets lathered and massaged over every fiber of those beautiful muscles. I take extra time on Kyle's spectacular, tight, athletic ass. I remind myself this isn't a dream.

"I showered with girls before," he says. "It was expected of me, but it wasn't exciting."

"How about in the locker room?"

"I don't know. I really didn't look at guys all that much in the locker room. If I got a hard-on, I'd jerk off and everyone thought it was cool. But taking a shower with you, oh man, this is magic."

"For me too!"

Kyle grunts as I work my way up the sharp, bulging muscles of his upper legs to the last part, now as hard as my own. Big, thick, well-shaped, the huge, reddish-purple head completely exposed by foreskin stretching back, Kyle's dick is sticking straight out, so hard he's grimacing. I'm lightly holding his sacks, big, low-hanging, bulging, ready to explode precious jewels.

"Oh no," I groan, remembering the mall. "Are you hurt? Oh, shit, Kyle, I'm really sorry."

"Just a bit sore. I've had worse playing touch football," he says, straining and gasping to talk. "After what I did, you had every right."

Still, I figure I should make up for almost crushing his balls, and I can't hold back any longer anyway. I've only felt a few cocks before, Matt's in Austin and a couple of guys in the club restroom, but this spectacular cock is so hard, it literally feels like steel. It doesn't budge when I press down.

Still on one knee, my tongue flicks at it rapidly. Kyle's body jolts as he moans. I kiss it, a deep, tongue-massaging kiss, getting the entire head into my mouth, massaging every bit. With one loud grunt, Kyle bucks forward, almost doubling over. My hand tightly cups his ass, feeling powerful muscles clench and thrust. Kyle's body heaves and jerks in frantic, electric spasms; he shoots long, ropey strings all over the place. With each thrust, an earthy, pained grunt fills the shower. He's still shooting! Seven … eight … holy shit, nine, until finally, a long string dribbles from the tip. Even more impressive, he's still hard.

Exhausted and panting, Kyle is almost doubled over. I help him gently, as we both stand and embrace.

"Oh, my God," he gasps, almost crushing me with his heaving chest, "I've never shot a load like that in my life." We kiss hard, deeply, our breaths heavy, tongues probing, hands clawing and gripping. Two hands grab my head; two light gray eyes sparkle.

"Your turn," he grins.

My own hard-on is so intense I might explode for real.

"Jesus Christ!" he shrieks when he looks down. He reaches but hesitates. I guide his hand all the way. "How big is this thing?" he asks.

"Nine. At least it was last year."

Kyle's head rolls back, mouthing a silent "holy shit" before he squeezes a dollop of shampoo into his hand. He edges closer, our dicks two crossed swords, two new companions playing their own little game. The fingers of Kyle's perfect hands massage through my scalp. It's one of the most pleasurable, wonderful experiences I've ever had. He doesn't flinch when his hand kneads the back of my head. Our hips pressed together, our dicks pressed straight up against each other's bellies, Kyle guides me to lean into the hot spray to rinse my hair off. Then it's on to the rest of me. I nearly shoot at the feeling of his hands washing and kneading and massaging every inch of my body.

Down on one knee, Kyle peers up with an oddly intense look. Gripping my ass with both hands, squeezing and kneading, he does the unexpected, pulling my cock into his face. Moaning in pleasure— well, I am too—he's rubbing my super pumped-up cock all over his forehead and closed eyes, cheeks, his partly open lips, all through his hair, everything. He pulls back.

"Kyle, don't force anything. Do only what you're comfortable with and the rest will come later."

He continues to nuzzle. It's when he imitates me, kissing the entire head, swishing his tongue all around to send jolts of electricity into every part of my body, that I shudder in a massive, uncontrollable spasm so powerful my legs buckle.

Kyle stands to hold me up as I explode. It goes on and on, a non-stop cannonade, the most amazing shoot I have ever experienced.

"Wow," is all he says as he rises to his feet. I collapse into his embrace. "I've seen other guys shoot their loads, but that was unbelievable," he whispers in my ear.

"My old bedroom," I explain as I pull down the covers. "I still use it once in a while." For good measure, I plump up both pillows. When I hold up a corner of the blanket, Kyle hops in and squiggles over a bit.

"I can't believe it. This is like a dream," he says as I snap off the light.

"That's what I was thinking. This is like a dream. I'm going to bed with Kyle Faulkner!"

After a few awkward tries, we find a comfortable position with our bodies tightly entwined, pressing every possible inch of skin together. I stroke his temple; his fingers trace lightly over my hand.

"Welcome home, Kyle, and welcome to your real life."

"How did you find the right words? How did you know what to do?" he asks.

"I tried everything, but nothing was working, so I prayed real hard. God must have answered my prayers."

"Yeah, Bobby-dude, he sent a beautiful angel," he whispers.

The boy who I thought I'd lose forever but who chose to live, the boy I always thought could never be mine, leans closer to give me a soft kiss.

"You're safe now," I whisper. "It's all over and I'm yours."

Kyle responds with a deep, contented sigh when I run my fingers over his face with the lightest touch.

"Kyle?"

"Mmm."

"What did you do in the ICU to save me?"

"The ICU? Oh," Kyle moans. "I was told by Mr. Lessard to go because you said my name in the ER—Bobby, somehow you knew you needed me—so when I was there, I felt really uncomfortable, you know, you being messed up so awful. I got up to leave, but when I got to the doors, I couldn't push them open. I just couldn't leave you all alone, hurt so bad. So I went back. I pleaded with you to be strong and to live. And I prayed, harder than I've ever prayed in my life, asking God to let you live and get better."

"Thank you, Kyle. You saved my life too." I sigh deeply and whisper to Kyle. "God must want us to be together."

I'm just barely touching his ear when I realize—he's sound asleep. I'm just as exhausted. That was one amazing day. A new life for me, too, not … just …

Epilogue

June 2004

Relaxing after a long, hectic day, Kyle and I are snuggling in our favorite spot, the comfy love seat set close to the sliding glass doors of our cozy den. From here, we can view our small but beautifully landscaped backyard patio (with a hot tub, of course), and beyond that, the spectacular view of the San Francisco hills, twinkling with thousands of evening lights.

"Is Mike all packed?" I ask Kyle.

"If I know him, he'll pack tomorrow morning just before the airport limo shows up."

"The limo's here at six."

"I'll bug him again when he comes in," Kyle says.

We used to introduce him as "Kyle's little brother," but now that he's six feet one and off to Boston University this fall, we just call him Mike. Good-looking, blond like his mother, outgoing like his dad, athletic but lankier than Kyle, Mike is a really nice kid (although there were some pretty wild times during high school). Ever since Kyle came out to his family the week before our high school graduation, Mike has been amazingly accepting and supportive. Too bad his parents didn't react as well back then—they kicked Kyle out.

"Did you make an appointment with the Realtor?" Kyle asks.

"Yeah, next Wednesday morning."

"Hey, wouldn't it be cool if we could get a condo on the water?"

"Totally cool. It will be our gift to ourselves," I tell Kyle with a smirk.

He grins back and leans close for a gentle kiss.

Provincetown. So many special memories.

"Will we ever stop talking about that first trip?" I ask.

"Nope." He's looking at me with an impish grin.

Kyle and I set out on our first vacation adventure a few weeks after we graduated from high school. We started in New York City with a visit to Kyle's Sicilian grandmama, who had heard him sing at the prom over his dad's cellphone. Kyle was scared when Grandmama said his dad had called and told her about Kyle being gay. He thought she'd disapprove, or worse, throw us out. Instead, she told a story about her own journey to America when she was sixteen, despite her mother and father's protests, and how important it is to pursue one's dreams. "Kyle, I'm old and tired. I just want to know my precious grandson will be truly happy," I remember her saying. She hugged and kissed Kyle as he cried on her shoulder.

We continued on to Boston to meet my Internet friend Paul, the guy who gave me all the party and prom ideas. He turned out to be a terrific guy and took us sightseeing all over town the first two days. He took us to Hingham the following day. I showed Kyle my old house—it was weird seeing someone else living there—and my old school, and where my little gang of friends and I used to hang out. Then we went to the cemetery so I could put flowers on Mom's grave. I hadn't been there since I moved, and worse, I didn't know if they'd ever find Dad and bring him home. I was glad Kyle and our new gay friend were there for me.

We finished with a ten-day visit to Provincetown. From the moment we stepped off the ferry, we saw gay guys everywhere. It didn't take long before we were holding hands in the street and even kissing in public. It was so exciting! And we went to our first gay beach, Herring Cove Beach.

"As long as I live, I will never forget my birthday gift on the beach," Kyle says.

Our eyes lock. Our lips unite in a deep, passionate kiss.

I found out that Kyle would turn eighteen during our stay in Provincetown. It was at Herring Cove Beach that I gave him a very special birthday gift. Nestled in a secluded spot in the dunes under a wispy-blue, late afternoon sky, we made passionate love for hours. Not long after, as we cuddled exhausted on our blanket, the entire sky glowed with a spectacular sunset. It will forever be the most special sex of our lives.

We're quiet for a few warm, special moments.

"We wouldn't have even gone on that vacation if the judge hadn't suggested it," I say to Kyle. "And as long as *I* live, I will never forget that day in his office."

Kyle and I had been summoned to the judge's chambers a couple of days after graduation. The judge was concerned about how taxing the year had been for both of us and suggested we get away. Take a vacation; maybe Boston and Provincetown, he told us. Then he disbursed ten thousand dollars from Dad's trust!

The judge went on to say that since I had graduated, he could finally tell me all of the trust provisions. First, he and Dad had agreed on forty thousand a year for college. Forty thousand!

Then he explained that the trust would be dissolved when I graduated from college, and any remaining funds would be paid to me. I asked if there'd be much left after all those big payouts. He sat back in his chair with a hint of a smile. "Oh, now I think there might be, me boy," he said in his best Irish brogue. "Somewhere in the neighborhood of 3.8 million dollars." Neither Kyle nor I could even breathe.

"I remember how uncomfortable I felt when we left the courthouse," Kyle says, "like you might think I had some expectation of getting rich or something." He snuggles a little closer. I know what he's going to say because we've told this story countless times. "You grabbed me and gave me one of those intense looks of yours, and you said, 'I meant it up at Ivie when I said everything I have is yours. I could be rich or I could be poor—'"

"—but as long as I'm with you I'll be happy," I say.

Kyle squeezes me tight and kisses me.

"I love you, Bobby Fowler," he whispers.

"I love you too," I tell him as we kiss again.

We're quiet for a bit, arms around each other, our love for each other stronger than ever.

"So what do you think is up with the judge?" I ask.

"The judge? I think it's serious. Jeez, when he was here last month, he spent most of his time with Richard," Kyle says, referring to an older gay guy who has become our close friend and mentor. He and the judge hit it off the first time they met. Boy, did they ever!

Kyle reaches for his bottle of water. A much-sought-after fitness model as well as a successful personal trainer, Kyle tries to be careful with what he eats and drinks.

"What are you looking at, sweetie?" I ask as I follow his gaze to the shelf across the room where we keep our most special awards and mementos. "Your NCAA championship medals?"

My sweetheart's thoughts are off somewhere. Maybe he's remembering that day, just before our first vacation trip, when he got a call to meet Coach Meyer, his high school swim coach, at the pool. No details, no explanation, just *be there*. So when we got there, another guy was with him. Coach Meyer introduced him as the men's varsity swim coach from Stanford University. Stanford! One of his swimmers had unexpectedly returned to Spain, the Stanford coach explained, and he was offering Kyle a tryout.

Kyle swam like I'd never seen him swim before. But after just two time trials, the Stanford guy told Kyle that was all he needed to see. Kyle was devastated, thinking it was just one more rejection. But a few minutes later, the Stanford coach shocked us by offering Kyle a full scholarship. Later, we learned that he had seen enough because Kyle had unofficially broken the Texas high school record in the 200-meter individual medley. What irony—the star football player who was supposed to get a scholarship to a big-time football program instead went to Stanford on a swimming scholarship. When we asked him how he had heard of Kyle, Kyle's high school coach answered, "Oh, it seems that a certain varsity swim coach and a certain high school principal were college roommates." Another day we will never forget.

Kyle stirs and comes back from wherever.

"I was thinking about the skinny little high school kid competing in a bodybuilding contest," he replies with a nod across the room. Next to his NCAA medals is a handsome trophy with a plaque that reads, "Bay Area All-Natural Classic. First Place, Novice Class, 2002."

"I still can't believe I competed," I tell Kyle.

"Honey, you worked your ass off and you never took steroids," he says.

"Remember how surprised I was when Jason showed up?"

"Surprised?" Kyle screeches. "You just about shit your pants."

I was in the pump room doing pushups when I looked up to see Jason standing there with a big grin. He had flown all the way from Fort Benning, Georgia, just to cheer me on. I will never forget he did that.

And during our junior year at Stanford, almost the same thing happened at Dad's funeral. We had received the stunning news that the remains of an American turned over to our people in Pakistan had been identified as my dad's. We called Jason with the news and mentioned the memorial service in Hingham, never expecting that he could take leave from his unit. Somehow, Jason talked his company commander into letting him and six of his Army Ranger buddies travel to Boston to serve as the military honor guard. We arrived at the church and found out that the handsome guy in the dress uniform was Jason.

"What an amazing guy," I say, more to myself.

Kyle tenses, leans his head back, and blows out an uneasy breath. I tense too.

"Fucking Iraq," he says. "Why'd he have to volunteer for a third tour?" he goes on, louder and with a bitter edge to his voice. "Why'd he have to go into the fucking army in the first place?"

I gently stroke his arm. It was only six weeks ago that Mum called with the awful news that Jason had been killed by a roadside bomb in some remote place called Fallujah. It was a very sad and tearful service at Evergreen Cemetery in Dunston.

"He was doing what he loved, sweetie," I tell Kyle as gently as I can. He knows. It just hurts so much, for both of us.

We're quiet once again, just sitting back, taking comfort in holding each other closely.

"You think Danny will show up?" Kyle asks.

"I really don't know. I kinda doubt it."

"Didn't you track him down in Seattle?"

"Yeah, but he didn't seem too enthusiastic."

Kyle sighs. "I guess *friends forever* sometimes falls short on the forever part," he says. "Weird how friends turn out. Helen always wanted to be a schoolteacher, and now she's writing software for some high-tech Internet company."

"And Josh always wanted to play baseball, and now *he's* the high school teacher," I reply. "Well then there's you," Kyle says with a gentle nudge. "Everyone thought you'd do nothing but music stuff all your life."

"Hey, I'll still do lots of music *stuff*." Kyle sniffs a chuckle. My music interests—the jazz band, my teaching post at the Conservatory and directorship of the Bay Area Youth Symphony, a few deejay gigs here and there for charity events, and my composing—keep me going full time.

"But running for the city Board of Supervisors this fall?" Kyle goes on. "Dude, I'm all for it, but what a surprise. You know what I think? Not only are you going to win, but someday you're going to be United States

Senator Bobby-Dude Fowler. Maybe even President Gay-Kid Bobby Fowler!"

"Yeah, that'll be the day."

Kyle looks up when we hear the slam of the front door. "Mike, we're up here!" he hollers. Feet clomp up the stairs from the front hallway. A tall, good-looking boy sticks his head in.

"Yes," Mike states.

"Yes? Yes what?" Kyle asks.

"Yes, I'm all packed," he explains with a self-satisfied grin.

"Don't forget," I tell him. "The limo—"

"—will be here at six," he responds from further down the hallway.

Kyle yawns and stretches his arm way back. "Honey, it's getting late," he says. "We've got a long day tomorrow."

Before heading to our bedroom, Kyle stops to pick up a picture off the shelf. It's a photo of me looking like a twelve-year-old in a tux with tails, holding the trophy I won at my first music contest. Kyle is lost in thought.

I gently rub his back.

"Amazing," he says. "How far you and I have come."

"It is amazing. August will be ten years since I first saw you in Mr. Sawicki's freshman English class. It's been quite an adventure."

"Yeah, Bobby-dude, quite an adventure."

Four days later

Late in the day, when the low sun casts that magical glow and every little boat in Provincetown's harbor is lit up in gold, the scene is so beautiful and compelling that sometimes Kyle and I watch spellbound from the town beach, like we did tonight. Now nearing twilight, and with dinner not for another half hour, our guest house's handsomely decorated, dark-paneled common room is quiet and empty, except for one tall, blond teenage boy hunched over his laptop.

"Hey, Mike, what's up?"

"Oh, hey, Bobby. I was just editing my daily journal," Kyle's brother says.

"Sorry. I'd better leave you alone."

"No problem. Here, you can read this part," he says with an impish grin.

Mike hands me his Mac. I get through the first few words of today's entry and stop. I have to sit and re-read them. Those few simple words still don't seem possible, but they're real, so joyfully, wonderfully, impossibly real. I read them one more time, letting those magical words sink into my soul.

Sunday, June 27, 2004
Provincetown, Massachusetts

Kyle and Bobby were married yesterday morning on the deck of the Boatslip, overlooking Provincetown Harbor. It was warm and sunny, a big crowd of friends and family were there, and everything was perfect. Who would have ever thought that two gay guys could legally marry?

Mom, as usual, kept herself under control, but Dad cried. It must be the Italian in him. So did Bobby's mom, Mrs. Robles, and his best friend Chloe. Lots of guests from Provincetown and New York and Boston were there, and a few from Texas and San Francisco. Josh and Helen brought little Bobby and Chelsea and told us another's on the way. Brian Hale came up from New York City. Last month he graduated from Yale with some financial help from Kyle and Bobby. And was I glad Judge Garrity was really nice after the way he chewed my ass out pretty good in court last fall.

After the ceremony, we paraded down the street and everyone cheered. The reception was a total blast! A couple famous DJs were there and they made Bobby sit in. Later, he and Kyle danced and they twirled each other all over the dance floor. Suddenly the music stopped. This guy Tim from Ft. Lauderdale proposed to his partner Zane right on the dance floor. Everyone went crazy when Zane screamed yes! Then Judge Garrity and Bobby and Kyle's neighbor Richard announced they're going to live together in San Francisco. That was just as wild, although Mom almost fainted. After the party broke up, Kyle and Bobby disappeared, and they weren't at the guest house or anywhere.

At breakfast this morning, I asked where they went. All they said was they went to the beach, Herring Cove Beach, I think. Then they kind of smiled at each other. I thought I'd better leave it at that.

I'm smiling to myself reading the last part. Re-creating Kyle's eighteenth birthday gift in the dunes is a yearly ritual, but one we don't discuss with anyone.

It's still hard to believe we're legally married. I proposed to Kyle in the middle of a crowded restaurant last winter (he was surprised to see some our friends there), soon after the famous court decision in Massachusetts made marriage for gays legal. It took ten years of incredible adventure, however, to get here. Looking back, our high school years were, without question, the biggest adventure. It's harder for me now to remember exactly what it was like as a nervous thirteen-year-old reporting to Dunston High School on my first day. One memory, however, remains vivid: the moment I laid eyes on the most beautiful boy I had ever seen, the boy who said "I do" yesterday on the deck of the Boatslip.

Ten years. Some horrible times during high school. Some wonderful times. That crazy summer after high school graduation when we took our first vacation and discovered Provincetown. We discovered how much we like being with each other. And then we had to say good-bye to so many friends when we left for college.

College was almost as crazy. (I don't think we'll talk about some of the things we did freshman year.) It was fun, difficult, fulfilling, exciting. In the rich stew of a college music environment, I exploded with new musical interests. Kyle excelled both as an athlete and a student. College changed us, and we matured a lot. We lost most of our high school friends and kept a few special ones, like Jason, Helen and Josh, and Chloe. We learned that the friends you keep, you treasure.

We decided to live in San Francisco and bought our house right after graduation. A year of painting, furnishing, refinishing, replanting, remodeling, re-everything. It was work happily done because it was our first and it was *ours*.

Kyle and I never fight. Sometimes we disagree, but a long time ago, the judge told us that the world would be a better place if we could put ourselves in the other guy's shoes. He told us to remember that not only do we love the other guy, he's our best friend too. As usual, it was good advice. I've come to truly appreciate what the judge and Mum have done for me.

Our love has grown deeper; we've both grown in some unexpected ways. I'm starting to understand that life doesn't always progress on a neat, pre-arranged path. Sometimes it's because we change, sometimes it's because things both good and bad are thrown at us. Kyle teases me (but he supports me 100 percent) about running for political office. He, on the other hand, is becoming a serious and very successful owner of a fitness and training business.

Ten years. Yes, it's been quite an adventure. That wonderful, amazing, beautiful, caring, stunning boy I thought would never be mine, and now we're married. And to think we might not even be here. Kyle prayed hard in the ICU when they thought I wasn't going to make it. I prayed just as hard up at Ivie for Kyle to live. God heard our prayers. He must want us to be together. It's like He's telling us, it's not sinful to be gay, it's not just okay to be gay—it's beautiful to be gay. After all, He made us just the way we are.

Mike has been patiently waiting. The ship's clock strikes nine. It's time for dinner—with my husband.

"Have the courage to pursue your dreams and be truly happy."
—Carmella Faulkner

I remember Kyle's beloved grandmama saying that to him the very first time I met her in Queens, New York, during our first vacation trip. It was wonderful advice that Kyle and I have tried to follow all these years.

Robert Ellsworth Richardson Fowler
United States Senate
Northern California

CPSIA information can be obtained at www.ICGtesting.com

225765LV00004B/23/P